"Outstanding. The most accurat[e] ever read and it brings out the ex[...] SOG. It brought back memories I had not thought about in years. This is a great book."

SFC Howard "Karate" Davis

US Army, 5th Special Forces Group (Airborne), MACV-SOG, CCC, Hatchet Force Company A, Covey Rider, 1969-1970

"Vivid and interesting... A very strong narration with deep characterization. This story honors those of us who served in SOG."

Sgt. Lee Burkins

US Army, 5th Special Forces Group (Airborne), MACV-SOG, CCC, Recon Company, 1970-1971, author of Soldier's Heart

"Most excellent; I am excited at having our story told so accurately and so well, and I'm proud to be a part of it."

Capt. Pete Johnston

US Army, 219th Aviation Company, MACV-SOG, CCC, "SPAF-4", 1969-1970

"The author has the gift of capturing the very realness of the Vietnam War. Memories I have long forgotten have since returned with renewed focus."

Sgt. Anthony E. Adams

1st Air Cavalry Division, 1971-1972

For Pipes & Pages ; looking forward to an
honest review. Love your page!
Hope you enjoy the read.

GENTLE PROPOSITIONS

J.S. Economos

#237

This novel is a work of historical-fiction which includes a unique blend of both imaginary characters and real people who take part in both real and fictional events in time.

GENTLE PROPOSITIONS

Special Projects Media
specialprojectsmedia@gmail.com

Book and cover design by Jason Economos; inset illustration by Carleigh Sion.

ISBN-13: 978-0-615-99763-6

FOREWORD

Gentle Propositions is a story of men. Men cited for extraordinary heroism, great combat achievement, and unwavering fidelity while conducting unheralded top-secret missions deep behind enemy lines across all of Southeast Asia during the Vietnam War.

SOG recon teams were fiercely hunted – pursued by enemy trackers and even bloodhounds, yet these small teams frequently out-maneuvered, out-fought and outran a numerically superior enemy in an unwavering effort to uncover hidden North Vietnamese Army facilities. They planted wiretaps and high-tech electronic sensors; they rescued downed American and Vietnamese aircrews, captured enemy prisoners, mined roadways, ambushed convoys, marked targets for aerial bombardment, and inflicted massive casualties against a well-disciplined and determined enemy.

But do not mistake this for a simple, cliché war story about running and gunning. There is intimate insight into the mind-sets and motivations of young Americans thrust into a passel of foreign and strange cultures worlds apart from their own. And furthermore, the continued motivation these men reserved to voluntarily look their mortality in the face, day after day, under such insurmountable odds.

When duty, honor, and country aren't enough, what keeps them coming back? Are they just professional soldiers performing wartime duties? Are some of them there just for the adventure, their war – the great "game" – the subconscious need to feel the rush of combat? What common fabric ultimately binds these men together?

The characters in this story – both real and fictional – are a true composite of a myriad of personalities who found a home in Special Forces, and in SOG. It is in these characters, their relationships, their struggles and experiences that we find the answers to our quandaries, and the personal reflections of a young man who becomes a warrior.

Lynne M. Black, Jr.

US Army, 5th Special Forces Group (Airborne), MACV-SOG, CCN, Recon Company, 1968-1970, author of *Whiskey Tango Foxtrot*

ACKNOWLEDGEMENTS

To say writing this story would've been impossible without proper criticism and guidance would be a complete understatement. Writing about SOG has been such a fascinating journey but the most rewarding chapter in this whole venture has been the countless phone conversations and email threads I've carried on with those few who were actually there.

Thanks to Mike Soetaert who I pestered way back in January of 2005 to read my first draft. I'm pretty embarrassed about those first few attempts but I've come a long way since then and I thank you for your help and motivation.

Thanks to Lee Burkins, the very first SOG recon man I had the pleasure of speaking with. Lee's book, *Soldier's Heart*, taught me a great deal about the Montagnard people and their beliefs, practices, and their connection to the land. But perhaps most important are the subtleties of the relationships he had with the Montagnards on his team. Thank you, Burkai.

Were it not for men like John Plaster and Frank Greco, we'd likely not know a fraction about MACV-SOG, the mission, the people, nor those who supported their efforts. Plaster's trilogy helped serve as a timeline of sorts for my own undertaking, and Greco's books are treasure-troves of information for enthusiasts and researchers like me. Thank you both for having taken the time and effort to compile such magnificent pieces of history.

Thank you to Ken Snyder, Luke Dove, Tom Waskovich, Rex and Deborah Hill; to Joe Walker, Howard "Karate" Davis, Ed Wolcoff, John Stryker Meyer, Joe Parnar, Richard Noe, John St. Martin, Bob Howard, Billy Waugh, and Dick Meadows.

Thank you to Pete Johnston for helping me sort out all the particulars surrounding Sneaky Pete's Air Force, and their timeline. For taking the time to point out errors in my aviation scenes and for working with me to get them right, and for explaining the intricacies of landing a fixed-wing aircraft at the Dak Pek launch site. I am also obliged to say thanks for having included me in a rather comical email thread between Tom Waskovich, Luke Dove, Ken Snyder, and Howard Davis. You guys crack me up!

The very first books I read about Special Forces in Vietnam were authored by James C. Donahue and his experiences serving as a medic in the Mobile Guerilla Force. Having read his trilogy, I was immediately inspired to write about SF in Vietnam and as a result, I absorbed a great deal of writing style from him.

Thanks to Jason Hardy for his continued efforts in compiling and organizing SOG's recon team history. To put it simply, these books have been instrumental in helping me determine who was where and what they were doing while in SOG, which makes for a far more accurate story.

I must also thank Richard "Nick" Brokhausen, author of *We Few*, for inspiring me as a writer. *We Few* remains one of the best books I've ever read and I'm proud to say your writing style influenced my own. And thank you for entrusting me with the follow-up manuscript to *We Few*. If you were to ask for my advice, I'd encourage you to publish both titles through Amazon and finish what you originally started. You're an incredibly gifted writer and I thank you for the inspiration.

James Ernie Acre, author of *Project Omega: Eye of the Beast*, thank you for our continued correspondence, and for all your philosophy on combat, politics, and beyond.

Thanks to Carleigh Sion for painting an original piece of artwork for my book cover. It turned out great. Carleigh can be found on Instagram @carleighflower.

To all my friends and family who've listened to me ramble on about this project for so long, thank you for your continued support and encouragement.

Thank you to David Babineau, author of *Done With Death*, for all of your help regarding the self-publication process and everything associated with formatting. I would've had far greater difficulties had it not been for your advice and shortcuts.

And finally, I want to express my deepest gratitude to Lynne M. Black, Jr. for an immeasurable amount of assistance and continued correspondence throughout the duration of this project. Were it not for you, the direction of this book would have likely been lost, or worse yet, it might've mimicked a story that's already been told and that's not what I wanted to do. Furthermore, I thank you for your advice regarding my publication options, as well as an unquantifiable amount of minutia in between.

All of you remain an inspiration to me and I hope this book and the one to follow serve to preserve the legacy of such a legendary unit and those who were a part of it.

De Oppresso Liber

AUTHOR'S NOTE

It has taken me nearly 10 years to research, write, compile, edit, and rewrite this story, and the following chapters make up only the first part of a multi-part series. This story is an odyssey of war and survival – both mentally and physically – and the fidelity born between young men who voluntarily fight side-by-side against unimaginable odds.

Gentle Propositions is a unique blend of both fiction and nonfiction. When I set out to write about MACV-SOG, I knew my main character and supporting characters and their experiences would be based on fiction and creative latitude. But overall, I felt changing the names of those who were really there, or augmenting their deeds and sacrifices for the sake of this story would ultimately tarnish the history of such remarkable unit and its accomplishments.

Throughout the course of this project, I have been very fortunate to have had guidance and immeasurable insight into the inner workings of SOG and the Vietnam War by those who were there. I asked for and received criticism and input – not only from both Recon and Hatchet Force members, but from straphangers, Covey riders, chase medics, and aircrew members who flew in support of SOG's clandestine operations. I learned things about specific people and places, about aircraft, communications equipment, vehicles, and all manner of explosives, ordnances, and weapons systems. I was educated about cultures and religions that are foreign to me in experience, but somehow familiar now by way of research. And I took all of this knowledge and I attempted to apply it keenly to tell a story.

I know some may find it impossible to read fiction about the unit they once served in, and I fully understand that; rest assured my skin is far too thick to take that personal. Just know that I did my best to reach out and speak to as many of you as I could during this process.

To the average reader with no prior knowledge of MACV-SOG, Special Forces, or their roles during the Vietnam War, you needn't worry. This story requires none. Just keep turning the pages if you like what you read.

Thanks and enjoy.

Jason S. Economos

Isaiah 6:8

Then I heard the voice of the Lord saying, "Whom shall I send? And who will go for us?"

And I said, "Here am I. Send me!"

1

"Fuck," Mark complained in a low whisper. "Sun's barely up and I'm already sweating my ass off."

Ethan glanced at his friend and shook his head while the liaison officer thumbed through a clipboard full of humidity-soaked papers.

"Alright, listen up," he demanded. "Take the index card you've been given and write down the outfit you wish to volunteer for. Those of you aiming for Special Projects need to write down the exact project name. If you don't give a shit where you go, put that down and we'll be sure to pick a nice and cozy safe place for you."

Command and Control; arguably the war's best-kept secret, and the rumor mill back at Ft. Bragg loved to speculate on it. There were some who knew – Special Forces veterans who'd returned from Vietnam to instruct candidates at Training Group, but their lips were sealed. To Ethan Jackson, that was all just a part of the show – theatrics, the allure, the uncertainty. Command and Control was a big part of the Special Projects – that much he knew, and with that he figured it had to carry heavy priority which meant it also it had have strong support assets. All of those things would attract solid people with a lot of experience. That's where he wanted to be. At least that's how he and his companions had figured it the night before in the NCO club at Group headquarters.

Nha Trang, South Vietnam was an absolute paradise perched at the edge of the South China Sea – a bustling metropolis with the added charm of an ancient seaside community, home to several in-country R&R centers for GIs looking to escape the war for a few days. Nha Trang was also the headquarters for the 5th Special Forces Group in Southeast Asia and command sure knew how to pick the sweet spots. Unfortunately, Group headquarters also attracted a lot of ticket-punching careerists who lived high on the hog while their SF brethren were busy beating the bush for the enemy and actually earning their living.

Ethan and his four companions had passed up the offer of another downtown night. The crew they'd thrown in with the night before had been a rowdy lot – all Special Forces NCOs returning for their second and third tours of duty. Before the night was done, a guy they all called "Macho" had adjusted some arrogant sergeant-major's headspace, and then the whole bunch set about to dispatching at least two jeeps full of MPs. It had actually been a pretty good show, though enough excitement for one night with the hangovers to match, so they opted to lay low at the NCO club on base and discuss the finer points of the various units they could volunteer for. Paul was still trying to decide between joining an A-team or the MIKE Force, and Benfield had talked a little about Project Delta but Ethan had been the first to mention Command and Control. No sooner had he finished his sentence, a man approached their table from the bar and loomed over them. He pulled long and hard at the cigarette pressed between his lips, his narrow eyes somehow reflecting the orange glow of the cherry. He had all the heirlooms of an SF combat rat: sun-faded fatigues and beret, combat infantryman badge, jump wings, Project patch, RECONDO patch and on and on. A conversationalist he was not, yet when he spoke, no one's attention wandered.

"Which one of you assholes mentioned C&C?"

All eyes were on Ethan as he dipped his head in a pathetic nod.

"What do you know about it?" he pressed.

"Nothing really," Ethan admitted as he looked up and shrugged. "Just rumors."

The man nodded as if partially satisfied.

"I've been on two A-teams and in the MIKE Force," he said, dragging on his smoke. "Good people, tough outfits, hairy operations. I've been up at CCN for seven months now. Take it from me – if you're thinking about volunteering for it, you better get your shit squared away ricky-fuck'n-tick." He paused to finish the rest of his beer and then leaned in, "And keep in mind where you're at when you talk." He made a slight glance over his shoulder at the Vietnamese girls working the bar. "Nguyen's *always* close."

He smashed the butt of his cigarette in the dirty ashtray and slipped back into the shadowy crowd.

*　　　*　　　*

Ethan shifted his weight from one leg to the other as the line grew shorter and shorter until he faced an unenthusiastic processing clerk. With a dry throat, he delivered the requested information: name, rank, and serial number and the clerk processed his orders. He glanced back at the flooring; the wooden planks were stained red by countless pairs of muddy jungle boots, and an overworked fan circulated musty tropical air from corner to corner. Finally, the clerk produced a slip of paper that boasted his new orders. He palmed the slip and strolled out of the clapboard building and joined Benfield under the shady refuge of the roof's overhang.

"Well, what's it say?" Benfield's dark eyes looked eager and excited.

Ethan glanced at the slip in his hand and then read it exactly as it appeared in bold print.

"Jackson, Ethan, Special Operations Augmentation, CCC, MACV-SOG, 5th Special Forces Group, Airborne."

Benfield slung a massive arm over his shoulder and chuckled, "Just couldn't help yourself, huh? You just *had* to tag along with Big Ben." He flashed his orders for Ethan to read and grinned like the Cheshire Cat. "Looks like you're coming with us."

"Us?"

"Me, you, the wetback and Marky."

"Shit, this ain't good," Ethan kidded as they made their way through the compound towards their temporary barracks. In truth, he was glad they were all going to the same place, and they made light conversation about their new surroundings and of their orders. Over two years of constant training had finally come down to a matter of days before they would be in the field, and the anticipation and excitement was almost too much to handle.

*   *   *

As they waited for the aircraft to taxi from the runway, it was easy to see why they called them Blackbirds. The Air Force C-130 transport ship boasted a midnight-black and forest-green camouflage paint job. The nose cone of the cumbersome aircraft had been fitted with a twenty-foot Fulton Skyhook yoke system that was used for snatching intelligence agents and other personnel from enemy territory without even having to land the aircraft. It had interchangeable insignia plates that could be switched in the blink of an eye. On the inside, the forward section of the payload compartment was partitioned by a red curtain with the words *Top-Secret* written in bold black print. Ethan had never really considered the essence of the term *Top-Secret* before that moment, and he quickly found it a surreal term, something he'd only seen in spy movies and on TV. Filling the remaining section of the payload compartment was a mixing pot of nationalities and affiliations: Vietnamese, Chinese, and Thais.

Possibly Laotians and maybe Cambodians, Ethan speculated, but knowing for certain was almost impossible; to a cherry, all Asians looked similar despite distinctions.

Some were armed, some wore tiger-striped fatigues, and others wore blue jeans and button-up shirts with mirrored sunglasses. There were also a few Americans whom he assumed were Agency types. As the Blackbird lifted off the tarmac, he began to swim in elation. He searched through the curious faces of those who remained from his graduating class. He remembered how almost everyone flat-out swore they were going to volunteer for C&C once they got in-country, yet the only other guys who had were Benfield Washington, Mark Anderson, and Paul Alvarez. They had grown to know each other well over the past two years and Ethan was especially fond of Mark and Benfield. Nobody called him Benfield, though. He was "Big Ben" – a horse of a man who'd grown up in Harlem. At fifteen, Washington lied about his age to join the Army; he was twenty-six when he earned his beret and graduated from Training Group as a Special Forces soldier with Ethan and the others.

Then there was Mark – the "Yankee version of a redneck" as Benfield had so eloquently put it once. He was from backwoods Minnesota and all he seemed to talk about was fishing and hunting, both of which were topics that every self-respecting Southerner could weigh in on. Mark fit right in minus the obvious accent, which left Paul Alvarez – a proud blend between Native American and Mexican blood. He was from some dirty little village along the New

Mexico side of the border. Sharp and a bit too serious at times, the wetback had "lifer" written all over him.

* * *

The airfield at Kontum buzzed like a hornets' nest as incoming and outgoing aircraft accessed the small contingent of runways and helipads on offer. It was a hazy, hot place where the sun wouldn't stop until it melted everything caught its rays. The heavy, acrid smell of spent aviation fuel remained trapped beneath the atmosphere and billowy red dust stirred with every footfall or tire track. Southeast Asia didn't have the typical four seasons; there was only the wet and the dry seasons. During the dry season, everything quickly became covered in a thick, red, dusty film that lingered until the wet season brought the monsoonal rains, quickly turning dust into an absolute mire of sloppy mud. It was hard to say exactly which was worse.

"Get a load of this fucking thing," Mark gawked.

They collected their gear and watched a junkyard-worthy three-quarter-ton truck roar to a halt at the edge of the tarmac. The entire rig had been painted flat-black and the front end had been nearly shot to pieces, which meant the guy behind the wheel had a bad habit of driving towards gunfire. The soft-top over the bed and cab had since been discarded and the split fold-down windshield had only half its glass on the driver's side. Mounted to the dashboard in front of the passenger seat was a .30-caliber machinegun that swung freely on a custom-made pedestal. And topping the chariot of mayhem off in complete style was the skull and horns from a water buffalo mounted to the grille via bailing wire. The driver stepped down from the rickety beast and strutted over clutching an old French MAT-49 sub-machinegun in one hand and a beer in the other; his appearance was nothing short of deranged. He looked to be in his early-thirties and kept an immaculate English-inspired moustache with long curled tips. He wore an old helicopter flight helmet, an unbuttoned Hawaiian shirt, a ragged pair of tiger-striped fatigue pants, and a pair of Ho Chi Minh sandals. He wedged the MAT-49 against his hip and took a long swig of beer.

"You fairies goin' to Couch Commandos Central?" he drawled. No one could talk at that point so they just nodded slowly. "Well what the fuck y'all wait'n for, a goddamn invitation? Get in." He drained the rest of his beer, slammed the tinted sun visor down over his eyes and climbed back behind the wheel. One-by-one the four of them pitched their gear up into the back of the truck and climbed in while their chauffer opened a fresh beer and turned the engine over.

"Hey Turtle, hold up!" a voice called.

"Man, this limo ain't wait'n all day," he complained.

"Did you get that?" Mark whispered to Ethan with a nudge. "Apparently this cat's name is *Turtle*. I never met a Turtle that wasn't a fucking two-bit whack job," he sighed. "God only knows what kinda unit keeps a joker like *that* on staff."

A man outfitted with an odd-looking harness, a CAR-15 and a camera jogged over and climbed in the passenger's seat behind the

.30-cal. *When Johnny Comes Marching Home Again* suddenly began playing loudly over two speakers that hung from the windshield frame. Turtle hit the gas and the old rig began growling forward, leaving a trail of red dust and black smoke behind them. They rolled out of the airfield and into an immediate swarm of civilians. Children clothed in little more than rags ran barefooted beside the truck along the potholed road. Some shouted for cigarettes while others held up bottles of Coca-Cola for sale. The two up front talked amongst themselves while glancing back every once in a while, almost as if sizing Ethan and the others up.

The one apparently called Turtle was odd-looking enough but the other man was a study in peculiarity in his own right. His fatigues were completely sterile and he hadn't had a haircut in probably two months. It wasn't long, only wild, spilling over an olive-drab cravat tied bandanna-style around his forehead. He carried a 35mm camera of some kind and wore a leather necklace that held a small jewel of Buddha, and around his right wrist were several homemade brass bracelets. He was armed with a CAR-15 – the sub-machinegun "commando" version of the M-16 rifle. The little carbine had a shortened barrel and a collapsible stock, and he carried several bandoleers stuffed with 20-round magazines across his shoulder.

"Hey," Mark said while leaning forward into the cab of the truck. "You guys are from CCC, right?" Mark was always good at breaking the ice, or tension, as it were, but neither of them seemed to care what he had on his mind. "So what do y'all do there?"

9

"Me, I'm just a clerk," the passenger laughed.

"Tough crowd," Mark shrugged.

No matter, Ethan figured. *We'll find out soon enough.*

The truck's heavy tires pounded Highway 14 into submission, and it quickly became painfully clear that whichever state-side manufacturer had designed the three-quarter-ton rig hadn't been too concerned about a nice, comfortable suspension. The airfield quickly disappeared in the dust while shirtless children scrambled along the road's edge, and scantily clad hookers sashayed slowly past, making devious eyes and calling out their prices. Farmers wearing black pajamas and conical hats plowed rice paddies, slopping through knee-deep muck behind bridled water buffalo. Paddy dikes divided the hamlets into squares, and small hootches with grass and palm-leaf roofs sprouted up in clusters adjacent to the paddies. Dark, fog-ridden mountain peaks carpeted by triple-canopy jungle slowly crept up far to the west. Over and beyond were Cambodia and Laos, and the Ho Chi Minh Trail.

The CCC compound was originally an ARVN truck repair facility and far from a Special Forces show camp. The compound was relatively small, around a few city blocks in size with guarded gates at its center where Highway 14 bisected it into eastern and western sections. A pretty standard affair of sandbagged bunkers and frothy bundles of concertina and barbwire surrounded the whole show.

Turtle stopped the truck in front an administrative building.

"This is as far as you twerps go for now. Get your shit and get out. The SMAJ will break it all down for you and then you'll go have a chat with the orderlies."

They climbed down and took a quick look around. The few Americans standing about offered yet another extensive study in the bizarre and oddity. Most of them looked like escaped convicts or mental patients. They wore a hodgepodge mix of fatigues, none of which matched and none of which were even close to US Army regulation. There were Fu Manchu and handlebar mustaches, pork-chop sideburns and wild, unruly hair. One guy was dressed in a silk suit and tie, and wore a filthy pair of jungle boots with old WWII leggings. He'd sewn his SF insignias onto the sleeves of his jacket and swaggered around with half a six-pack of Budweiser in one hand and a carton of Pall Malls in the other.

An orderly herded them inside a briefing room where they were instructed to sit and wait for the sergeant-major. The room itself was rather boring except for a large red veil that hung from the back wall which warned *Top-Secret*. They all sat quietly and speculated as to what was behind the curtain until the door swung open and a short, stocky man bearing no rank approached the wall and pulled the curtain aside. Everyone exchanged wide-eyed glances while examining the map which detailed the tri-border region where South Vietnam, Laos, and Cambodia all merged.

"Welcome to Command and Control Central," he said while gnawing on an unlit cigar and waving a hand at the wall map. It was completely blanketed with intelligence information, thumbtacks and all sorts of grease pencil markings. All of this information had been penned in amongst an entanglement of lines that extended from North Vietnam, through eastern Laos, and into eastern Cambodia, splitting off in multiple arrows that curved eastward into South Vietnam. The entanglement represented what was the Ho Chi Minh Trail system.

"Well I'm guessing from the looks on all your faces that y'all might have some questions, so allow me to elaborate.

"SOG stands for Studies and Observations Group, and that's what you gents have volunteered for. Our mission here at CCC is cross-border reconnaissance and information gathering. For those of you who are a little slow, cross-border means Laos, Cambodia, the DMZ and north."

CCC's area of responsibility began along Laotian Highway 165 and extended southward into Cambodia by roughly eighty klicks, or kilometers. Command and Control North operated in Northern Laos, along the DMZ, and into North Vietnam, while Command and Control South picked up the rest of Cambodia.

"Aside from reconnaissance, we also pull ambushes, prisoner snatches, wire-taps and surveillance, rescue missions, raids, sabotage, and all sorts of crazy shit that'll likely get you killed."

As the sergeant-major explained, SOG's OPS-35 employed two types of ground forces: platoon and company-sized raiding elements called Hatchet Forces, and smaller, more precision-minded reconnaissance teams. CCC's Recon Company had roughly twenty teams on-hand, all led by two or three US Special Forces soldiers and manned by nine or so indigenous mercenaries per team. The indigenous team members were a blend of ethnicities: Montagnards, Chinese-Nungs, Vietnamese, Cambodians, and even former NVA.

"Those of you going to Recon Company will receive team assignments as soon as possible," he said, working the saliva-soaked cigar from one corner of his mouth to the other. "Keep in mind that most of the men on these teams are very tight. They do *everything* together and you will have to earn your place among them. Each team has its own personality and that depends largely upon the One-Zero, or team leader. We always choose team leaders based solely on experience."

He pulled the veil back down over the wall map.

"On paper, we're still a part of the 5th Special Forces Group. But for SOG to operate to its full potential, we must remain of little or no interest to the conventional military and public eye.

"Don't keep journals or diaries, don't write home about what you're really doing over here, and don't run your mouths off to the uninformed. If you do, you're gone. Plain and simple. Are there any questions?"

Silence prevailed.

"Gentlemen, I guarantee you this is the most dangerous assignment in Southeast Asia. This *is* the real deal – *this* is what Special Forces was intended for. Welcome aboard."

Following the briefing, they went before the orderly to decide their fate. He sat comfortably behind his desk, basking in the glorious efforts of a straining air conditioning unit. Of the four of them, Ethan was the first in line. The processing clerk motioned him forward while looking him up and down.

"What can I do for you, specialist?"

Ethan sucked it up and said what he had to say.

"I'd like to volunteer for Recon."

"Recon, huh? Wanna be a goddamn war hero, do ya? Well that's good cause Recon needs warm bodies to fill the ranks and y'all sad sacks ain't gotta choice in the matter anyways cause you're *all* goin' to Recon."

Paperwork and in-processing done, they each signed a contractual agreement that bound them to secrecy for a minimum of twenty years after their military service. Then they each selected unique radio codenames and made it official.

*   *   *

Staff personnel flowed into and out of Snowden Hall as Ethan and the others scanned the recon team roster, looking for their names and team assignments. When he found his name, he read discretely to himself while dragging his index finger down:

Recon Team Utah

(1-0) SSgt Cameron

(1-1) SSgt Lawrence

(1-2) Sp4c Jackson

As he mumbled the names off, two guys came through the door and paused to look him over. The rusty spring stretched in loud protest and finally banged the door shut behind them.

"Lemme see that," one of them said. Ethan quickly recognized him as the guy who had jumped a ride from the airfield earlier that day. The other guy stood behind him peering over his shoulder.

"You Jackson?" the first guy asked with a stiff southern accent.

"This the twerp you were telling me about?" the second guy butted in before Ethan could answer.

"Yeah whatcha reckon?"

The second guy sucked at his teeth for a moment while looking Ethan up and down.

"He don't look like much."

Ethan just stood there with a bemused look on his face while the pair went on as if he wasn't there.

"I know but the *Dai-uy* says we gotta get somebody or else he'll find somebody for us. Last thing we need is some flatfooted clerk from the TOC."

"True."

"What's your name again?" the guy from the airfield asked.

"Jackson. Ethan Jackson."

"Well I'm John and this here's Mitch," he said as they shook hands. "Welcome to Recon. C'mon, the team house's this way," John waved. "Where you from?"

"Charleston, South Carolina."

"Charleston huh? You gotta girl back in the World?"

"Not that I know of, sergeant."

"Good. Now before you ask me – yes, all those buildings you saw just outside the wire are houses of ill repute. You're new, so the girls will try to swindle you. Never pay more than eight-hundred P for a short-timer and always use a rubber when you get your ashes hauled. We constantly inoculate the local pussy supply but guys still get VD. Keep your weapon and feet clean and dry and always purify your drinking water."

"Anything else?"

He laughed, "We ain't even scratched the surface yet."

A grouping of about ten buildings made up the team houses along the south side of the compound. Each building was divided into four rooms that measured around ten-by-twenty feet, just big enough to house the Americans from each recon team. Ethan stepped inside the musty hooch and dropped his duffle bag on the clean, concrete floor. Three racks were positioned in the back half of the room; one against the very back wall and the other two stacked into bunks along the left wall in the corner. Wedged into the back-right corner was a mini-sized refrigerator that sat atop an empty ammo crate; beside it, along the right wall were three wall lockers. The walls had been painted flat-white, giving the room a larger feel by exploiting the natural light. The forward half of the room had a single footlocker in the center serving as a coffee table and five folding lawn chairs. They had built several shelves using the lids from ammo crates and those hung from the wall above the fridge and were cluttered with personal effects and photos. In the front-left corner, a reel-to-reel tape player rested atop another empty ammo crate while a Jimi Hendrix poster hung on the wall behind it. Painted on the space above the room's door read: YOU HAVE NEVER LIVED UNTIL YOU HAVE ALMOST DIED. FOR THOSE WHO FIGHT FOR IT, LIFE HAS A FLAVOR THE PROTECTED WILL NEVER KNOW.

"Where'd that come from?" Ethan asked.

"Unofficial motto," Mitch said. "Dunno who first came up with it."

"Well the top bunk is mine," Ethan boasted sarcastically. "You guys are shit outta luck." His new teammates chuckled as it was the only bunk available.

After settling in, Mitch took him over to the S-4 Supply shop to draft his equipment.

"You're in luck," the clerk declared from the back of the room. "This is the last CAR-15 I have right now." He emerged from behind the racks and rows of weapons and crates of ordnance toting the little carbine by the carry-handle. He handed it across the counter and Ethan gingerly accepted it with awed enthusiasm while looking it over with a burgeoning smile.

The aluminum anodizing had been worn away from the corners on the receivers and it had a very dulled and smoothed finish. He laid the carbine on the counter and dug through the rest of his gear. Among the goodies was an indigenous rucksack, a Hanson extraction strap, combat harness, five two-quart plastic canteens with covers, one large collapsible water bladder, compass, strobe light, URC-10 emergency radio, pen flares, two Claymore mines, leather gloves, signal mirror, orange signal panel, gas mask and a huge stack of 20-round M-16 magazines. The supply clerk added a custom SOG recon knife and a Colt .45-caliber pistol to the lot while Mitch rifled through it, making certain it was all there. Barely able to carry it all, he and Mitch lugged the equipment back to the team house and dropped it on the floor. Ethan stood before the pile wondering where to begin. He quickly learned that every man had certain preferences as to how to rig his combat harness and where he wanted to carry certain things. Yet some things everyone carried in the same place so they all knew where to look in a pinch.

"You want the most important things like your emergency radio, signal mirror, morphine Syrettes, compass, and signal panel in your pockets so you'll never be separated from them," John explained. "String your compass with some parachute cord and wear it around your neck."

Both Mitch and John showed off their harnesses and where they'd placed their equipment; each of them could locate anything they wore without the slightest hesitation.

They laid out all his gear beginning with the combat harness – the platform of which was the standard issue M-56 pistol belt and H-suspenders. Ethan chose to use canteen cover pouches, six in total: four pouches for magazines, one for assorted grenades, and one for water. The canteen covers could fit seven 20-round magazines for his carbine in each – nearly double the number of magazines in each pouch compared to the smaller standard ammo pouches which could only carry four magazines. Although M-16 magazines were designed for a full twenty rounds, the springs and followers were notorious for tilting inside the magazine body which caused failures in feeding and extracting. His teammates advised him to pack no more than eighteen in each.

Like everyone else, Ethan taped his SOG recon knife and sheath upside down to his left suspender strap, and fixed a serum albumin kit to the back of his harness, right behind his head. He also carried a six-foot coil of climbing rope used to tie a Swiss seat with. The Swiss seat was used extensively as a rappelling and climbing harness, and could also be used for rope extractions beneath helicopters.

Dispersing the equipment evenly on both sides of the harness ensured a very balanced system with ammo and ordnance, water and first-aid within easy reach. Items that weren't extremely vital were stuffed inside his rucksack. Things like rations, a poncho liner, Claymore mines, additional canteens and ammo, assorted grenades, teargas powder, salt and iodine tablets, wrist restraints, det-cord, blasting caps and C4 plastic explosives. Fully loaded with ordnance, water, and rations, a recon man's equipment weighed nearly a hundred pounds – a hundred pounds that had to be lugged through dense triple-canopy covered mountains infested with enemy soldiers, booby-traps, and all manner of natural hazards.

He was busy making the final adjustments to his harness when the team house door suddenly flew open and something rolled across the floor.

"Shit!"

"Frag!"

Sure enough, not more than a few inches from Ethan's left foot was an M-67 fragmentation grenade – no pin, no spoon. He scrambled and kicked it back through the door in a squeaking furry of panic, then dove on the floor and squirmed up under one of the racks. He waited for it to cook off, expecting an ear-splitting explosion but heard howling laughter instead.

"You motherfuckers," Ethan cursed as he crawled back out and got to his feet.

"What's the matter, you wanna live forever?" someone called as he came through the door holding the grenade.

"Damn Bill, he got your number on that one," John howled with laughter. Mitch was still in stitches.

"Kid's got good reflexes," he admitted with a chuckle.

He reached out and shook Ethan's hand, then snaked a beer from the fridge and took a seat. His fatigue pants had been cut off into shorts and he was wearing a dirty pair of white flip-flops, a faded Rolling Stones t-shirt, and a short-brimmed boonie hat with "RT Missouri" embroidered on the front.

"Boy you're as green as the grass, ain't ya," Bill grinned as he looked Ethan up and down. "How long you been in-country for?"

"Five days."

"Three-hundred-sixty and a wakeup!" he guffawed.

"May as well be a lifetime," Mitch teased.

"How long you been here?" Ethan asked.

"First tour was with A-333 at Chi Linh back in '67. Extended, got shot to pieces during Tet, healed up and came back, and I wound up here with all the other misfits."

The door was suddenly kicked open again and in stepped a lean, square-jawed man wearing a black nylon windbreaker and cutoff jeans and a pair of black Chuck Taylors. Like everyone else, he too wore a church-key around his neck. He also wore a long length of parachute cord tethered to the handle of a Smith & Wesson .38 Combat Masterpiece which he kept tucked in the front of his waistband, and he smelled as if he'd just bathed in Aqua Velva aftershave.

"What's going on, *Dai-uy?*" Bill innocently quizzed as the man stepped into the team house.

He just stood there for a moment with his hands on his hips and his lips tightly pursed; the rest of his face hid behind a pair of mirrored aviator sunglasses while his beret covered most of his salt-and-pepper-colored hair.

"Which one of you fuck-ups stole the colonel's jeep last night?" he finally asked.

"What makes you think it was us?" John replied with deceitful innocence.

"Cause the goddamn thing's shot to shit and those fuckheads from CID just gave me the third degree."

"Oh really – what were they asking about?" Bill led on.

"Apparently a buncha ARVNs had their jeeps fired up in town last night. Although I don't know why I'm tell'n y'all about it since you sons-a-bitches are likely behind it. Reckon none of y'all are men enough to 'fess up to the crime, though."

He waited impatiently for a few silent moments with his right hand resting on the handle of his pistol – almost as if waiting for someone to draw. The others were trying hard to stifle their amusement.

"Honest *Dai-uy,* we don't know shit," John pleaded.

"Yeah, y'all *never* know shit... Who the fuck are you?" the captain asked.

"Spec-Four Jackson, sir," Ethan saluted. He was pretty-well sure that CCC had a lax policy regarding the formalities usually reserved for officers, but he figured he'd play it safe anyways.

"Damn, you must be one of my FNGs," the captain beamed. "I can't remember the last time one of these limp-dicks saluted me and called me 'sir'. It might not be too late to save you from these gangsters. I might be able to get you a cushy gig over at the TOC as my personal assistant. What say you?"

"You're too late *Dai-uy* – he's ours," John interjected as Mitch slung an arm around Ethan's shoulder and pulled him back.

The captain frowned, "Well then, I can see it won't be long before he's fucking up the order of my universe." He reached into the refrigerator, hooked a beer and punched a hole into the top with his church-key, then stormed out of the team house. "Fucking nightmare assignment for a career soldier if I ever saw one," he scoffed as his voice trailed off. Everyone broke out into a fit of laughter once the captain was well on his way.

"*That* guy's a captain?" Ethan asked as he glanced around in bewilderment.

"Yeah, that's Recon Company's commanding officer, Captain Jim Yates," Bill chuckled. "Don't let that old fart fool you, though – he was running recon with Project Delta at the beginning before transferring here; pulled recon for a while and lead a Hatchet Force company, too. He's done it all, knows his shit."

"And he takes a lot of heat for our escapades," John added. "I love that man."

"So what happened to the colonel's jeep?" Ethan asked.

"Those fucking ARVNs shot it up last night while we were in the bar," Mitch said as he finished the rest of his beer. "So we paid them the same courtesy, except we stole one to replace ours and then we shot the others to pieces."

"Y'all were *shooting* at each other? I thought the ARVNs were on our side."

"Shit, most of 'em are worthless and the ones that ain't, are commie sympathizers," Mitch spat.

"That's not entirely true," Bill argued. "There's plenty of hard chargers in the ARVN ranks, they just have piss-poor leadership. Too much corruption."

"So who stole the colonel's jeep?"

"Hell we did," Bill proudly admitted. "Vehicle ownership is a very fluid concept around here. Plus, it's part of our job to piss the *Dai-uy* off. It's a love-hate relationship."

*   *   *

It was barely after dark as Ethan curiously approached the source of all the loud racket echoing through the humid evening air around the compound. Illumination flares drew flickering, black silhouettes against a stark-white backdrop. A heavily drunken NCO lay passed out in the dirt next to the club's open door while his staggering buddies tried their best to wake him, pouring beer onto the ground as they leaned forward. Another herd of NCOs played a drunken game of dodge ball with what appeared to be horseshoes and wailing with maniacal laughter in the process.

A choking cloud of smoke filled the inside of the club as almost every man on the compound crammed themselves inside the building, which wasn't any bigger than half a basketball court. Strands of Christmas lights were hung everywhere and glowed in red, blue, green, and orange haze, while a set of speakers blared the Zombies' "Time of the Seasons". Off in the back-right corner, a cluster of NCOs crowded around a table playing a dangerous game of liar's dice while two young Vietnamese women danced on the bar wearing next to nothing. Ethan strained hard through the commotion and found his new teammates on the far side of the bar, harassing Captain Yates and clawing after the dancers.

24

"Drink up, cherry, it's on the house!" someone slurred while filling Ethan's hand with a full glass and slapping him hard on the back. It was none other than Bill Allen, and he was looking well-oiled and in good spirits.

The shots continued to flow as nearly everyone in the club offered to refill his glass throughout the night. Their urgings were tough to deny and Ethan was not one to turn down a free drink. Another hour was all the twenty year-old Green Beret would remember of his first night in Kontum – the first of many to come.

*   *   *

A muffled voice called from the open door of the team house, "Jackson, get your ass over to the club, Barnes is look'n for ya."

With soiled fatigues and matted hair, he dragged himself through the club's door and inspected the scene. It looked like an absolute train wreck; broken glass, overturned tables, chairs, and barstools showed signs of the previous night's events. The musty building reeked of stale alcohol and cigarette smoke and suffered from bad lighting. Standing behind the counter was Bob Barnes, the club's manager. "Big Bob" was an intimidating sight, about the size of a household refrigerator, and at one point, the One-Zero on RT California. His days of running through the bush had been cut short because of his size; his teammates were worried they couldn't carry him out if he got wounded. So instead of taking a staff job, Big Bob decided to manage the club, where he felt he was doing the most for the men.

"You seem like a good kid, Jackson, and I hate to do this to ya but you owe the house a pile of money for last night." Bob passed the tab across the countertop.

"Fucking Bill Allen," Ethan moaned.

"Lemme guess – stuffed a drink in your hand and told you it was on the house, and then everybody else offered to refill your glass?"

Ethan just stood there feeling like the village idiot.

"Oldest trick in the book. Think of it as an initiation fee. And believe me," Bob chuckled, "it coulda been *a lot* worse."

Ethan emptied his chit-book on the bar and massaged his pounding head at the temples. After settling the tab he promptly reported to the mess hall in search of something to abate his hangover. Coffee always seemed to taste better to him after a night of drinking so he loaded up on the typical Army breakfast of powdered eggs and toast, and poured himself a tall cup of freshly-brewed coffee, complete with two creams and plenty of sugar. He sipped the scalding brew quietly and scanned the room for familiar faces and soon recognized several recon men gathered for their morning rituals at a nearby table. He tried to place their names before closing in but it was far too late to spin on his heel and slink back to the sanction of Utah's team house – they'd already spotted him. He was a loner in there and he *had* to break the ice. Using his coffee mug and breakfast as camouflage, Ethan moved in slowly and cautiously, hoping to buy himself a few seconds to remember at least *one* of their names.

"Some of Recon's new meat," one of them grinned as Ethan neared the table. "C'mon over here, lad; have a seat," he demanded. "What'd you say your name was again?"

"Jackson," he admitted nervously.

"Yeah, we can see your *last* name is Jackson, smartass," another scolded with a smirk while flicking at the name-tape on Ethan's jungle shirt. "You gotta first name?"

"Ethan."

"Where from?" another asked.

"Charleston."

"Well I'm Joe Walker," he said as they shook hands.

Joe Walker was a slim,wiry man who just happened to be one of SOG's most accomplished One-Zeros. Behind a pair of horn-framed glasses, he looked almost out of place – more like a pharmacist from a small-town drugstore, or maybe a window teller at a bank. Make no mistake about it though, Walker's RT California was one of SOG's most successful teams and was constantly slated to run the toughest targets.

"This handsome screw-up is Tom Waskovich but we all just call him 'Ski' or 'Woji'." Tom had come to CCC just a few months earlier, first running recon with Wyoming before taking over the One-Zero slot on South Carolina. He sneered at Joe and shook Ethan's hand.

"These two degenerates are Rex Hill," Joe pointed, "and Pete Johnston. They don't do much except get in our way, so don't pay 'em any attention," he smirked.

Pete and Rex were officially part of the US Army's 219th Aviation Company, but had volunteered for a small unit that flew O-1 Bird Dog spotter planes exclusively for CCC. Unofficially, they were known as SPAF pilots, which stood for Sneaky Pete's Air Force.

Next he met Joe Parnar, a well-respected medic who worked at the camp's dispensary and took turns flying across the fence as the chase-medic. He also ran recon as a straphanger whenever teams were undermanned, and operated with the Hatchet Force when needed. Parnar's role was one of the most diverse of anyone there and his experience across the fence was held in high regards.

And last but certainly not least was Tom Waskovich's partner-in-crime, Ken Snyder – the venerable, baby-faced RT Iowa One-Zero.

"It's not normal for all of us to be on stand-down at the same time," Ken said. "Usually most of us are either in isolation, on the ground, or out at the launch site running Bright Light. So we're just kinda savoring the moment before the weather breaks and we get sent back out."

"The operational tempo is high in this outfit," Joe added.

They asked him what team he'd joined and when Ethan told them, they all nodded in approval. Apparently Utah was a strong and tight team.

2

His first few weeks passed with little sleep. Firebase Mary Lou's big guns shattered the nighttime glass from only a few kilometers away, sending a pulsating vibration echoing through the countryside like a summertime thunderstorm. Illumination flares slowly drifted to the ground, delivering a shimmering, flickering glow that sketched spooky shadows across the compound. As if the noise wasn't enough, the stagnant, humid air was nearly suffocating and the entire place seemed to be infested with rats. When nights were simply too hot to move or sleep, he would lay awake and listen as artillery boomed and small-arms fire rattled away in the distance. And it was during those restless and humid hours he came to know his teammates better.

John had been running recon since early '68 and was two months into his second tour. He was a seasoned recon man and came from a little town nestled in the mountains of eastern Tennessee.

Mitch was from Southern California and looked the part; tanned, icy blue eyes, cleft chin, sandy-blonde hair. He'd been in-country since August of '68 and had run recon for the duration, leading his first mission as the One-Zero a month before. He'd done well and showed the prowess of a potentially solid team leader, and was sure to inherit a team of his own before long.

Ethan found himself sitting on the concrete steps leading up to the team house's door on one such sleepless night, listening to the outbound artillery crack and thunder across the otherwise silent countryside. A slight breeze tickled the torrid post-midnight air as the screen door creaked open from behind and John plopped down beside him. They sat silently for a few minutes while absorbing the ambience and becoming acquainted with each other's presence.

"You'll get used to the nights," John finally said as he yawned. "So what brings you to the party?"

Ethan thought to himself for a moment as another outgoing artillery round from Firebase Mary Lou boomed overhead.

"College didn't sound too appealing and I sure as hell didn't wanna get drafted, so I volunteered… Seemed like the right thing to do, I guess."

"College huh?"

"Yeah."

"Your folks got money?" John asked as he yawned again.

"We ain't rich if that's what you're ask'n."

"Sorry, that was a bit personal."

Ethan shrugged, "S'okay."

"So Charleston, huh?"

"Born and raised," Ethan nodded. "Do a lotta fishing and spend a lotta time around the beach – some hunting but not a whole lot."

"Never been there before," John admitted. "Lots of history. I hear it's nice. Your father serve or are you the first?"

"My old man rode around in a Sherman in Europe."

"A tanker."

"Yeah. Did his best to convince me to go into the Air Force instead of the Army. Said the Air Force was the only outfit where you're guaranteed clean sheets and warm food every night."

"Yeah you probably shoulda listened to your pop," John chuckled. "My old man was with the 11th Airborne in the Pacific from '43 till '45. He's gotta few nervous ticks about him." He stood and stretched before pushing the door open and stepping back inside. "Better try to get some rack-time; we're gonna hold an equipment inspection with the little people tomorrow morning, so it'll be the perfect chance for you to meet 'em. Then we start training."

Low clouds socked the countryside in as they walked to the north side of the compound the next morning. Ignoring the unpleasant humidity, Ethan's new teammates elaborated on the quagmire of Southeast Asia's cultural and racial tensions.

"Everybody hates somebody," Mitch said. It was deeply woven into Southeast Asian history – well over a thousand years of racial and cultural despise between Montagnards and Viets, Laotians and Cambodians, and just about any combination of the four, not to mention the Chinese. When the French came to Southeast Asia, they called the tribal inhabitants of Vietnam's Central Highlands, "Montagnards", which literally translated to "people of the mountains". The Montagnards were Vietnam's version of Native Americans; though truly indigenous to the region, they had been forced from their coastal homelands to the Central Highlands. The Vietnamese viewed them as an ancient and uncivilized people but Special Forces had established a blood-like bond with them and to the Green Berets who lived and fought with them, the "Yards" were forever loyal.

"All of our Yards are from the Bahnar tribe and they're all from the same big village just to the southwest of here," John said. "There're several significant tribes – Sedang, Jarai, Rhade, Bru and Halang, but it's said the Bahnar are the most educated. Nay is the Yard team leader and Hyuk is the interpreter. We're just gonna introduce you to them and inspect their equipment and weapons today."

They approached a group of nine little brown people that swarmed around a picnic table beside the indigenous barracks. Immediately, a short, round-faced character spun and greeted them in clear English.

"*Trung-si* Cam-run," he grinned.

"Hey partner, y'all ready for inspection?" John replied, not wasting any time.

"We ready," he grinned with a nod and a smile.

"Good, tell Nay to have them put their harnesses on while we check everything."

He turned and translated John's instructions to the Yard team leader. Without hesitation, Nay fired quickly at the others and the giggling and horseplay ceased abruptly as each Yard pulled his equipment on and stood shoulder-to-shoulder. John and Nay started their inspection with Hyuk first. John was meticulous and thorough as he checked the buckles on Hyuk's gear, making sure the edges were filed down to round corners. He inspected the layout, admiring how ordnance and magazines were within quick grasp; he checked grenades, making certain the spoons were secured with tape and the pins correctly folded over. Next, they inspected Hyuk's CAR-15; John pulled the charging handle back and eyeballed the ejection port, breech and bolt. Satisfied, he reloaded the magazine and chambered a live round, then made certain the safety was positively engaged. Everyone at CCC carried loaded weapons at all times. As John and Nay moved through the team, Mitch talked of each Yard in detail, beginning with Hyuk.

"He's like everyone's slightly-older brother. The younger ones look up to him but he's definitely not above the grab-ass and horseplay." He comfortably sported cut-off blue jeans, loosely-laced jungle boots, and an unbuttoned jungle shirt. A worn-out, hand-me-down green beret sat on his head with the 5th Group's flash aligned perfectly above his left eye.

Nay was the catalyst of the group and held great influence over the others, which made him a natural leader. He was in his thirties which made him the second oldest of the jovial lot and carried himself in a prideful, experienced manner.

33

"Nay's been fighting the communists for over a decade," Mitch said. "Most of the others have been fighting for a few years with Special Forces but they never question Nay. On some teams, power struggles emerge between the indig team leader and the team interpreter but not on this team. Nay doesn't take any shit and they respect him as their leader; his father is the chief of their village, too."

Lost in thought, Ethan found it impossible to believe that he'd soon lead this group of tribal warriors into combat.

What the hell can I possibly teach them? he wondered.

Reaching barely five-foot-two was Luc, the team's pointman. His brilliantly white teeth beamed through a pair of fat lips that stretched across his weathered and narrow face. He was the oldest of the lot and seemed like a quiet giant of sorts. As the team's pointman, it was Luc's responsibility to guide them safely through enemy territory; it was a deadly job that required second nature and a sixth sense.

"He smells the NVA *long* before the rest of us can."

"What do you mean? Like actually *smell* them?

"Yeah, their body odor," Mitch said. "Your diet makes you sweat a certain way and that scent travels through the woods. I know it sounds crazy but it's the same reason why we eat indigenous rations several days before we go out. It's so that our scent will be like everyone else's out there. Piss, shit, sweat – it's all a part of your scent."

"Can you smell the enemy?"

"Definitely; you'll see once your bush ESP starts to develop. Takes a few missions but it'll come. It'll save your ass, too. Believe me."

Like all the others, Bo looked funny too – like a cartoon character with a thick head of jet-black hair topping off a scrawny toothpick-like frame. A deep, purple-colored scar drew a diagonal line from the left corner of his mouth almost to the back of his jaw line; when he smiled, four of his upper teeth, from center to left, glistened in gold.

"He took a shot in the mouth from a piece of shrapnel a few months ago," Mitch said. "That side of his mouth was peeled back and all four teeth were pulverized." Like most of the other Yards, Bo was simply a gunfighter and had no special status. "Me and John pitched in and got his teeth fixed. He smiles a lot and we're afraid the NVA can see him all the way from Hanoi."

Like the others, Ti Tu, Nui, Sol, Tang, and Noon were all combat-hardened gunfighters, none of which looked to be a day over seventeen.

The Montagnards loved bright, flashy colors and Utah's Yards were no different. All wore the colorful Special Commando Unit pocket patch along with Utah's custom recon team patch, and the US Army Special Forces insignias on their jungle shirts. They all had flashy Rolexes or Seiko knockoffs and homemade brass friendship bracelets, and they loved Hawaiian shirts. And though they held John and Mitch in high regards, John was quick to point out that Ethan would have to gain their confidence and respect.

35

"You will hafta prove yourself to them," he said. "They'll follow you into the gates of Hell if they believe in you."

With the inspection completed, John held a quick team meeting regarding the week of training ahead of them. As the horseplay commenced between the other Yards, Ethan could hear them laughing while sounding out the syllables of his last name, "Yok-sun." They gathered around him and touched his arms and held his hands, inspecting him, judging him. It was awkward at first but John and Mitch assured him that he'd get use to it. It was a strange customary that Ethan didn't understand; they were in his personal space and it was uncomfortable but he wrapped his head around the concept and made an effort to honor their rituals. It was just one way for him to earn their trust and that was as important as anything he'd ever learn in combat.

The next day, under his teammates' tutelage, they began with the basics: weapons and small-arms training. The firing range was located a few kilometers south of the compound but instead of loading up in the deuce-and-a-half, John had the team don full equipment and cover the distance to the range on foot, claiming that it was the best way to become accustomed to the weight of their gear. The firing range itself was nothing more than a sun-parched field of red clay pock-marked by dozens and dozens of small craters from ordnance testing; there was also cluster of shot-up targets down at the far end. Five minutes into his first training session, Ethan could see the past eighteen months in the Special Forces training pipeline had only served as a foundation to what he would eventually learn. He watched the team train briefly before John and Mitch began to work him into their drills and procedures. They showed him how to engage and fire at the enemy at uncomfortably close ranges.

"Forget aiming with your sights," John said, stepping back about thirty meters. "Just about all of our firefights occur within this little bit of distance, so you gotta have your weapon at-the-ready at all times or you're dead. A split second is all that matters."

Because the jungle was so thick and heavily vegetated, recon teams usually didn't see the enemy until they were literally face-to-face; there simply wasn't time to shoulder a weapon, aim and fire. Shooting from the hip had to become a reflex and Ethan sought to perfect it by means of endless practice. He also learned his teammates were big believers in frag grenades and could throw them so perfectly they seemed to float like feathers before exploding just above the ground. The harsh reality was that firing a weapon in dense jungle was the last line of defense because the muzzle blast would give away the team's location. Grenades inflicted severe casualties and disrupted enemy ranks without exposing the team. Over time and with lots of practice, John and Mitch had perfected the technique, but the Yards were a different story all together; they lacked the arm strength and were notoriously terrible at throwing things.

They also experimented with smoke grenades, white phosphorous, and CS gas grenades, carefully examining their effective uses.

"Never use green smoke – pilots can't see it against the jungle," Mitch warned.

Smoke grenades were used to mark targets or identify positions for aircrews but the problem was the smoke took too long to disperse through heavy foliage. For this very reason, recon teams preferred white phosphorous instead of colored smoke. When mixed with oxygen, the phosphorous would burst into a mist that burned at five-thousand degrees Fahrenheit, forcing a billowing white cloud instantly into the sky. White phosphorous grenades, also referred to as Willie Pete, were perfect for marking targets but could also inflict serious casualties upon the enemy.

As John instructed, Ethan would carry at least two WP grenades on his equipment while in the field but the chance of one being punctured while hanging from his harness was always entirely possible. White phosphorous grenades represented both extremes of the spectrum: a life-saver when used correctly but having one ignite accidentally would surely be a most unpleasant experience if it didn't kill outright. CS gas grenades were also extremely effective against enemy ranks, especially when coupled with a WP grenade. When mixed together, the two chemicals created a nauseous and deadly gas, and the humid climate caused the gasses to billow into a thick cloud that hugged the ground like a blanket of fog.

As the One-Zero, the team's organization was left to John. The team's pointman, Luc, was naturally placed at the head of the column. In order to exploit as much of an edge as possible, Luc sometimes wore an NVA uniform complete with a pith helmet and even Bata boots.

"It's real simple," John claimed. "The NVA will hesitate to fire when they see him because they're not certain he's the enemy." That slight hesitation was no more than a few seconds' time, but those few seconds would allow the team to engage first, and that would mean all the difference in the world.

The second man in file behind Luc was Bo, who would also be dressed as an NVA soldier. Instead of packing a CAR-15, Bo was equipped with a sawed-off Chinese-made RPD light machinegun. The RPD fired 7.62mm rounds out of a 120-round drum magazine and was significantly lighter than the M-60 machinegun. Sawing the front section of the barrel off just forward of the gas tube made the weapon far more maneuverable while maintaining accuracy. Just the tool needed to chop a large NVA formation up without sacrificing maneuverability.

Directly behind Bo was John, directing the team's route of travel while Ethan followed with the team's radio. Behind Ethan was the Yard team leader, Nay, then Hyuk. The last two slots were reserved for Mitch and one more Yard – usually Nui; they worked rear-guard and were responsible for covering the team's tracks, erasing all signs of their passage while listening and watching for enemy trackers who may be shadowing them. It could prove to be a difficult job if the One-Zero steered them through unfavorable terrain making it all but impossible to erase their tracks.

SOG recon teams were constantly outnumbered by heavily-armed NVA troops who could reinforce by the hundreds once a recon team was cornered. It wasn't uncommon for a recon team to be outnumbered by a hundred-to-one. Stealth was of utmost importance to a recon team's survival and it proved far easier to maintain stealth with fewer men. Utah was run as an eight-man team, and John always took the most experienced Yards. With eight men, the team could maintain stealth yet have ample firepower in case they made contact. If a man was wounded, it would require two men for his aid while leaving five to fight.

When a recon team made enemy contact, it was paramount they react quick and with violence of action. This controlled response was a team formation referred to as the immediate-action drill. It was quite simple. When enemy contact was initiated, the pointman would drop to his knee and fire off a full magazine while the rest of the team would split in half to either side. When the pointman emptied his magazine, he'd then turn and sprint back through the corridor his teammates had created while they covered his movement with controlled suppressive fire. One-by-one, each team member would cover the other as they peeled away in pursuit of the pointman, who would then be leading the team to safer ground. All this would occur in the matter of a few seconds. It was absolutely vital for a team to establish fire superiority from the outset, hit the enemy hard with a high volume of fire and grenades, then make a hasty retreat while calling for air support and an extraction.

The concept was simple and easy and the Yards had been thoroughly trained in all the subtle techniques, but they started fresh for Ethan's benefit. John and Mitch lined them all up in their respected positions and then moved them through the motions of the immediate-action drills one-by-one, going slow while Hyuk interpreted. This proved to be a timely process, but after a solid week of repetitive training, Ethan knew all the ins and outs. All that was left to improve upon was the quickness and agility of the team's reaction time. They practiced the IA drills constantly, starting with simulated gunfire, and eventually graduating to live ammunition.

"They like to creep up on us overnight and surround us and then hit us at dawn," John warned. "When you let 'em close the door on you like that, it usually means you're fucked, so it's best to hit *them* hard before they hit you – to knock *them* off balance."

The act of initiating contact was similar to the IA drill, but instead of responding to contact, the team would initiate it by moving towards the enemy's position. Once the team opened fire, they would either roll through and overrun the enemy's position or peel away into an IA drill. It all depended on how many NVA there were.

Like most teams at CCC, Utah trained in the nearby jungle, moving as they would if they were deep behind enemy lines in Laos or Cambodia. They employed stealth and stalking tactics perfectly executed with absolute silence, using only rehearsed hand and arm signals, and facial expressions. Soon, they found themselves sneaking up on wild game without ever revealing their presence.

John would have them pretend it was an NVA soldier and they'd remain totally motionless while observing the animal only meters away. Other times, they'd break away into an IA drill and kill whatever poor critter happened to be caught in the ambush. After they were done training, the Yards would collect their kills, tote the carcasses back to camp and prepare a great feast.

They practiced taking enemy fire from any and all angles so there would be no delay or confusion in their reaction.

They practiced carrying wounded teammates while responding to enemy fire.

Some days, they practiced chopper insertions, making sure to dismount quickly and move around the front of the aircraft and into the jungle. This gave the pilots a visual of the team and allowed the door gunners clear fields of fire. However, not all landing zones were large enough to land a chopper into, so they practiced inserting and extracting by aluminum ladders which were rolled out of the aircraft; they also rappelled in. When things got real bad and an LZ wasn't readily available or close enough to get to, teams were often pulled out on "strings" by way of the Swiss seat or the Hanson extraction rig. Being yanked from the jungle and dragged behind a Huey going a hundred miles per hour at eight-thousand feet made static-line parachuting look like something from Boy Scout camp.

3

Special Forces was a unique and thriving community – a strange mix of wayward and colorful personalities. Recon was a young man's game and the hazards of the job had a way of bringing out the animal in even the most placid individuals. The club was common ground, the one place where everyone came together to discuss combat lore, commiserate over lost friends and naturally, to party. It was a dangerous place for the uninitiated and the indiscretions and mayhem that transpired under its roof were often as wild and nefarious as the mission profiles.

During his first few weeks, Ethan made a good habit of venturing into the club with his teammates; they knew the score – who was safe to drink around, who had a short fuse or a nervous tick. Every man knew his place among his peers and for those first few weeks, Ethan's place was in the corner, watching and listening. It wouldn't always be that way, he knew, but until he earned his seat among them, that's just where he happened to fit in.

Utah had been training hard for weeks. They'd burned through thousands of rounds of ammo, several crates of grenades and even some heavier ordnance like B-40 RPGs and 60mm mortars. It was the kind of stuff that made grown men as giddy as children. Cleaning weapons, hot showers, then food and drinks over at the club was the order of business after a long, hot day at the range.

"But do you see how much more effective it is?" John lamented. "Ain't got time to shoulder and aim – ya gotta snap it up and work the trigger from your hip." He finished the rest of his beer and then used the bottle like it was his CAR-15 to illustrate his point. "It takes time," he nodded at Ethan, "but you're definitely getting better."

"Snap it up and work the trigger from your hip, aye?" Ray Fuller mimicked with a sneer. "Ya'll talk'n recon or whorehouse tactics?"

"I'd say both," Mitch chuckled.

Randy Reynolds just sat there snickering behind his beer. He was from Amarillo, Texas and had a soft spot in his heart for explosives and practical jokes, and it wasn't long before he figured out how to marry the couple.

Captain Yates bounced through the door, made straight for the bar, and grabbed four cases of ice-cold Budweiser.

"Shit *Dai-uy,* where you goin' with all that booze?!" Reynolds chortled.

"Private party. You pinheads ain't invited," he growled and strutted back through the door.

44

"C'mon," John motioned. "Something's up."

They caught up with Yates outside and got the scoop.

Bill Allen's team had attempted a prisoner snatch on a small group of NVA somewhere in Laos earlier that day.

"They blew an ambush, grabbed one of them little fuckers and tried to run," Yates explained. "Buncha Nguyens came running down the trail, shot the goddamn place up and hit the poor bastard they'd grabbed."

"Everybody get out okay?" John asked.

"Yeah, came out on strings."

A large crowd was forming on the helipads, anxiously awaiting the air package that had pulled Bill and his team clean off the ground. It had become an important tradition in Recon to greet returning teams with open arms and cold beers, especially after close calls. Minutes later, RT Missouri shimmered into view, dangling like yoyos beneath the helicopters. Normally they would've gone back to the launch site at Dak To but bad weather had forced them straight to Kontum. Bill and his teammates were surrounded as soon as their boots touched the ground. They looked tired and so dirty, yet relieved and happy to be back. Yates went around and filled each man's hand with a beer and then passed the rest around. Everyone helped them collect their gear and the whole crowd began shuffling back towards the company area. The S-3 Operations officer, Major Carl Zune, made his way through the pack and shook their hands.

"Glad to have ya'll back. Too bad about your kidnap victim," he chuckled. "You boys come see me as soon as you get settled, while the details are fresh." Then he turned and smirked at John and Mitch, "And I'll be see'n you gents bright and early tomorrow." The major glanced at Ethan and sighed, "Damn shame ya got mixed up with the likes of these felons." He chuckled at himself and pushed on through the crowd.

"What's that supposed to mean?" Ethan asked.

"Means we're getting a warning order tomorrow," Mitch said.

"No, the felon part."

"Work hard, party hard," John grinned. "Sometimes our antics don't go over so well with command."

"So what's that got to do with the major?"

"We call Major Zune, Major *Doom*," Mitch said. "He and Yates basically hold our fate in their hands."

"See, Zune is our S-3 Operations officer and he gives us our target assignments and warning orders. He has these *gentle propositions* reserved just for special occasions, like when a bunch of us get into trouble."

"So I'm guessing these *gentle propositions* ain't so gentle," Ethan said.

"Doom learned his tradecraft alongside the likes of Billy Waugh and Dick Meadows."

"...Oh shit."

"You're getting it," John laughed. "So when you fuck up and word filters through camp, Zune conjures up a real *choice* mission as a way for you to repent for your sins. And since he cut his teeth with

Waugh and Meadows, he's pretty much seen and done it all. He can get real creative, too. He's got special pull down in Saigon and usually gets his little suicide ops approved."

"I think he's got dirt on some higher-ups down there," Mitch speculated. "Maybe even Chief SOG himself."

"So this is the penance y'all owe for stealing the colonel's jeep and shooting at the ARVNs a few weeks ago," Ethan concluded. "And since I'm a part of this team now, that means I get to pay it, too. Great."

"Penance," Mitch chuckled. "Have you ever heard anyone in this outfit use a word like that?"

"I told you the kid was sharp," John grinned.

The following day, Ethan and his teammates shuffled into the TOC and received a warning order for a Prairie Fire target located a few kilometers across the border on the north side of Highway 110.

"Reckon you boys think since you got a new guy, it means you get a softer target," Zune grinned. "Don't worry; Jim has informed me of the crimes in which you two are guilty of. I'll just bide my time and wait until you're *all* guilty of some misdeed or three. Won't be long considering the company you keep."

"You shouldn't believe everything the *Dai-uy* says," John advised. "We don't recollect having 'fessed up to any recent indiscretions. He's a pathological liar."

"Yeah," Mitch elaborated, "that's why they sent him to OCS and gave him a commission."

Zune cackled and handed John the target folder.

"Just a simple area recon this time. No sense in punishing the kid for something he hasn't done yet. Aerial observation of truck traffic in this area has been thin lately and S-2 thinks the NVA may have built a secondary route specifically around this stretch." The major motioned to a boxed-in section of Highway 110 on the large wall map.

Like cancerous veins, the Ho Chi Minh Trail system spread from North Vietnam, through the far eastern edge of Laos and down into Cambodia with an uncountable number of branching roads, trails, and footpaths linking it all together before spilling into the border regions of South Vietnam. With SOG's help, American airpower had been secretly bombing the main routes of the Trail on a very regular basis in an attempt to stem the flow of troops and supplies.

"Our bombs often cut the trail and make it impassable," Zune explained to Ethan, "but it doesn't last long. They either work all night to smooth it over using bulldozers or they cut a hidden bypass around that part of the road that we can't spot from the air."

There was still a lot about SOG's mission that Ethan didn't know but the blanks were beginning to fill in. Going into Laos meant they could receive air support from fighter bombers and helicopter gunships. But unlike Laos, Cambodia was a far more complicated affair. Since it was declared a "neutral" country by Prince Sihanouk, this meant no fixed-wing air support could aid SOG ground forces inside Cambodia – only helicopter gunships. The North Vietnamese denied all accusations of having enemy troops located within Laos and Cambodia, as did the US and South Vietnamese. Still, both Laos and Cambodia were sanctuaries for the NVA and it was up to SOG recon teams to monitor their activities and report their findings.

The trio started by scouring the target folder which contained the latest intelligence collected on the area. A few weeks before Ethan had gotten to CCC, RT South Dakota had been inserted into the same target with the same mission. They'd gotten in clean but low clouds and soupy weather soon closed in. Dean's team was trapped for five days but that didn't stop the NVA. They had a predictable habit of exploiting the weather conditions knowing that US air strikes would be delayed. Being the sneaky and slimy recon misfit that he was, Dean managed to slip his team through the cracks and came out under light ground fire.

After Zune's briefing, Ethan and his teammates moved into isolation to begin planning and training. There would be no late-night partying or fraternizing with other teams about the specifics of their mission. Later that day, John flew a visual recon of the target-area aboard a SPAF O-1 Bird Dog spotter plane piloted by Captain Bruce Bessor. The slow, yet nimble O-1 glided over southern Laos while John familiarized himself with the terrain, looking for suitable landing zones for the team's insertion and extraction. The ideal LZ was critical for a successful insertion: Too obvious an LZ would likely have enemy LZ watchers close by, who would then report the team's location to a larger enemy force. Obvious LZs were often ringed by antiaircraft positions which meant bad news for the air packages. The perfect LZ was usually one that was so small only one chopper at a time would be able to squeeze in. A hole in the jungle canopy so small and inconspicuous, no enemy LZ watcher would suspect a helicopter could actually fit down inside it. John also kept close eyes on the surrounding terrain, looking for possible enemy locations, bunkers, trails, hootches, and anything else that may be of intelligence value.

That night, Ethan and his teammates held conference with Covey Rider Howard "Karate" Davis in their team house to review the mission. As a Covey Rider, Karate's job was to fly with SPAF and Air Force forward air controllers in support of CCC's cross-border operations.

"This is how it usually works," Karate explained to Ethan. "We fly out real early and check out the area that you guys will be working in. If the weather's clear and there's no real fresh sign of Uncle Ho's little cousins, I radio the launch site and you get the green light to insert. Then it's game-on."

But that was only half the equation.

Covey Riders also collected situational reports from inserted teams and helped SPAF and Air Force forward air controllers coordinate air support for besieged teams. In short, FAC pilots and their Covey Riders were a recon team's only lifeline.

"Shit sometimes, when we get a bunch of those suckers out in the open, we dive and hit 'em with Willie Pete until the big guns show up," Karate nodded. "Hell, we'll even hang out of the window with our CAR-15s and fire 'em up or drop frags on 'em when we can."

"Oh the life of a Covey Rider," Mitch mused. "Don't egg him on, E. His ego's plenty big as it is." Karate just sat there cheesing like the Cheshire Cat.

John and Mitch set about planning the mission while Ethan listened in to better understand the process. The following day, they presented a brief-back to Major Zune and Captain Yates. The brief-back outlined their overall plan and included possible insertion and extraction LZs, the general area where the team would conduct their reconnaissance, escape and evasion routes, and everything in between.

Yates and Zune conceded and Utah got the go.

The remaining time in isolation was spent going through their weapons and ammunition and all the tools of their trade. They packed and repacked their gear to be certain they had everything they would need and within close reach when needed. They worked on all forms of nonverbal communication to include hand, arm and even eye signals. They also tested various antitank mines at the firing range, both modified and unmodified versions. The practiced burying the mines in puddles, which provided perfect concealment; they buried them in soft dirt and in hard-packed clay, making sure to sweep the surface clear and erase the evidence. They also worked on uniform camouflaging.

In an effort to exploit the shadows of the jungle, recon men often used black spray-paint on their OD-green fatigues. They'd start with a fresh pair and spray them with random and erratic black stripes. Once done, they'd pull their combat harness on over their uniforms and connect the lines, spray-painting over straps and pouches, and then finally repeating the process with a rucksack on. The end result was a custom camouflage which worked brilliantly to blend all of their equipment together and into the shadows.

*   *   *

Lying on his back in the cool confines of Utah's team house, Ethan listened to Firebase Mary Lou's howitzer battery pound away while a few bursts of small-arms fire rattled off in the distance. Gunfire always sounded much closer at night and infinitely more terrifying, but as John put it, "It's just the home-guard VC doing their daily part to support the cause."

They ate indigenous rations the following morning then turned their personal effects over to the acting Recon Company first sergeant, Bob Howard. Never before had Ethan met such an impressive and dedicated Special Forces NCO than Sergeant First Class Bob Howard. He had recently returned to CCC after recovering from nearly fatal wounds he'd received while on a Bright Light mission back in early December. And the actions he performed on that mission, Howard was submitted for the Medal of Honor for the third time while at CCC. Third time must have been the charm for Bob because there would be no down-grading the citation like before. He was set to receive the Big One, the Pale Blue – the Medal of Honor. But the truth was that Bob cared not for combat citations and the shiny uniform ornaments that came along with them. If he had it his way, he'd be in the field, running recon or commanding Hatchet Force operations for SOG. Quite simply, the man was "Mr. Special Forces" through and through, almost to a fault.

"You'll do fine," Bob said with that slanted Alabaman smile and humble, penetrating eyes. Ethan just nodded at his encouragement and returned his firm handshake.

The only advice Captain Yates gave him was, "Don't fuck up."

Out to the helipads they trundled under the weight of their equipment and that special type of mental stress and excitement that only sudden annihilation and suicidal odds could inspire. John paired the team off into two groups and sent them to their respective ships. Ethan piled onboard with John and a few of the Yards and then they were up and out over CCC.

Lush greenery blanketed the rolling hills and mountains of the Central Highlands for as far as he could see while red-clay roads created irregular seams. He could see shallow rice paddies and small clusters of villages; far to the south, columns of black smoke twisted skyward without offering much of an explanation. Twenty minutes later, the convoy set down on the airstrip at Dak To, one of CCC's forward launch sites. It was situated precariously close to the tri-border region where Cambodia, Laos, and South Vietnam all merged together. Supporting the airstrip was a twelve-man Special Forces A-camp and their contingency of Montagnards. Also stationed at the remote outpost were elements of the 4th Infantry Division and the

173rd Airborne Division, who had fought one of the war's bloodiest battles on the adjacent Hill 875 in November of 1967. Roughly fourteen kilometers northwest of Dak To was the SF camp at Ben Het, and some twenty kilometers beyond were Dak Seang and Dak Pek SF camps. These remote launch sites were used when recon teams were targeted for missions along Laotian Highway 165, the northern-most area of operations for CCC.

Quietly following his teammates into the perimeter of the launch site, Ethan pondered the sign by the gate that flatly warned outsiders against taking photos of what was beyond. The launch site at Dak To was a completely restricted facility to nonessential personnel. A handful of small buildings stood inside the barbed-wire perimeter with mounds of sandbags piled around each. The exposed airstrip was a remote place with few creature comforts to offer; a communications shed, the airfield control tower, and a canvas-roofed hooch which served as the Bright Light team house was about all there was. Recon teams from CCC ran a week-long duty at Dak To code-named Bright Light and rotated in and out every Saturday. A Bright Light team's sole purpose was to either rescue or reinforce, either for downed American pilots or teams who were engaged in their death throes with the NVA. It was basically a waiting game to respond to disaster.

Trouble from Texas emerged from the commo-shed and manifested itself in the form of Randy Reynolds and Pete Mullis. "Rodeo" Reynolds and "Texas" Pete were both from the Longhorn State and were the One-Zero and the One-One, respectively, of RT

North Dakota. Reynolds had been trying forever to convince the guys on RT Texas to switch team names with him, insisting that it was only natural; he and Pete had even thrown together a tidy lump sum to purchase the rights to the team name but the guys from Texas weren't selling. Being that they were dead serious about the matter made it all the more comical.

"Shit boys," Randy called to them. "Karate says the weather's look'n good out there. Guess y'all will get your shot at the title, first thing."

"Y'all pulling Bright Light?" John asked.

"Yeah; pretty quiet so far."

"Who's out?"

"Just Hawaii. Had some movement last night but nothing major."

John and Randy walked over to the commo-shed to monitor the radio traffic while Mitch and Ethan settled the Yards in and made any last-minute preparations. About twenty minutes later, John emerged from the communications shed and walked straight over.

"*Dai-uy* Shepherd and Karate gave us the go."

The chopper crews were already pulling on their flight helmets and flak jackets and cranking their birds to idle. Ethan sat on the ground with his back against his ruck and slid his arms through the straps. He reached forward into John's hands and pulled himself to his feet.

"Okay, listen up," John said. "I know you're nervous. Just keep your eyes and ears focused and remember what you learned over the past few weeks."

Ethan nodded nervously while cinching the shoulder straps of his ruck down tight.

"You'll do fine. Bounce around on your feet to make sure nothing in your pack rattles or moves." After several hops, John was satisfied and slapped him on his shoulder.

As the eight men of Recon Team Utah filed through the gate towards the cranking choppers, they fired a single round at a sand-filled 55-gallon drum just to be certain their weapons functioned properly. Afterwards they each applied a plug of green tape over the muzzle of their weapons to keep the dirt out. They bristled outside the wire, crossed the drainage ditch, split into two parts and boarded the slicks.

Ethan began to feel a sinking sensation in his stomach; his nostrils filled with exhaust as the rotor wash stirred a halo of dust around the launch site. Nervousness and anxiety owned him as a burst of pure adrenaline dumped into his veins and surged through his body. Though he refused to acknowledge it, he had mixed emotions about the moment. He couldn't deny the excitement that coursed through him, yet he realized that death was all-too possible now.

Whatever happens, God I pray I'm not a coward.

The cabin flooded with a gust of cool air as the air package pulled off the airstrip and began to climb with altitude. The mist and fog had slowly begun to burn off the high ridges to the west. At eight-thousand feet, the red clay hills of Ben Het passed quickly below and soon, the rolling hills of the Central Highlands gave way to the Laotian frontier. It wasn't difficult to distinguish the border between South Vietnam and Laos – heavy, lush greenery gave way to a maze of thousands of pock-marks resulting from heavy Arc Light B-52 air strikes. Surrounding the blemish-like smudges were seared and splintered tree trunks. Massive entanglements of debris fanned out from every hole; some craters were filled with murky green water while others were only a few days fresh. Beyond the moonscape of craters, the devastation yielded to more heavy triple-canopy jungle, cavernous ravines and steep mountains.

John leaned beside Ethan, pointing down to the dirt road that formed a section of Highway 110 – a branch of the Ho Chi Minh Trail. The once lush green jungle had been vaporized on both sides of the east-to-west roadway, leaving only craters and gray, pulverized earth. Astonishingly, the roadway was completely intact despite US efforts to keep it closed with B-52 air strikes; it snaked around deep defilades and into blotches of jungle before reemerging just before the border. Employing many thousands of engineers and manual laborers, the NVA constantly repaired and maintained the Trail, using bulldozers to fill in craters and smooth the roadways as soon as the bombs stopped falling.

Anxiousness, excitement, nervousness, anxiety – it all boiled inside him. He would come to find that it would *never* get much easier; it would *never* feel much different, no matter how many times he went across the fence. Ethan knew because they'd all told him so. As he searched the hills and valleys several thousand feet below, he knew there were no friendlies beneath the canopy, and there was no place safe to go in case it got bad. He had only seven other men to rely on to make it back out. A sobering realization indeed, but he felt well-trained and confident in his teammates, and that was enough to make all the difference.

Shortly after crossing over the Laotian border, a pair of Cobra gunships broke loose and made a rapid descent towards the canopy. They made racey, low-level passes in a figure-eight formation over a tiny hole on a sloped hillside several kilometers away. They were baiting the LZ for any form of hostile ground fire or antiaircraft fire before Utah's slicks dropped in for the insertion. All too often, choppers committed to LZs only to be shot out of the sky by heavy ground fire; if the NVA opened up, the Cobras would be ready to suppress them.

Satisfied, the guns pulled out and hung close, ready to respond to hostile fire. Karate circled safely to the east and began directing the insertion. John readied himself in the open doorway on the starboard side with Luc to his right, their weapons at-the-ready. Bo readied himself beside Ethan in the opposite doorway and offered him a smile that stretched the purple-colored scar across his face.

"*Trung-si* no worry!" he shouted and patted Ethan's arm.

Lower and lower the ship fell, dropping into the LZ as trees raced past in blurs of green and brown. Ethan prepared himself in the open doorway as the downdraft washed the heat and humidity up from the bottom of the LZ. He trained his CAR-15 on anything his eyes focused on, tracking shadows, trees and anything else that may conceal the enemy. He strained to see barking muzzle flashes from enemy AK-47s, or exploding flak from antiaircraft guns but they weren't there. Anxiety burned through him as he felt the eyes of a million NVA cast upon him, waiting to kill him and his team.

Just as it seemed they were going to crash, the pilot pulled power and eased them in. The nose flared and the bird pulled into a perfect hover for barely a second, which was all John needed to determine if the LZ was hot or cold. As the One-Zero, if John didn't like it, he wouldn't go and *none* of them would go.

The bird lurched as he and Luc dropped into the swaying elephant grass five feet below; then Bo was gone, and then Ethan as quickly as he could. The fall was short and he clambered to his feet, struggling under the weight of his equipment. His right fist clutched his CAR-15, while he pushed himself to his feet with his left arm. His jungle boots clawed at the soft earth but the damp grass made traction difficult at first. His eyes watered and his vision blurred while light debris from the Huey's downdraft floated through the air. He followed his teammates around the nose of the lifting slick just as John had instructed which gave the door gunners clear fields of fire. Slipping quickly into the woods, John situated them in a slight defilade among a thick tangle of saplings and ferns.

The second ship came in and Mitch and the remaining Yards – Nay, Hyuk, and Nui – slipped out and bolted through the waving grass and into the perimeter. By the time they were whole again, the choppers had pulled out and were gone. The beating of their rotors slowly faded as they climbed high and into a holding pattern several kilometers to the east in case the team needed an immediate extraction. Karate continued to draw circles far in the distance, barely within earshot, waiting on them to call in a situational report, or sitrep.

Holding that tight perimeter, all eight men lay motionless, quietly observing their surroundings in total and complete silence. The foul stench of mold and mildew mixed with expended aviation fuel and permeated Ethan's nostrils, assaulting his sense with incredible presence. His ears and head throbbed to the beat of his heart as it pounded like a drum inside his throat. He slowed his breathing and eased into his surroundings, listening for anything unusual, but all that remained was an incredibly eerie silence – a silence so loud it became disturbing. Quietness was good but complete silence was bad. Seconds bled into minutes while the jungle began to resume its normal ambience of chirping, chattering and howling. Then John nodded at him, and with the volume so low only he could hear, Ethan slowly pulled the radio handset to his head and relayed the team's sitrep to Karate with a simple "Team okay." With that, Karate cut the choppers loose and sent them back to Dak To to refuel. Soon, the FAC's engines were gone as well and they were left to fend for themselves.

John motioned Luc to take the point, moving uphill to the west. He slowly rose to his feet while clutching his CAR-15 and began leading them away from the LZ. One-by-one, each team member followed accordingly until they'd formed up into a tactical column. Mitch and Nui worked deliberately to erase their existence from the jungle by repositioning foliage, plants, small saplings, erasing boot prints, and other signs of nature that betrayed the team's passage. It was up to them to see to it the enemy didn't pick up the team's back-trail, but even when everything was done right, sometimes luck simply ran out. The NVA knew of SOG's existence all too well and devised special units tasked with hunting, tracking, and killing SOG recon teams. They were counter-recon elements and they were among the toughest, most well-equipped and well-trained outfits the North Vietnamese had.

So like the others, Ethan moved with extreme caution, analyzing every shadow, every tree, every blade of grass for enemy movement. He was sure not to step on anything noisy like rotten bamboo stalks or anything too soft, like mud. Rotting bamboo had a bad habit of generating a silence-shattering crunch when stepped on. In the depths of the woods, a noise that loud could be heard from a long ways away. Likewise, soft earth was nearly impossible to erase boot prints from. In the NVA's backyard, every little thing had to be considered hostile – trees, rocks, shadows, bushes – everything could conceal an enemy soldier or ten. Ethan moved slowly, pausing, listening, looking, stepping, and then repeating it as proficiently as he could. As John and Mitch had shown him, he avoided all shafts of sunlight and moved from shadow to shadow, tree to tree, keeping good cover close by in case they got hit.

The column zigzagged silently through dense underbrush on a western heading for a solid hour, covering several hundred meters from their landing zone. With the wave of a hand, John shifted their course more to the north and put team parallel to the ridgeline, which loomed several hundred meters uphill. By changing directions at random intervals, enemy trackers had a much harder time predicting where a team was heading. If they were being shadowed and continually moved in a straight line, trackers could predict where they would cross a trail up ahead and alert reinforcements to ambush them. Usually, a recon team had no knowledge of any trails until they were crossed and moving in straight lines would invite certain annihilation.

Several more hours crept by with the team finding or hearing no fresh sign. The remaining light of day began to dwindle away as the sun dropped below the ridgeline and the shadows grew darker, bigger, and deadlier. Ethan's face throbbed and sweat ran aimlessly down his face and into his eyes with a stinging presence. The straps of his rucksack hacked deeper into his shoulders with every step. Insects swarmed around his head and the blunt taste of dried salt emerged when he licked his lips; his fatigues were drenched with sweat and coated with salt rings but he paid little attention to his ailments. He could not preoccupy his mind with anything else; he *had* focus if he was to survive – if *they* were to survive.

Very little sunlight penetrated to the jungle floor even during the peak hours of daytime, making it hot, humid, and dark beneath the canopy. With the retreating sun, the woods quickly morphed from shades of vibrant green into fuzzy gray. John signaled Luc to button-hook around so they could observe their back-trail in case they were being tracked. For ten minutes, they sat in utter silence, observing and listening to the pulse of the jungle, but seeing nothing.

Satisfied, John began searching for the team's RON – remain overnight position – where they would deploy into an extremely tight defensive perimeter until dawn. He was looking for the ideal spot – a spot so inconspicuous and so small, the enemy would never imagine eight men could actually fit. Several large cypress trees stood just uphill to the left. Although the entire mountainside was littered with cypress, this cluster contained three mature trees with large trunks. The sprawls of their roots reached out and down with a grappling effect, meshing into the soft soil making it the perfect RON site. The grade of the mountainside was plenty steep to keep the enemy from being able to perform continual sweeps if the team was located. John also took into consideration the distance they were from the ridgeline, about a hundred meters uphill. Being too close allowed the NVA to pitch grenades down-slope where they would explode right on top of the team.

Satisfied, John motioned Luc who slowly and quietly led the team into the RON site where each man deployed as rehearsed. Once settled in, Ethan crept about five meters outside his position and wedged his Claymore on the opposite side of a tree trunk, positioning the mine so that it faced outward. The Claymore was a curve-shaped mine, containing steel balls and a piece of C4 explosive; it could be detonated by time delay, trip-wire, or electrically. It was a directional affair and when detonated, the mine would expel a devastating barrage of fragments in a fan shape. But because of the C4, it had a deadly back-blast; teams had learned to place them in front of obstructions, like trees or rocks. Keeping the mines danger-close to the RON kept the enemy from being able to trace the mine's wires back to the team or turn the mines around.

With his Claymore out, Ethan leaned against his rucksack using its bulky form as a prop, positioning the straps to where he could simply slide his arms through them if they were hit overnight. As he had learned, he would keep his combat harness fastened securely around his waist and the radio handset close to his ear. His CAR-15 would never leave his side, nor would his Claymore detonator and he dare not move a muscle unless it was absolutely imperative.

The squelch broke and Ethan gave Karate an encrypted grid coordinate of their location and a last-light sitrep; all was well. With most everything taken care of, all that was left to do was to eat and try and sleep some. He reached into his armpit and removed the little baggie that contained his dinner – a dehydrated ration of rice and chicken he'd added water to earlier. His teammates had shown him the trick: add water, knot the baggie off and place it next to the skin so that body heat warmed it. Splash some Tabasco into it and voila, dinner. As he shoveled his ration down, he concentrated on memorizing everything in his sector while listening to the ambience for anything unusual. Soon, gray transformed to a total and complete blanketing void of blackness. He slowly waved a hand before his face but not even at an inch away, could he see.

John decided against having assigned watches, which assured him the entire team would constantly be alert and on edge. The slightest sound would jerk them from an uneasy slumber, driving their hearts into their throats while adrenaline pulsed through their veins. But with the exception of a few far-off signal shots, the restless, uneventful night finally unfolded into predawn grayness.

Watching the shadows take form, Ethan ate silently yet poised and prepared for whatever might come with the turn of day. If the NVA had located the team overnight, they'd hit them at dawn, hoping to catch them off-guard.

The radio crackled and Ethan put the handset to his head and breathed a "team okay" into the mouthpiece. In minutes, their Claymores were in and they were on the move, tracking northwest, angling towards the crest of the ridge.

Operating in dense jungle over mountainous terrain, recon teams regularly covered less than a thousand meters in a full day of movement. Visibility was often cut to just a few meters in all directions and everything was green – billions of shades of green. Not only was the terrain and climate inhospitable, but the Ho Chi Minh Trail was quite literally the most heavily defended and regularly patrolled corridor on the face of the earth.

The NVA had base-areas complete with field hospitals, tunnel networks, outdoor and underground classrooms, supply depots, and camouflaged truck parks. From Hanoi, down through

Laos, and into Cambodia were an estimated 10,000 antiaircraft emplacements while the roadway networks were serviced by some 30,000 support troops, with an additional 60,000 security troops. And that didn't include the counter-recon units that continually hunted SOG teams. More than once, SOG recon teams had simply vanished without the slightest trace.

*   *   *

By midday, they had reached the crest of the ridge without finding a single sign of enemy presence. With a thinner canopy, the sun poured through the trees and illuminated wispy patches of vibrant green elephant grass and groves of waist-high ferns. The air was cooler and lighter, more refreshing. John signaled Luc into a group of moss-covered boulders and everyone quickly deployed into a defensive perimeter. Every day, from noon till around 2pm, the Vietnamese sought refuge from the unrelenting midday heat – a tradition called *pok*-time. It was in a recon team's best interest to honor this tradition; any movement during these hours would be a written invitation to the NVA to come to the big dance.

They ate quietly, watching their Claymores while monkeys frolicked in nearby trees. Somewhere just beyond their position, likely poised on a tree branch with its throat swollen into a balloon, an Asian gecko groaned a *"phuc-yuu"* while birds flocked above the treetops. Ethan admired the peacefulness – how the woods seemed to ignore their presence.

Squelch broke yet again and Ethan passed John the handset while Mitch readied a signal mirror and John reported the team's sitrep.

"We gotta stay high-and-dry," John whispered, as he passed the handset back to Ethan. "There's a team in contact farther up north."

Ethan's eyes narrowed, "Any idea who it is?"

John shook his head no.

Going "high-and-dry" meant they had to avoid enemy contact because all available air assets were committed to helping whoever's team was in trouble. If Utah made contact, they'd be on their own until the other team was extracted and air assets diverted. Looking around the perimeter, Ethan knew they had a superior defensive position, being staggered among large boulders atop a steep ridge with clear fields of fire at all sides. Because the jungle was thinner there, the enemy was less likely to come wandering about. So for the next two hours, they waited in utter silence, hoping for the best for whoever's team was in trouble.

Another radio check with the FAC and they were back on the move, driving north along the ridge for about sixty meters, then switching back southwest and moving downhill towards wrinkles of undulating hills and small valleys blanketed by heavy jungle. With nightfall pending and the air becoming crisp, they found another perfect RON site and bedded down for their second night.

Just before dark, John moved the team a few hundred meters into another RON site, a tactic many One-Zeros used in hopes of throwing the NVA off if they had lucked into finding the team. Dusk quickly poured into blackness with no sounds other than the jungle itself, breathing.

4

He opened his eyes and searched frantically from side to side, trying desperately to see light, any light at all. Still engulfed in an endless sea of complete blackness, a cold, lonely feeling trickled down his spine while his nostrils flooded with the musty smell of mold and cool moist air. A million thoughts burned instantly through his brain before he regained his awareness, but something wasn't right. No crickets, no lizards, no birds; the jungle had completely silenced itself into a deathly hush. Complete silence was bad. His ears strained against it as his brain tried its best to process anything – any sound.

There it was.

A rustling sound – something so unnatural, it simply didn't belong. It was a sound that reminded him of home, of someone tearing through a mountain of fall-colored leaves while the seasons rolled. Anywhere else, it would have been a warm, friendly sound, but not there. Adrenaline flooded his veins as his heart pushed up into his throat, beating hysterically like the main rotors of an approaching helicopter and he was certain the entire hillside could hear it.

Slow moments passed in utter silence, a silence so loud it hurt his ears. He tried desperately to slow his heart rate and his racing pulse, but the surge of adrenaline overwhelmed his efforts. He was terrified. In his left hand, his Claymore detonator; in his right, a frag grenade; his CAR-15 lay comfortably across his lap with a full load, one round chambered and eighteen left in the magazine. An eerie chill swept back down his spine as more faint rustling resonated through the woods; there was no doubt something was there.

Silently rolling to his left side, he placed a hand on John's right leg and breathed as quietly as he could.

"Movement; uphill, fifty meters."

"Shhh," he softly hissed.

A relentless eternity bled away in cold silence before a bone-shattering *crunch!* gouged and chipped echoes away from the depths of black. Ethan squeezed his eyes closed as tight as he could until he saw white; his heart had all but punched a hole through his chest. It was the unmistakable sound of rotted bamboo giving way under a man's foot, not more than twenty-five meters away. Bamboo stalks collided with a resonating *whack!* as they were parted aside. A heavy waft of stale urine and intense body odor drifted downhill and polluted the cool, damp air.

Then came voices; a low chatter of Vietnamese tongue flowed calmly between unseen faces and shadows within shadows.

The sloshing of half-full canteens and then drifting beams from flashlights became discernable. Ethan had never before been in such a life-threatening situation, and certainly not voluntarily. He knew the Yards would keep their cool; he just hoped he could keep his.

Claymores first, then grenades; don't shoot unless it's unavoidable, he reminded himself. *Then, break contact and run like hell while getting Karate to bring in air support.*

Only problem was Karate wasn't there, not until first-light and it was far too dark to run.

One, two... five, six, seven...

He counted silently to himself as their flashlights slowly floated and bounced past. He didn't need to see them with his eyes to gauge their numbers – that's how close they were. He could barely breathe for fear they might hear his deep exhales and he could feel his pulse throbbing through his face. Burning embers of lit tobacco glowed through the foliage as the offensive stench slowly rolled over their heads and assaulted their senses. For a brief moment, the burning cigarettes brought a relief to the rotten, stagnant air.

This is fucking nuts, he thought. *I can't believe this is actually happening... Thirty-two, thirty-three...*

It seemed a never-ending column of NVA not twenty meters beyond his Claymore. Slowly they wandered past without the slightest idea of what was literally right under their noses. They drifted through the jungle like the smoke that twisted from their cigarettes. Number ninety-eight was on the tip of Ethan's tongue as the last man slipped past. They listened to them for what seemed like a long time as they made their way down the hillside by way of an apparent trail the team hadn't found when they moved into their RON site. Such was the risk of moving into an overnight position after sundown.

Ethan finally slowed his breathing while listening to the silence. A cold sweat ran profusely down his face before soaking into his fatigues as his nerves began to ice down. He had been consumed by an emotion he had never experienced before – an emotion that couldn't be explained by tears, or laughter, or even anger. Ethan realized that he would've killed them, as many as he could without a hint of doubt, or hesitation, or remorse. He would kill for self-preservation, for survival, for those seven men whose lives depended upon him. It was a mental state of preparation that he willingly accepted and it was as important for his survival as any weapon.

*   *   *

After SPAF-1 dropped by for the morning sitrep, John, Luc, and Bo pushed forward, leaving the rest of the team to cover their advance. About twenty meters from their RON, they found their first trail, no doubt the one the NVA had used the previous night. It looked to be a lightly-used trail, showing a fair amount of growth on its surface, but it wasn't wide enough to accommodate vehicles. Overhead tree branches had been pulled and lashed together creating a dark corridor that aimlessly meandered through the Laotian countryside, completely invisible from passing aircraft.

Ingenious, he thought.

His head swam as he forced one leg in front of the other, carefully stepping over the trail's surface. His CAR-15 floated by his side and his palms flooded with sweat. An eerie, uneasy feeling mingled and meshed with sheer exhilaration and stifling anxiety. It didn't break his heart to put the trail well behind, but Ethan knew the NVA were close – the way they smoked their cigarettes, talked, and pushed through the brush under the cover of night. They were noisy and careless, and best of all, they weren't counter-recon types.

Just before noon, they crossed another trail, taking careful consideration not to disrupt the surface. Just as the first trail, this one showed recent signs of use. They documented it, shot several photos and moved on. As *pok*-time approached, the team moved into the deepest cover they could find and setup for a small bite to eat while they waited. Then they were back on the move, cresting a low, gradual ridge while moving deeper into Laos. The backside of the ridge opened up into a wide, dense valley that ran from north to south. Shifting northwest, the team slowly moved down the hillside, towards the valley floor.

Barely fifty meters from the ridge, Luc halted the team and relayed the signal – another trail with the same hints of recent usage as the previous. Elephant grass and rooted saplings had begun to reclaim the trail for the jungle but the grass had recently been parted, and the center was well-matted and damp. It was an alarming trend that indicated the NVA were moving back into the area. Unfortunately, none of the trails found so far were large enough to support vehicles, only infantry, but the odds of finding something good were improving.

The rest of the day passed without incident and soon, they were settled inside their RON while the bottomless void of another night claimed the jungle. Ethan nestled into the bamboo thicket and propped himself against his ruck. He was tired of his own stink and the grit and grime that stuck to his clammy skin. His head pounded from dehydration and his eyes were as dry as wheat. Survival was an exhausting task and he knew he wouldn't get much rest if he couldn't bed his mind.

Against his better judgment, his thoughts wandered off to a little street in Charleston, South Carolina lined with two-story brick homes. Dusk was settling upon his street while children ignored the waning summertime twilight and continued to play. The faint hint of a backyard barbeque wafted overhead, surely coming from the Crumbs' house two doors down.

He shifted his position just slightly enough to pull himself from home and back into southern Laos. He felt his equipment clinging and his matted hair pressed against his scalp. A brief vacation was all he needed to reset his awareness. The damp night carried him into a light, uneasy sleep that remained uninterrupted until predawn.

*   *   *

He pulled the charging handle back and ejected the live round from the chamber insuring the brass casing hadn't swollen and seized inside the breech from the nighttime moisture. Ethan gave a quick glance, pressed the loose round back into his magazine and quietly reloaded his carbine. John gave SPAF-1 a positive sitrep while the team reeled in their Claymores and prepared to move.

Hyuk peered from under his boonie hat and offered Ethan a broad smile with a thumbs-up. The Yards appeared at ease and full of confidence with the turn of day. They formed up behind Luc and got the show on the road.

The jungle was alive with all its children talking in full voice, which was an encouraging sign. They drifted quietly through a spooky area covered by a stagnant blanket of fog. Moss-covered teak trees towered endlessly with thick rope-like liana vines hanging aimlessly about. As they made their way silently into the trough of the valley, the ancient hardwoods yielded way to thick sapling groves and razor-sharp thorns. The thorns pulled and ripped away at uncovered skin, leaving bloody abrasions that burned like fire as sweat seeped in. With every step, Ethan's ruck grew heavier and heavier; his shoulder straps never seemed to have enough padding, and what was there certainly wasn't always in the right places. His feet bled sweat and the soles of his jungle boots grew thoroughly unforgiving. Insects swarmed about his face and neck, though only curious; apparently, they didn't like the camouflage stick and bug repellant smeared over his skin which suited him just fine. Through the mist, they silently traversed over a maze of fallen hardwoods. As Ethan threw his leg atop the first trunk, Nay grabbed his arm and pulled him back down. Puzzled, he watched Nay slide his bamboo machete across the trunk right where his leg had been. He scooped a small green snake onto the blade.

"Two-step," he whispered as he flung the critter into the woods. He swiped his index finger under his throat indicating the snake was poisonous.

Ethan sighed with slight frustration and then nodded. Watching for the enemy was one thing, but keeping an eye out for poisonous snakes was something he just hadn't thought much about. Nay cracked a smile full of white teeth and patted Ethan's shoulder. It was a bamboo viper, a nasty little guy with enough venom in one drop to kill a man dead-cold in the time it would take to walk two steps.

They continued to creep through the deadfall for the better part of two hours with only the slightest hint of sunlight poking through the canopy in brilliant beams of dusty luminescence. There, the stink of the jungle was at its greatest as timber decomposed away into the rich and moist soil.

*   *   *

For the next two days, they swept to the northeast and eventually took on an easterly heading. Pushing into a neighboring valley, they found more high-speed trails and dodged a few patrols, but still found no indications of a secondary roadway large enough to support vehicles. Shortly after *pok*-time on their fifth day, they discovered an NVA bicycle supply line. The right side of the pathway was narrow and rutted in some areas with bicycle tire tracks stamped perfectly into the muddier sections while the left lane showed hard-packed earth.

In an effort to remain hidden from overhead observation, the NVA often resorted to moving supplies via bicycle in many locations. A few weeks ago, Ethan had inspected a captured bicycle that one of the teams had brought out of Laos. The heavy steel frame could easily carry several hundred pounds of equipment and the left handlebar had been sleeved with a long section of bamboo. Instead of riding the bicycles, the NVA used the extended handlebar to walk the bikes when loaded down with supplies. Once unloaded, they'd ride them back to a base-area and load back up. Soldiers were often assigned specific routes and trails and used them on a regular basis, eventually learning them so well that they were able to use them in complete darkness.

The bicycle path had been their biggest find yet and it almost ruled out the possibility of there being a larger roadway in the immediate area aside from Highway 110. John pulled the team up against a nearby hillside to monitor the path for a few hours before finally deciding to mine it. After some careful deliberation, they selected the most opportune spot, moved down and established security. Ethan looked on as John buried the antitank mine brilliantly in a rutted section where rainwater had collected in a murky puddle. The track was too narrow for a passing bike tire to miss the mine, and with hundreds of pounds of equipment strapped to its frame, the weight was certainly plenty enough to trip the pressure-plate. It was early in the afternoon and they'd been on the ground for six days; they were all exhausted and out of food and water. Satisfied at what they'd found and the conclusions they'd drawn, John grabbed the radio and called for a last-light extraction.

*   *   *

The thumping of the Huey's rotors and the whine of its engines were the loudest things any of them had heard in almost a week. The cool air tugged and pulled at Ethan's fatigues while ripples in the soiled fabric jerked and popped in the wind. Only after sitting on the cool aluminum flooring of the chopper did he truly feel his exhaustion; his entire body ached and his stomach growled from hunger. They were all both physically and emotionally spent.

John looked over at the crew chief while talking into the headset, nodded and grinned. He then aimed his CAR-15 out of the open door and began squeezing rounds off on full-auto. Then Luc rattled off two full magazines and then Bo started chopping away with his sawed-off RPD from the other side of the bird.

Ethan pointed his barrel out the open door and clamped the trigger, and before he knew it, the bolt had locked back on an empty magazine. He reloaded, closed the bolt and squeezed the trigger again while howling into the frozen air with his teammates like a pack of madmen, and it felt absolutely incredible. Empty magazine after empty magazine, his anxiety and anxiousness fluttered away in the wind. He had never felt more alive.

*   *   *

As the Huey spiraled towards the helipad on the south side of the compound, Ethan watched as a crowd quickly formed up to receive their return. Being in-country for all of two months, he'd been among those waiting by the helipad on more than one occasion, but only now did he realize the raw impact it had on a returning team. Standing amid a billowing cloud of red dust were a select few who understood what Utah had been through during the past six days. It was a feeling he had never experienced before – an emotion of complete elation and exhaustion and total relief all mixed into one. As they dismounted the choppers and stepped into the crowd, they were greeted by warm and ecstatic faces who were thrilled to see them back. Any recon team that returned back in the same physical shape it had left in was all the reason they needed to celebrate, and there was sure to be a party later that night.

Ethan and Mitch walked the Yards back to their barracks while John scrambled over to the mess hall to rustle up dinner and a case of beer. They mixed things up with the little people for a few minutes and then headed straight for the showers with all their equipment.

The standard post-mission procedure was to hit the showers with a cooler full of beer and lawn chairs, and just sit there until the hot water rinsed everything clean. That done they trundled back to the team house and set their equipment out to dry, grabbed their shaving kits and went back to the showers to clean their good selves.

Captain Yates suddenly materialized out of thin air and swaggered up to the stalls.

"Well, how'd he do?"

"He's alive, ain't he?" John winked.

"So this riffraff's a keeper, huh," he sighed while eyeballing Ethan over. "Knowing the new company you keep, it ain't gonna be long before you become a pain in my ass."

"Don't worry *Dai-uy,* I aim to please," Ethan snickered.

Yates pawed at the grip of his .38 while fishing a beer from their cooler, then strutted off towards the club.

"That man never goes anywhere without that pistol, does he?"

"Inseparable," John nodded. "Of course, when you wise up some, you'll tote firepower with you at all times around these parts."

After showers they all herded into the club to start the beginning of their stand-down. Mark and Benfield and several others new to the job of recon were already there, and though Ethan had been the first among them to go on a cross-border mission, the others had received team assignments and were well into their training cycles.

Dean Garrett hadn't heard but maybe three words come out of Mark's mouth before he asked him what part of Minnesota he was from.

"Hibbing," Mark said with a suspicious look.

"Grand Rapids," Dean grinned and that was that. He scooped Mark up like he was his long-lost twin. They had a lot in common, those two – always going on about walleye and pike fishing or hunting deer up in that frozen tundra they called home.

Benfield was Rhode Island's new junior man and Paul had taken up with the likes of RT Georgia.

After an early breakfast the following morning, the three of them shuffled over to the TOC and made their way into one of the briefing rooms where Major Zune was waiting. Debriefings were usually conducted right after a team returned while the facts and events were still fresh, but they occasionally got pushed back.

"Morning, gents," Zune offered. "Let us get right into it so I don't take up anymore of your stand-down than absolutely necessary."

The debriefing was a long and drawn-out affair. Zune started by congratulating them on an outstanding job as it was becoming increasingly difficult for teams to get on the ground and stay there without being discovered, especially around major roadways. Each of them recounted everything they'd seen, heard, and done over the course of those six days. They described in detail all the trails and footpaths, what direction they ran in, how many NVA they'd seen, if they'd noticed any unit patches, the type of gear and weapons they were carrying, how their canteens were sloshy and that they'd used flashlights to guide their way down the trail. It was all important stuff and it was all catalogued for future reference. Then they talked about the lack of a roadway and about the bicycle path they'd mined.

"The jungle is all triple-canopy here and we were a good three klicks north of the main drag," John explained. "When we found the bicycle path, I pulled the team back and we watched it for a few hours but didn't see or hear anything. I sent Mitch and Nui down and they buried an AT mine in the track."

John was a very meticulous One-Zero. Zune and another Operations NCO were busy poring over the photos and reading the notes they'd all jotted down in their personal notepads. The S-3 shop seemed satisfied.

After the debriefing, the guys gathered the Yards up and headed over to the club to watch a movie. Although the movie selection was anything but diverse, it was a good way to unwind and enjoy a lazy afternoon while between missions. The Yards were a curious bunch and were easily entertained by John Wayne's *The Searchers*, though they were a bit miffed about the cowboys being at odds with the Indians.

"Don't worry about it," John said. "It's all been sorted out and we're all friends now."

*   *   *

Creedence Clearwater Revival's "Green River" lashed out from the speakers of John's Teac reel-to-reel tape player. The importance of music to everyday life in a war zone was almost immeasurable and Mitch and John had accumulated quite a collection between themselves. Besides CCR, their library included Iron Butterfly, The Beatles, Johnny Cash, Simon and Garfunkel, Jefferson Airplane, Jimi Hendrix, The Animals, and plenty more. Most of it came from their families back in the states, so when somebody got something new, plenty of copies were dubbed.

No matter how long a recon team was on the ground across the fence, once they returned back to Kontum, they generally received several days' worth of stand-down time with no company formations; they were also exempt from the daily detail roster.

Their second day of stand-down had developed into an uneventful affair by all accounts. Since the shooting incident between a handful of recon guys and some ARVNs a few months back in downtown Kontum, Recon Company had been pressured to let things cool off. Things seemed quiet in the secret war that was being fought in Laos and Cambodia, and even though teams were on the ground, very little was happening.

It was a luxury that would not last.

The sweet acrid smell of WD-40 drifted around the team house as they finished cleaning their weapons, drank beer and jammed to the Doors. Their buzzes soon set in, so they shuffled off to the club to keep the good vibes rolling. A few drinks later, they'd been recruited by Bill Allen to do a bit of rat hunting in the perimeter bunkers. Hearing him explain how the hunt worked, Ethan almost laughed himself to tears.

"You wanna earn your CIB?" Bill grinned. "Grab a flashlight, some ear plugs and a pistol, and come with me."

They snuck across the compound and poured into a large bunker on the perimeter, and positioned themselves on one side. Bill took a piece of raw meat he'd gotten from the mess hall and tied it to a length of para-cord, allowing it to dangle about a foot above the dirt floor. They giggled in the dark for a few minutes while drinking until the rodents came scampering after the bait.

"Okay… now!" Bill ordered; all their flashlights beamed on at once and they opened fire.

The rats had no chance.

They baited the trap and repeated the ambush several more times, giggling like little kids. Eventually, the dead carcasses attracted more rats and ammo began to draw thin, so they moved on to blasting caps. Standing outside the bunker and laughing uncontrollably, they waited until the rodents scurried through the carnage before setting the caps off. The inside of the bunker would go from pitch-black to a bright flash that filtered through several firing ports, accompanied by a series of muffled pops. By that time, their little firefight had drawn a few more onlookers and participants, and everyone was trying to get in on the hysterics. At some point, somebody took a Swedish-K sub-machinegun into the bunker and ripped off a magazine on full-auto.

"What the fuck are you halfwits doing over there?!" Captain Yates barked from somewhere in the shadows.

"Shit, that's the *Dai-uy*," Mitch laughed. "Sounds pissed."

"Party's over," Bill said as he pitched a teargas grenade into the bunker to disperse the rodents.

The next morning, Ethan awoke with a pounding headache and an empty team house. Squinting painfully at the bright sun and already sweating from the humidity, he stumbled outside just as John rolled around the corner with an electrical circular saw, hammer and nails, and a tape-measure.

"What's going on?"

"Here," John said, "plug me in."

Ethan grabbed the end of the cord and plugged it into the wall just inside the door.

"What are you building?"

John was too busy making measurements in the wall to the left of the door to answer Ethan's question. He juiced the saw and cut a square hole into the wall and inspected his handy work.

"What the hell are you two retards doing to my team house?" Captain Yates demanded as he turned the corner.

"Nada mucho, just a little home improvement," John said.

"And where the hell might Mitchell Lawrence be?"

"Couldn't tell ya, *Dai-uy*," John lied.

"Great. I'll probably have to go bail his hide outta Long Binh before the day's over," he complained. "Fix that damn hole and clean this shit up before the Old Man sees it. And if I catch you twerps shooting rats in the perimeter bunkers again, I'm gonna transfer y'all to a leg unit down in the Mekong. Ya hear?"

"I don't recall being caught," Ethan grinned.

"You'll recall my boot in your ass if you don't show me some respect," Yates warned.

"Roger that, sir." Ethan said as he clicked his heels together and hacked out a form-fit salute.

"Fool," the captain snapped and tugged at Ethan's arm while looking around nervously. "You trying to get me killed?"

"Ain't no sniper gonna shoot at you when he's got plenty of better officers to shoot at," John giggled.

Yates gave them both the finger and slipped back between the team houses.

A short while later, Lieutenant Colonel Abt walked over and surveyed their project. Now a veteran of three wars, Fred Abt proved to be the type of commander who led from the front and all those under his command at CCC held him in the highest of regards. Word had it that he had accompanied two recon teams on separate missions into Laos simply to observe what it was like. Naturally, when Chief SOG in Saigon learned of his escapades across the fence, Abt reluctantly agreed not to do it again. But his actions meant much more to the men of Recon Company and he quickly won their total admiration and respect.

"Gentlemen," he greeted with a slight grin, "how are we doing this morning?"

"Just fine, sir," John promised.

"Good, good – I noticed you're in the middle of some remodeling here," he pointed, "and I'm curious as to what will be filling this rather large hole in the side of my team house." He waited patiently with a bemused look on his face.

"Just a little climate-control, sir," John offered.

"I see, and I would assume Sergeant Lawrence is *acquiring* the hardware?"

"As we speak," John nodded.

"Well then," the colonel shrugged, "carry on." He turned and meandered on about his way towards the TOC without another word.

"What just happened there?" Ethan asked, somewhat bewildered. "I thought we were done for."

"One of the perks about this outfit is the freedom. As long as we get the job done out in the field, nobody gives us any shit."

"Except for Yates," Ethan laughed.

"Hell, the *Dai-uy* would hate his job if it weren't for us," John laughed.

By sundown, the hole in the side of the team house had been filled with a brand new air conditioning unit that Mitch had "found" down in Pleiku. Daytime temperatures in South Vietnam commonly soared to over a hundred degrees but cooled off to around the mid-seventies at night. With the addition of a little climate control,

Utah's team house would hover at a dry and comfortable seventy-eight degrees, night or day.

The last bit of stand-down was spent lazing around the team house and mingling over at the club while SOG's cross-border mischief continued to plague the enemy.

While the Special Forces camp at Ben Het remained under siege, Company A from CCC's Hatchet Force inserted onto a Laotian hilltop overlooking a stretch of Highway 110 and proceeded to carry out Operation Nightcap. Their primary objective was to shut down that portion of the Trail, and that's exactly what they did by using a host of heavy weapons including machineguns, mortars, and a 90mm recoilless rifle. Word passing through camp was that the recoilless rifleman had been severely wounded, but that Tom Waskovich had volunteered to take his place while his team was out at Dak To.

And while Tom stood behind the recoilless, Utah began to train up for their week-long Bright Light duty at Dak To. Bright Light teams were expected to respond to a number of tactical emergencies in a matter of minutes, whether it was a distressed recon team or downed aircrews. Since Bright Light teams were called in for the direst of situations, they carried very little food and water. Instead, they went in heavy, carrying as much ammunition and ordnance as physically possible as well as a small assortment of medical supplies.

For two full days, the team drilled from sunrise to sunset, placing emphasis on suppressive fire, assaulting formations, firing and maneuvering, and immediate-action drills. They practiced mounting and dismounting helicopters by means of rappelling and by aluminum ladders, and rode strings for emergency extractions. Many times, Bright Light teams were inserted right in the thick of battle and had to shoot their way through to a beleaguered team, therefore, John decided against using NVA uniforms, reasoning that confusion might cause friendly fire. Early Saturday morning, the entire team boarded Hueys bound for the launch site at Dak To where they'd relieve RT New York of Bright Light duty.

5

The "Mortuary" was little more than a canvas-roofed building and whoever had named the place had a real sick and twisted sense of humor, regardless of how appropriate it really was. It stood in between the control tower and the communications shed and served as the ready-room for Bright Light teams waiting to respond to tactical emergencies out across the fence. It even had its namesake hand-carved into a sign that hung above the door.

Ethan lay on his back, catnapping as the midmorning sun punched tiny sparks of light through the canvas while a feathering breeze carried dusty heat in through the windowless frames. No matter how much shade the Mortuary provided, the heat at Dak To was stifling and inescapable. He sat up from the cot and glanced around the room at what appeared to be snoozing teammates. In truth, sleep was a lost concept with the heat. Occasionally one of the Yards would shoo a fly away from his face or toss to a more comfortable side. Piles of weapons and equipment lay beside every cot ready to be pulled on at a moment's notice.

Minding his steps, Ethan ventured outside and slipped into the commo-shed to monitor the radio traffic with John, Mitch, and the launch site commander.

South Dakota had gone into Laos the day before, and Ethan had monitored their situation closely since it was Mark's first time across the fence. Their insertion was smooth but they picked up a few trackers while moving away from the LZ. Dean, being the cunning and sneaky sort, had concealed their passage and shaken their trackers by nightfall. At sunrise, they'd given the all-clear and got on with the show. It would be a few more hours before another sitrep, so the team all headed down to the river to cool off.

They lounged in the shade and goofed around with the Yards for about an hour before a pair of deuce-and-a-halfs and an M-48 Patton from the 4th Infantry Division rolled up and parked in the muddy flats a short while later. It seemed the grunts were in need of a midday siesta as well, though they didn't take their suspecting eyes off the Yards for one second. Ethan couldn't blame them; even though the boys were cutting up and horseplaying in the river, they were all armed to the teeth and looked just like the enemy.

The next day, South Dakota's luck ran out after they got caught snooping around in a truck park. A quick firefight gave way to a hard run, and they grabbed some high ground and called for air. Covey showed up with several sets of Skyraiders and worked the area over with napalm and cannons while the slicks came in and whisked them out and back to the launch site. Ethan and his teammates were waiting on the airstrip as the Hueys landed. Dean was grimacing and limping as he led his people off the strip and back into the security of the launch site.

"Dude, you hit?" Mitch asked.

"Just some scratches."

"Turn around, lemme see," Mitch demanded and spun him around. "Just some scratches? Your ass is peppered."

"Goddamn B-40 went off behind me."

"Fragged in the ass," Dave shook his head and smirked. "You're supposed to *face* the enemy, Dean-o."

"Get in there and lay down," Mitch ordered

John swatted at Ethan and chuckled. "Mitch clucks like a wet ol' hen whenever he gets to play medic and dig frag outta somebody's ass."

Dean grumbled while Mitch herded him up into the Mortuary. The Yards from both teams had all gathered around and were beginning to break out the foodstuffs and clown around – a pretty standard affair among their simplistic circles. Mark trundled over and dropped his equipment into a tired pile; he looked ragged.

"How was it, what happened?" Ethan asked him.

"Don't really know," he shrugged with furrowed eyebrows. "Shit happened fast."

Mark dug a pack of smashed Lucky Strikes from his pocket, fished one out with trembling hands and lit it, taking a long hard pull. He was still high and jagged off the adrenaline.

"We heard trucks stop in a stretch of woods yesterday morning. They pulled out after dusk; we didn't hear any other vehicles come in so first thing this morning, we moved down out of our RON and had a look around. Established security, found fresh tracks all over the place, shot some photos. They'd tied branches together in the upper canopy to hide the place."

"Yeah yeah, a trail we found two weeks ago was the same way," Ethan said.

"Yeah so I'm standing there, snapping away with this fucking camera and before I know what's going on, a few of the Yards are firing up a clump of trees just to my left. We broke into an IA drill and dumped a few mags and some grenades into the bushes and ran back uphill and then – *BOOM!* – something big went off behind us."

"B-40?"

"Ask Dean-o," Dave giggled.

Dean looked up and scowled behind a pair of middle fingers while Mitch continued to dig fragments out of his hindquarters.

"So what happened after that?" Ethan asked.

"We got back up high and rigged a few trees with some det-cord so we could open the LZ up better. The Spads rolled in and started shooting up the truck park and we got a buncha secondaries." He took another long drag from his cigarette and ran a grubby hand through his hair. "Then the slicks came in and pulled us out."

"Sounds like fun," John smirked.

Mark just nodded and dragged on his smoke.

Mitch finished suturing Dean's wounds as the Yards began shuffling by with food they'd prepared from leftover rations and heaps of leafy delicacies they'd gathered from the jungle floor. No matter how serious a target was, the Montagnards always seemed to have food on the brain and were never too busy to stop and pick up a few edibles along the way. After feasting, Dean and the boys packed up and caught the last few Hueys back to Kontum.

*   *   *

Ethan tossed and turned himself awake sometime in the wee hours of the morning and lost the fight to go back to sleep. He picked and felt his way through his snoozing teammates and outside under a depthless, star-studded sky. The air was crisp and damp and his breath instantly turned to fog. He strained to see the mountains silhouetted against the stars and felt an eerie presence fill in around him.

"Did they wake you?" a voice whispered over his shoulder. It was one of the Yards.

"Did who wake me?"

"The spirits. They are all around you, warning you of danger. That is why you not sleep."

"The NVA are close, aren't they," Ethan said as Nui sat down on the sandbags beside him. He shivered against the chill as he gazed out at the distant hills. He could somehow feel their presence – faint and distant but he knew they were out there.

"Can you see them?" he asked.

"VC?"

"The spirits," Ethan whispered while spacing out at the cosmos.

"No no," Nui chuckled. "You look in wrong place, Yok-son. Only bad spirits live in sky. Good spirits live in ground. They protect you."

"So you can see them?"

"I not see them, I feel them. They all around us, even now," he smiled as he waved his hand. Nui studied Ethan for a moment more and finally smiled, "Do not worry. You are strong with good spirits."

He patted Ethan's head and wandered off into the darkness towards the Mortuary while the Central Highlands loomed quietly in the distance. Ethan fought the chill for a while longer and considered Nui's apparent connection to the spiritual world and the meaning behind the cryptic conversation. Some of the men in Nui's lineage were shamans of his village and historically, the Montagnards had always maintained good rapport with the spiritual side of things. If the Yards believed Ethan to be in the caring embraced of good spirits, so be it. He would need all the luck and good fortune he could muster to survive the balance of his tour and he knew it.

Ray Fuller and his people were at the launch site bright and early the following day and Covey wasted no time clearing them for insertion. RT Oregon was going into steep terrain several kilometers west of the Golf Course – an area with miles and miles of high-speed trails, layered antiaircraft nests, and who knew what other cute little surprises the NVA had stashed away.

Fuller wrapped up his pre-mission briefing and they all headed out to the choppers where the engines were warming up. The aircrews were busy settling in and making final preparations to their ships while Oregon climbed aboard under the weight of their equipment and weapons. Mitch was riding along as the chase-medic and he was all smiles. The turbines spooled up in a maelstrom of power and rotor wash and off they went, noses down and climbing high into a cloudless sky with the sun on their tail-rotors.

Ethan was still trying to get used to the anxiousness and anxiety that always crept in after seeing friends off, and it wouldn't abate until they were all back at the launch site safe and sound. In the meantime, all they could do was crowd into the commo-shed and huddle around the radio bank and listen to the traffic.

First came the false insertions and then the Cobras trolled in over the actual LZ but got nothing.

"Gladiator Three-One and Three-Two, make your approaches from the south," Covey directed. "Keep that high ridge to your left, should help conceal the drop."

"Uh copy that... Okay, Three-One approaching short-final... Okay Covey, they're out clean."

"Roger Three-One, head back to the orbit point. Three-Two, go ahead and make your approach."

"Roger Covey... We're right above the hole... Whoa fuck! It's hot, it's hot! We're hit, we're taking fi...," the pilot's voice suddenly drowned in a cacophony of rattling metal and mechanical strain.

"Three-Two, get off the deck," Covey begged. "Three-Two... Bro, talk to me."

John's attention was glued to the wall map and he was furiously scribbling marks and circles with a grease pencil.

"Get the Yards ready," he ordered without looking away.

Ethan ran back over to the Mortuary and found Ti Tu and Bo huddling over a small fire cooking breakfast while the others were busy horseplaying. He called them in and told them to get their gear ready.

"Helicop crash?" Hyuk asked.

"They shot one up pretty bad but they're not down yet."

"*Trung-si* Mitch?"

"...C'mon, ya'll hurry up and eat, and get your stuff ready."

Back in the commo-shed, the launch site commander, Captain James "Guerrilla" Shepherd, was scrambling to order another air package up from Kontum. He'd just earned command of the launch site and was still figuring out how to juggle it all, but was exactly the type of officer needed for the job. Captain Shepherd had spent several months running recon under Joe Walker, which meant he knew precisely the dangers the teams faced.

The radios continued to hum and from what Ethan and the others could discern, the second slick had been hit bad and had no working radios, but was limping back to the launch site with the rest of the air package.

"Fuller's in light contact," John said. "He keeps saying he's missing a Yard from the second bird."

"Probably got hit when they leveled off," the captain speculated.

"Covey, this is Three-One. Still don't have comms with Three-Two; they're smoking like hell and the tail rotor looks like it might shake itself loose any second now."

"Three-One, Covey. Just stick with 'em all the way back to the lima-sierra… Three-One, can you see inside the cabin?"

"Covey, I can't see much but it looks like they're working on somebody."

"At least one wounded," Captain Shepherd said. He got back on the radio to update Kontum and find out how far away the second air package was.

Twenty minutes later and they were all racing out onto the airstrip to receive the crippled slick. It poured smoke from the main rotor compartment as it yawed a few times before finally bouncing to a rest. Ethan turned back to grab the closest fire extinguisher he could find and then ran back out to help just as the rest of the ships came in and landed on the far side of the airstrip.

Thick smoke streamed down from the top of the bird with the rotor wash and swirled in big dusty circles; it smelled of cooked hydraulic fluid and fried electrical wires. Ethan shielded his eyes as he ran through the wash while trying desperately to make out the commotion amid the smoke.

"Get his legs!" someone shouted.

"Hurry, grab 'em!"

"Easy, easy!"

No talking – only shouts; the Huey's engines were still winding down and the noise made communication almost impossible, even when standing shoulder-to-shoulder.

"Ethan," John shouted and kicked the fire extinguisher from his grasp. "Help them get that Yard!"

He scrambled across the aluminum flooring – the smoke and dust burning his eyes and throat – and slipped on something thick and wet. It was blood and it was smeared all over the floor of the chopper. He ignored it and collected the wounded Montagnard under his arms, and helped two crewmembers carry him away from the ship. They placed him on the ground about fifty meters away and ran back. John and Captain Shepherd emerged from the smoke struggling to carry another casualty, and as Ethan closed in on them, he knew it was Mitch. Without a word, he scooped up one of his legs. He looked down as they scurried away from the chopper and saw the compression dressing covering his lower-left abdomen. They placed Mitch next to the unconscious Montagnard and John immediately went to work.

"Ethan, help me!" Captain Shepherd called.

They ran back to the chopper where the two crewmen were working to free the pilot from his safety harness. He'd caught a bullet in the fleshy part underneath his chin and had slumped forward over the cyclic, but the straps were too tight to loosen under his weight.

"Hold him" Ethan said as he reached up and cut through the straps with his recon knife. The pilot fell forward and out into their waiting arms. The top-back of his flight helmet had a hole the size of a golf ball in it, and the ceiling above and behind his head was coated in a thin layer of blood and brain.

They carried him back and gently laid him down, careful not to place his body too close to the living; it was a psychological thing. The crew chief and the door gunner were trying to talk to the copilot but he had gone catatonic the second he'd landed the slick. It was a miracle he'd been able to hold himself together for that long. And while Captain Shepherd tended to the wounded Montagnard, John continued to work furiously on Mitch.

"Caught two here," he said, pointing at a pair of perfectly round, black holes just beneath Mitch's ribcage. "I need your help changing the bandage on his back."

Ethan nodded, sleeved the sweat from his forehead and gently scooped Mitch up under his arms, straining slightly to roll him. John carefully removed the bandage and examined the exit wound. It was about an inch shy of his spine and close in size to a tennis ball; ripped flesh, torn and swollen tissue – just a gory hole packed with blood-soaked gauze, but the hemorrhaging had stemmed. John applied a new compression bandage and checked Mitch's vital signs again.

"Shep, I need one of those slicks to get us down to Pleiku now or he ain't gonna make it," John pleaded. "He can't take any more morphine; his heart rate's too low. We gotta go now."

The captain turned and bolted down the airstrip without a word.

*   *   *

Ethan slipped the headset down around his neck and felt the wind rush in around his sweaty ears as he gazed out of the Huey.

Laos.

It stretched for as far as he could see: high mountain peaks and deep, wide valleys. There were bomb craters, too. Thousands upon thousands of bomb craters mostly clustered around Highway 110 – some new, some old. Thirty minutes ago he had watched John fly off with Mitch and the wounded Montagnard, bound for the 71st Evacuation Hospital down in Pleiku. Mitch was in bad shape and if he had any chance at all, John would have to keep him alive during the flight. But not ten minutes after they took off, the net flooded with a mayday call that no one wanted to hear. The NVA had shot up another aircraft – a Cobra gunship – and this time, they'd brought it down.

Fuller's team was only a few klicks west of where the Cobra had crashed but they were still in contact and were fighting a man short. Covey had been working air on the NVA while trying to guide them to an alternate LZ when the gunship had gone down. Aside from the NVA, there were also several steep ridgelines blocking them from the crash site.

The crew chief slapped Ethan's leg and motioned for him to put his headset back on.

"Hey, the FAC needs to talk to ya!"

He cupped the headset down over his ears and heard his call-sign.

"...Hollywood, you with me? Hey bro..."

"Yeah Covey, I'm here; go ahead."

"Hey man, I need you to stay on comms."

"Roger, sorry." But Ethan was just too nervous and too terrified to be embarrassed. He had neither his One-Zero nor his One-One – just the Yards and *none* of the experience required to lead a Bright Light mission, yet there he was, and he was going to lead those men all the same.

"There's a small spot about three-hundred mikes below the crash I might be able to put you in on," Covey offered. "That's about the best I can do." He was way down on the deck, circling wide, just above the treetops.

Ethan had studied the topography map of the immediate and surrounding areas back at the launch site and had tried hard to picture the layout of the crash – how the gunship had settled in relation to the mountainside and the adjacent hills and ridgelines, but seeing it firsthand pulled his perspective together. He could barely make out the crash; the bird had settled on its right side in thin single-canopy, nose pointing downhill. The tail section had bound up and was partially broken beneath the exhaust port where it connected to the fuselage.

"Put me in right on top of the crash," Ethan decided. "I don't wanna hafta fight uphill if Nguyen's already between us and the pilots."

They hurried to make ready for the rappel just as one of the gunship pilots started talking to Covey over the emergency frequency. Ethan pulled the headset off and braided one of the ropes through his carabiner, then quickly checked his Yards. A gaggle of toothy smiles and a few pats on the head, and they were ready. The Huey sank down and came through the draw, exploiting the terrain for every possible advantage before slipping in over the crash. Fluorescent-green streaks burned across the sky as Ethan and the Yards maneuvered onto the skids and locked their heels into place. Squatting slightly, he glanced down over his right shoulder and scanned the hillside beneath them. There was a man on the ground and he was waving an orange signal panel wildly above his head. Then the crew chief started hammering away with his M-60.

Ethan kicked off the skid as hard as he could and zipped down the line at a blistering rate. He hit the brakes right as he blurred past the tail-boom of the Cobra and crashed into a thick stand of brush. Rather than wasting time trying to free the rope from his carabiner, he implemented his training and the philosophy behind it: "Don't fiddle-fuck around with the rope," John had told him. "Aircrews are gonna cut you loose once they see you're on the ground anyways."

He fetched his recon knife and cut the rope right above the carabiner, then pulled the tail-end free just as the slick banked and dropped out of sight. He could hear the gunships swooping in on the adjacent hills, trying to suppress the antiaircraft threat. Then came the second Huey thumping in overhead with the rest of the little people sliding down ropes and into the trees around him. Another gun nest opened up somewhere along the ridgeline above them but only for a quick burst.

"Hey man, you okay?"

Ethan looked up to find one of the Cobra pilots standing a few feet away holding the signal panel.

"Yeah... You?"

"Couple scratches; my gunner's a little banged up, though."

Ethan crawled out from the bushes and got to his feet; the Yards had already fanned out and were busy securing the crash.

"Hey, do me a favor and stash that thing," he said, pointing at the bright-orange signal panel. "NVA can see that from a mile away."

The pilot quickly folded it up and stuffed it into his flight suit and led him down to the front of the aircraft where the gunner was leaning against a tree.

"Hey Jerry," he moaned. "Any of these guys medics?" He was in a considerable amount of pain.

"Sorry," Ethan said, "I fell asleep the day they taught first-aid."

"C'mon man," he offered a chuckling complaint, "this hurts like shit. Don't make me laugh."

"Dislocation?"

"Yeah," he grimaced. "Shoot me up and help me reset this thing."

"Sorry man, can't do it."

"Can't do what?"

"No morphine, no resetting," Ethan said. "You ain't bleeding and you ain't dying. I need you alert and able to move under your own power."

He untied his cravat and fashioned a sling for the gunner's arm, then gave Covey a sitrep and began sorting out the particulars of the extraction. The air assets were all drawing low on fuel and the Cobras were nearly out of ordnance as well. And making matters more critical, antiaircraft positions were opening up faster than the Cobras were able to knock them out.

"Spads in five mikes," Covey promised. "As soon as I'm able to start working this AA over again, I'll send you some slicks. Get ready because I already got 'em prepped for ladders."

One glance around their position and Ethan knew he had some quick work to do. He handed Hyuk two coils of rope and instructed him to help the pilots tie Swiss seats. While the rest of the Yards pulled security, he retrieved a long stretch of det-cord from his ruck and set to work. The mountainside was steep and the aluminum extraction ladders were a little over thirty feet long, which meant the Hueys were going to have to hover low enough for them to reach the ground. They needed a clear hole in the canopy and they needed it fast. He made three wraps of det-cord around every tree trunk inside a fifty-foot circle, priming each with an acoustical blasting cap, save the last, which he rigged with a standard pull-fuse. Covey's O-2 Skymaster suddenly streaked across the valley and loosed a brace of white-phosphorous marking rockets into a series of folds on the valley floor while a storm of green tracers tracked him across the sky. Big red tracers and the unmistakable buzzing of a 20mm cannon ripped apart the marked area. An A-1E Skyraider coasted across the valley, pulled up and banked away as a second Skyraider lumbered in behind and pickled off two canisters of napalm. Ethan momentarily marveled at the torpedo-shaped containers wobbling through the air just as they crashed into the trees and engulfed the entire position in molten flame. Around they came again, Covey marking targets and the Spads dropping ordnance and shooting the place up as perfectly orchestrated as anything he'd ever seen. It was beautiful.

"Uh Hollywood," Covey called, "get your people ready." The sound of approaching helicopters began to reverberate off the surrounding mountains. He yanked the pull-fuse and herded everyone behind the crippled gunship. The sharp *clap!* of high-explosives and a quick whiff of expended plastique and vaporized fauna, and he knew they were in business.

He sprang to his feet with an orange signal panel clinched in his fist and scrambled over into the middle of his smoldering handiwork. The explosion from the pull-fuse had tripped the acoustical fuses causing everything to go up at once in perfect cadence. The Yards quickly hustled the pilots over and fanned out while Bo and Nui machete'd the hanging debris away from the swath. Ethan waved the bright-orange signal panel as the first Huey hit short-final right over the hole – the ladders fluttering and swaying in the downdraft. Four of his Yards quickly made the ascent, but cresting and actually climbing into the cabin was an almost impossible feat; the trick was to hold on and ride out until the Hueys could find a safe place to land and bring everyone fully onboard. With some help, the two pilots struggled onto the ladders and straddled the rungs. Ethan snapped them into the center cable with the carabiners that hung from their Swiss seats, ensuring they'd not fall off during the flight.

Everyone was set.

He waved the ship off, and up and out they went, just barely clearing the tree tops and the tracers. The second Huey slid right in behind the first, and then – *BOOM-BOOM-BOOM!* – green streaks and a big fiery muzzle blast above their position ripped the sky just beyond the hovering bird. M-60s returned fire as the helicopter yawed and dipped away.

He turned and bristled through the clearing and uphill into the woods, gritting his teeth against the fear while moving decisively towards the threat. First he heard them conversing and then he caught movement inside a little nook hollowed out of the hillside; he leveled his carbine off and fired them up. Red tracers skipped and sparked against iron and steel, ricocheting skyward and then a light machinegun opened up to his left; Nui had moved up on-line and was chopping at the enemy position from behind his RPD. Then something screamed overhead with a sizzling whistle, a smoky contrail and a hot explosion.

"RPG!"

Ethan rolled right and fired his M-79, then pulled himself to his knees and pitched a white-phosphorous grenade. Back downhill he stumbled and slid as the Yards covered him and then peeled off behind. The WP grenade cooked off and he was on the radio pointing Covey towards the gun they'd just hit and begging for a ride out.

"Last chance, get ready," Covey warned. "We're all on fumes, here."

Minutes later and they were soaring out across the valley floor, buffeted by the wind, white-knuckled and teary-eyed, several thousand feet above Laos while the NVA filled the skies with tracers and bursting flak. And when he was finally able to catch his breath, he roared his lungs out against the blistering wind – his entire existence momentarily frozen in tension while his veins coursed with a maniacal blend of endorphins and pure adrenaline.

*   *   *

They were back at CCC late in the afternoon, straight off the choppers and into a massive celebration right there on the helipads outside the wire. Warm smiles and backslaps, handshakes and congratulations issued mostly by faces he barely recognize. And before Ethan could really soak up the vibes and bask in the elation, he was being ushered from the crowd by the S-3 Operations officer, Major Carl Zune. Straight from the party and into Zune's debriefing chambers inside the TOC. While everyone else partied on, Ethan and the Cobra pilots walked through the entire operation with the major and his staff – start to finish. And when they were done with that part, in came the S-2 Intelligence shop to get a better fix on where all the antiaircraft positions were, what calibers they'd encountered, if they'd seen any NVA up close and what they looked like, if they'd spotted any trails and if so, what direction they ran. Everything down to the tiniest of details was pertinent intelligence.

Exhaustive, extensive, thorough.

Many details were things Ethan had never even considered but the Operations and Intelligence gurus expected that and made use of what he was able to give them. After the debriefing, he learned that both Mitch and the Montagnard had made it to the evacuation hospital down in Pleiku, and with that news, his spirits began to lift. Up until then, he had been relatively subdued by what he'd seen earlier in the day when that shot-up Huey had first landed on the airstrip at Dak To.

"So this's the plan," Randy Reynolds slurred as Ethan walked into Utah's team house. "We gonna fuck'n party hard with this goddamn hero tonight," he declared as he slung an arm around Ethan's neck, "and come tomorrow, we'll catch the early bird down to Pleiku to hook up with Johnny Cameron, and see Mitchell Lawrence. How's that sound?" He stared Ethan down out of the corner of one eye while arching his back and turning the last of his beer up and slightly leaning forward into a brilliant display of balance and alcohol consumption that only an inebriated Texan could achieve.

"Say yes," Mark said, spinning the cap off a fifth of Jack Daniels. He took a big pull and passed it to Ethan.

"I love how you jerks see fit to party at our house even when we ain't home," Ethan smirked. He collected the bottle from Mark and threw back a worthy swig. It went down warm and easy and he could feel his nerves calming and the edge slowly dulling. Combat and the subsequent adrenaline crash had left him jagged and shaky, but the alcohol helped.

He collected his shaving kit, traded his boots for a pair of white flip-flops he used as shower shoes, and shuffled himself over to the showers for a proper bath. The boys, obviously having nothing better to do, packed a cooler full of beer and followed Ethan over to the stalls – both as a form of harassment and to hear the full scoop on how it all went down. And being such *humble* and "Quiet Professionals", it was only natural they Monday-morning-quarterbacked the entire operation. But Ethan didn't pay them too much attention; the beer was cold, the shower hot, and the night before them promised enough nefarious indiscretions to satiate even the darkest misfit in Recon Company.

*   *   *

He could feel the heat in his throat and taste the alcohol on his breath even before he opened his eyes. Ethan groaned and rolled over in his rack while the air conditioner purred steadily across the room.

God bless that AC unit, he thought aimlessly. *Better thank Mitch when I sober up…*

Then he remembered.

"Shit." He bolted up in his rack and scrambled to reach his watch as his head spun and his temples pounded. "Goddammit," he sighed as he read the time; they'd missed their morning flight by a good hour and fifteen minutes.

"Relax, buddy," John said. "They medevac'd him to Japan at first-light."

"How's he doing?"

"He's in rough shape but he's gonna make it," he said. He was busy boxing up Mitch's belongings to send home.

"We were supposed to catch a ride down," Ethan promised, "but it got a bit wild last night."

"Those Aussies put on a good show, huh?"

"Yeah," Ethan chuckled.

"Had a word with Zune; he told me about the Bright Light op." He placed some more of Mitch's things into the box and looked up at Ethan. "I'm sorry I put you in that position, man. It's my responsibility as a One-Zero to lead this team and I wasn't there to do that."

"You crazy? If you hadn't gotten on that bird, Mitch wouldn't have made it," Ethan said. "And Fuller's Montagnard – you kept 'em both alive, John. That's all that matters. That *is* leading." He sat up and popped two aspirins and washed them down with a few swigs of lukewarm canteen water. "All I did was get lucky."

"Yeah," John nodded. "Lucky, sure, but you showed good sense out there."

Ethan shrugged.

"Dude, you rappelled right in on the crash, got the pilots out, knocked out a damn fifty-one position, and got the team out. Nobody even got a fucking scratch. That's Audie Murphy shit right there."

"Yeah? Reynolds said I pleased the gods somehow," he joked as he crawled slowly out from under his sheets and massaged his temples.

"Pleased the gods," John chuckled, "the gods being Zune and Yates and the first sergeant. And Reynolds was right," he nodded, "you pleased them alright, because you're my new One-One." He reached over and slapped Ethan's shoulder. "Congratulations! Before you know it, you'll be a bona-fide One-Zero like me. Now get your ass outta bed; we got work to do."

*   *   *

The machine that was SOG continued to steam ahead with teams inserting or extracting on a daily basis. As the third week in April approached, there had still been no voiced protests from Prince Sihanouk of Cambodia regarding President Nixon's top-secret bombing of the "Fishhook" region along the border near Quan Loi, South Vietnam. It had been such a well-kept secret that no one in

SOG had learned of it until the second wave of B-52s went in. Because of vital intelligence gathered by SOG recon teams from inside Cambodia, the Nixon administration quickly became wise to the massive numbers of NVA troops concealed there. The first B-52 Arc Light air strike had hammered the Fishhook a month earlier. With peace talks in Paris still in a stalemate, the Nixon administration launched a second Arc Light strike into the Fishhook, but this time, their target was COSVN, the Central Office for South Vietnam – Vietcong headquarters proper.

On the morning of 24 April 1969, the second Arc Light went in. Immediately following the air strike, a hundred-man SOG Hatchet Force company from Command and Control South launched from Quan Loi to raid the bombed area. Joining the raid was none other than Special Forces legend Sergeant First Class Jerry "Mad Dog" Shriver. There wasn't a soul in Special Forces who didn't know who Shriver was. Now into his third tour with SOG, Shriver had earned the nickname "Mad Dog" by North Vietnam's Radio Hanoi. He was fiercely close to his Montagnards and elected to live amongst them in what became known as "going native".

Minutes after the bombs stopped falling, two platoons of the Hatchet Force landed amid the destruction. In seconds, enemy machinegun nests opened fire on them, killing anyone who wasn't able to find immediate cover. Shriver and his Yards were pinned down and unable to maneuver; no one could move an inch. Desperate to seize the initiative, Shriver mustered his Yards' courage and assaulted the machinegun nest head-on. That was the last time anyone saw him or the Yards who followed his lead, and it took the rest of the day to extract the tattered and torn Hatchet Force platoons. Several Yards were dead and wounded, Shriver was missing in action but presumed dead, and both Sergeant Ernest Jamison and Lt. Greg Harrigan had been killed in action. MACV's COSVN raid had been a total disaster and it proved the preconceived notion that nothing could survive a B-52 Arc Light strike was indeed only a notion. SOG headquarters in Saigon was stunned and the Special Forces community took a hard hit when the news made its rounds. The loss of SFC Jerry Shriver had many recon men questioning their own abilities to survive the bush, and that was a dangerous question to ask. But despite the losses, SOG's secret war continued to roll on and soon, Utah was back in the sling again.

6

They were going into Cambodia to pull an area recon in the hopes of sniffing out some high-value targets, and to get a general idea of what the NVA were up to out there. Back in March, RT Illinois had a near-miss just a few kilometers north; they had gone in to find an enemy 85mm artillery piece which had eluded both California and Wyoming earlier. Trackers had pursued them and a large sweeping force had literally moved right through their hillside RON, but they managed to avoid detection and extracted two days later without incident. Over a few drinks in the club, John Plaster speculated for a while about where the NVA might have moved the gun, but finally just shook his head in frustration. In his estimation, it'd take a miracle or plain dumb luck to dig it up again.

The next day, John and Ethan flew a visual recon over the target-area in northeastern Cambodia. Gliding in a pair of SPAF Bird Dogs high above the jungle, they watched for antiaircraft fire and scanned their target for any signs of recent activity. While consulting his map-sheets, Ethan used a grease pencil to mark the coordinates for several possible LZs he liked on the plexi-glass windscreen. He also took careful note of the terrain so that an escape and evasion plan could be devised before the mission. After a few passes, the Bird Dogs banked east and sped for Kontum. In the team house that night, they deliberated with Covey Rider Luke Dove about which LZs to use. Luke had held down the One-Zero slot on RT Delaware for a good stint and had recently been recruited to fly as a Covey Rider. As it was, only the best recon team leaders were selected as Covey Riders and Luke had earned his spot among their ranks on more than one occasion. But just like in Laos, LZs in Cambodia had to be carefully selected to avoid detection during insertion. Luke shot down several potential landing zones because they were simply too obvious and had been used too many times in the past. The NVA were quickly growing adept at dealing with recon teams and the insertion proved to be the most dangerous and critical part of any mission. Many recon men speculated that there was an NVA mole somewhere inside SOG headquarters in Saigon who was relaying intelligence about recon missions and team locations back to Hanoi. It was a chilling thought but entirely possible. It just seemed all too coincidental when teams attempted to insert. Sometimes, there'd be hordes of NVA troops waiting in silence for them to land and occasionally, teams would disappear without the slightest trace. But no matter how large the enemy numbers, Cambodia still claimed to be a neutral country. Therefore, the only air assets available to SOG teams were helicopter gunships, which is why Nixon's top-secret B-52 Arc Light strikes were such a big deal. And after experiencing firsthand how critical fixed-wing air assets were to a team in contact, Ethan didn't want to think about being in trouble on the ground without those assets. Finally, John made the decision to use the lower-left corner of a large grassy clearing they had spotted earlier that day.

*   *   *

He watched anxiously as the slender, menacing Cobras trolled over the LZ far below. Covey Rider Luke "Vigilante" Dove directed the first slick into the LZ from the side-seat of a circling O-2 Cessna. The Huey spiraled crazily towards the landing zone, its olive-drab hull contrasting sharply against the magnificent green saturation of the elephant grass below. Suddenly, the bird's nose flared as the pilot pulled her into a perfect hover over the fluttering ground. Ethan could see his teammates standing on the skids with their weapons at-the-ready but something was wrong. The slick seemed to drop deeper into the grass and then they were out and gone. As Ethan's chopper pulled hard and flared, he could see why his teammates had hesitated – the grass was far deeper than perceived during their visual recon. What Ethan thought had only been four-foot tall grass was well over eight feet high and extremely thick. He shifted his eyes and muzzle to the tree-line, scanning quickly for any signs of the enemy. Nay stood to his right while Hyuk and Nui perched themselves on the opposite side of the ship, waiting for him to jump. The grass whipped violently beneath them in the down-draft, and he could see it was at least a ten-foot drop; eighty pounds of equipment would make it feel more like a hundred. He waved the pilots to go lower and when the bird sank deeper into the grass, he jumped off the skid.

He landed hard and fell to the side as his knees buckled under the weight, then scrambled to a crouch inside the rotor-wash and consolidated with his half of the team, and waited for the grass to settle. They found John's back-trail and began moving towards the tree-line which stood about fifty meters to the west. John and the others had set up a hasty perimeter inside the grass instead of moving directly into the tree-line.

"What's wrong?" Ethan asked, making his whisper as soft as possible. He didn't like being in the clearing for long; the tree-line offered hard cover.

"Trail just inside the tree-line," John whispered. "Luc's check'n it out."

A few minutes later, the little Montagnard quietly pushed back through the heavy grass.

"*Beaucoup* NVA, Cam-run."

Ethan looked at the Yards one-by-one and could see the tension beginning to creep into their faces. Thankfully, Covey was still circling off to the south, waiting for John to give him the all-clear; that also meant the slicks and gunships were still on station.

John leaned in to Ethan's ear, "We sit tight and wait for the guns to come back in," he whispered. "We'll initiate contact, put the guns on 'em and hop on the slicks. When it happens, we'll move towards the far side of the clearing."

Ethan nodded.

Nerves wore thin as the tension piled on, and their senses heightened. A light breeze feathered through the grass as he swiped his forehead dry with his sleeve. He could feel the sweat bleeding from his pores as he watched for any movement. He could barely hear John breathing into the radio handset, talking to Covey. He hung the mic up and signaled everyone to get ready; they were about to initiate contact. Ethan's throat tightened as he mentally prepared himself. Grenades and M-79s first, then he suspected they'd be running like hell while Luke Dove sent the gunships in.

John gave him the look he had been waiting for. Pins out, spoons *pinging* away and through the air they flew, and into the tree-line. The Yards thumped away behind their M-79s. Booming explosions and then everyone was up and running through the grass while ear-splitting pops and cracks whipped and tracers spun overhead. Deeper into the grass they pushed which seemed like the worst idea imaginable; there was no cover, only slight concealment and their back-trail was so impossible to conceal, Ethan and Nui didn't even bother. The contour of the LZ began to climb slightly, and he could see the grass moving and parting out to their left.

"They're trying to outflank us!"

"I'm talking to Covey; gunships are almost here," John called back. "Put some forty mike-mike on those assholes."

He stopped Nui and pointed, "Right there, hit 'em with some frag!"

Nui fired a brace of rounds which sent them scattering but it wouldn't be enough. What they needed was a delaying action while they waited for the slicks to come back in. With slightly higher ground to their advantage, he rigged a Claymore mine across their back-trail while Nui and Hyuk covered him. After setting the mine, he placed both a white phosphorous and a teargas grenade in front of it and backed away about fifteen meters.

Approaching choppers began drumming the sky and up until then, the heat had been the last thing on Ethan's mind, but it was inescapable now – the sun was almost directly overhead and the earth seemed to sweat almost as much as he did. Suddenly a row of pith helmets came bobbing through the weeds. He waited for what seemed like forever then gave the detonator three quick squeezes. An ear-ringing explosion and a plume of white phosphorous and teargas billowed up into the sky while a hot wave of shredded grass and debris wafted over them from the back-blast. Hyuk and Nui were already on their feet, pulling at Ethan's harness, urging him to hurry. Brush began to break just inside the jungle to their left and Vietnamese voices began shouting.

"*Beaucoup* NVA, hurry!" Nui begged.

Ethan tossed a frag into the tree-line to his right and followed the Yards through the grass just as a pair of Cobra gunships dove in and immediately began working the area over with rockets and cannons. A shocking amount of small-arms fire opened up all around them as the first pair of slicks arrived on station. The first Huey came in fast and just to the west of the team's perimeter, both door gunners blazing away behind their M-60s. Nui and Bo and Hyuk, then Ethan climbed on and they were roaring out, firing their CAR-15s at the muzzle flashes and NVA out in the open. He saw the second slick drop in and then out it came as quick as ever. Ethan tugged the radio headset on and listened to the traffic while gray puffs began stitching the sky from the west.

As the last ounce of adrenaline expired and the cold air dried running sweat, Ethan closed his exhausted eyes and leaned back against the bulkhead; he could still smell aviation fumes and combat clinging to his skin and hair and equipment. He reached for a canteen on his hip and brought it to his lips only to find two holes where enemy rounds had ripped through the plastic. He just marveled at the near-miss while the Yards all patted his forearms and nodded toothy approvals.

*   *   *

In a lawn chair beneath hot running water in full kit, Ethan watched the mud and loose debris puddle up around his feet and wash away. The exhaustion of combat, the subsequent adrenaline crash, and the extensive debriefing session had left him shaky and drained. Muscle soreness, mental fatigue – he was growing familiar with all the rigors that plagued a recon man fighting a secret war.

"Hey," John rapped on the shower stall. "You alive in there?"

"Barely."

"You were good out there today, man... You made good decisions that kept us alive."

Vivid images of the firefight began to streak through his mind again. He fished another PBR from the cooler and opened his boot laces; there was nothing quite like drinking a cold post-mission beer while sitting under a hot shower. His thoughts sunk further away from the present and focused on the imagery, sounds and smells of Cambodia as they burned into his psyche; explosions and white phosphorous, teargas, the smell of expended gunpowder and the crack of small-arms fire, pounding rotors and the mechanical whine of the turbine under great stress. The way those pith helmets had come bouncing through the grass just seconds before he'd blown them to smoldering bits. He suddenly realized that he'd killed men in combat. Assaulting the antiaircraft position in Laos a week before had been different; he hadn't actually seen any of them go down. He quickly buried that notion as deep and in the darkest place he could find because he was alive, and he was glad.

"Hey, John."

"Yeah."

"You really think Charlie was wait'n for us out there?"

"Better believe it, GI."

"What makes you so sure?"

"You notice how the whole goddamn countryside started shooting at us when the Hueys came back in?"

"Yeah..."

"We were on the ground for what – twenty minutes, tops?"

"Yeah, sounds about right."

"Not enough time for 'em to mass on us if they'd just gotten lucky. But we didn't land in the middle of anything either. That's why their air defense wasn't too accurate, and they didn't count on us sniffing 'em out before they could close the door on us."

Ethan thought for a moment about what was said in the debriefing, in particular, how John had described moving them away from the tree-line and back across the clearing. He'd done it to draw the NVA out into the open so the gunships could pound them. It was the type of tactic that rarely worked – so much so that it didn't merit repetition of any kind. Even John had admitted as much in the debriefing.

"They wanted us on the ground and without any assets so they could kill us, plain and simple."

The beers had them feeling primed and the edges were beginning to grow dull again. They hung their gear out to dry back at the team house, collected their shaving kits and went back to the showers to clean themselves. That was how it was done: gear and equipment first, bodies second. Then they'd break down and clean all their guns, magazines, grenades and ammo, and then repack it all. It was an exhaustive, time-consuming process but was of life-or-death importance.

"So how exactly does it work?" Ethan asked. He inspected the folded pin and then replaced the old wet tape that secured the spoon to one of his fragmentation grenades before moving to the next.

"How does what work?"

"Hanoi obviously has moles in the South Vietnamese government and the ARVN, and they're obviously getting intel on what we're doing and where. But *how*?"

"We're required to share target assignments and other intel with our VN counterparts and somewhere in that process, that information is finding its way north." John loaded another magazine and tossed it in the pile on his bed.

"Okay but how?" Ethan pressed. "Physically, I mean."

"Could be done by wiretap, could be a guy taking photos of documents with some kinda little spy camera... Hell, it could be as simple as a guy with a briefcase who makes the drop while he's out at lunch," he speculated. "All I know is that we're required to share classified intel with our ARVN counterparts, and somewhere in that exchange the NVA are learning about our planned targets, the LZs we pick, our mission objectives, what team is or will be on the ground and how many of us there are... Shit, sometimes even our names, rank, and where we're from. You realize every time we give Covey a fix on our position, it gets reported up our chain-of-command? And guess what's included inside the intel packet we share with the ARVNs..."

"You serious?"

"Unfortunately, yeah," he sighed. "That's part of the reason why we wake up surrounded sometimes."

They retrieved their harnesses and began repacking all their magazines and grenades and other assorted war-waging doodads and recon trinkets. They were preparing for yet another target, but there was to be no stand-down in between; in three days, they'd be crossing the border again and Ethan would have his first real taste of life as a recon One-Zero.

7

They could see it from miles away – a bright bald spot in the middle of a long, steep, jungle-covered mountain range.

Leghorn.

It had been the brainchild of RT Colorado One-Zero George "Ken" Sisler way back in late 1966 during the infancy of SOG's cross-border operations. As teams penetrated deeper into Laos and Cambodia, the dense vegetation and steep mountains made communications spotty and unpredictable. Realizing the need for a cross-border radio relay site, Lt. Sisler happened upon the perfect location for such an installation – a thousand-meter peak with near-vertical slopes that towered high above southern Laos. On the second day of the new year, 1967, Sisler and his team were inserted on the tiptop of the precipice with a slew of radios and everything they'd need to defend their new digs from the NVA that were sure to pay them a visit.

Two years later and the place was still in business.

The Vietnamese pilots swung the Kingbee in a wide bank around the remote perch giving Ethan and his teammates the grand aerial tour. It appeared to be little more than a sandbag fort built atop a barren wedge of earth and rock. There were about three or four main bunkers facing out at all points of the compass with a few scraggly trees and several radio antennas at the very top. About fifty yards beneath the bunker detail was a small shelf-like landing zone barely large enough for a single helicopter. The helipad was made of sandbags and looked a lot like giant cobblestones from the air, while the terrain fell sharply away on all sides except that which led up to the top. Repeated airstrikes and defoliant agents had kept the jungle cropped back, making it all but impossible for the NVA to assault with any real effectiveness.

They hit short-final, flared, and were bouncing on the sandbagged helipad in a matter of seconds. The massive, old reciprocating engine struggled in the thin air so landing wasn't a problem, especially with a full load. Weapons and equipment in-hand, Utah scrambled out of the Kingbee and off she chugged, sinking rapidly into the valley to gain airspeed before climbing back out, rotors slapping through the afternoon air. There was a dug-in bunker off to the right of the pad and a sandbagged staircase that meandered up to the top. All likely approaches were blocked by thick coils of concertina and barbwire with rock-filled C-ration cans hanging from the wire – the most sophisticated early-warning ground assault system in the entire world.

"Whatta place," Ethan said, taking it all in. "Whose Yards are those?" He was glancing up towards the top, and could see about a half-dozen little people – a few lounging about while the others scanned the surrounding ridgelines with binoculars and scoped rifles.

"Hatchet Force," John said as he led them up the staircase. "Squads rotate in every week to pull security for the NSA team, and to monitor our radio comms."

An American emerged from one of the bunkers above and paused to watch them climb up. He was shirtless and unshaven but seemed glad to have them there.

"Hey," he called, "where's the women and booze at?!"

"It all got diverted back to Group Headquarters," John teased.

"Why am I not surprised…"

"So what's the skinny?"

"Ain't shit," he leveled. "The occasional potshot but mostly just for harassment's sake. Ya'll stepping off tomorrow?"

"Yeah," Ethan said as they all met at the top.

"Y'all know how it works, right?" he asked. "New rotation comes in and unloads, bird takes off. Resupply ships come in, all hands on deck, and then our ride comes in last," he whistled and waved his hand for effect, "and off we go. Those cats don't like to linger on the pad for too long. Charlie might not be able to press us up here, but that don't stop 'em from lobbing eighty-twos and RPGs at us, especially when choppers sit down."

"We're gonna step off about a half hour before all that," Ethan said. "Find a spot to hole up in for the shift change. Then we'll move."

"Right, well you guys can drop your shit in that far left bunker," he pointed. "My guys were kinda sprawled out but we made some room for y'all – it's pretty tight living up here."

Tight was an understatement. The ramshackle bunkers were around twelve-by-fourteen feet, which was ample room for two or three guys but stuffing a whole eight-man recon team in one for the night was going be tough. All the bunker roofs were walled-up with sandbags and doubled as 60mm mortar pits; there was also a 90mm recoilless rifle position covering the main approach. The largest bunker was where the SOG-employed NSA team eavesdropped on enemy radio transmissions and worked to break their codes. Several sheets of plywood, some 55-gallon drums, a few plastic tarps, several long radio antennas and some wiring, and the place was complete.

They stowed their gear inside the bunker and settled down for the afternoon while the Yards broke out their cookware and foodstuffs, and mingled with the others. Nay and Luc were all business, though; they bummed a scoped and suppressed XM-21 and set up a little observation post inside one of the mortar pits and went to work. They looked like a pair of pros at first – Nay spotting and softly mumbling corrections in Bahnar while Luc tracked with the rifle until he acquired his sight-picture. A sharp crack followed by the hiss of escaping gasses from the suppressor made them grin like crocodiles. A few shots later and Nay was pestering Luc to switch positions, insisting that it was his turn.

"Are they hitting anything?" Ethan asked.

"Maybe a few monkeys," John chuckled. "They just like shooting with the suppressor."

Ethan leaned back against a mound of sandbags and laid his CAR-15 across his lap while the sun sank deeper and deeper before finally slipping beneath the horizon. Low clouds turned from pink and red to dark purple as the cooler air sank and mist began to form in the surrounding valleys. The view Leghorn afforded was astonishing and yet, he knew not to grow comfortable there. They were effectively surrounded by thousands and thousands of NVA – many of whom would be hunting them in the coming days.

"Yok-son?" It was Hyuk; he could tell by how he spoke. He was their translator and his English was the best.

"Yeah, what's up?"

"You come sit with us," he said. "We ask you questions."

"What kinda questions?"

"Come come," he insisted.

He crawled down off his sandbag perch and crossed the shelf over to where the Yards had all congregated around a very conservative cooking fire.

"Tell us things," Hyuk said. "What story of God you believe?"

"Story of God? Like, my religion?"

"Religion, yes," he smiled and placed a hand on Ethan's forearm. "Tell us what is your religion."

"I... I'm not sure I have one." He looked up and found the stars to be even more brilliant in a moonless sky. "I mean, I believe in God and all but I'm just not real religious I guess."

"Yes, which god?"

"Just... God." He could tell they wanted more. "It's tough to explain." He thought for a long minute. "I believe there's a higher being, something greater than any man or animal... That when we die, our spirits move on to something infinite." He looked at their faces and found them hanging off his words as Hyuk translated softly in Bahnar. "But I also want to believe that Karma's real... that doing good in this world for others will make it so that good things happen to me while I'm alive, and that my soul will go to a good place, be it Heaven or wherever... Does that make sense?" Their faces were awash in the soft, flickering orange glow of the tiny fire. They seemed satisfied in some capacity and he was glad because he didn't know how else to explain it.

"Nui has told us your spirit is strong and good. No need to worry."

Hyuk patted his forearm and handed him a broad leaf stuffed with freshly-cooked monkey meat. He ate quietly and listened to them chitchat in Bahnar while thinking about the days ahead. They were going in to monitor a series of river rapids about six kilometers south of Leghorn, and it was Ethan's mission – his to plan and his to lead, and the anticipation had made him an anxious, nervous wreck.

*   *   *

He was paralyzed, suspended somewhere between a state of consciousness and dreamland – almost as if his mind was awake but unable to will his body to move. He was vulnerable and he knew it, and he could feel the NVA creeping in around him.

C'mon Ethan, move... wake up, he beckoned. *They're coming through the wire, move!*

He could feel his head shaking back and forth and a slight twitching motion in his lower legs. He was close.

They're on top of us by now – gotta be... cutting our fucking throats while we sleep.

An icy hand grabbed his forearm and he was startled awake, on his back in a cold and dark place but the hand that still gripped his arm was warming as they shared body heat. It wasn't the grip of a man trying to kill him, but of someone trying to reassure him – a comforting touch.

"They're coming through the wire," Ethan whispered. "I – I think I hear sappers coming through the wire." He started to sit up but the hand on his arm squeezed convincingly tighter.

"Bad dream numba ten," Nui whispered.

A few of the others stirred by his side just enough to touch him and let him know they were there and everything was okay. He reluctantly lay back down while searching the darkness intently for the sounds of an approaching enemy, but all that was there was an infinite silence. It tormented him for a few long moments, letting him hear faint noises that weren't really there until he finally let it go and eased back to sleep.

They were off Leghorn and inside the tree-line by sunrise, waiting for the early-morning light to sift down through the treetops. Soon they were on the move, side-hilling on a southern azimuth while keeping the main ridgeline up to their right. The down-climb from the helipad had been treacherous enough, but side-hilling in such steep terrain was a far more dangerous proposition, so every step they took was calculated and deliberate. They found themselves traversing through a double-canopy mixture of matured growth with areas of thick underbrush. After about two hours of steady movement, they buttonhooked above their back-trail and stretched out in a staggered line across the mountainside, and waited for the shift change back up top. With heightened senses, they methodically searched the woods while Ethan and John monitored the radio traffic between the pilots and Leghorn. It had taken him all morning to calm his nerves and settle in, to tap into nature's frequency and become part of the ambiance. That was the only way to be successful at staying alive, the only way to hear the unnatural sounds the enemy made; the rest was just plain luck.

It was an hour before they picked up and continuing on-course to the south, working their way towards a finger that extended off the taper of the mountain range and jutted out into the river valley. The trees tall and the underbrush thick, but where the canopy parted just right afforded them a grand view of the target-area and the mountains beyond. It was a beautiful day, bright and sunny with low fluffy clouds drifting east – a real tropical look. Moving through dew-covered underbrush had soaked them all in short order, and it would've been Heaven to stop and strip down, and dry out in the warm sun. Instead, they skirted around bright piercing shafts of sunlight and remained focused on the task at hand.

Pok-time came and went without incident and by mid-afternoon, they happened across their first trail. Choked, overgrown and narrow, it obviously hadn't been used in quite some time. Orienting themselves with their maps, Ethan and John both made mental notes about the location and direction of the trail, but made no marks on their map-sheets. Pertinent mission details including their line-of-march, E&E routes, discovered trails and other intelligence would all be filled in during the debriefing process once they got back to Kontum. So with flank security established, they crossed without incident and continued side-hilling towards the finger.

He liked the way that spot looked on the map – how it extended out into the valley and dropped down right into the river basin. He wanted to find an RON site somewhere on that finger, and then slowly make their way into a river-watch position the following morning. It was a good plan that would keep them on higher ground over night, but it was far from a safe bet. And as they made their approach to the saddle, it was easy to see why. The ground they were on quickly squeezed into a narrow spine and fell sharply away on either side. It was a natural chokepoint – an excellent spot for the enemy to trap them against the terrain, and even if they were able to make it downhill, they'd be pinned against the river with nowhere to run and the NVA holding all the high ground. But even with that prospect at the front of his mind, Ethan still liked it because it was an unlikely spot for them to be. And the only way the NVA would be able to get to them would be by crossing the same narrow saddle; the other three sides of the finger were simply too steep to mount an assault over and there'd be no way to climb up from the valley without making a lot of noise.

They swung around in a buttonhook to observe their back-trail for a bit and then searched out an RON site. It was late in the afternoon and the shadows were beginning to stretch out and grow long and dangerous. They ringed their position with Claymores and then worked out an E&E route should they get hit and have to run. Luc and Nui came crawling back in after conducting a thorough recon of the finger and were happy to report nothing out of the ordinary. So they settled in as best they could, eating in pairs while the shadows bled to black and the night slowly closed in around them.

*   *   *

He could just barely make out Nui signaling them from down inside a bramble thicket at the river's edge, right where the trail climbed up the riverbank and back into the woods. It was a gift from above – a natural gift from the gods of recon themselves because a more perfect place to setup and grab a prisoner probably didn't exist.

"Two coming across," John whispered. "You pick."

They flashed the signal up the trail to where Luc and Ti Tu had established flank security, and then broke squelch on the radio to alert Leghorn. They'd been counting heads for three days, just waiting – biding their time for the right pair to come waltzing down the trail. They'd seen everything from squads to platoons moving in both directions, but none fewer in numbers than five. In Ethan's mind, two was the magic number. Two meant the possibility of grabbing them both, or having to kill only one. Two also meant being able to initiate the grab'n-go with suppressed weapons instead of Claymores.

Two was the perfect number, and the second he saw them crawl up the riverbank and back onto the trail, Ethan knew he wanted the one in front. He was older, skinnier and far more weathered. Chances were he'd been on the Trail for much longer and likely had more intelligence value than his teenaged companion.

He signaled John and made ready.

Relax, relax… Just let 'em come past you and then step out behind 'em. Grab the kid so you can ease him to the ground when it's done. John's got the old man, Nay and Hyuk will back us up. No sweat.

He adjusted his sweaty grip on the suppressed .22-caliber High Standard and watched them as they shook the mud from their Bata boots and got on with their stroll.

Don't look into their eyes.

Around the bend in the trail they sloshed, and then he rolled deftly out from his hide. A fistful of the kid's rucksack strap and he pressed the muzzle to his head just behind his left ear. The suppressor coughed twice and Ethan struggled to control the kid's deadfall. He laid him face-down on the trail and felt the jungle sucking in around him in a head-spinning blur.

Fuck... Keep it together. Search his shit and deal with it later.

Dexterity escaped him as he stripped the kid's gear away and emptied his pockets into a tidy pile. Wallet, cigarettes, Zippo, knockoff Rolex and a few balls of cold rice; the older one carried that plus a handful of papers wrapped in plastic and secured with a rubber-band. Solid intel, plus whatever they carried in their rucks but there was no time to explore the contents.

Things were beginning to happen fast. John and Nay had their prisoner cuffed, gagged, and hooded and ready to move, and the rest of the Yards had security hemmed up tight. No words spoken, only deliberate action. They stashed the body deep in a bramble thicket while Nui and Bo sterilized the incident from the trail. Time to move, and move they did – uphill to the northeast for a short distance before stopping to make radio contact. Ethan was so shaky and excited he could barely whisper into the handset, but Covey had a solid copy and was already scrambling the air package. It was all coming together so perfectly that something just *had* to go wrong. It was inevitable. Murphy's Law, and a few hundred meters later, it caught up with them in the form of yet another trail – wider with fresh sign moving in both directions. A dangerous proposition to cross, particularly with a prisoner in tow, but their LZ was on the far side and there was no way around it.

Carefully, slowly, quietly, Ethan eased himself beyond the veiling foliage and out into the open – eyes and muzzle moving as one, foot placement being of a conscious and deliberate nature. He glanced up and down the corridor before probing slightly into the woods beyond. It felt like minutes had trickled by but in truth, it had only been seconds; any faster and noise discipline would've been all but impossible to maintain. Luc stepped out behind him and came up to find a way through the brush ahead while Bo and Nay pulled security for their crossing. John, Ti Tu, and Hyuk shuffled the prisoner across while Nui backed out and meticulously repositioned the fauna behind him in order to conceal their passage.

Ethan felt the air in front of his face crease with hot lead even before he heard the muzzle blast, then his ears were ringing and he was stiff-arming Nui and Bo into the brush behind Nay and the others. The woods began to blur as his vision tightened; they were running as hard as they could, bulling their way through a tangle of branches and vines that grabbed and snatched at everything they carried.

Fuck, is anybody hit?! How did they get the drop on us? How many? Fuck, we need high ground so I can call Covey. Fuck!

His thought process was spinning into a maddening quandary.

Relax, focus, stay alive. Luc'll get us to a high-point; check your people, then get Covey on the horn.

They broke through the underbrush and spilled out onto yet another trail; Luc had cut right and was leading them down the corridor, using the footpath to gain distance without all the noise generated by crashing through the woods. Running and running, constantly glancing over his shoulder to make sure Nui was keeping up and that the NVA hadn't filled in behind them. His brow flooded with sweat and he could feel it stinging its way through all the little abrasions on his face and neck. He considered the bobbing heads of his teammates as they ran and then CAR-15s and AKs suddenly chattered at each other up front. Low and moving forward under the *crack!* of small arms fire and tracers – his team split on either side of the trail while Bo established a steady base of fire for them to maneuver behind.

"Go left, go left!" he heard John shout.

Several Yards bolted across the trail with the prisoner, the sharp *crump!* of a hand grenade and then Bo's RPD ran dry.

On his stomach, Ethan lobbed a grenade from his M-79, rolled across the trail and pushed Ti Tu up into the woods. Then Nui was firing as he and Bo peeled off, leaving Ethan to cover their withdrawal. He snatched the pin from a teargas grenade, let the spoon ping away and flung it into the haze. Then he was scrambling uphill behind the others – hands clawing at the earth, legs pumping and feet digging for purchase, lungs burning in the humidity, heart in his throat and his pulse pounding in his ears. He climbed for maybe a hundred meters, just barely able to see his teammates above him while shouts and signal shots echoed through the woods below.

Tracers suddenly cut into the hillside all around him, splintering trees and ricocheting up into the sky. He rolled over, swung his CAR-15 around and emptied a magazine into them, knocking several down and momentarily scattering the others into the woods. He changed magazines and started climbing furiously again, eyes fixed on a moss-covered boulder up to his right. That was the hard-point he needed. From there, he'd make his stand and do everything in his power to keep the NVA off the others long enough for them to get out.

Behind the rock just as more AK rounds came skipping his way. He calmly stacked magazines to his left, grenades to his right, and then went to work on semi-auto. Two, three... five... seven, eight – they just kept coming and he just kept knocking them down like bowling pins. Someone slid down beside him and he hoped it was one of the Yards; he didn't want to be alone any longer but it was just too late in the game to be scared.

"You lost your goddamn mind?!" John shouted.

"I'm slowing 'em down so y'all can get out!"

"Get your Audie Murphy ass up that fucking hill!" John pitched a frag and hit them with a jolt from his CAR-15. "Let's go, let's go!"

They scrambled, scampered, clawed and climbed their way up until they broke through the woods and into a raggedy clearing.

"Is this our LZ?"

"No choice, prisoner's slowing us down."

"What, why?"

"He got hit back on the trail," John called over his shoulder.

The Yards already had the wagons circled from the safety of a few scattered bomb craters and Covey was on the way with the air package, but their prisoner was hemorrhaging.

Blood-soaked shirt ripped open and a quick rinsing of the wound with iodine-treated canteen water. Ethan applied direct pressure to the wound with the palms of his bare hands – the blood making it a warm and slippery affair while John tied a hasty tourniquet above his left elbow, and then probed for a vein to start an IV drip.

"Oh man, they're mushy... His blood pressure's too low."

"Shit, he's puking!"

"Roll him my way, quick!"

He coughed and vomited, and jerked with abdominal contractions omitting a fetid waft of bile and bodily waste. Ethan splashed water on the man's face and wiped the vomit away while John flushed and dressed the lime-sized exit wound in his lumbar. Once more on his back, pressure on the wound until John finally got an IV started, and then a fresh compression bandage to seal the leak.

An RPG came sizzling by and clapped off in the treetops beyond them and what followed was an absolute maelstrom of small-arms fire and booming explosions. He could barely hear Covey calling for him over the radio, and then he saw the O-2 Skymaster roll across a ridgeline to the east. He fished his pen flares out, pointed one as high and straight up in the sky as he could, and popped it off.

"Covey, spot my flares!" Ethan fumbled to reload another and then fired again. "Spot my flares!"

Out of nowhere, two Cobras flashed across the sky. He shook open his orange signal panel and waved it madly overhead. The gunships banked, turned inbound, dropped their noses and went to work.

It was beautiful.

Pass after pass, they juked ground fire and worked the NVA over, eventually pushing them back with cannons and rockets until the ground fire slackened while distant antiaircraft fire stitched the sky. He looked down at his prisoner and was relieved to find him still clinging to life. And then, with bound hands, the NVA soldier waved him closer until he could just hear his whisper.

"*Do'i mot cho cai,*" he stammered with a smirk – the life slowly ebbing away while Covey's voice crackled through the radio handset and the Cobras hunted.

8

"Life's a bitch."

"Excuse me?"

"That's what he said."

"Who?"

"The NVA we grabbed… Waved me in and whispered right into my ear."

"And that's all he said to you?"

"Word-for-word."

"Then what?"

"Well then he died," Ethan said, glancing down at his trembling hands – dried blood and dirt still trapped under his fingernails. It was all just a few hours old.

"In English?"

"Huh?"

"Did he whisper to you in English?"

"Oh. No, Vietnamese."

"Well how do you know that's what he said?"

"I asked one of my little people when we got back to Dak To."

"And you remembered the phrasing exactly?" another analyst pressed.

"*Do'i mot cho cai*," Ethan repeated. "He whispered that into my ear, smirked, and died. Y'all know the rest."

From the debriefing, John and Ethan went straight to the showers in full kit with a pair of lawn chairs and a cooler full of beer. Post-mission decompression and the water was warm and rejuvenating. They sat side-by-side in silence, savoring beers while the rest of the compound hummed around them in the late-afternoon sun. The solitude was much-needed and after a couple of beers, Ethan's edge had dulled and the shakes had smoothed out.

"Hey... You good?"

"Yeah," Ethan nodded.

"Close enough to shave, huh."

"Which part?" Ethan quipped.

"Wish I hadn't pointed Luc down that trail," John sighed. "That was a bad call."

"Hey dude, forget it." Ethan reached over with his beer and they toasted. "So how about all that surveying equipment they were carrying, you reckon they go that far when selecting a place to build something out there?"

"Beats me," John shrugged. "I always just assumed they simply pointed at a spot and started building. But if they're actually out there *surveying* areas beforehand... that says a lot about their knowledge and commitment to see this thing through. That's why we respect those little fuckers, ya dig?"

"Definitely," Ethan nodded.

"So I talked to Bob Howard and *Dai-uy* Yates while you were still in the debriefing."

"Yeah? What'd they hafta say?"

"I think they wanna give you your own team."

"…Oh shit."

"Yeah," John chuckled. "You better do something dumb quick because I don't feel like breaking in another new guy."

"Gimme a few days. I'm sure I'll thinka something."

They ate steaks and drank off the top shelf in the club but left early before the night grew too rowdy. The Yards had a small cookout planned the following day and neither Ethan nor John had the energy to party all night and suffer through hangovers. But by noon the following day, their little grill-out had grown into a company-wide pig picking. The indigenous members from all the teams had pooled their resources and had set up two big fire pits and were cooking a pair of golden pigs on spits. They were also steaming leafy pockets full of shrimp, squid, monkey, chicken, vegetables, and plenty of fruit. It was an assortment of cuisine unlike anything Ethan had ever seen, smelled, or eaten before. Nay waved him over, carved off a big chunk of pork, piled on a host of leaf-wrapped delicacies, and topped the plate with rice, fruit and vegetables.

"Eat, eat," he urged with a big smile and patted Ethan's shoulder.

Beer and food in-hand, Ethan drifted through the gathering to where John, Mark, Pete Johnston, Ray Fuller, Randy Reynolds, and Luke Dove were sitting in a circle of lawn chairs.

"I'm tell'n ya," Fuller lamented, "I was in there last night and she was working."

"Bullshit. Who was she with?" Reynolds fired back in denial.

"Beats me, some leg from the Fourth."

"What's he talk'n about?" Ethan whispered. Meanwhile, Reynolds and Fuller continued their volley.

"Randy's girl used to work at one of the houses in town," John said. "He became one of her regulars and they hit it off, so he put her up in an apartment in downtown Kontum but word is she's still working."

"All this according to Fuller," Luke reminded them with a smirk, and for good reason: Reynolds was known to fall in love at the drop of a hat, and Fuller had a reputation for being just the type of *customer* to prove to Reynolds that his girl was indeed still working.

"The perfect storm," Ethan giggled.

Five minutes later, Reynolds was shoving a reluctant Fuller towards a company jeep and promising castration lest he receive total cooperation for whatever schemes he was conjuring up within his demented little Texan mind. Bob Howard just stood there smoking a Lucky Strike and wearing that bemused half-grin he'd perfected over the years.

They partied on, eating and drinking, recounting boorish jokes and embarrassing one another for no other reason than to share a laugh and be merry. Three months ago, Ethan never would've imagined he'd be sitting in the middle of such hard men – the most dedicated and bravest, most dangerous men he'd ever known. He never considered himself to be any of those things, yet he had somehow found a place amongst them.

A successful mission earned the team a few well-deserved days off from both combat duty and from the menial tasks that kept them busy around the compound. And while they rested and recovered, everyone else seemed to be preparing for a mission or ready for insertion. RT Illinois inserted into Cambodia two days later to perform a damage assessment after another wave of B-52 Arc Light strikes. It wasn't long before they ran across a mob of NVA and extracted after a running gunfight, leaving two of Illinois' Vietnamese critically wounded. Then the following day, Covey Rider Mike Scott and SPAF pilot Bruce Bessor were attempting to make an early-morning radio check with a team when their radio transmission was abruptly broken off. The team reported hearing a heavy antiaircraft battery pumping away in the distance, meaning only one outcome: Bessor and Scott's O-1 Bird Dog had been shot down over Laos. There wasn't a man in recon who didn't volunteer to go in after them, but a fast approaching monsoon system denied them a Bright Light attempt.

By morning, the monsoon had enveloped the entire countryside in a blur of rain, wind and fog, halting CCC's operations in both Laos and Cambodia. That night, those from Recon Company along with Pete Johnston, Rex Hill, and others who knew Bessor and Scott best gathered in the club and toasted drinks in their names while recounting their fondest memories. With his own corner staked out, Ethan leaned his stool up against the wall with the intentions of only observing once again the ethical rituals that were to follow. Continuous combat over an extended period of time, coupled with the secrecy of SOG's existence, had eroded things of unimportance away. All that remained was a rollercoaster of raw emotions: elation, depression, anxiety, fear, and rage – all at the most extreme ends of the spectrum.

The bad, unpredictable weather translated to suicide for both ground and air operations along the Trail, so for five days, CCC's covert war was mostly put on hold. Ethan took time to catch up on mail and spent the rest inside the club shooting pool or watching movie reruns. Just as cabin fever began to set in, the weather finally broke and everyone quickly picked right back up where they left off. Nearly every team was back in training again, running small patrols around camp or down at the range practicing tactics and live-fire drills. A few teams had received replacements while others remained slightly short-handed. Two days later, Utah received a warning order for another Prairie Fire target.

"The Bra" was arguably the hottest, most dreaded block of real estate inside southern Laos, and consisted of four target-areas: Hotel, India, Juliet, and November-9. Of those targets, Juliet-9 seemed to have the worst reputation among recon men at CCC.

While NVA activity in other target-areas cooled down at times, The Bra was always hot. It was where Highway 110 broke away to the east from Highway 96 – another major north-to-south route of the Trail. And as if that wasn't bad enough, somewhere deep inside the velvety folds and jungled valleys was the NVA's *Binh Tram* 37 – a major network of bunker complexes, field hospitals, supply depots, and truck parks.

"The river that runs straight through the target draws a pair of half-loops and it looks like a woman's bust-line from the air, and on a topo-map," John illustrated with his finger in the air.

"How do you know what a woman's bust-line looks like, you queer," Bill Allen chided from the comfort of his seat.

"If dicking your girlfriend on my last R-and-R makes me queer, so be it," John sneered.

"You ever been in there?" Ethan asked, breaking up the catfight.

"Yeah, last September. We were on the ground for two days before the NVA had dogs on our asses."

"Dogs? You're shitting me."

"No lie, GI. We could hear hounds yelping all day and night."

"Fucking unnerving when that happens," Bill added. "It's like slow death; they just keep getting closer and closer and there ain't much you can do about it."

"So what'd you do? How the hell did you shake 'em?"

"Dusted our back-trail with CS-powder and rigged a few Claymores with CS. Guess they finally gave up or we killed the dogs and their handlers, whichever."

Ethan threw back the last few swallows of a Coke and finished his ham sandwich just as Bill Delima and Glen Uemura strolled into the club and joined their table. A few months back, Delima and his RT Hawaii had been hit hard by a counter-recon force while inside Juliet-9 and had barely escaped with their lives. Glen's eyes went cold just with the mentioning of that target-area.

"We've had four Medal of Honor recipients here at Kontum, and two of those were earned while inside Juliet-9," John said.

"Zab early last year," Bill nodded, referring to Fred Zabitosky, "and just a few months later, John Kedenburg earned his posthumously."

"Who were the others?" Ethan asked quietly.

"George Sisler in early '67 and it sounds like Bob will get his soon," John said. "Big footprints to follow in, huh?"

"Huge."

For the next three days, Utah trained hard and long, from sunup until sundown. Since their mission was a simple area recon through a long, sweeping valley, they dropped the specifics and rehearsed everything. Every formation and tactic was hammered out with live-fire, while small mistakes were analyzed and smoothed out. They practiced carrying wounded teammates while having to fight and run; they practiced riding strings; they practiced subduing and snatching prisoners; they rehearsed wiretap procedures on

150

enemy communication lines. Everything. They rehearsed live-fire IA drills at all angles so they'd know exactly how to react should they get hit from any direction.

With two days before their scheduled insertion, John and Ethan flew a visual recon of Juliet-9 to map and mark favorable LZs, and terrain features. From the backseat of Pete Johnston's little O-1, Ethan peered downward at The Bra with weary eyes and a knotted stomach. Juliet-9 consisted of the most inhospitable terrain he'd ever seen. Heavy, triple-canopy jungle blanketed steep folds of earth while shadows suppressed the deepest pockets of valleys from the sun's midday rays. Banks of ghost-like mist drifted through the treetops and lingered against the steep mountains. Thousands of bomb craters plucked away at the earth on both sides of Highways 96 and 110; in the disturbingly round voids were pools of stagnant, murky-green water deposited by the monsoon from two weeks earlier. At the craters' edges was shattered earth and heavy tangles of splintered growth; the trees that managed to stay upright were stripped of all their foliage and bark, and wore only a suit of black charcoal. Astonishingly enough, the roadways were perfectly intact despite the constant bombing of the Trail and its infrastructure. Ethan marked several possible LZs as well as a few abandoned antiaircraft positions that had been etched into the mountainsides. He noted the positions of several bomb crater clusters in case they needed to scramble for a fast extraction.

The night before their insertion was one of sheer anxiety and anticipation for both John and Ethan, and neither of them could quell the emotions of running such a menacing target. With Norman Greenbaum's "Spirit in the Sky" jamming over the speakers in the team house, they prepared two Claymore bags with what John called "specialized ordnance" consisting of a variety of grenades. They taped packets of powdered teargas to white phosphorous grenades, rigged M26 frags with time-delay fuses, and packed several V40 golf ball-sized mini-grenades for good measure. John was back in the driver's seat as Utah's One-Zero and that suited Ethan just fine.

*   *   *

Ethan stuffed his bare feet into his boots and slung his CAR-15 across his shirtless back – the forged aluminum receivers cold and rigid against his skin. Outside, a few of the boys were huddling around a burning chunk of C4, waiting for a pot of water to boil while everyone else milled around one of the perimeter bunkers just across the way. Distant inbound choppers from Kontum beat the moist air as the echoes rolled through the valleys around Dak To. The sun slaved laboriously from the east attempting to draw back the heavy cloud curtain but it had a long ways to go. The only rays of direct sunlight stretched far across the horizon in milky strokes of fire before being smothered above the cloud cover. John and Luc were working quickly to get the .50-caliber tripod situated while Nay linked several belts of ammo together.

"Ethan!" John shouted. "Get those goofballs under cover and bring us more ammo!"

He ran back inside the Mortuary and grabbed the radio, then scrambled Ayatt and Ti Tu to help him with several more cans of .50-caliber ammo. The trio sprinted back across the launch site and clambered up on top of the bunker where John and Nay were busy finishing their preparations. They dumped out all the ammo and worked quickly to link all the belts together into one neat stack. Nay fed the first few rounds of the belt in from the left, slammed the receiver top down, and then John stroked the charging handle back.

"Delta-Tango-Lima-Sierra," the radio crackled, "this is Panther Two-One, over."

"Go ahead, Panther." Ethan replied.

"Any sign of a welcoming committee this morning?"

Ethan concentrated hard through the binoculars as he and the rest of the team gazed out past the airstrip and into the dark green mountains facing the launch site.

"Nothing yet Panther."

"Roger that, we're coming in." The air package dropped down into the valley from high up in the clouds, banked back around and flared out over the airstrip across the drainage ditch. Just as their landing skids kissed the tarmac, the atmosphere suddenly split open with a terrible *crack!*

Whumpf! Clumps of earth geysered a hundred feet skyward at the far end of the airstrip; John sat poised behind the heavy gun with his knees pulled into his chest, waiting for the next round to fall. The choppers were pouring on the power and were lifting off right as three more rounds splashed in front of each other as the

NVA began to walk them closer to the launch site. In the blink of an eye, John swung the .50-cal's muzzle around and closed the butterfly trigger.

Boom-boom-boom-boom-boom! Bright red tracers lasered through the air and pounded the hillsides over a thousand meters downrange. The big gun's muzzle blast beat a steady cloud of dust from the sandbags while hot empty brass collected at the base of the tripod. Nay's gritty smile reflected insane delight as he hand-fed the belted ammo into the receiver. Every twenty rounds or so, the gun would jam and John would reach forward and work the charging handle back to cycle the bolt.

Whumpf-whumpf! Another pair of rounds impacted in front of the others as the enemy continued to walk them closer to the launch site. Hot concussion waves belted through the bunker with terrifying power. Smoke and dust, and shattered earth roiled across the tarmac, drifting on the morning breeze. Nay quickly dumped another can of ammo onto the sandbags and linked it before John could run dry. Between the staccato pounding of the .50-cal's bolt and the outgoing gunfire, Ethan could barely hear the lead gunship pilot transmitting, asking them to cease fire.

"John, the gunships are rolling in; hold your fire!" Ethan yelled.

John kept the butterfly trigger pinned – his face showing stoned emotion, but his eyes transmitting wild obsession. Just then, the Cobras rolled in from the right and fired several 2.75-inch rockets. Bursts of fiery explosions were seen before their thumping impacts could be heard. Devastating 20mm cannons buzzed overhead while shredding the jungle against the distant hillside. Another call for the .50-cal to stop firing – the pilots fearing their aircraft could take hits from skyward ricochets. Suddenly, the gun went silent and all that was left was a scalding hot pile of empty brass and belt links. Distant thumping from exploding rockets echoed, while the sounds of helicopter turbines and rotors scorched and diced the atmosphere. Ethan's brain and heart pounded in a rhythm of headache and exhilaration and sheer terror. His nostrils burned from the wafting gun-smoke and the odor of fear that his body emitted.

John exhaled a deep, slow breath as he stood up from behind the gun; the radio handset crackled in Ethan's grasp as the gunship pilot requested a sitrep on the rocket fire. He gazed at John with uncertainty and confusion as he pulled the mic to his mouth.

"Negative contact, Panther; we're clear."

Across the drainage ditch, the choppers settled down again, delivering RT Colorado for their week-long Bright Light duty. The rest of the Yards emerged from below and began shoveling the expended shell casings back into the ammo cans.

"Karate's gotta be over Juliet-9 by now, maybe we'll launch today," John said as he climbed out from behind the heavy gun.

"Did you not hear me yelling?"

"I heard you."

"Dude, that was bad," Ethan admonished him. "That was really fucking bad. That coulda been a fucked situation."

"Then maybe they shoulda thought about that before they fucking flew into my line of fire," John snapped. "Square the gun away, I'll be in the commo-shed." A brace of pilots went bristling after him, seething about the situation and Ethan could hear them arguing as they walked off.

After helping rearm the gunships, Ethan made his way into the commo-shed. John had his feet up on the desk where the radio bank sat and was teetering back on the legs of his chair.

"Well, what's the deal?"

"Same shit," John said flatly. "We're grounded."

"Any chance S-3 will scrub the mission?" Ethan pushed.

"We're here until the weather breaks over the target. Until then, we wait for Karate's call."

He slid the chair back and pushed his way past chase medic Joe Parnar and RT Colorado One-Zero Willie McLeod.

"What's with him?" Joe asked once John was beyond earshot.

"He's been on-edge for the past week," Ethan said.

"Any word from Karate?"

"It's still shit."

"How many days have you guys been out here?" Willie asked. "Feel like I ain't seen y'all in a month."

"Eight days," Ethan sighed.

"S-3 won't scrub it?" Joe asked.

"Guess not."

"What target?" Willie asked.

"Juliet-9."

"John tell you about the last time he was in there?" Joe asked.

"No... Why, what happened?"

"NVA tracked 'em down overnight and had 'em surrounded by first-light. They got hit hard and the One-Zero – Foster I think was his name – was killed outright. Two Yards were hit pretty bad too. So John got on the horn and declared a Prairie Fire emergency and started putting air on the NVA. They finally got an extraction that afternoon but had to leave Foster's body behind; Bright Light never recovered it and John inherited the team."

"Fuck man," Ethan mumbled. "He never told me any of that."

By midday, Karate radioed back with a negative on an early-afternoon launch, and a last-light launch looked unlikely as well; Utah would soon be on its ninth day of standby at Dak To. Some of the Yards were horseplaying quietly while a few others began to prepare food and check their equipment. Ethan grabbed a seat beside John atop a perimeter bunker and dug into a bag of cold rice and chicken, but not before a liberal application of Tabasco sauce. They ate in silence for a while, listing to the crickets while the little people from both Utah and Colorado milled about the launch site.

"Joe told me what happened the last time you worked this target," Ethan said, breaking the silence. John nodded and continued eating. "Is that what's eating you?"

John was quiet for a few more moments while gazing out across the tarmac.

"The odds are stacked *too* high against us in there, Ethan. You don't know – you ain't never been in there." His hands were trembling. "I shoulda died so many times before now," he said, staring off at nothing in particular. "I know if I go back in there, I ain't gonna make it out again."

"Then let's just pass this target," Ethan urged. As soon as the words left his mouth, he felt dumb for even suggesting such a thing. He knew John would rather roll the dice than pass on a mission and lose face, even though no one at CCC would really have thought less; everyone knew of The Bra's reputation and nobody wanted that target.

"What if we passed it," he said. "What if we passed this target on to another team and *they* went in there and got all shot up? I couldn't live with myself, Ethan. No way." He was right and Ethan knew it; they both felt the same way.

They sat in silence again for what felt like an eternity while listening to the nighttime creatures.

"I sometimes forget what my parents look like... I mean, I have to look at a fucking picture, man. Their faces, I forget their faces... But I'll never forget what a dead Vietnamese or Montagnard looks like. And I sure as hell won't be able to forget what a dead American looks like," John sighed. "This place ain't nothin' but a beautiful fucking world of suffer and human wreckage."

The next morning, Karate again denied Utah a first-light insertion due to the harsh weather stalled out over Juliet-9. With the arrival of the air package tasked to insert and extract teams that day, Joe Parnar was back at Dak To, riding chase as usual. Ethan offered him a good morning and pulled him aside, filling him in on the conversation he shared with John the previous night, and Joe was concerned to say the least.

"We need to get him out of the field," he said. "Normally, I'd say it's just the stress talking, but he basically predicted his own death. He'll just will it to happen if he honestly believes it to be true."

"So what the fuck do I do?" Ethan stressed. "You know him, Joe – he won't back down from any target."

"Still no word from S-3?"

"Nothing."

Ethan could see Joe conjuring for a moment as he led him into the commo-shed. He radioed Kontum and reported that John had come down with amoebic dysentery. It took a few minutes of explanation before they finally got what they so desperately needed. S-3 had finally caved and scrubbed their mission.

"Don't sweat it," Joe encouraged Ethan. Besides Zune, those guys in Operations never leave the air conditioning, and Zune will understand. We bought John a few days' rest, which should help, but I still think he needs to get out of the field for good."

"Thanks a lot man, I'll see ya back at Kontum."

Though relieved, John was still irritable and temperamental so Ethan elected not to tell him how he and Joe had gone about getting the mission scratched. Regardless, he knew he'd done what was best for the team and that's what mattered most. John crashed into a deep slumber as soon as they dragged themselves into the team house, waking briefly twelve hours later only to shower and eat, and was down again for another ten hours. Though he knew Joe was probably right, Ethan feared a few days' rest wouldn't be enough for John. He had sensed a change of being in him way back when Mitch had been medevac'd six weeks earlier. He remembered searching John's eyes a few days back and what he had seen was a young man unraveling behind his sense of duty and loyalty while aging well before his time. Duty and loyalty to close friends, both killed and missing. It was a process of slow mental and emotional erosion caused by dangerous levels of high stress and a constant struggle against the odds.

There was also the team to consider; who would lead Utah if John quit? Amongst the other teams, RT Illinois One-Zero Ben Thompson finally called it quits earlier that week and transferred to Long Thanh to teach at SOG's One-Zero school, leaving John Plaster the only American on the team. And although he'd proven to be an excellent recon man, Lieutenant Colonel Abt felt Plaster wasn't ready to lead just yet. Glen Uemura was in line to inherit RT Hawaii from One-Zero Bill Delima, and a young John St. Martin had taken over RT New York only a few days earlier just as the team was boarding choppers at Dak To.

Teams were being pushed harder than ever and replacements simply weren't filling the holes quickly enough. It wasn't like playing a pickup game of baseball at the neighborhood diamond – jumbling teammates together in a hodgepodge fashion could get men killed. There had also been a change in first sergeants while Utah had been at Dak To. Bob Howard was scheduled to return stateside shortly in preparation to receive his long-overdue Medal of Honor, making former RT Florida One-Zero Norman Doney Recon's new first sergeant. Like Bob Howard, Norm Doney was what most considered the epitome of a Special Forces soldier. As a member of the older generation of SF, Doney had extensive experience in Southeast Asia and had served in the top-secret CIA-run Project White Star in Laos during the early '60s; he'd also run recon with the 5th Group's Project Delta before coming to SOG.

In the days that followed Utah's ordeal at Dak To, it became apparent that changes had indeed settled within John; he remained distant and somewhat withdrawn from the day-to-day happenings around the compound. Ethan's concerns were genuine enough that he began to contemplate taking it to Captain Yates and the first sergeant, but decided to wait a few more days in hopes that John would come around.

The monthly awards ceremony was held a couple of days later and Ethan was proud to finally have his CIB pinned to his chest for the Bright Light mission but that wasn't all. He also received a Bronze Star for valor for the same operation, and was told that a second decoration was awaiting final approval for his actions during the attempted prisoner snatch and subsequent delaying action he'd fought just a few weeks earlier. The Bronze Star dangling from his pocket flap felt big but what he was truly proud of – what he coveted most was the combat infantryman badge.

He listened to the various citations being read aloud as the Awards and Decorations cadre shuffled along with the Colonel through their ranks. And when they finally reached John, they presented him with a varnished MACV-SOG service plaque and a shiny presentation bolo knife, both engraved with his name and time served in Recon Company. That was it; it was official: John Cameron had quit recon.

The drinks were stiff and the music was loud in the club that night as they all ogled over a pair of Vietnamese dancers twirling around on center stage. Meanwhile, all the Covey Riders did their best to convince John to join their ranks without success. The dangers of running recon were unparalleled, but a close second was flying as a Covey Rider. John had spent eighteen months beating the odds along the Trail but riding Covey was hardly much safer. At a glance, Ethan thought it strange that a man could endure almost two years of nonstop combat, yet crack under the pressures of waiting for a mission to drop. Yet he too had felt the pressure mount while at Dak To and knew that waiting only made things worse. He awoke to an empty team house the following morning; John's rack was bare except for the rolled-up mattress and his wall locker had been cleaned out. He'd left without a single goodbye or good luck.

"Can't believe he just up and split like that."

"The man lost his nerve, Ethan," Karate said flatly as he sipped his coffee. "Imagine trying to face these guys after realizing you can't hack it any longer."

The next few days brought steady monsoonal downpours to the Central Highlands leaving Kentucky and Arizona socked in and everyone was worried they'd find trouble before the weather could break. Later that afternoon, Captain Yates told Ethan that Utah had been assigned a new One-Zero.

"Well, who is it? Do I know him?"

"Congratulations numb-nuts," Yates smirked, "you're the proud owner of a SOG recon team."

*   *   *

The team house was a cool, empty environment necessary for his mental and physical repair and preparation. Mark, Ben, and Paul made themselves at home as usual and drank all his beer without replenishing the stock, but it was good to spend time with them again. They were proud that Ethan was the first of them to become a One-Zero, but they couldn't understand his reluctance. John and Mitch were both gone now and the only man left to lead was him; so much rode on his shoulders and he didn't know if he was ready for the responsibilities of being a team leader.

Paul slung his arm around Ethan's neck and spoke low, "Be happy that John was lucky enough to survive two tours of recon and still walk outta this fuck'n place, man."

He was right.

Mark came through with a new album his brother had just sent him – Led Zeppelin I. The British rock band pumped liberating electric guitar riffs, thunderous drum solos, and rusty vocals into every corner of the team house while they played cards and ignored the pitter-patter of rain for the better part of two days. In between hands, Ethan pored back over a few letters from home but they always seemed to ask him to write more. But what more could he say? Government censors were always on the hunt for classified terms like "MACV-SOG", "Prairie Fire", "Ho Chi Minh Trail", "Salem House" or anything else they deemed a potential breach of security. There were always rumors circulating around the compound about someone who knew a guy who was friends with a guy who had written home in detail about everything. When the censors caught him, the punishment was always the same: "They sent his ass off to some leg infantry outfit."

"Intelligence gathering" is the term Ethan used to describe things in his first letter – truthful, just not elaborated. At first, he felt like a little kid keeping secrets from his family, but as the months passed, it began to eat at his conscience. What bugged him most was the fact that his family would never learn the truth if he was killed or went missing while across the fence. He wanted them to know more, but he just didn't know how to say it without sending up a red flag.

He aimlessly scoured the room for a moment, knowing he'd find what he was looking for right at the moment that it occurred to him. He snatched up the 35mm Pen EES-2 he'd forgotten to inventory after coming back from Dak To; the photo lab technician, Jonesy, had been nagging him for the better part of a week to turn it back into the lab, but Ethan had simply forgotten. He started with the room itself, snapping away at all the creature comforts, then got a few of Recon's finest to pose for a few group photos. He toted the camera into the club that night and took some pictures of the theater the following day. He shot a few of the colonel and the first sergeant throwing horseshoes over at the pits, and of a typical shirts-versus-skins game of basketball, complete with elbow-throws. He went to the Yards' barracks the following day and told them of the recent changes, and snapped a few group photos.

Though Jonesy was glad to finally get the camera back, he wasn't thrilled about the contents of the film.

"This is not meant for your personal use," he lectured Ethan. "If the colonel or the first sergeant knew I was developing these prints, they'd probably make me burn shit for the rest of my tour."

"Relax," Ethan advised. "They won't give a shit even if they did find out. Besides, they're for my folks."

"Wait, you're sending these home?"

"Yeah, why?"

"Well the censors may not like it, man. You took pictures of your team down at the range; might be a little too much info here, ya dig? A photo is worth a thousand words, ya know…"

Despite Jonesy's warning, Ethan sat down that night and wrote short captions on the back of each picture, making sure to leave out anything classified or questionable. He studied one photo he'd taken of the team house and realized the large painting of the team's old patch on the wall was perfectly visible in the background of the photo. There were other hints in the photos too – field gear, weapons, little brown people wearing field gear and toting weapons. He sealed the photos in an envelope without a letter and dropped it in the mail without another thought. He'd know sooner or later whether the censors didn't approve.

*   *   *

The Yards were crushed to hear that John had left but were surprisingly upbeat when Ethan told them he was their new team leader. Their reservations about him had seemingly dissolved after the walk-off mission from Leghorn. Even still, he knew he had to tread lightly for the time being, so he focused on smaller things. Probably the best thing he did to help foster cohesion was sit everyone down to design a new team insignia; the original insignia was several years old and resembled Colorado's and Hawaii's team patches too closely. Ethan wanted to breathe fresh air into his team's identity and after a day of deliberation, they had finalized a new design. It was an oversized 5th Group beret flash; to the right of the diagonal Vietnamese flag stripes was an eyeball suspended by a parachute with two bolts of lightning meant to symbolize the art of reconnaissance, their airborne training, and their ability to strike anywhere, like lighting. Above that was the team's name and port of call: "RT Utah – CCC". And lastly but most certainly not least, they added a Bengal tiger in the bottom left corner to represent the Montagnard people and their ferocity. They were all excited about their new team patch and the only thing left to do was to head into town and have it embroidered by one of the local tailoring shops.

A few days later, Ethan called a quick meeting with Nay, Luc, and Hyuk – the three most senior Montagnards on the team; he sought their advice on how to pick up where John had left off in terms of training cycles and team organization, and they were quick to receive his leadership. With Ethan the lone American on the team, Utah's training cycles were slow to start and he tried hard to coordinate and orchestrate it all on his own. Nay, Luc, and Hyuk worked tirelessly to help the team along, and Mark, Ben and others often pitched in to help. Occasionally he would take them down to the range just to observe and study other teams in training. Things persisted in that manner for close to two weeks before a second American was finally assigned to the team.

Ethan and Randy Reynolds were making their way back from the showers one day when they heard Captain Yates bellowing at them all the way across the compound. The club had been in an absolute uproar the previous afternoon and the colonel's executive officer had ordered it closed for the night. Disgruntled and irritated with the decision, Ethan, Reynolds, Bill Allen, and a host of other culprits from Recon had carried the party on back in the company area well into the wee hours of the morning. At some point, Reynolds and Pete Mullis had wobbled back to their team house, grabbed a 60mm mortar and a case of rounds and met Ethan and the

167

others out by the perimeter bunkers. They started dropping illumination and white phosphorous rounds way outside the wire while at the same time Mark was behind one of the .50-cal machineguns ripping off long bursts and yelling like a maniac. In a matter of minutes all the staff personnel had scrambled from their cozy racks in full battle-rattle and into the perimeter bunkers, expecting a full-blown Kamikaze assault reminiscent of those executed by the Japanese back in WWII. The entire compound went on high-alert and during the ensuing confusion, they'd managed to get away with their little stunt – that was until they heard Yates yelling after them.

"Shit, we're fucked," Reynolds croaked.

They searched for a quick E&E route lest they be reprimanded for their late-night shenanigans but the Captain was already upon them and he wasn't alone.

"Move an inch and I'll plug ya," he threatened. Neither of them recognized the guy backing the Captain. "Not you, Reynolds – beat it."

Randy wasted not a second scurrying out of sight between the team houses, snickering at Ethan and giving him the finger as he slipped away.

"Aight *Dai-uy*, what's this all about?"

"Relax, you ain't in trouble," Yates scoffed, "not yet anyways. This is Staff Sergeant Eddie Davis, your new One-One."

Davis stepped forward, locked eyes and they shook hands.

"Davis comes from L Company, 75th," said Captain Yates.

"Ranger," Ethan said.

"Guilty as charged," Eddie proudly confessed.

"A Shau?"

"Know it like the back of my hand."

The A Shau Valley was one of the most notorious and heavily-occupied NVA sanctuaries in South Vietnam, sitting right on the Laotian border up north in I-Corps. CCN constantly pulled operations in the valley as did long range recon teams from the 101st Airborne Division and the newly formed 75th Infantry Regiment (Ranger).

"How long were you there for?" Ethan asked.

"A year. I put in for a transfer to Group when I extended and I've been serving on an A-team for the past six weeks."

Twelve months of running around in the A Shau Valley mixing it up with the NVA qualified Davis as a potentially solid teammate and Ethan took an immediate liking to him. Long-range recon patrols and SOG recon teams operated similarly, but there were distinct differences. LRRP teams didn't operate across the fence and were usually comprised of five or six Americans with one indigenous scout. Ethan knew Eddie had the experience and figured that he'd soon get his own recon team after a few missions with Utah.

"You snore?" Ethan asked as they made their way across the compound. Eddie chuckled and shook his head no.

"Smoke?"

"Bad for your chest," Eddie advised. "Hard to run from the NVA when you're suck'n wind."

"Yeah well I'm glad to hear you like to run, because I can guarantee we'll be doing a good bit of that," Ethan promised. "You ever work with any Montagnards?"

"We used Kit Carson scouts sometimes, but no Yards. I hear they're tough as shit though."

"You ever lead a team?"

"Yeah, a few times. What about you – how long you been working this gig?"

"Came to CCC straight from Bragg in January," Ethan said. "Been running recon ever since."

"How many times have you been out there?"

"Four, once was a Bright Light."

"Four?"

"Yeah man," Ethan replied flatly, "steep learning curve."

9

The false dawn cast an eerie glow of dull light as it filtered through the canopy, transforming black into one blurry color totally void of detail. Brush continued to break a little more than a hundred meters upslope near the team's RON site as the NVA continued their steady downhill sweep. To avoid encirclement, Ethan had slipped the team out of their overnight position before the false dawn and silently crept downhill. But as the jungle slowly gained shape, it occurred to him that their predicament had grown far worse. Without realizing it, he had walked them into a trough on the mountainside. Steep embankments funneled them in tight, leaving them with only one feasible option – back the way they'd come. His guts began to knot and twist even worse than before; they'd done their best to shake their trackers for the better part of two days but nothing seemed to keep them fooled for long. He scanned the embankments for a likely escape, but knew they'd have to smash their way through the underbrush and the noise would surely advertise their position and intentions to anyone in the area. Looking downhill, he could see the hitch only getting deeper and narrower.

Goddammit, he cursed himself. *Luc is your pointman. Next time, let him do his job.*

He clutched his fist and signaled the team to form a perimeter amid an entanglement of underbrush and hardwoods, hoping the tree trunks would help provide better cover while the ground clutter supplied concealment. Claymores went out barely five meters from the perimeter, carefully wedged in front of tree trunks; three covered the upslope approach, one covered the rear and each flank were covered by two.

Either we'll blow a hole in them and run like hell, or they'll kill us where we lie, he figured. *Either way, I hope it's quick.*

The Yards were tense and uneasy about the situation and he worried if they held any confidence in him at all now. He looked to his right at Eddie and figured that the chances of letting him down were entirely possible.

"I trust you so long as you don't get us all killed," Eddie had laughed in the club a few weeks back. But sarcasm always carried with it a tone of true concern or intent, and Ethan could sense that Eddie had doubts about his experience and abilities as a One-Zero. All that was of little consequence because the NVA were coming.

The cracking and crunching had grown close – inside a hundred meters, and the crickets were quickly tapering off in silence all around them as if trying to listen. There were no voices though, only intentional noise from a well-disciplined enemy trying to flush the team from hiding. Their line extended roughly sixty meters across Utah's front and as they continued closing in, the ends began to wrap around the edges of the trough, drawing ever closer to a complete circle. The noose began to tighten around the little recon team's neck – Ethan's eye's bulged through the slowly growing light, trying to get a visual while his lungs begged for deeper breaths. He made eye contact with Luc and pointed upslope, giving his crack pointman a direction of travel once it started. He glanced back at Eddie and nodded. Movement stopped and the silence grew eerie and deafening.

BOOM-BOOM! BA-BOOM! Claymores thundered on both flanks and then from behind, blowing splinters of hot debris and earth and nature all across them. Ethan clapped the detonators in his hands while pressing as flat as he could to the earth. Another series of trembling earthquake-like vibrations shuddered through his insides, yet he heard absolutely nothing. Terrible heat washed over them like a high tide as the remaining three Claymores capped off only five meters away. Instantly, the Yards drew to their knees and flung grenades into both flanks while Luc rushed uphill through a blanket of smoke with the others fast behind him. He tore through a hollow void in the underbrush which had been instantly disintegrated by the blast before coming upon a line of shattered bodies.

Nothing was the way it should be; limbs that hadn't been severed were bent at all the wrong angles and where joints were not. Entrails, brain matter, and bone fragments were everywhere. Pushing past, they could see others struggling through the thicket, dragging themselves back from the blast radius while moaning and screaming in pain. Luc drove on while firing short clacking bursts into the wounded, leaving nothing to second-guess. Ethan choked on the wet-metal aroma of blood and bone as it marinated in the smoke of expended explosives. He spun behind a hardwood and counted heads as his team hustled past, quick and tight on Luc's lead. He could hear nothing except his own heartbeat and deep breathing amid a piercing ring. Signal shots and blind gunfire cracked from below and to the right as the NVA licked their wounds and regrouped. Flashes of khaki and green began to zigzag through a thicket thirty meters to his right. He hugged up tight against a tree and drew a bead on the first group while caressing the trigger of his CAR-15, but they melted into the brush before he could stroke them.

Bo and Hyuk suddenly pulled him to his feet while Eddie worked to raise Covey on the radio. Then they were up and hustling to catch the others, following broken brush and churned soil; there was no time to camouflage their back-trail.

"We gotta ride yet?!"

"There's a bomb crater about four-hundred meters up ahead; Vigilante says we can get out there," Eddie called back between breaths.

"Air?"

"Slicks and Cobras inbound and he's trying to get us some Spads, but we gotta haul ass before they out-flank us."

Ethan's face and lungs burned as his rucksack straps hacked away at his shoulders. Sporadic gunfire close behind and they could hear the NVA cautiously breaking brush and talking on their back-trail.

"We gotta slow them down or they're gonna be all over us."

"We can outrun 'em," Eddie argued.

Ethan shook his head and signaled Bo to drop his ruck.

"We'll slow 'em down a bit; just keep moving for the LZ. And tell Vigilante we're gonna hafta come out on strings."

They quickly gutted extra ammo and grenades and Claymores from their rucks while Eddie talked to Covey.

"Slicks are prepped for strings; you two better not be late," Eddie warned.

"We'll be right behind ya so don't blow us away," Ethan said as they pounded fists.

Eddie and Hyuk grabbed their rucks and slipped into the brush. Silence settled for a moment as Ethan scanned the immediate area for the best cover where they could lay in wait to ambush. Once it began, they'd leapfrog over each other in a shoot-move-communicate fashion.

Working quickly, they daisy-chained a pair of Claymores together to cover the approach, and then took up individual fighting positions safely behind the mines. Ethan nestled in behind the trunk of a fallen tree just off their back-trail while Bo moved into a shallow depression just above him.

Vietnamese voices echoed hollow and broken against the hillside.

His throat tightened as the first flickers of khaki uniforms began to bristle through the woods slightly below them. Their numbers were thick and staggered behind a three-man tracking team, AKs at-the-ready. Closer they came, trudging uphill like an incoming tide washing over a desolate beachhead. Twenty-five meters, then twenty and fifteen, and the trackers were just beyond the Claymores, creeping. The adrenaline burned through his veins again as he flipped the safety off the clacker and blew the ambush.

He squeezed his eyes tight against the brilliant orange bubble that engulfed the hillside just as the fiery concussion flattened him on his back. Sounds ceased to exist and he remained transfixed in a daze that seemed dreamlike while thousands of leaves in every shade of green imaginable fluttered to the ground in epic slow-motion. He lay there for a brief moment, gazing at the skylight as it filtered through millions of perforations in the upper canopy.

Fuck... Hurry, shake it off, shake it off, he coughed as he rolled over on his stomach and found his carbine. *No way that was only two Claymores... Fuck!*

Blood dribbled from his nose and from the corners of his eyes, and he tasted it faintly in his mouth. Small boney hands clutched at him and helped him to his knees; it was Bo and his eyes were pleading. Ethan glanced back down the hillside amid the commotion expecting to see swarms of NVA massing upon them but they weren't there. The explosion had blown a hole through the underbrush, annihilating both man and nature, and all that remained in the blast-radius was thick lingering smoke and bits of fleshy gristle and tattered shreds of clothing. He began to panic as he wrestled his survival radio from his thigh-pocket. He fumbled it clumsily as he switched it on and cycled to the emergency frequency but all he could hear was a sharp ringing in his ears. Bo pushed him forward in what Ethan hoped was the right direction but all he could do was stumble. He was dazed nearly beyond function but Bo kept him moving and he was soon able to hear recognizable voices over his emergency radio.

"My One-Zero's back there somewhere. Can you see anything?" Eddie's voice crackled faintly over the net. A SPAF Bird Dog coasted over the treetops a minute later, banked high, and made a second pass.

"I can't see anything except a smoky hole," Luke Dove replied.

Ethan keyed his radio a few times to clear the net before transmitting.

"Vigilante, this is Hollywood," he stammered groggily as he and Bo kept moving.

"Hollywood, what's going on down there? Give me your sitrep, bro."

"We're on the run," Ethan panted, his ears and head splitting.

In minutes, the team was whole again and back on the move for the LZ while more signal shots continued to crack from behind, letting them know the chase was still on. By the time they hit the landing zone, Luke Dove had several pairs of Spads making gun-runs all around the clearing and on their back-trail, and there was little for them to do but hunker down in the bomb craters and wait for the air package to show up.

Ten minutes later they were yanked out clean on strings, looking back as the Spads and Cobras continued to work the NVA over with hard-bombs and cannon fire. They locked arms to stabilize and then shivered uncontrollably as the adrenaline and anxiety fluttered away against the buffeting wind, high above Laos.

They were back at Dak To by lunchtime – delivered straight from death's cradle into a small celebration put on by Paul's team, which was on its last day of Bright Light duty. They lounged around the launch site for the rest of the day, splitting the afternoon between the Mortuary's shade and the shallow waters of the Dak To River. They got back to Kontum that night, hoping to clean up and spend an evening in the club, but the colonel had closed it down for the night after a brawl had broken out earlier that day. Nothing new really; what more could be expected from an inebriated mob of bloodthirsty cretins separated from a handful of Vietnamese strippers by only twelve feet? After getting the Yards squared away, they feasted on steaks and mashed potatoes at the mess hall and called it an evening. The next morning's debriefing was a long, drawn-out affair, and afterwards, Captain Yates pulled Ethan aside to his office.

"I should ream you a new asshole for splitting your team up like that," the Captain barked. His comment was confusing and Ethan knew his facial expression showed it. "Look," Yates continued with a more relaxed tone, "you're a One-Zero now and on top of everything else, you gotta make sure to take care of your people out there. You did good, but what worked once may not work twice, see?"

Ethan nodded.

"You got a promotion board hearing day after tomorrow in Pleiku; you're on the early bird tomorrow morning so don't piss me off between now and then, cause I might just yank your little South Carolinian ass off that manifest. Savvy?"

"No sweat, *Dai-uy*. I read ya," Ethan nodded.

"Good, now get the fuck outta here," he shooed.

*   *   *

House 8 was just one of SOG's safe-houses scattered throughout South Vietnam, and was little more than a handful of rooms with a small bar downstairs. The house itself was of colonial French design with a high concrete wall sealing the perimeter, while a rusted cast-iron gate and a small contingent of SOG security personnel regulated access. The outside wall, like the rest of the buildings in downtown Pleiku, showed scores of pock-marks and bullet holes, revealing the heavy fighting that took place there during the Tet Offensive the year before.

Paul had gotten his hard stripes last month, and Ethan and Mark were up for theirs; Ben and Ray Fuller were both up for staff sergeant, and Bill Allen was up for sergeant first-class. Bruce McNeil showed up late after spending the day scrounging some badly needed medical supplies for CCC's dispensary. McNeil was a tough character to pin down at a glance. Just looking at his name, most figured him for a typical Irish-American, but in truth, Bruce was full-blooded Puerto Rican.

"Me and my mother immigrated to Miami in '59 and she remarried about a year later," he said as he swigged on a glass of Beam and Coke.

He was widely intelligent and had made it through SF's toughest, longest training to become a medical specialist. He stood at a squatty five-foot-nothing with bronzed skin, black hair, a face as round and as flat as a frying pan. He came to CCC around February and was assigned to the dispensary right off the bat, which kept Joe Parnar riding chase. Whenever he got the chance though, he tagged along as a straphanger but had only been across the fence a handful of times. Yet with all his time on the compound, McNeil grew to be one of the best card players at CCC. Whatever the game was – poker, blackjack, spades – didn't matter; he was impossible to read with dark eyes and rough stubble. He would look his hand over while speaking smartly about whatever the current subject happened to regard: politics, music or fine arts, women – whatever. He'd smile and crack a joke but never once showed any emotion as to what cards were in his hand. No matter how much he won though, he never kept the winnings for himself; instead, he'd buy drinks for everyone in the club until his haul went dry. Few were sore about losing to Bruce.

Later that afternoon, a small contingent of guys from CCS showed up for promotions as well. After a few drinks and the typical introductions, everybody was mixing things up, swapping close-calls and comparing scars.

"You guys think the Bra is bad? Go hang out in the Fishhook or the Parrot's Beak for eight days and then come talk to me," one guy scoffed. With that comment, a clash of egos sparked which lasted the rest of the evening, though no punches were thrown or furniture broken.

The next morning's review board was a standard affair; a lot of detailed questions were asked regarding weapons and rates-of-fire, as well as the proper usage of various ordnances – specifically, the minimum safe distances at which they could be used near friendly forces. Those "by-the-book" numbers were never really applied or followed in recon though. There were a few questions geared towards the military code of conduct, and discipline policies and procedures. As advised by the first sergeant, nobody wore any unauthorized unit patches on their fatigues, but the board knew what unit they had come from and probed each of them with a litany questions regarding their unit's operations.

"Sir, I'm not at liberty to discuss any specifics regarding my unit," was the typical answer and the review board knew not to probe any further.

Instead of heading back to House 8 afterwards, the group strolled around the sprawling airbase that made up Camp Holloway and the 71st Evacuation Hospital. They tried to ignore the pain and hurt that had accumulated around the hospital, but it was everywhere – unavoidable and raw. Slicks were constantly landing and unloading stretchers of wounded and dead that had just come from distant battles in places that most couldn't even pronounce.

Sobering and depressing.

They poked around in the PX for a while, trying to space themselves from the war and its victims, but had little success. Ethan stewed over a shiny new stainless steel Rolex while the others urged him to hurry up and either buy it, or quit window shopping. He had managed to save most of his monthly pay since he'd arrived in-country, but most guys in recon believed in the philosophy of "spend now."

"Why save?" Ray asked. "If you run a mission next week and get blown away, you'll have nothing to show for it." Not exactly the most picturesque philosophy but it was logical enough.

"Fuckit," he decided. "It's only two-hundred bucks."

"I wouldn't flaunt that thing around here though," Bill warned. "Wait till we get back to Kontum unless you want it ripped off your arm by some little shit on the back of a passing Honda."

Good advice, Ethan thought.

With the setting sun came growing appetites for steaks and alcohol.

"I know just the place," Ray said, jabbing Bill's ribs with his elbow.

They took point, leading the group back across the camp, finally stopping at the entrance of an unmarked building stashed discretely among others – the type of place that was easily missed at a glance. They staked out the entrance for a moment and finally turned back on the younger guys.

"Play it cool and follow our lead," Bill whispered.

Once through the door, they piled up behind each other, unsure of what was happening up ahead, but unwilling to abort the mission for a less exciting option. The bar was close in size to the club back in Kontum, but was a little more lavish in décor and employment. A handful of pretty, petite young Vietnamese waitresses sashayed around the room, their almond-shaped eyes casting glances back at them as they took orders. The group tried to make themselves unseen and discreet, but six men in green berets was not something easily missed.

Bill and Ray confidently pushed deeper into the bar, passing a few vacant tables before settling upon a larger one against the far right wall, but close enough to the door in case a hasty exit was in order. They sat quietly, exchanging glances while observing their surroundings. Overall, things appeared quiet – only a few groups huddled over drinks at their respected tables while waiting for the evening to kick into full swing. Their presence was the new topic of conversation now as the club's regular guests whispered back and forth while firing curious looks back at them from across the room.

"Are you kidding me?" Mark whispered loudly while pointing across the room. "Leather couches? Where the fuck do you get leather couches from?"

Bill jabbed his ribs a little too hard, making Mark grunt and suck for air. It was impossible not to laugh, but they stifled the noise fast as one of the waitresses approached. But before she could close the gap, an older NCO made it clear that he was "handling" this one. He moved in slowly and unamused.

"You mongrels must be lost. The SF bar is *that* way," he said, jerking a thumb towards the door.

The rest of the bar looked on with uncertainty at the unfolding tension. The man's name-tape read "Collins" – a sergeant first-class with all the charm of a gut-shot polar bear. Ethan recognized the unit patch on the big man's sleeve but couldn't quite place it for the moment.

"Ya see, this here bar's for the Headhunters; you fellas certainly ain't no flyboys so you must be look'n for trouble."

He was protecting the bar as if it were his daughter's virtue.

"Sarge, if we wanted trouble, we woulda caused it already," Fuller nodded. "We're old friends with a mutual acquaintance – goes by the name of *SPAF*."

The unit patch sewn to Collins' sleeve was the US Army's 219th Aviation Company, the Headhunters – the very same company that had detailed a special all-volunteer unit to fly Bird Dog spotter planes exclusively for SOG operations at CCC. The pilots affectionately referred to themselves as SPAFs, Sneaky Pete's Air Force, which was of course an unofficial title.

Collins was suspicious, "Who the fuck are you guys?" His dark eyes cut back and forth, waiting.

"We're SPAF's best customers, sarge; we give him all our business," Bill winked, trying to lighten the mood.

"We're from CCC," Fuller said.

Just then, a short gray-haired man in an olive-drab flight suit approached the table. He was slightly aging, clean-cut and handsome with a raspy voice. Ethan thought he'd seen him in the club back in Kontum before, but wasn't quite certain.

"Recon or Hatchet Force?" he asked quietly.

"Recon, all of us," Allen replied. "Except McNeil, here, he's a medic at the dispensary."

"Dick Larson, Headhunter-09," he said as he smiled and shook their hands.

Just about every pilot and crewmember that flew in support of CCC's operations hung out in the club back in Kontum, whether they were chopper crewmen, SPAF or Covey pilots. And even though the Headhunters didn't fly for SOG, the 219th Aviation Company was SPAF's parent unit. And as it was, those flyboys were all too happy to welcome them in. It wasn't long until the little establishment was at maximum capacity. Two hours later, Bruce was hard at work outlining the finer points of having a solid medic as a teammate, and since all other teams represented were full, Ethan was his target audience.

"I'm sick of that damn dispensary," Bruce declared. "Inoculations, fucking STDs – I gotta get outta there."

It really wasn't his style to complain, but with the right amount of alcohol, Bruce's so-called "style" was as blurry as his vision. He did present a good argument though, and before the end of the night Ethan promised to give him a fair shake when they got back to Kontum.

At some point during the night, the six of them managed to get themselves back downtown to House 8, but nobody could recall much of the trek. The only thing Ethan could remember was running drunk through a dark alley while being chased by three MPs for curfew violation.

"Looks like they nearly got you," Ben laughed, pointing at the missing buttons on his jungle shirt the next morning.

The top three buttons had popped off after an MP had grabbed him from behind, but he'd somehow managed to wiggle free. That was when the group had split up and recognized the unwritten law of "every man for himself." They spent the rest of the morning battling hangovers and arguing about who had gotten back to the safe-house first. They arrived in Kontum late that afternoon but had to hitch a ride from the airfield back to the compound; apparently, somebody had forgotten to send the deuce-and-a-half for them.

Paul and Eddie were spacing out in the team house to a foray of electric rhythm courtesy of Jimi Hendrix while the AC unit worked overtime. Though he'd only been gone for three days, they were quick to catch him up on the happenings. An Australian rock band and a small contingent of strippers had passed through the day before and put on a good show, but things had gotten rowdy in a hurry as clothing hit the floor. Ethan knew he'd missed a good time by the way they talked about it, and everyone shared a hard laugh when Paul explained that Captain Yates had started the whole fiasco.

"A CCN team almost got blown away a few days ago in the A Shau," Eddie said, changing the flow of conversation.

"What happened?" Ethan asked.

"They got in and cut the choppers loose and got ready to move, but overheard the team's name mentioned in some of Chuck's radio traffic."

"Apparently, the NVA knew every American's name, rank, the team's name, and exactly when and where they were going in," Paul added.

"Holy shit. Did they get out?"

"Yeah they called the slicks back and got out without a shot fired."

"Scary shit. Reckon there really *is* a mole in Saigon."

Even though SOG was a clandestine unit, they were required to report current recon team locations and other information to their ARVN counterparts and a select few in the South Vietnamese government. There was a great deal of speculation among recon men that somewhere along the way, information was changing hands but no one had proved anything yet. It was all too coincidental; far too many teams had simply vanished for it to be a matter of bad luck, and it was the only logical explanation as to how the NVA had come across specifics on the CCN team. That thought alone was unsettling enough, but there was absolutely no comfort in the thought of SOG headquarters having sprung a security leak.

Ethan talked to Eddie about interviewing Bruce for the third slot on the team; as the team leader though, he knew it was ultimately his decision to bring a new man on, but he valued Eddie's experience and wanted to know what he thought.

"I don't see any reason why having a medic on the team wouldn't be a good idea," Eddie said. "How many times has he been out?"

"He's been a straphanger twice and flew chase a few times," Ethan said. "Let's just fit him into the training routine tomorrow and see what happens; maybe shuffle a few things around."

They did an informal interview with Bruce later that night just to get a feel for what his field experience was. He'd been in a pretty thick firefight while on one mission and fired a few rounds while riding chase, and was quite eager to step into the slot as Utah's One-Two. Bruce met the Yards the next morning, who immediately took a liking to him. He was the same height as they were and his skin color a close match, and the Yards kept asking him what tribe he was from. They ran through the motions down at the range, starting with basic hand and arm signals before moving on to tactics and immediate-action drills. Bruce proved to be adaptive and a fast learner and felt comfortable as the team's One-Two.

With the IA drills comfortably rehearsed, they moved on to live-fire drills and ambush techniques. The amount of firepower they were capable of was astonishing and their peeling movements were almost fluid. They rehearsed numerous scenarios with wounded teammates, making Bruce's job twice as hard. In a conventional unit,

188

medics were non-combatants, but in recon, every man played an intricate role in the team's survival. If Utah took wounded, Bruce would have to tend to their needs and fight at the same time.

They took a break for lunch and watched Vermont and Iowa train for a bit before getting back at it. For the rest of the day, the team practiced firing their weapons on semi-auto in controlled bursts of three or four rounds, and then had reloading contests to see who could change magazines the fastest. By the end of the day, Ethan and Eddie both agreed the team needed Bruce a lot more than the dispensary did, but knew it would be a hard fight to convince them to let him go. As luck would have it, they caught Lieutenant Colonel Abt deep in a game of horseshoes over by the club the next day. He was good and there was no doubt that if those shoes had been grenades, the ringers wouldn't have stood a chance. He listened to Bruce's request much like a father would his son, and with that, had only one question to ask.

"You're sure about running recon?"

Bruce nodded without hesitation, "Sir, the dispensary isn't exactly what I had in mind when I came to Kontum."

The colonel nodded, Yates shrugged, and that was that.

10

Dak To. Bright Light duty. Mid-morning and the situation was growing worse by the minute. The air package carrying Ray Fuller's team had linked up with Covey at the orbit point over their target – a small section of real estate in southern Laos where Highway 613 split south from Highway 110 and ran off into Cambodia. Fuller was going in behind the fork to monitor trail traffic south of Juliet-9. Right as Covey got the ball rolling and sent the guns down to probe, the net flooded with a mayday call. An O-1 Bird Dog had been shot down while on a visual reconnaissance flight in the mountains north of Leghorn. As soon as the call had come over the net, Fuller's target had been scratched and the entire show had raced north with Covey to find the crash. And while they searched for the wreck, all anyone could do at the launch site was wait and listen to radio chatter. Kontum hadn't yet said who the Bird Dog belonged to but everyone already knew: The only unit flying O-1 Cessnas with any business over Laos was SPAF. And then CCC confirmed the inevitable. SPAF-5 had been flying a VR with RT Rhode Island's team leader when it had been knocked down by enemy AA fire. Ethan's stomach hit the floor; Benfield Washington – his close friend since Jump School – was in Dale Forsythe's backseat.

Just then another air package thundered up to the airstrip and set down. Ethan left the commo-shed to receive the aircrews while Eddie and Bruce gathered the Yards and made final equipment preparations. They all knew they'd be in the thick of it before long, and in the most impossible of ways, it was where they *wanted* to be. Their friends were on the ground, hurt or dead, and more were about to go in after them. The only silver lining to the whole mess was that Jim "King Arthur" Young's team had flown up from CCC.

"You're a day early," Ethan said as Jim led his Yards off the airstrip.

"Always was a sucker for a gunfight," he half-smiled. "How bad is it?"

"Ain't look'n good; Forsythe's O-1 went down in a valley north of Leghorn. Him and Big Ben were flying VR this morning. Covey's already spotted dozens of ack-ack nests and I think he's about to put Fuller's people on the deck. Nobody's come up on the emergency freq yet, and Ray's birds gotta be getting low on fuel by now."

King Arthur's team, RT Arizona, was going in the following day but hitched a ride up early to help support the Bright Light effort. They walked back to the commo-shed and listened to the radio squabble right as Fuller's insertion unraveled into utter chaos. Covey had found a useable LZ about four-hundred meters south of the crash. Fuller and half his Yards had gotten on the ground but when the second ship approached short-final, the entire place opened up with RPGs and machinegun fire.

"We're hit... going down, going down..." The transmission was noisy and garbled but everyone listening knew what was happening.

Then Covey came up.

"Panther Three-One is down, Panther Three-One is down. Shit. Can anybody see anything?"

They listened as he began sorting the mess out, keeping one eye on each crash site. Then Fuller came up on the net with a sitrep; somehow, miraculously, his team was whole and relatively unscathed. The second half of his team had apparently jumped clear of the slick right as it flared and the NVA opened up. They had consolidated on the LZ and were shooting their way through to the downed aircrew.

Covey began working the area over with Spads and Cobras to Fuller's direction. He was also trying to work air around Forsythe's Bird Dog but the skies were beginning to fill up with large caliber flak. Now he had to put air on dozens of antiaircraft positions that were opening up in addition to directing gun-runs for Fuller all while keeping the NVA off the crashed Bird Dog. It was a tall order to fill.

The launch site commander pointed at Ethan and told him to go.

"Secure Forsythe's crash. I'm gonna have Covey blow you a hole with some five-hundred-pounders to the east. Get 'em outta there, no matter what."

He streaked out of the commo-shed with King Arthur, Kyle "Twig" Dean and Mike Wilson close behind. Like any savvy One-One, Eddie already had Bruce and the little people geared-up and ready to go. King Arthur ran ahead and got the air package winding up while Twig and Mike escorted Utah across the drainage ditch and onto the airstrip. As they were loading up, the slicks and gunships from Fuller's lift came limping onto the tarmac puking hydraulic fluid, smoking, windscreens shattered, shot to pieces. A brief conference between the pilots, some last-minute offerings of advice and good luck, and they were up and away, noses down, rotors slapping and grabbing for airspace.

Pulling the headset on, Ethan listened closely as Covey continued to work air around Fuller and both crash sites. It was a prioritized affair. Birds with low fuel were sent immediately into the fight depending on what type of ordnance they carried; everything else was stacked accordingly at the orbit-point, or was sent in to hit targets of opportunity.

The orbit-point was an absolute racetrack of loitering aircraft but Covey had no intentions of delaying the Bright Light. Ethan listened to the call-signs and then watched as two sets of Spads peeled off and lumbered down to a smoldering hole at the edge of the valley floor. They rolled in, sprinkling 20mm cannon fire all over the area, lifted up, banked out, and lined up for another pass.

"There's your LZ," the crew chief called over the headset while pointing. "When they finish hosing it down, we go in."

A few hundred meters to the left was the crashed Bird Dog in thick, tangled canopy and it didn't look good. About the same distance away, to the southwest, was the wrecked Huey at the edge of the only natural landing zone within three kilometers. The broken slick was on its side, tail-boom blown off, rotors pretzeled into twisted metal. Two more sets of Spads were taking turns working their guns around Fuller's people. Green tracers were lasering across the sky in every direction possible while fast-movers streaked in and pickled off their hard-bombs and napalm loads. Then Covey cued up the call-signs and led them down the rabbit hole to the LZ. He'd worked hard to hollow out a flight corridor for the insertion package to travel through – a safe, yet, narrow crease of airspace where the enemy AA couldn't reach them. Along the fold and down onto the deck, rushing over the treetops and then they were above the clearing while the gunships dove in to silence any objections.

Leaning out, Ethan watched the LZ materialize beneath him. The bombs used to blow the hole had been set for air-burst instead of impact and it created a nice, clean little scar clear of any debris aside from a few shattered tree trunks. Out went the aluminum ladders and then they were down-climbing as fast as they could. It was the first time his team had used ladders on a mission and no matter how many times they trained with them, the first few rungs were always slightly awkward. Finally on the ground, the Yards fanned out and kept their eyes and guns out while the second ship came in and dropped the rest of the team off. They consolidated quickly while Covey gave Ethan an update on the whole ordeal. Fuller had shot his way through to the crashed Huey and found the aircrew banged up but alive.

"We've got a clean approach to the LZ so I'm gonna try and extract them while the slicks still have enough fuel," Covey reported. "Keep your ears on and stay in touch."

Ethan and Nay quickly strung the team out on-line and began their sweep to the west, towards the crash site. The bush was moderately thick but they cared not for complete stealth. Fuller was still in sporadic contact to the south and fast-movers were busy pasting enemy positions all around them, but somehow, it remained strangely peaceful and serene in Utah's little world. It wouldn't last, not with the ruckus they were causing, but they had to make that sacrifice if their friends were to have a fighting chance – albeit, a small and waning chance. The emergency frequency was still clear and Covey had spotted no signal mirrors or orange signal panels around the wreck. They moved for what seemed like only minutes before Luc suddenly halted them.

"Does he see it?"

Hyuk whistled softly and made a diving gesture with his hand and nodded forward. They were nestled in a thick stand of bamboo and as Ethan let his senses settle he could faintly smell fried electronics and leaking aviation fuel. Nay moved quickly through the team and tied the little people off into a solid perimeter.

Good ol' Nay. What would I do without him?

He radioed Covey with a sitrep while Luc and Bo snuck forward to assess the crash and see if the NVA had gotten there first. Covey came back and told him they'd already extracted the air crew and were pulling the first half of Fuller's team out. Meanwhile, the Air Force was busy tending to the layered antiaircraft threat, and there was still a bit of sporadic gunfire coming from where Fuller's people were. Luc and Bo returned and signaled the all-clear, and they formed up and swept forward, closing in on the wreck. As they enveloped around the demolished Bird Dog, Ethan knew neither man had survived the crash. The engine compartment was pancaked back into the forward half of the fuselage where the pilot sat. Forsythe's upper body had punched through the windscreen and hung limp over the smashed engine compartment. He was very dead. Luc took Nui and slipped away into the woods to recon the immediate area while Nay hurried to get the rest of the Yards into a perimeter. Out came the machetes and they hacked their way through the tangle to what was left of the front of the aircraft. Bruce dropped his rucksack, which contained all his medical supplies and tools, and climbed up to Forsythe. He loosened the chinstrap on his helmet, felt for a pulse and examined the trauma.

"Several fractures in his skull… broken neck." He tried to pull him the rest of the way out but couldn't move him much. "Shit Ethan, he's pinned."

"Great. What about Ben?" Ethan started to choke up but forced it back.

Bruce climbed his way around the side of the fuselage and stuck his head inside a broken window. "He's not in here."

"What?"

"There's nobody in the backseat."

Ethan grabbed the handset and keyed the mic.

"Covey, Covey, this is Hollywood."

"Go ahead, Hollywood."

"I need a headcount and confirmation of exactly *who* was in this aircraft. I got one KIA and another possible MIA. Copy?"

"Roger, wait one."

"I'm gonna go cut a few sections of bamboo," Eddie whispered. "See if we can pry him free."

Ethan glanced up and pondered the swath the careening Bird Dog had created as it crashed through the trees. The left wing was caught in the upper canopy about fifty meters behind and the right wing had collapsed and was partially blocking the door to the fuselage.

"Hollywood, you're looking for two Straw Hats: SPAF-5 and Bigfoot."

"Roger Covey. We got the scene secured. I have SPAF-5 but Bigfoot's not here. I say again, Bigfoot is *not* here. We're still looking."

Ethan had hoped it had all been a mistake and that his friend hadn't been in the backseat, but all that hope was gone and his team was left facing a totally new problem.

Where was Washington? Had he survived the crash only to be captured by the NVA? Was he evading through the bush?

Bruce and Eddie managed to maneuver the collapsed wing out of the way of the side-door. Peering in, they found only the camera that Washington had been using during the flight, and a slew of shell casings and several empty 20-round magazines scattered about the floor where the backseat used to be. Eddie scooped some brass up, sniffed and rolled them around in his hands, and glanced around as if combing through a crime scene.

"There's no fresh sign here aside from our own," Ethan said. "And there's no way he woulda just let Nguyen walk up and take him without a fight, not Big Ben. He probably burned through those mags while they were over the target-area."

"S'what it looks like," Eddie figured. "Hot target."

"This area was completely free of tracks when we came in," Bruce surmised. "And he didn't climb down from there because the door was blocked by the wing. Not only that, but the crash woulda killed him, *for sure*. There's no blood or anything on the radio bank in the backseat."

They all stood scratching their heads for a minute while bombs continued to fall in the valley and surrounding hillsides.

"Did he fucking *jump* out?" Ethan looked at Bruce and Eddie as they considered the possibility. Luc and Nui reentered their perimeter and came straight to them.

"*Trung-si,*" Nui said, pulling Ethan's arm. "We find other 'Merican."

"Where? Is he alive?"

Luc shook his head, "He not live, *Trung-si*."

Ethan rubbed his face for a second, and accepted it with a nod. "Where is he?"

"In tree," Luc said and pointed the way.

"NVA?"

"Not see," Luc tapped his nose, "smell."

"Shit." Ethan huddled together with Eddie and Bruce and solidified the agenda. "You two stay here and get Forsythe outta the cockpit. Me, Nui and Luc are gonna go get Ben. We rally here and then move back to the LZ. Everybody switch on your emergency radios in case we get hit while we're separated."

Ethan dropped his rucksack and retrieved a long length of rope and three 120-round drums for the cut-down RPD he was carrying. He favored the light machinegun over his beloved CAR-15 on Bright Light missions simply due to the high volume of fire he could put down on the enemy. Nay flashed him a smile and a thumbs-up, and off they went.

It wasn't far – about seventy meters or so, when Luc pointed up into the mid-level branches of a young hardwood. He was hanging upside down, arms stretched out, CAR-15 caught askew in his harness, flight helmet still strapped to his head, fatigues ripped, about thirty feet up. His left leg was wedged between some branches and was very broken at the knee.

He must've tried to bail as they came into the canopy and the Bird Dog lost speed, Ethan figured.

"Nui, I need you to climb up there with this rope, throw it over one of those higher branches and slip this loop around his upper body." Ethan quickly tied off a bowline rescue knot and handed it to Nui. "When we lift him up, take your machete and hack through the branch, and we'll lower him down."

Nui nodded, stripped his gear off except his CAR-15 and machete and picked his way into the tree. He was perfect for that sort of job; he was skinny and taller than the others, yet plenty strong to support more than his own weight. Luc stayed close to Ethan and kept his eyes focused on the woods; he was lost in his own little world. With the loop around Washington's upper body, Ethan collected the slack and took a few wraps around a nearby tree trunk; Benfield was a heavy man and he didn't want to drop him from thirty feet up.

"Now take that limb out."

Nui hacked away at the branch with his machete until it broke free and crashed to the ground, then he reached out and pushed Washington's lower leg out of the notch. The rope caught him and he was free, twisting and swaying. They were taxed against the weight, lowering him hand over hand until he was finally on the ground. A set of Spads lumbered by and a .51-cal opened up not more than a hundred meters away, tracking them across the sky.

"Must go, must go," Luc urged. "*Beaucoup* VC come."

Ethan tossed Nui the Claymore bag he carried all of his nasty little surprises in and told him to pepper their back-trail with toe-poppers and whatever else he saw fit.

"You carried me through Training Group," Ethan whispered to his friend as he strained to get him into the fireman's carry. "I'm sorry I waited this long to return the favor."

He hefted Washington to his shoulders and stumbled back to the crash site while Nui booby-trapped and disguised their back-trail.

"You guys hear that fifty-one open up?" Eddie whispered as he and Bruce helped lower Washington off Ethan's shoulders and on the ground next to Forsythe. "Fuller's out and Covey said our ride is fueled up and heading this way. Where was he?"

"Thirty feet up in a tree." A pair of small explosions erupted back where they'd found Washington. "Shit, they already found our back-trail."

He glanced around their position and didn't like their options. Carrying Washington and Forsythe back to the LZ was going to be all but impossible: four-hundred meters uphill with the NVA closing in – he knew they'd never make it. The Yards began fortifying their pathetic little positions as best they could by hacking the bush back a few meters and using whatever debris from the crash they could get behind. Natural cover was hard to come by.

"Covey, this is Hollywood." Static poured through the mic for a few tense moments. "Covey, come back. Talk to me."

"Go ahead, bro."

"Hey, we found Bigfoot. Both Straw Hats are KIA. You get that?"

"Yeah, solid copy. Slicks are inbound. How do you wanna do this?"

"Nguyen's too close and our KIAs are too heavy to carry. I need you to work air danger-close around the crash until you can get a slick to drop us some strings in here."

Ethan kept the plan simple by design. Under heavy air cover, they'd send Washington and Forsythe out on strings and then run hard to meet their ride at the LZ. He relayed the suspected position of the .51-cal machinegun, hunkered down and let Covey vector in the air show. The first pair of Spads dove in and doused the area all around where the heavy machinegun had opened up from; the second set came in right behind them and loosed a rack of 250-pounders and napalm. They came back around and began working the area around the crash site over with their cannons and slowly extended their reach outward while another pair dumped CBUs to the southwest. Cluster-bomb units were an absolute nightmare for infantry formations, and whatever bomblets didn't explode in the initial drop would sit there until some unlucky cousin of Uncle Ho's disturbed its unstable existence. Ethan made a mental note of it; he had no intentions of moving to the southwest but if a team ran the same target in the future, it would be prudent information for them to know.

More gun-runs and then the Hueys came thumping in from the southeast. Covey came up on the radio and told them to get ready. They'd situated both Washington and Forsythe in Swiss seats and lashed them together to keep them stable. It was the best option they could conjure up under the circumstances and they all prayed the enemy AA wouldn't get them as they came out. The first Huey slid in over the crash and down came the ropes. Ethan quickly snapped both men in and then waved the Huey off. He stood there and guided them as gingerly as he could for as long as he could, clinging to their legs, then their boots, and then finally letting go. It became a heart-breaking visual that would stay with him for the rest of his days, and he just stood there, staring at them as they slipped up through the trees and into an impossibly peaceful sky. Then he felt arms pulling him down while green tracers streaked past and punched holes into the wrecked Bird Dog. His men were pitching frags and firing short bursts into their southern perimeter, yet he remained calm and focused on exactly what he had to do.

"Covey, my KIAs are out and we need a ride," he replied flatly. "They got through the gun-runs and are coming at us from the south. When you see the Willie Pete, I want you to paste this position with whatever you got. I'm also gonna need some LZ prep."

A B-40 rocket sizzled past and clapped off high in the trees, and he watched Bo quickly shift his fire. Eddie yelled for them to get small and blew the Claymores and the concussion deafened him for a moment. Then he was running with Nay and Nui and the rest of his team, following Luc and the others back to the LZ. A brace of Cobras came in hot over the hole and pounded the place with rockets and cannon fire. Ethan could hear the guns flexing on the LZ up ahead, then Spads rolled in and dumped a rack of napalm onto a nearby knoll.

They hit the LZ just as the first Huey sunk in and bottomed out. Eddie threw Bo and Hyuk and Bruce onboard, then jumped on and they were out. In came the second ship while the guns swarmed around and covered the approach. They were up and running and Ethan tossed his Yards on the Huey before he allowed himself to be pulled in. Then they too were up and out, the turbines whining as the pilot poured on the power and hugged the treetops to escape the antiaircraft threat.

Two pairs of F4 Phantoms came swooping in from the east – the first dropping napalm onto the crashed Huey while the second pair unloaded on the Bird Dog, reducing both to little more than greasy smudges and molten metal on the jungle floor. The crew chief reached over and handed Ethan the headset. He pulled it on with trembling hands while aircraft of every flavor streaked across the sky. He talked to Covey for a bit, making sure everyone on his team had gotten out and were okay. That was it for him. He flipped the boom mic away from his mouth and leaned back against the bulkhead, shaking, hoping it would all just turn to dust and blow away in the wind.

11

Ethan drifted through the crowd, making his rounds and sharing drinks with Tom Waskovich, Ken Snyder, Bob Howard, Joe Walker, John Plaster and others before sidling back over to his table. The air quickly turned stuffy and hot inside the smoke-filled bar; large red, green, blue, and orange Christmas lights hung in long strands, shimmering through the haze. The jukebox rolled over another tune, but this time it was the Beetles singing "Give Peace a Chance".

"It's like clockwork," Bruce laughed and shook his head. "Somebody always plays that fucking song."

It lasted a mere five seconds before a huge roaring chorus of "Fuck peace!" filled every corner of the bar. The jukebox's cord was yanked from the wall and the music died; a few seconds later, Creedence Clearwater Revival's "Run Through the Jungle" controlled of the airwaves.

Ethan sat alone in thought as those around him engaged in conversation. Things didn't feel the same as when Mitch had been wounded and medevac'd some months back – he knew Big Ben's family. Since his family lived right there in Fayetteville, Big Ben would often drag Ethan and Mark home with him, insisting they'd make it their official home away from home; the Washington household had always been a warm and welcoming environment.

"That sumbitch was like a walking motivation poster for the Army. Y'all remember that shit?"

Ethan and Paul smiled while chuckling at their memories of Jump School and Training Group while Mark reminisced.

"We use to pretend like we were gonna drop out just to fuck with him," Mark laughed. "He'd look at us for a few seconds and get all fired up, and start making his case for going Airborne."

"You don't wanna be no fucking leg, do ya?! Airborne, goddammit!" Ethan shouted.

The laughter drew quiet again as each of them drifted off into their own thoughts and memories. Pete Johnston and Rex Hill cut through the commotion of the crowded barroom and joined their table. It hadn't even been two months since the tragic loss of Captain Bruce Bessor, and yet, another SPAF pilot had been killed in action. Pete and Rex expressed their deepest sorrow for Big Ben and thanked them for recovering Captain Forsythe's body. Dale was both respected and irreplaceable, and his loss marked a staggering casualty rate of nearly fifty percent among the small five-man SPAF detachment. They all chatted for what seemed like a long time, buying rounds and getting drunker and drunker. Finally, he carved his way through the crowd, out the backdoor and into the bottomless shadows of a moonless night. He found a nook in the dark where no one would find him and cried until his tears simply ran dry.

The team was up early for a winded debriefing with S-2 and S-3. Since their mission had been a Bright Light rescue, they had little intelligence to report, but were asked individually to recount the events as they had transpired. With several days of stand-down just beginning, Eddie jumped a flight up to Camp Eagle near Phu Bai in I-Corps to hang out with some old buddies from the 101st. As Ethan walked back to the team house, he heard his name being yelled from the direction of the club. Turning around, he saw Bill Allen waving at him and heading his way.

"What are you doing for the next few days?" he asked.

"Nothing man, we're on stand-down for a bit."

"You guys wanna go to Saigon for a few days?"

"Hell yeah, I'll go," Ethan eagerly volunteered. "I've never even been south of Pleiku."

"Shit are you kidding me, Jackson? You've been here for almost seven months and haven't even been to Saigon yet?!"

"Nope."

"Pack your trash and meet me at the gates in a half hour," Bill said as he trotted off.

Ethan knew he needed to keep his mind occupied on something other than the loss of his friend; he simply didn't want to dwell on it any longer.

On their way out they made a quick stop at one of the local Vietnamese-owned tailoring shops just outside CCC's wire. Bill picked up a pair of jungle shirts he'd dropped off to have the lower pockets removed and reattached to either shoulder. It was a common modification that many recon men swore by because the lower pockets were useless when wearing field gear unless they were relocated to the shoulders. Among the shirts were also six battle flags, three NVA and three Vietcong. All were tattered and worn out and a few even had splotches of dried blood splattered across their soiled colors.

"Holy shit, are those real?!" Ethan asked, pointing at the flags while Bill stuffed them into his rucksack.

"Nah," he laughed, "but most grunts and REMFs can't tell the difference. I trade them when I'm in Saigon. I used to make 'em myself but I got tired of doing it, so I just pay her to do it now." He unfolded a medium-sized red and blue flag with a yellow star at its center. "She even sprinkles a little chicken blood on some of 'em."

He paid the wrinkly old *mama-san* several hundred piasters, equivalent to a few dollars US and thanked her. From the tailoring shop, they walked through the hard-packed dirt road of crowded downtown Kontum before stopping at another open-air cafe for lunch. A leathery old *papa-san* shuffled up to their table with a gleeful smile.

"Ahh yes, *Trung-si* Allen, nice to see again! I cook numba one, like always. You wait here."

Before Bill could even greet him, the shriveled old man plodded back behind the dingy curtain that separated the kitchen from the small open-air patio. While they waited, they watched the passersby with intrigue and curiosity while chewing the fat.

Bill loved being in Special Forces – the man simply knew how to work the Vietnam "gig". He was a lifer by all accounts but not of the typical breed. A Special Forces lifer thrived on operating in a covert environment by means of unconventional methods, and because of that, none of them ever saw rank past colonel.

"You run a decent team, kid," Bill admitted with a nod. "Too bad you're just now get'n here; damn war's almost over."

"Over? How do ya figure?" Ethan asked.

"Well, look at our situation," Bill replied. "All these kids get'n drafted and get'n hurt or killed over here… Folks back in the World ain't buy'n this shit no more. This ain't World War Two."

"My ol' man told me the same thing before I left," Ethan said, shaking his head.

"Yeah well, we never came here to win anyways," Bill added. "Too many folks back in the World showing sympathy for Charlie and hate for GIs."

The old *papa-san* emerged from the kitchen with a round of Cokes, and dragging in his trail was the magnificent waft of Vietnamese cooking. A gaggle of filthy local kids strolled over toting a variety of goods for sale ranging from bottled Coke, cigarettes, to female companionship. Out in the street, well-used prostitutes waded among the crowd wearing westernized outfits while trolling for potential customers.

"In a few years, we'll be pulling out for good," he added, swigging his Coke. "There's already rumors about the 5th Group going back to Bragg soon." He produced a smashed pack of Marlboros, stuffed one between his lips and fired his Zippo. He held the pack and gestured for Ethan to take one.

"No thanks," he said, waving the offer away.

Just then, the old man came over with two armfuls of hot food. A feast was served up consisting of cooked chicken seasoned with choice Asian spices and a large steaming mound of fried rice. The frail old man then brought a bowl of cooked fish out and placed it on the table. Using chopsticks, Ethan and Bill piled their plates high with generous helpings and topped everything off with a dash of Tabasco sauce.

There were a collection of smells in Vietnam Ethan knew he would never forget: tight moldy jungle air, the pungent odor of diesel fumes mixed with burning human waste, the smell of blood and gunpowder after a firefight, and the indescribable aroma of Vietnamese cooking. The latter was, by far, his favorite and nothing could compare to the taste of Southeast Asian cuisine.

"So when's our flight leave?" Ethan asked as they finished cleaning their plates.

"Not sure yet," Bill replied in a nonchalant manner. "We'll be able to wrangle something from the airfield, no problem."

"*Wrangle?*" Ethan's voice hinted a little uncertainty and Bill caught it.

"No worries, kid; I'll handle it," he said, with a raked smile.

An hour later, the Central Highlands flushed beneath the Huey before giving way to the sprawling reaches of the airbase at Pleiku. The chopper settled on the busy tarmac next to a large stack of cargo that was to be loaded onboard. In exchange for the lift, Bill offered the crew a case of beer.

The crew chief smiled, "Ya got it on ya right now, sarge?"

"Well no," Bill laughed with both palms up. "That don't mean I can't get it, though."

"Tell ya what. Y'all help us get these supplies onboard and we'll call it even." And that was that.

From Pleiku, Bill managed to get them onboard an Air Force C-123 cargo flight down to Bien Hoa, which was just a hop northeast of Saigon. Since the flight was vacant, it didn't cost them any favors and it was more comfortable than a noisy Huey, but not by much. Over the droning rumble of the plane's engines, they talked for the rest of their trip – a luxury the loud chopper ride hadn't afforded them.

"How do you know how to get around like this without being on the flight manifest or having orders?" Ethan asked with genuine curiosity.

"It ain't real hard – kinda like haggling, but you definitely need shit to trade with, like flags and Ho Chi Minh sandals, and junk like that," Bill said. "There's also a few things that you don't wanna leave home without." He opened the top of his ruck and pulled the flap back so that Ethan could browse through his "tools". Besides the flags, there was a sterile pair of OD-green fatigues, a change of civilian clothes, a Browning Hi-Power 9mm pistol, two CS grenades, an Air Force survival knife, and a small rectangular wooden box.

"I thought we weren't allowed to carry weapons in Saigon."

"Better safe than sorry," Bill smiled, lifting up his jungle shirt and revealing a leather shoulder holster that secured a suppressed .22-caliber High Standard. "You need to put yourself a street-kit together."

"Street-kit?"

Bill nodded, "Just a small assortment of doodads I never leave home without. "

"So what's in the box?"

"Paint supplies," Bill said. "I'm an artist!"

"My ass; what's it for?" Ethan laughed.

"Vehicle acquisitions," he winked.

The more they talked, the more Bill resembled the character "Sergeant Peterson" from the movie *The Green Berets*, starring John Wayne. The movie had done its best impression of an A-team in 1968 Vietnam, and "Peterson" was the team's scrounger and often "found" things that were in high demand.

"Hold up now – I'm no scrounger," Bill declared. "You wanna talk to a scrounger, go talk to Turtle over at the motor pool. I'm what you'd call… *resourceful*," he said with a grin.

They spent the last few minutes of the bumpy flight laughing at *The Green Berets* – mocking The Duke in how he looked in webgear and carried an M-16.

"The day I see a bird-colonel busting brush and tripping enemy booby-traps is the day I die happy!" Bill guffawed as the C-123 made a typical bouncy landing on the Bien Hoa airstrip.

A hot irrepressible wave of humidity and fine red dust wafted through the fuselage as the crew chief lowered the cargo ramp in the back of the aircraft. Ethan and Bill shouldered their rucks and stepped from the plane, making sure to thank the crew chief for the lift. The mid-afternoon heat was unbearable – much worse than it was in the Central Highlands.

"It's a fucking nightmare when it rains here," Bill said. "It's nothing but a giant mud hole."

The tarmac was stained with red tracks and there were deep mud-filled ruts all over the place. Fixed-wing aircraft continued to access the strip while choppers jockeyed for position at a large helipad on a gentle hilltop that overlooked the strips. There were several large fuel bladders and a few bunkers off to one side; two shirtless GIs were busy rearming and refueling a pair of Cobras while another directed traffic with his radio.

Ethan slid his beret on, cocked the flash, and pulled the flap down over his right ear. He followed Bill across the tarmac and toward a collection of buildings and bunkers where a vacant convoy of deuce-and-a-halfs waited. Just past the convoy was a formation of about forty GIs in freshly starched fatigues and shiny combat boots standing before an NCO holding a clipboard. The NCO's voice bellowed over the noise of the airfield as he went through the various do's and don'ts for all the new guys. They strolled past the formation, catching wide glances from such innocent faces – young and terrified, full of uncertainty and apprehension. Though he didn't want to admit it, Ethan knew he had worn that same look almost seven months ago. He had tried so hard to appear like he knew what he was doing and where he was going at the time, but he knew he hadn't fooled anyone.

"Goddamn, new meat! Check this shit out," a voice called from behind. "You cherries don't believe whatcha hear now – y'all gonna love the 'Nam!"

Ethan turned back to see two GIs heckling the group; standard initiation for all FNGs new to Vietnam. Bill and Ethan continued across the airfield, heading toward the hilltop LZ situated about a hundred meters from the edge of the tarmac. They stopped at the bottom of the hill and moved off the dusty rutted road while dodging a jeep full of ARVN Rangers as they sped past.

"Wait here while I try and wrangle us a chopper to Saigon," Bill said. "You see any guys from Group drive by, flag 'em down – see if they'll give us a lift into town." He ambled up the road towards the LZ, "And keep a close eye on our shit!" he shouted over his shoulder.

There was activity everywhere, like colonies of ants hastily working on hundreds of separate tasks. Some line grunts were lounging on top of a row bunkers while trying to enjoy their brief time in the rear, while staffers appeared to be hassling a group of GIs burning barrels full of waste out by the perimeter. A few more slicks taxied in and out as Ethan glanced around at dozens of passing

214

ARVN jeeps. He considered flagging one of them down for a ride but he was leery to trust them. Earlier in the war, the ARVNs had earned a bad reputation for corruption and poor leadership among its ranks but had fought hard in recent years to improve their image. The ARVN Rangers and Special Forces units were tough but when it came to his own life, Ethan wasn't about to put it in questionable hands. Just then, a jeep came screaming downhill and slid to a dusty halt beside him. The pair up front were a couple of Rangers from the 1st Infantry Division – LRPs in the Big Red One.

"Hop in," Bill waved.

They roared past the big PX, blew through the gates and swerved into a chaotic sea of afternoon traffic on the main drag. Horns blared furiously from an endless mob of Lambrettas and Vespas, rickshaws and cyclo-cabs, overloaded buses and jeeps, all while bicycles zipped magnificently through the tightly-packed traffic as if threading a needle. They talked shop with the LRPs for several crowded blocks and then hopped out among a long line of curbside vendors swamped by faithful patrons. A dirty little Vietnamese kid ran up to them carrying a box.

"I give numba one shoe-shine for you, GI. One-hundred P," he offered.

"No shoe-shine, kid. *Di-di mau*," Bill ordered, waving the boy on. "Go on, *di-di*."

"You want pussy? Special Forces eat *beaucoup* pussy," he persisted. "My sister, she numba one, young sucky-fucky. How 'bout it GI?"

"Shit kid," Bill laughed and handed him a few piasters. "That sales pitch was worth a few bucks."

"You *beaucoup dinky-dau*," he laughed and turned down the sidewalk, melting back into the mix.

They moved down the sidewalk, passing vendors and turning down more offers for sex, drugs, weapons, jewelry, cigarettes and just about anything else one could imagine finding in a warzone. Bill led him through a discrete doorway right off the sidewalk and into a narrow, dimly-lit shop. Right beside the door was an old wooden countertop with an archaic cash register. Beside it, a porcelain ashtray collected a wad of smashed cigarette butts still smoldering – the smoke twisting around in the hot stale air.

"The owner's an old French paratrooper, Edmon Durante," Bill said, speaking low while walking towards the curtain at the very back of the shop. "Take a look around; buy something – he's a good connection to have here in Bien Hoa."

Ethan's eyes scaled the walls and the cluttered floor before him. Every nook and cranny of the room was shelved, and the shelves were piled high with anything imaginable – from pottery, local artwork and crafts, scattered military equipment, even other trinkets like pocket knives and Rolex watches. Ethan shuffled his way through the tight aisles looking for the ideal gift to give to the Yards' village chief at his upcoming visit. His teammates had extended the invitation to him and Bruce as a way to symbolize their gratitude and loyalty. After some careful deliberation, he decided on a few stainless steel Swiss Army knives. He knew how much the

Yards loved flashy objects and he figured the stainless would polish up easily enough. He also grabbed an old whistle figuring it might be of some use while in the field.

*   *   *

The road from Bien Hoa was fast and uneventful but the ride felt good. The wind whipped through Ethan's hair with a liberating howl, much like riding in the open door of a slick, only nobody was shooting at him. Bill's larceny skills were tried and tested true; he'd stolen them a fresh set of wheels from an unsuspecting Air Force major and repainted the unit designation in an alley using the art supplies he carried in his ruck.

Entering Saigon's city limits, they ran head-on into a wall of traffic and it took them another half-hour to negotiate their way through barking horns and thick exhaust fumes through to SOG's downtown safe-house. They checked in with the duty sergeant at House 10, showered up and kicked back at the bar downstairs for a few early-afternoon cocktails.

"Cushy gig ya got here, Patty."

"Bill fucking Allen!" the bartender beamed as he glanced up. "What the hell are you doing back here?! Last time I saw you, we were bleeding all over each other in a medevac over Loc Ninh."

"We didn't need no damn dustoff," Bill gloated. "How ya been?"

"Good 'nuff I reckon," Patty shrugged. "Fuck'n got shot up again."

"Jesus, how many Purple Hearts does that make?" Bill kidded him. "Heard you were up at CCN for a bit."

"Yeah, serious business up there, bro. Took a burst from an AK in my left leg in the A Shau about eight months ago," he said as he mixed a brace of Jack and Cokes.

"You always were a bullet magnet."

"No shit. So who's your partner?"

"Ethan Jackson, Pat Tolson," Bill said, and they shook hands.

"Special Projects? Who you with now?"

Bill nodded and swigged his whiskey, "CCC Recon."

"Serious business," Pat lamented.

"You said it. So who all's in town tonight?"

"Few regulars from CCS and a couple guys from some other project but they're all downtown already," Pat said. "It sure is good to see ya, man. Seems like everybody else I know got themselves smoked in the past year."

"Yeah there's a lot of that goin' around," Bill sighed.

They finished their drinks, thanked Pat and caught a cab down to the nefarious Tu Do Street – Saigon's version of the Las Vegas strip. The traffic was unlike anything Ethan had ever seen before. Drunken GIs and ARVN regulars reclined in rickshaws and cyclo-cabs while their Vietnamese cabbies pedaled their hearts out, jockeying for position with Renaults, Citroens, jeeps and buses. Vietnamese cowboys wearing Stetson hats and aviator sunglasses darted through the congestion on mopeds, snatching expensive watches off the wrists of unsuspecting GIs who hung their arms outside taxi windows. Anyone who walked or stood too close to the street ran the undesirable risk of becoming an instant hood-ornament. They stepped out of the cab and right into the middle of the strip among crowded cafés and restaurants, tattoo parlors and whore houses – the red-light district, proper. It was the very place where all manner of nefarious indiscretions transpired right out in the open for all and sundry to see.

"Don't wander off in there by yourself," Bill warned of the alleys.

He strolled casually while Ethan did his best to swim and not drown in the sea of exotica. The smells were incredibly overwhelming – a heavy mix of exhaust fumes, kerosene, raw waste, perfumes and incense, and Vietnamese cooking all made a hundred times heavier by the humidity. As dusk settled upon Tu Do Street, the hot sexy glow of flashing neon signs marked late-night hotspots while black marketers tempted their every step with stolen goods, carnal pleasures, and everything in between. Rock'n-roll music blared and a thousand different conversations pinballed up and down the crowded street all at once.

"You're gonna love Mama Bic's," Bill promised.

He went on to explain that Bic was an infamous Saigon restaurateur who also ran a massively successful prostitution ring. She was also a savvy black marketer and hawked everything from medical supplies to alcohol and cigarettes.

"She used to own the Sporting Bar but it was demolished during Tet," he continued while leading them through the crowded sidewalk. "Nowadays, bar owners on Tu Do hire her out for a few months at a time to manage their joints. They know she'll bring in all the prettiest girls and all the best clients, like us." And whichever bar Mama Bic was running at the time also naturally served as the official *unofficial* Special Forces rendezvous and safe-house in Saigon.

"Back in the early days, about the only thing you had to watch out for around here were Saigon cowboys. Shit's changed now," Bill continued. "That's why we need street-kits, but you ain't gotta worry about a schoolgirl dropping a frag at your feet at Mama Bic's." It was well-known that Bic greased whatever wheels necessary to avoid any heat from either side of the coin. "There's something else you need to know." He stopped and leaned in close to Ethan. "Bic's a Phoenix agent."

"You serious?"

"Think about how many connections she's made in Saigon – either by running bars or by dealing goods on the black market," Bill said while scanning the crowd. "Ain't hard to figure why Phoenix and the CIA would want her. And the connection has its perks. She's close with SF and the Special Projects. That's why she don't charge us for a night with one of her girls. Instead of money, she'll get you to run by the PX and buy her a few cartons of smokes or a case of whiskey."

"Which she unloads on the black market for a hundred percent profit," Ethan figured. "So you mentioned something about Bic's girls being free," he smiled devilishly.

Bill grinned, "Only if one of 'em picks you. That's how it works."

They wove through the undulating crowd at Mama Bic's, searching for a safe place to sit down, order drinks and eat a decent meal. It was an eclectic bunch – a vibrating mix of GIs and Viets, prostitutes, waitresses, a CIA spook or two and the typical American reporter with their photography entourage thrown in for good measure. Within a few minutes of finding a spot to post up, they each had girls in their laps.

"First time Mama Bic's?" one of them asked Ethan. She was pretty and petite with big European-inspired almond-shaped eyes, supple olive skin and silky black hair cascading just past her shoulders.

"Yeah," he smiled sheepishly.

Am I making it that obvious? Try to relax, be casual.

"Special Forces numba one," she giggled and ran her hand along the inside of his thigh, massaging him under the table. "You got girlfriend back home?"

"No, no girlfriend," Ethan stammered.

He took a long pull from his drink to dull the edge a little more while she leaned in and nibbled on his ear. He remembered what it had been like when he'd first arrived in-country, days before he'd gotten orders to CCC. Barroom foreplay and the inevitable exchange of money for sex, and afterwards, she'd gone right back downstairs into the bar to fish for new clients – a strange and impersonal experience. But Mama Bic's girls were different; they were *all-night* girls, clean, beautiful – Eurasians.

"My name Lahn," she smiled. "You buy Saigon tea," and before he could answer, the drink slid across the table. But Ethan was privy to the scam; GIs bought them by the dozens thinking they were getting girls sauced up but the drink contained no alcohol. It was expensive to boot, and girls would split the profit with bar owners making it a lucrative enterprise. Even still, Ethan eased back into his seat and played the game as cool as he knew how.

Bill had a popular face at Mama Bic's and seemed to know just about everyone there – a surprised look, warm smile, the obligatory "Holy shit, Bill Allen, you're *still* here?" token followed by typical Special Forces warzone parley.

Three hours later, Ethan was drunkenly searching the undulating crowd for Bill while the MPs prodded the masses to get to their final destinations. He heard his name being called from the street and then a cream-colored, four-door Citroen maneuvered up to the curb in front of him. Lahn was perched seductively on the backseat.

"Ethan, you come wit me," she beckoned and swung the door open.

He studied her over with lusting eyes as her cream-white linen trousers and aqua tube-top popped against the bright-red interior. He swayed slightly while leaning in, and she slid across the seat to the far side, tempting him deeper like a Siren from Homer's *Odyssey*. Ethan felt the driver's eyes searching him coolly from the rearview mirror.

Round face, wide flat nose, broader build... Nung, mid-thirties.

"Come," Lahn stroked the seat beside her. "I cook for you at my home."

He scanned the rowdy horde around him.

"You look for Bill," she smiled.

"Bill, yeah, where is he?"

"He wit Hai," Lahn smiled. "She live wit me. You see him soon. Come."

Ethan glanced back into the cab again, fixing his eyes on the driver. He didn't like it – the lack of control; exactly why he dreaded cross-border insertion flights. No control.

Backseat, passenger's side; keep him in sight. If it goes bad, put two behind his ear.

He lowered himself into the squatty cab, right hand discretely on the silenced .22-caliber High Standard concealed in his waistband, eyes on Lahn's driver. Away from the curb they pulled, and Ethan was committed to the ride and whatever else might transpire in the depths of the night. Tu Do materialize through the windshield before being lost in a glowing bloom of flashing disco signs and nightlights blurring behind them.

"Chee," Lahn said with a cute nod. "He drive me and, how you say, guard?"

"Bodyguard. He protects you."

"*Bah-dee-guard.*" She said it slowly, pronouncing every part of the word while Chee downshifted and scanned the road ahead before entering a traffic circle.

He's focused on getting us safely off the strip, searching for threats, avoiding roadblocks, never comes to a complete stop, professional...

"You've worked for us before."

Chee's eyes cut to the rearview and caught Ethan's.

"...Phoenix. I work security for Mama Bic, for Lahn and Hai," Chee said. "There is no danger for you here, my friend."

"Nung?"

He nodded.

Almost perfect English... I should be safe here.

Ethan cautiously relaxed back into the seat a little more and slowly freed the knot from his throat.

"You like me, Ethan?" Lahn smiled as she held the back of his hand to her soft face. "I like you. I hope I pretty for you."

He knew she could sense his tension.

"You're *very* pretty, Lahn. What part of the city do you live in?"

"My home in Cholón, not far."

Cholón. Chinatown; the business epicenter for Saigon which sat astride the Newport Docks on the west bank of the Saigon River. It was a black market hotspot, and it was also where thousands of American and Vietnamese deserters, junkies and gangsters sought refuge. Gun-runs and airstrikes had nearly leveled that part of Saigon during Tet, and just like everywhere else, the destruction was still apparent.

Ethan tried his best to remember the route that Chee had taken from Tu Do but he was utterly lost. All he knew was that he was south of everything – south of Tu Do and Mama Bic's, SOG headquarters, and worse still, south of House 10.

They pulled up to a high-walled compound with a tall wrought-iron gate, the headlights revealing another Nung with a hairy face as he opened the way.

"My partner, Lum," Chee said. "He drive for Hai."

He pulled past the gate and into a lush garden of palms, banana and mango trees and other floral exotica. The villa was a predictable mix of colonial French and Vietnamese design and architecture – white stucco and wrought-iron railings, bamboo and teak. Bic rented the place and many others like it all across the city for her best girls.

Lahn offered him another Jack and Coke but he'd decided during the ride that sobering up was a wiser decision, so she poured some green tea and gave him the grand tour. It was a beautiful, cozy place with teak and tile flooring, colorful rugs, bamboo and rattan furniture, candles and incense, and sculptures of Buddha and his deities. She led him into her room and closed the door behind and before he could fantasize what it might be like, he was inside her. She arched her back and undulated, digging her short nails into his shoulders and it went on for a long, hot while until their passion peaked and they both melted back into the sweaty linen sheets. The room glowed in naked flickering candlelight and smelled of smoldering incense and humid sex.

She reached across him, pressing her bare chest into his while retrieving a bamboo pipe and a little ornate tinderbox made of teak from the nightstand. Ethan watched her pack the brass bowl on the end of the pipe with a soft blonde-colored chunk and a few liberal pinches of vanilla pipe tobacco.

"You smoke," she said, handing him the pipe.

"No no, I'm okay."

"Smoke," she insisted again with a giggle.

"Opium, heroin – what is it?"

"No opium. Hashish wit tobacco," she said with doughy eyes. "Numba one sleep, you see."

He reluctantly put the piece to his lips and pulled as she matched the bowl. His cheeks ballooned and he inhaled deeply, letting the thickly-coiled smoke flood his lungs with sweet vanilla and a burnt resin aftertaste. Three hits and he was swimming through clouds, numb, save the tingling sensation that sparked across his skin in the most peculiar and indescribable of ways.

On his back, in the clouds while she cashed the bowl-pack and snuggled in against him. His eyelids drew heavy and he let sleep carry him away to the rhythm of her gentle breathing.

12

CCC, Kontum Province, South Vietnam, and back to realities of fighting a secret war. While Ethan and Bill had been gallivanting in Saigon, RT Hawaii had gotten hit and lost two men while inside Juliet-9. It was the same target Utah had been assigned only weeks before but never got to run due to bad weather. That night was probably the quietest night at CCC that Ethan could remember since being in-country. Nobody felt like partying and those who were in the club drank quietly and kept mostly to themselves. Laying low in the team house for the night, Ethan and Bill listened while Bruce recounted what exactly had happened to RT Hawaii the day before.

It was Bill Delima's last mission before rotating back to the states, so he and Glen Uemura had traded spots, making Glen the One-Zero. Hawaii had gotten a late insertion into The Bra two days before, and had taken NVA artillery fire during the night, but came through unscathed. After their morning radio check, they moved out but made heavy contact with a large number of NVA which turned into a running gunfight. Covey instructed Uemura to go high and dry because Florida and Washington were both in dire straits as well. The whole scene was one that Ethan had feared from the very beginning: multiple teams in big trouble but having to wait according to which situation was worst.

Hawaii managed to lay low for a few hours, after which Covey brought in the choppers. Tragically, during the extraction, Hawaii's Montagnard pointman was shot and killed and Dennis Bingham was fatally wounded by shrapnel from an RPG blast. What's more was that there had been a fourth team in heavy contact at the same time as the others: RT Arkansas, led by one of SOG's most established One-Zeros, Ralph Rodd.

Rodd's team had been hit hard by a volley of RPGs and AK fire and all anyone knew was that Rodd had been severely wounded as well as One-One Sam Barras. Worse yet was that the beleaguered recon team was still out there, socked in by torrential monsoon rains and surrounded by an unknown number of NVA. Nobody in Recon would deny that 17 July 1969 had transpired into one of the company's darkest days. The rain continued well into the next day and it appeared that Rodd and his team wouldn't be getting an extraction until the weather broke. After a light breakfast, Ethan shot a few rounds of pool with John Plaster at the club; John was up by one game just as the Lieutenant Colonel Abt and Captain Yates joined the rotation.

"Any news on Arkansas?" Plaster asked Yates as he smashed the neatly-racked triangle with a loud *crack!*, dropping two solids and a stripe.

"Ain't look'n good today; goddamn weather just won't break."

Everyone feared the worst for Arkansas; the longer they had to wait, the weaker they became and everyone knew it wouldn't be long before the NVA mounted a final assault.

"Y'all pick your heads up, now. We're gonna get 'em outta there," Lieutenant Colonel Abt encouraged. "Who's got winner?"

"You do, sir," Plaster offered.

"We'll play doubles – me and Jim versus you two," he said, nodding at Ethan and John.

An hour later and they were still at it, having drawn several new teams of two into the rotation. The captain wasn't a bad shot, but Lieutenant Colonel Abt was far better at horseshoes than a billiards shark. The rainy day competition was a good way for everyone to blow off a little steam and ease their minds, but everybody was careful not to have too much fun – Arkansas was still out there: cold, wet, wounded, and surrounded.

Despite the terrible weather the next day, Covey pilot Don Fulton took a gamble and flew his 0-2 Cessna low-level beneath the cloud bank, buzzing over miles of ridgelines before he managed to find the valley where Rodd's team had holed up in. He then aimed the nose of his aircraft skyward and shot blindly through the clouds and radioed a pair of A-1E Skyraiders, advising them to watch where he broke through, saying that the center of the valley was directly beneath. Sure enough, the Spads saw right where he punched through and were soon buzzing over Rodd's team while Fulton led a group of Kingbee helicopters back down through the rabbit hole. Minutes later, Arkansas was extracted without a single hostile shot fired. Both Ralph Rodd and Sam Barras were medevac'd to Japan for emergency medical care and then back stateside for yet more surgery, and Captain Don Fulton was awarded the Distinguished Flying Cross for his selfless actions. Moral seemed to jump back up with news of RT Arkansas' rescue, but July had been a devastating month for Recon Company and it still wasn't August yet.

Eddie wandered back to Kontum the next day and that afternoon, the three of them grabbed a jeep and drove out to the Yards' village near Plei Te. It was a relatively short drive down Highway 14 some fifteen klicks before turning west on an old rutted logging road that led deeper into the Highlands. They kept a steady pace in the jeep, knowing the possibility of an enemy roadside ambush was all too great in that area. Soon, they began passing tribesmen and young children walking beside the road wearing nothing but loincloths and carrying crossbows, and machetes fashioned from sharpened leaf springs. Before reaching the village they met Bo and Hyuk walking along the road and offered them a ride for the rest of the way. Every hundred meters or so, Hyuk would tell them to pull over and pick someone up, and soon, the jeep had half the village riding on its hood.

The village itself dominated a gentle rise dead in the center of a small valley that overlooked several low-lying slash-and-burn fields. The road stopped at the fields, so to access the village, everyone had to walk the remainder of the distance in along a weathered footpath. The open valley and fields served as an excellent security measure against any unfriendlies who were forced to cross the open ground to get to the village. The perimeter was guarded by an ancient fence cut from tree branches, some of which had sprouted new roots and gown back into trees. A series of five longhouses dominated much of the actual village and stood several feet off the ground on stilts. The largest of the longhouses belonged to the village chief and his family while four separate families owned the others. There were around twenty other smaller hootches which also stood on stilts while crowding around the larger longhouses; the smaller dwellings were owned by smaller families. There were a few buildings used for storing what little supplies the village acquired from the outside world, but overall, it remained self-sustaining. The longhouses and huts were all constructed of bamboo and hardwood saplings with grass-covered roofs. Fires burned constantly inside each dwelling while the smoke filtered through the grass roofs and kept the bugs at bay. It also gave the Yards a very distinct aroma that reminded Ethan of his time in the Boy Scouts – that smoky, wood-burning fire smell that could only come from standing around an open flame.

Dirty little children mobbed their jeep with gleeful delight as they came to a stop in the mud beside the hamlet. Nay and Hyuk shooed them away, but once they got out and started walking across the dikes, the little kids turned the jeep into a playground. Nay latched on to Ethan's arm and guided him across the paddy dike and into the center of the village where the chief was waiting. He was a short and shriveled old man with sinewy extremities and very little muscle. His cheekbones were high and definite and his lower jaw very slim; his eye sockets were deep and his yellow eyes bugged. He wore several necklaces made from bone and leather, and a large collection of brass bracelets jingled from his wrists. His clothing was little more than an olive-drab t-shirt and a loincloth, no shoes, and he chewed endlessly on an unlit hemp cigar. Nay introduced them in their native tongue to his father, Y Lap. He smiled broadly, showing a large amount of purple-colored gum where his two front teeth once were; the rest of his teeth were stained oily-black from decades of chewing beetle nut.

"Give him gift, Yok-son," Nay quietly advised while standing to their left.

Ethan reached into his pocket and produced one of the stainless steel Swiss Army knives he'd bought in Bien Hoa and held his hand forward while slightly bowing his head. The old man smiled again while reaching forward with both hands, taking Ethan's gift. His eyes lit up as he opened the blades and checked their sharpness; the stainless was so shiny he could see himself in it. The chief spoke quickly in Bahnar as he fumbled with the knife.

"He is much happy, *Trung-si*; you have given him great gift," Nay smiled. "Now, we will drink rice wine. Come."

They followed Nay and Hyuk and the chief across the village and up into the great long house. The inside was dim and smoky-smelling from the fire, but somehow inviting and friendly. Each family member had their own sleeping quarters sprawled out on the floor of the house. The rest of Utah's Yards flooded in behind them as the chief and Nay squatted around a large urn filled with a murky-looking brew with bits of rice floating aimlessly about. Several long bamboo straws lay across the rim of the urn; on the shaft of each straw was a perpendicular splinter that served as a drinking mark.

"Each time you drink, must drink until wine reaches splinter. You see?"

Hyuk dropped one of the straws into the brew and pulled hard on his end until the wine dropped to the splinter. Nay then refilled the urn with water and took his turn until his share had been sucked down; Bo went next. Once again, the urn was topped off and the straw passed on; it was now Ethan's turn. He dropped his head over the rim of the urn with the straw in his mouth and took one final glance around the room; his whole team was watching him now as was the chief with his unlit cigar and several other Montagnard tribesmen. A stiff, pungent odor tickled his nostrils; he pulled hard on the straw and felt the heavy liquid flow into his mouth. Just when he thought he couldn't fit another drop in, the sliver emerged and he pulled the straw from his pressed lips. He forced the wine down in two large throat-burning gulps before passing the straw to the chief, who smiled and nodded with approval.

"Big drink, *Trung-si*, big drink!" Hyuk beamed and slapped his back and all the tribesmen smiled and nodded with their approval.

The straw was passed around several more times before coming back to Ethan again. By now, his head was swimming in wine and his vision was starting to tilt and blur with each blink; Bruce and Eddie weren't doing much better and the Yards were having a hearty laugh at their expense. Ethan dropped the straw back in and pressed the end between his lips and formed a tight seal. He sucked as much as he could, but the splinter just wouldn't surface. He was barely able to force the brew down just as Nay and Hyuk leaned over the urn to inspect the straw.

"More! More!" Nay demanded while pointing at the straw; his eyes were huge.

"You finish drink, *Trung-si*, Hyuk shouted. "You must!"

Ethan's mouth and throat were burning now and his face tingled from intoxication. He knew he couldn't handle a single drop more of the rice wine, but he shuddered to think what might happen if he refused to finish his stick. Such an insult would not be forgotten among the village and neither him, nor Bruce, nor Eddie would be invited back. He put the straw in his mouth again and sucked until the stick surfaced, but that was only half the battle. He still had to swallow it. He held his breath and forced the liquid down his scorched throat, but his stomach refused to allow any more. With his mouth still full of wine, he coughed, forcing the brew up and out of his nostrils. It exploded from his nose and ran down over his lips and chin, and soaked the front of his jungle shirt. His eyes and nose burned and watered as the laughter reached his ears. Looking up through hazy, swirling vision, he could see the Yards laughing hysterically at him. He composed himself the best he could and sleeved his nose and chin dry of wine.

"Good *Trung-si*, good! You do fine. No problem," Hyuk assured him while trying to quell his laughter. Ethan smiled wryly and passed the straw to Eddie who immediately quit laughing.

The Yards were incredible hosts and served a massive feast consisting of wild boar, chicken, fish, and rice. They cooked the food over open flame while the children clung to the Americans' legs and arms, demanding that they stomp around with them still hanging on. They celebrated long into the night, stopping only after passing out with numb teeth and swirling brains, and they slept late into the morning. Every time Ethan stirred, his pounding head felt like it was being smashed in a vise. The rice wine was the heaviest brew he'd ever swilled and although his teeth weren't numb any longer, his face was still a bit tingly, and the sun was incredibly bright. They spent the rest of the day nursing their hangovers and mingling in the village. Bruce conducted an informal check-up session and tended to any minor afflictions or ailments the Yards complained about while Eddie and Ethan helped them with some of the domestic chores. In turn the Yards showed them how to shoot crossbows and spearfish in the nearby stream. Nui managed to convince Bruce to give him the keys to the jeep so he could practice driving; before long, he had every kid in the village hanging on while he swerved up and down the old road. He wasn't a bad driver, but he hadn't yet figured out how to shift the gears and use the clutch simultaneously.

Before leaving late that afternoon, the chief gave one of his brass bracelets to Ethan as a sign of friendship. It was made of brass shell casings that had been hammered into shape by hand. He thanked him the best way he knew how – both hands pressed together as if he were praying, while slightly bowing, and the Yards smiled and thanked him in their best broken English.

With Bruce at the wheel, Ethan and Eddie waved bye to the village while the little kids chased them down the old road for as long as their little legs could keep up. Watching their peaceful little existence shrink in a cloud of red dust, Ethan believed the Montagnards to be the most civilized people he'd ever encountered and he couldn't understand why the Vietnamese felt so threatened by them. He sat quietly for the duration of the return trip while bouncing with the ruts and reflecting on the past day, and he hoped he'd be invited back soon. They kept their CAR-15s close as the sun dropped lower to the west and the humid air grew cooler over Highway 14. A foreboding twinge of excitement coursed through his body as he thought about the upcoming days: Stand-down was over and Utah would soon be jumping the fence again.

13

Ethan held the magnifying glass up to the photo again and concentrated hard on the details, but it was still quite difficult to be absolutely certain. He passed the photo to Eddie before picking up another from the pile on the table.

"I ain't sure, man – camera lens coulda been dirty. I mean, it could be anything," Eddie said as he compared two photos side-by-side.

"Well you were at the briefing just like me and Bruce; S-2 thinks those are caves," Ethan lamented.

"That lieutenant seemed too sure of himself," Bruce offered as he rifled through the pile of photos again.

"He's a photo analyst; I would hope he knows his shit," Ethan shrugged.

SOG headquarters in Saigon had sent the photos back to CCC along with one of their analysts to review the intelligence that had been collected from the images. The S-2 shop was convinced the aerial photos showed caves and the photo analyst supported their theory, so S-3 Operations passed the show on to Utah.

The target-area was tucked way back inside Cambodia, scraping the southwestern reaches of CCC's area of operations. The photos showed a rugged combination of single and double-canopy jungle and limestone rock faces, but the elevation was tough to gauge. On top of that, the target-area was way out of the reaches of Ben Het's artillery fan and the rules of engagement still prohibited any fixed-wing air support inside Cambodia. Yet despite the odds, Ethan's confidence was high and his excitement was growing. They weren't going to be simply roaming through the woods this time. They had a near-exact location with a six-digit coordinate fix; they had detailed aerial photographs of what appeared to be multiple openings and gaps in several limestone rock faces, and high-speed trails galore. S-2 advised them to expect anything when dealing with caves because the NVA were masters of disguise and used their natural surroundings to no limits. The high possibility of caves meant they could run into anything from base-areas to enemy artillery emplacements, to American POW camps. That thought alone was enough to transmit the very importance of getting a team in there undetected as soon as possible, and Ethan was glad his team was going in.

They spent the rest of the afternoon studying the target folder and the folders of the surrounding target-areas. Usually, the S-2 shop had a good idea about specific NVA units operating within a particular area. That type of intelligence generally came from captured documents pulled straight from the source by SOG teams or the CIA. Sometimes it came from conventional US and ARVN units operating along the border regions, but S-2 didn't have much intelligence on Utah's new target – it was simply too remote. Ethan was eager to get the team back down to the range to begin their pre-mission training regimen, but the Yards weren't due back until the next day.

Over the past month, several new bars had surfaced on the compound. While everyone still frequented the main club over by the mess hall, the officers had started their own bar, the senior NCOs had a spot, and the Covey Riders had theirs. RT Iowa One-Zero Phil Rice and teammates Ray Harris and Tom Lois took it upon themselves and decided that it was time for the junior NCOs to have their own little watering hole as well. They took half of their team house and turned it into a bar, while the other half served as their personal living quarters.

By late-afternoon, Ethan, Bruce, and Eddie found themselves drinking in Iowa's new bar, effectively named the "RON" as indicated by the wooden sign that Ray Harris had hand-carved. Underneath the sign was a brass plaque that read "PF Travel Agency" – PF meaning Prairie Fire. Iowa had done a bang-up job with the place and had somehow acquired a ten-foot bar to serve drinks from; they had also outfitted the joint with an AC unit, a reel-to-reel tape player, radio, and turntables which supplied plenty of music. One wall was painted to resemble a bamboo thicket and another wall had been decorated with crossed Thompson sub-machineguns which were locked and loaded.

The RON was an immediate success and everyone was enjoying the new atmosphere. Ethan had a little more than he intended to, but Mark was the first one to pass out inside the bar. The punishment for such an infraction was usually mild embarrassment, like being stripped naked and left outside overnight, tied down to a heavy piece of furniture. And since it was Mark's 21st birthday, that's exactly what they did. Paul, Bruce, and a few others stumbled their way over to RT South Dakota's team house and stole Mark's rack and mattress, carried it out to the helipads, and set it up. Eddie helped Ethan carry Mark over to his new quarters while everybody else laughed and catcalled from the open door of the RON. Somebody suggested tying him to his bed in nothing more than his "birthday suit", jungle boots and his beret… so they did. It was quite a show when the air packages thundered in the following morning.

Later that morning, First Sergeant Doney held a formal debriefing session for all recon One-Zeros whose teams had either just returned from a mission, or were about to insert. In the past, that type of debriefing had been largely informal and had gone down in the club over drinks. While those "pow-wows" were effective and beneficial to all, Doney's vision of a One-Zero debriefing session was far better organized. Since Utah's next target was so remote, Ethan directed most of his questions to guys like Joe Walker and RT Maine One-Zero Dave Baker – guys who had experience with running the more remote target-areas and coming out unscathed.

Joe's team was one of the most flexible teams in SOG and could effectively run light or heavy in numbers and weapons. RT California often ran heavy and used RPGs and 60mm mortars which gave them the appearance of a much larger force than simply an eight-man recon team. Sometimes the trick worked and the NVA would hesitate before pursuing. Joe suggested using the 60mm French "knee" mortar since it was shorter and lighter than the US-issued tube. The French tube also had a base-plate that helped the user stabilize and aim when firing. Ethan's mouth practically watered at the thought of dropping mortar rounds on the NVA, and as soon as he could, he planned on paying the guys over at the S-4 shop a visit. Dave Baker and other One-Zeros warned him about the thinner ground clutter that grew beneath the canopy in northeast Cambodia. Thinner undergrowth meant faster, quieter movement and greater visibility, but those advantages were shared with the NVA.

Doney's sessions proved to be highly effective and were also a great way to learn which teams were going where. John Plaster and RT Illinois were heading way north, some forty miles northwest of Dak To, to recon a treacherous valley along Laotian Highway 165. Plaster's new One-Zero, John Allen, was a solid team leader who had run recon out of CCN a year earlier until his entire team had been wiped out over the course of two days. Allen was the sole survivor of RT Alabama and for reasons only he knew, he was back running recon again.

*   *   *

The roar of the wind and the thumping rotors made hearing nearly impossible inside the cabin. Ethan's perspiration had long since been blown dry and his nervous anxiety refused to let his heart rate settle.

He searched the faces of his Yards; Luc and Hyuk appeared calm, almost placid and bored, but Ethan could tell they were trying hard to ignore Tang's fidgeting. He'd be fine for a few minutes and then adjust his rucksack straps again or tap his foot on the aluminum flooring. Tang was a good kid by all measures – handsome and agile, but young and inexperienced. Up until now, all he'd done was train and run small patrols around Kontum with the rest of the team. He was a bit of a cutup and clowned around a lot, which was good for a few laughs. During training though, he seemed as good as any of them and was an excellent shot with the M-79. Nui had turned his ankle a few days earlier while rappelling from the Dak Bla River Bridge, so Tang was filling in.

Ethan began to run back through the mission prep one last time; he was certain everyone was squared away. He decided against Joe's 60mm mortar recommendation after playing with it on the range for a few days. Mortars were excellent for defending stationary positions against massing enemy forces, but Ethan just couldn't seem to find a place to fit it in. It was an indirect-fire weapon, which meant the rounds traveled in an arc unlike a bullet or a recoilless rifle round, which traveled in a straight line to meet the threat. A mortar would certainly give them greater reach – out to about eight-hundred meters – but he wasn't planning on engaging the NVA at that range, nor did he envision sending any of his boys out into an open area to fire it. Between their M-79s, RPDs, and CAR-15s, and a sky full of helicopter gunships, Cambodian target-areas didn't seem *that* much different than the northern targets of Laos. The LZs they had selected were small and the E&E route was thoroughly planned should it come to that.

The bomb-scarred and pock-marked tri-border region passed quietly beneath Utah's aerial convoy several thousand feet below. Heavy clouds from a stalled cold front had moved into position way to the north across Laos, while broken clouds littered the sky above Cambodia. The early-morning mist blurred the steeper ridgelines and peaks, while thicker blankets of fog filled in the valley floors and smothered the terrain from view. The bright sunlight blasted through the passing clouds in shafts of moody luminescence, creating an almost majestic feel.

But despite the natural beauty, the insertion flight was the most dreaded part of any mission. They were each stuck in thought, carousing and searching through the jungles of their own minds, unable to escape the mechanical popping of the rotors and the cold rushing wind.

Mission prep was the first thing Ethan usually thought of, and once all that passed, then came the "What if's" and the "In case of" scenarios. Rarely did his thoughts find passage through those narrow mazes, but this flight was dreadfully long. He hated long insertion flights – they all did – and he didn't want the extra time to think. But he couldn't help it – the letter from his older brother, David, was still fresh on his mind. It was the first letter he'd gotten from him since being in-country. Usually, his parents and his brother would all write their own letters and mail them together. It made it easier to keep up with everybody when they all came in one envelope, but as the months passed, more and more separate letters showed up.

It felt good to hear from David; he'd finally gotten into graduate school and was chipping away at a Master's in Finance. He knew a lot about various investment vehicles and how to play the stock market without getting too ambitious.

Movement in the cabin scrambled his thoughts; the crew chief was talking into his mic while moving behind the starboard side M-60 as the other door gunner saddled up on the other side. The crew chief tapped Ethan's leg and pointed down to a wide-open valley as it materialized through the fog. The primary LZ he had picked during the VR flight was on the upslope of a low-lying secondary ridgeline that intersected at the northwestern corner of the valley. They'd spotted the suspected cave network several days before in an adjacent valley farther to the northwest, nearly a kilometer from their insertion point. There was also an alarming number of abandoned antiaircraft positions scattered in the surrounding foothills, most of which were blanketed by fog.

He reached down and adjusted the cuffs of his vintage WWII leggings he'd gotten from Ray Harris earlier that week. For about five bucks a pair, Ethan, Eddie, and Bruce all chipped in and bought enough for the entire team. The leggings made a nice snug fit around the top of their boots, which kept the leaches out and their pant legs tucked in. When moving through dense jungle, briars and ground clutter no longer snagged and pulled at their pants, but the leggings served as an even greater device in deception. No American units used leggings anymore, so by wearing them, they appeared to be Australian or British at a glance.

The slicks began to orbit high above the valley while the Cobras played ball over the LZ, zipping around through the fog as the rising tropical sun burned the haze away. A pair of Huey gunships orbited slightly above the Cobras and searched feverishly for hostile targets but the NVA didn't take the bait.

"Get that fucking thing outta my face!" the crew chief shouted while leaning away and pointing at the white phosphorous grenade hanging from his left shoulder strap. He shifted to his right to give Hyuk room between him and the crew chief.

A minute later, Ethan's slick quickly began plummeting through the air in a psychotic spiral while the pilot aimed for the little LZ. Fear grew inside him and sweat began to bead up on his painted face, while adrenaline seized control of his entire existence. He knew being scared didn't change a thing when it came to war, but only fools and lunatics weren't scared. As far as he knew, he was no fool and was still mostly sane.

One last glance over his shoulder ensured Luc and Tang were ready and in position on the other side. He braced himself in the open doorway with the arcs of his boot soles locked onto the Huey's landing skids. As they sank lower, the dot-sized clearing quickly morphed into a hole only big enough for one chopper to fit. The rolling hill above the LZ loomed over them with an ominous presence as patchy fog banks drifted up and over the top glowing orange from the rising sun. At twenty feet, he searched through the canopy for any NVA-furnished surprises while taking mental notes on the terrain features. He scanned the immediate area looking for the best place to set up a defensive perimeter and soon realized just how thin the undergrowth was. Instead of towering hardwoods and cypress, there were mostly Asian pines and scraggly sapling thickets – neither of which offered much in the way of cover or concealment.

At five feet, he dropped from the ship and hit the ground, tumbled once, and moved quickly for a slight depression off in the tree-line he'd spotted from the air. They piled into the defilade and set up a perimeter just as the second bird sunk into the landing zone and repeated the maneuvers. Bo, Eddie, Bruce, and Nay moved quickly away from the lifting ship and into the tree-line; in a matter of seconds, the team was whole and silence had once again settled back upon the little clearing and the surrounding countryside while the choppers climbed high.

Dave Baker and others had described the terrain exactly as it materialized before him. Peering out from their little perimeter, he could easily see what he figured was almost sixty meters in all directions. Knee-high grass and waist-high ferns filled in the holes around the Asian pines and sapling thickets; slabs of exposed moss-covered limestone protruded from the ground and offered the only effective cover within view. He eyeballed the terrain to his front and made out the narrow saddle that intersected the main north-to-south ridge. Taking a quick look at his topography map, he quickly identified the same terrain features, got a rough fix on their location and took a compass reading. Insertions were always the most confusing and dangerous part of a mission; everyone's biggest concern was getting in unnoticed and moving off the LZ and into cover as quickly as possible. It was easy to become disoriented and almost lost once under the canopy since most prominent terrain features couldn't be seen from the ground.

Ethan brought the radio handset to his mouth and gave Karate the all-clear, then leaned over to Hyuk's ear and whispered his orders so that he could translate to Luc. Normally, he would just nod or signal Luc with his eyes, but the woods were far thinner than anything he'd ever operated in before and he wanted to take the necessary precautions to give them the sharpest edge.

"Tell him to head across the saddle but to stay close to any rocks in case we need cover," he breathed.

Hyuk translated quietly and Luc nodded. Slowly they rose in order-of-march and followed in the little pointman's every careful step. They moved without sound or any hint of existence other than their own individual heartbeats, just as they always did. He was uneasy about the team being so exposed at first, but the thinner ground clutter allowed them a much easier passage with less resistance. He spaced their intervals out a little farther to compensate for the better visibility and slightly staggered their line to the right flank. Luc took them exactly as he'd been instructed and wove meticulously around bright shafts of sunlight and avoided the more open areas, keeping them close to the boulder groupings and larger trees. The saddle was little more than a dip in the hilltop as the terrain fell casually away on either side.

Once at the intersection, the hillside climbed slightly higher above but Luc's body suddenly tensed up in mid-step and his CAR-15 slowly drifted across his front and to his left. The team froze in place and kept their eyes trained and Ethan could feel his pulse pounding in his temples. Then everyone went to a crouch.

"Bunker," Luc mouthed and pointed with a slow nod.

Ethan methodically combed the hillside with his eyes.

Staring down on them with a wide-open firing port was a log bunker etched into the hillside about thirty meters away. He immediately knew the structure was vacant because if it hadn't been, they would have already been dead. The bunker afforded a perfect field of fire right down onto the saddle.

He signaled quickly for the team to form up into a wedge with Bo and his RPD on the left flank and Tang's M-79 on the right. They moved fast, yet utterly silent, and cleared the bunker with an enveloping sweep. Ethan and Bruce crawled inside and scoped the approach out while the rest of the team deployed in a defensive perimeter. Cold-chills raced up and down his spine as he peered out through the firing port.

From that position, a light machinegun or even a few AKs could have wiped the entire team out without even breaking a sweat, and it would have been next to impossible to outflank the position due to the openness of the terrain. Saddles were always potential chokepoints and made excellent ambush sites. Even worse was the fact that the bunker had a clear line of fire down onto their insert LZ and any competent gun crew could have made a real mess of things.

They turned their attention to the bunker itself and noted its condition and structural integrity, and quickly agreed it would have taken several gun-runs to knock it out of commission. The structure was built using large hardwood logs that appeared to have been cut by chainsaws.

"Where the hell did they get the timber to build this bunker?" Ethan whispered to Bruce. "All I see are sapling thickets."

He shrugged, "Maybe they trucked it in."

Filling in all the gaps and cracks between the logs was an ingenious blend of mud and pulverized rock which made a crude cement-like mortar when it dried. The dingy dwelling had plenty of room to house a three-man gun crew and ammunition, but by the looks of things, the owners hadn't been around lately.

Ethan took several photos detailing the bunker's size and construction while Eddie took a few Yards and pulled a quick sweep of the immediate area. Where there was one bunker, there were bound to be more and they would all be linked together by a system of high-speed trails. Yet strangely enough, they found no trails leading to or away from the bunker, and none were spotted near their LZ during the VR flight a few days earlier. Just then, Luc pointed out a tree that had a symbol carved into the base its trunk. A few minutes later, they found several more markings and realized they were trail markers. With such a thin canopy and sparse underbrush, clearing a trail would have been a waste of time and far too obvious, so instead, the NVA were using tree carvings as a trail without actually having to cut the paths.

After being on the ground for almost an hour and having only moved about seventy meters off the LZ, Ethan could feel the team's luck wearing thin. There was no doubt the NVA were in the area and he knew they needed to put some distance between them and their LZ. He still couldn't believe they hadn't made contact yet and he figured they were on the fringe of a bunker complex or possibly a base-area. He put Luc on course to the south and planned to move away from where the caves were located, then swing up and approach the area from the west over the next two days.

They moved across the hillside, paralleling a low ridge to their right, while making sure to maintain a safe distance from the top so the enemy couldn't drop grenades down on their heads. Staying off the spine of the ridge also kept them from getting skylined by way of a bright day and a thin canopy. They staggered their direction of travel every hundred meters and buttonhooked around to watch their back-trail before stopping for *pok*-time.

One-by-one, they each ate a lukewarm lunch, repacked their trash and pulled in their Claymores. Eddie gave the FAC a sitrep while Bruce and Ethan studied the map and took more compass readings. They'd put about four-hundred meters between themselves and their LZ and hadn't heard or seen any new signs of enemy presence. The ridge was dropping lower the farther south they went, so they decided to cross over and move into the neighboring valley for the night.

Ethan's shoulders had been reacquainted with the weight of his field gear and rucksack, and the blisters on his feet had been reopened, yet he was just as excited and nervous as the first time he'd been across the fence. It was a sensation he couldn't put his finger on and one that he would never be able to put into words. It was a wild obsession to beat the odds and do things very few others had the will and temperament to do.

The team had performed well and needed rest for the upcoming days, so they began searching for their RON position late in the afternoon. The jungle had grown to a thick double-canopy and offered much better cover and concealment. Luc pulled them into a bamboo thicket atop a gentle rise and made a quick recon of the immediate area. Again, one-by-one, they took turns eating dinner while the rest kept eyes on the perimeter. Ethan always allowed them to cook their meals using a little ball of C4 while patrolling around CCC, but never allowed it when across the fence. A hot meal went a long way for a recon man while in the bush, but he just couldn't risk the possibility of the NVA catching their scent even though C4 burned without odor or smoke.

After everyone else had finished eating, Ethan pulled out a little plastic baggie containing freeze-dried rice and chicken; he added lukewarm water and a healthy dash of Tabasco sauce, then knotted the bag closed and tucked it into his bare armpit; fifteen minutes later, he was chowing down.

Right after dark, the team picked up and moved to a new RON site in case they were being shadowed by trackers. They moved for about a hundred meters before settling into another suitable location that Luc had found while on his perimeter recon. Making a tight circle with their feet at the center, they each cleared away their sleeping areas of any loose debris, then set their Claymores, gave Karate a goodnight sitrep and burrowed in for the night.

14

His eyes were wide-open, searching the depths of a moonless night while the ground rumbled and quaked beneath him. He slowly rolled over on his stomach and huddled down behind his ruck while bringing his CAR-15 around. He groped blindly for the Claymore detonators and found them where he'd laid them out at his side. The ground rumbled and vibrated in a strange rhythm – an odd, galloping-like way, and he could hear something big crashing through the underbrush just a few hundred meters away.

What the fuck is that?

Ethan caught ear of the Yards whispering feverishly among themselves; he reached over and squeezed Hyuk's arm and pulled him close.

"Be cool," he whispered. "Everybody be *real* cool."

His heart was racing and he began to feel woozy as the adrenaline diluted the blood in his veins. He was trying so desperately to stay calm and collected, but he had no idea what was barreling towards them. He couldn't see his own hand before his face and he began to lose control of his thought process. A cold clammy hand latched onto his wrist.

"That sounds like a fucking tank," Bruce whispered.

He focused again on the rumbling and listened for the mechanical groan of diesel motors and squeaking tracks, but they weren't there; only a continuous, lumbering thunder that shook the ground they lay on.

"That ain't no tank."

"Well I ain't try'n to stick around to find out."

It was moving in from the west and approaching their perimeter from the left, and what once sounded like a few hundred meters out was suddenly half that. Ethan thought about calling in a sitrep to Leghorn, but quickly convinced himself otherwise. If the NVA were trying to flush them out, they'd be monitoring the radio frequencies and would know they were close if he described the sounds. They also had radio directional finding equipment capable of triangulating the signal if he stayed on the frequency too long. Whatever it was grew closer and he began to notice a pattern, almost like giant footfalls on the jungle floor. A hundred meters quickly became sixty and suddenly, a terrifying roar ripped through the cool moldy air.

Trumpets… it sounds like a fucking trumpet or some kinda horn.

"Ollie-phanns, ollie-phanns," Hyuk whispered into his ear.

"Elephants?"

"Yes."

He'd heard stories about the NVA using elephants as beasts-of-burden to haul supplies down the Trail, but from the sounds of things, those were no NVA-employed elephants. He thought for a second about shooting them while the crashing drew closer and the ground continued to rumble beneath him, but seriously doubted their CAR-15s would have much stopping effect on such a large animal. Maybe the M-79 or the Claymores but they couldn't even see an inch in front of themselves.

"Hold your fire and stay put," he demanded.

He began to feel less and less in control of the situation and it was wracking his nerves, but it was too late for anything else. Bamboo crashed violently just to the left of their perimeter as the thunderous rumble drew down on them.

"Fuck, they're coming right through us," Eddie cried..

Something suddenly tumbled over Ethan's back. He tried to squirm out from under it, fearing it was the crushing weight of one of the elephants, but he could then feel the wiry limbs and torso of one of his Yards. They lay there in a motionless, silent heap while the herd crashed off into the night.

"Anybody hurt? Hyuk, Nay, Tang?"

He could hear the Yards whispering in Bahnar as they groped their way from the pile and back to their trampled positions on the right side of the perimeter.

"We okay," Hyuk finally whispered.

"Shit that was thin ice," Bruce sighed nervously.

They tried to settle back down for the few remaining hours before dawn, but everyone was simply too keyed up and on-edge to sleep. About an hour before sunrise, a faint hacking sound resonated down through the valley from the north – the telltale sound of enemy woodcutters taking advantage of the cool morning before the day's heat set in. They decided to pack up and distance themselves from the elephant trail just in case the NVA came along to investigate.

As dawn slowly filtered down through the upper canopy, they began to survey the damage done by the elephant herd. The right side of their tiny perimeter had been trampled and the contents of Nay's and Tang's rucksacks were scattered about, but nothing looked to be damaged. After snapping a few photos of the Yards' trampled equipment, Ethan took Bo and Eddie out onto the trail to get a closer look while the rest of the team covered them and watched for any NVA. They moved with caution, not sure of what to expect, while watching carefully where they stepped.

The destruction was absolutely spectacular; bamboo was rigid and strong, yet the herd had blazed a trail wide enough to drive a truck through. Eddie found one of their Claymores which had been completely crushed under an elephant's foot. They took a few pictures of the damage, salvaged the C4, and buried the rest. Before moving off the trail, Ethan posed in the middle with his arms stretched out to his sides to give the photos scale while Eddie snapped several frames. They gave Karate Davis their morning sitrep and began pushing silently to the northeast while keeping close ears on the woodcutters, and trained eyes on the bush. The undergrowth remained relatively dense but nothing like the triple-canopy growth they'd been through in Laos. They zigzagged for a few hundred meters before stopping to eat a late breakfast and then pushed on until *pok*-time.

Aside from the natural sounds of the woods, the rest of the afternoon remained quiet. Just before dark, they happened upon a shallow streambed that bubbled over slabs of limestone and granite. The stream was about eight meters wide, the water clean and flowing, not stagnant, which made it an excellent natural resource to the NVA. Glancing downstream, he could see the terrain becoming rockier and more rugged. The water was cold and crystal clear so they took a few minutes to refill their canteens and absorb the postcard beauty they'd discovered. The lush foliage spilled over the stream's low banks and created long dark shadows that loomed over the cool water, while shafts of sunlight speared downward and created a peaceful yet secretive mood. For some reason, Ethan thought it ironic that such unspoiled beauty could thrive amid a chaotic and violent world. He wanted to cross and set up their RON somewhere on the far side, but feared being spotted so late in the day.

They backed off about a hundred meters east of the stream and settled into a sapling thicket. As they waited for dark, Ethan checked his map and reviewed the terrain that lay ahead of them. Missions rarely went according to plan once a team was on the ground and plans were subjected to constant augmentation and spontaneous decision-making.

They'd spent the entire day pushing up through the target area, paralleling the creek while covering a respectable amount of ground without incident. After another lengthy map-reading session, they had a confident fix on their position and where they suspected the cave system was located. They appeared to be just a few hundred meters shy, but the safest way in meant crossing the stream in the morning and approaching the cave network from the west. Once darkness fell, the team quietly picked up and moved south for another hundred meters before crawling into a dense thicket for the night. Their false RON would throw off any trackers, but they had no way of knowing what was around their new spot since it was too dark to conduct a quick recon of the immediate area. They quietly strung Claymores and settled on an E&E route in case they were rousted during the night; Karate wished them a goodnight and promised to be back in the air at daybreak.

Ethan spent the first few restless hours thinking about what they might find in the coming days while keeping his ears tuned to the frequency of the woods. The nighttime air quickly grew cold and damp, and he did his very best to keep warm under his poncho liner. Sometime after midnight, a steady rain set in, soaking them all from head to toe. He quietly checked the radio and spare batteries to be certain they were staying dry. The sound of the rain falling through the vegetation made it impossible to detect any movement outside their perimeter, and the remainder of the night felt like a lifetime set in slow-motion. The night closed up around him in tight claustrophobia and he shivered under his wet poncho liner, at times feeling like he was suspended in a black void with only the ground he lay on to remind him of where he was. Nights like that were dreadfully long and offered little rest. A recon man's mind often conjured up some terrible thoughts during those cold, wet and lonely hours. Fortunately, the night remained uneventful but the rain continued its relentless assault into the following day.

Low clouds and heavy fog had settled into the valley overnight and choked out the sky. Eddie hooked up the long antenna for the PRC-25 while Ethan tried to raise Karate, but it was useless – the foul weather had rendered communications impossible. Their only chance of making radio contact was to find higher ground so their signal could travel farther.

By mid-morning, they had abandoned the approach to the cave system and moved back to the west, away from the rain-swollen stream. The driving downpour allowed them to move quicker as it masked their sound and partially covered their back-trail, but the fog had cut their visibility in half; if they ran into anything, they'd be face-to-face before anyone knew it.

By late morning, they were steadily moving up a thickly-wooded hillside when they happened across dozens of tree stumps. They moved in ever-so careful to inspect the stumps in hopes of gaining an estimation on how long it had been since the trees had been harvested. Many of the cuts were only a few days old while several more stumps were well on their way to rotting out. At their bases were the usual wood chips made from axes, but they also found numerous piles of fresh sawdust made from chainsaws. Ethan scooped a handful of wet sawdust up and stuffed it into his pocket – irrefutable evidence to give to S-2.

"Guess we know where they got the timber to build that bunker," Eddie whispered. "Probably spooked that elephant herd the other night, too."

Counting heads as his team filed past, Ethan glanced back down upon the stump grove one last time as the rain continued to pour.

How long does it take for one of these trees to reach maturity? And how long would it take for a stump to rot after being cut down?

He wondered silently while turning uphill to follow his team, searching the annals of his own knowledge for the answers. A few more minutes of silent movement passed before he realized his epiphany: If the NVA had time to wait for trees to grow into maturity, they were prepared to fight for the next century if that's what it took. They were dug in like ticks, well-motivated, and combat-hardened and all they knew was struggle.

Why the fuck are we fighting in South Vietnam when we should be fighting them here, in Cambodia and Laos, he wondered. *This is where we should be committed, and not secretly.*

Yet oddly enough, he had no regrets about his situation; he was one of the very few who had the temperament and nerve to constantly fight outnumbered. Ethan was where he wanted to be, with the Montagnards and other Americans like himself. He was a 20-year-old kid from Charleston, neck-deep in a secret war whose end was nowhere in sight. Yet he wouldn't have had it any other way.

They were on the hilltop by *pok*-time but the driving rain and the low clouds and fog had socked the entire countryside in. They found a thick stand of bamboo and stuffed themselves inside, hoping to find some reprieve from the elements but that was only wishful thinking. They sat quietly and shivered uncontrollably in the cold, wet weather, eating in pairs while Ethan and Eddie rigged up the long antenna. It was basically just a long, pre-cut length of antenna wire stretched out across the ground and aimed in the direction of the receiving station. It had worked brilliantly when they'd tested it at the launch site before insertion, but the weather had been fair. After nearly two hours without any luck with the radio, they decided to save the batteries and switched it off. It was the first time Ethan had ever experienced real radio trouble while in the field; there were plenty of times in the past where radio contact had been poor but they'd at least had it. It was their only lifeline to salvation and rescue, and without a solid signal, they were utterly cutoff and seemingly forgotten. Desperation began to crawl through his guts and he fought to put his mind at ease. The batteries and radio were still dry and the antennas were good; so far, the weather was the only factor not cooperating.

*   *   *

The rain hadn't let up for nearly seven days and the temperature was in the low sixties during the height of the day; at night, it was dipping down into the upper forties. Everything they had was completely soaked and morale was as low as Ethan had ever seen on his team. To keep from catching hypothermia, Bruce had them all doing jumping-jacks and pushups at times during the day. They still hadn't made radio contact since the weather had closed in and to keep from running into the NVA, they elected to stay on the hill. They had spent the first two nights in the bamboo stand but decided that a third night in the same spot was a bad idea. Luc managed to find them a grouping of boulders the day before that offered just enough dry ground for each man, but they were all still exhausted and miserable. Water wasn't a problem but each man had only packed enough food for six days in the field. Since they weren't moving around much, they wisely began to ration their food and conserve what little energy they could.

The days were long, but the nights were infinitely longer; security wasn't an issue because there was always a few who couldn't sleep. Over the past eight months, Ethan had learned how to sleep in the field without falling completely away. Every hour, he'd systematically wake up to listen for ten or fifteen minutes before allowing himself to nod off again. It had taken him the first few nights to get use to the rain, but he was now applying the same technique, and it hadn't failed him yet.

It was around midnight when the rain began to slack off and an hour later, not a drop was falling. Everything was as silent as it ever could be, but suddenly, the crickets and frogs began, and eventually the Asian gecko made his presence known. After listening to the constant hiss of the rain for nearly a week straight, it was a pleasure to know the jungle's creatures hadn't drowned. Ethan decided to give the radio a shot just in case the weather didn't hold, so he and Bruce quickly rigged the long antenna. They knew the chances were slim, but even the slightest possibility of reaching Leghorn made it worth a try. Bruce switched the PRC-25 to Leghorn's frequency and although he wanted to hear a friendly voice on the other end of the radio, Ethan decided to play it safe and communicate by breaking squelch instead. He keyed the handset twice and waited breathlessly for a single reply.

Seconds passed…

Nothing.

He keyed it twice more, but again, received no reply.

"Fuck," Bruce mumbled. "I doubt we could hit Leghorn with a mile-high antenna on a clear day."

He knew Bruce was probably right: The relay site was nearly fifty kilometers to the north. All they could do was wait until morning and hope that Pete Johnston or Rex Hill would be out looking for them. Maybe they could get an extraction before noon if the weather held out long enough. They packed the radio away and settled back down to catch what little sleep they could. Ethan's eyelids grew heavy again and began to draw tight, but his ears were suddenly alert and honing in on the sounds of enemy presence. A series of muffled putts and pops bounced around the woods before silence prevailed again. A few seconds passed before the sounds dribbled in again, but this time they were followed by the unmistakable signature of a two-stroke gasoline engine. The engine reached maximum output and RPM almost instantly.

"Generator," Eddie whispered.

And where there was one generator, there was bound to be another, and where there were generators, there was always a sizeable enemy presence.

15

The generators abruptly died just before the false dawn on Utah's ninth day. The uneventful predawn came and passed, and soon, the woods began to surface from the colorless void of yet another black night. The cool air was thick and heavy with a soupy mist that hissed and swirled around them. Ethan lay still while trying to shake the wet cold from his bones. He hadn't had much sleep; none of them had. A few hours each day is about all any of them could muster while the rain poured, and even that wasn't really sleep. His hands tightened slightly around his weapon as he listened intently; he could hear the fog ghosting through the underbrush, moving and swirling around them. A soggy green lump shifted slightly by his side as Bruce stretched out momentarily before propping himself up against his ruck. The rest of the team was beginning to stir and shift about in the early-morning glow. The rain was still holding back, yet large drops of dew continued to roll off leaves, falling to the ground after filtering through the different layers of the canopy with a *pitter-patter* splash. Ethan signaled Eddie to make a quick clover-leaf recon of their perimeter to make sure the NVA hadn't found them over night. Muzzles and eyes faced outward in all directions while Eddie took Bo and Nay and swept the area. Twenty minutes later, they reentered the perimeter one at a time, making sure to watch their backs in case they'd mistakenly led the enemy in.

"All's clear," Eddie muttered.

Ethan nodded and went about the morning tasks that had become routine by then. One-by-one, they each cleaned their weapons of the moisture that had built up over night, ensuring that nothing would stick in a time of dire need. Once done, they then took turns stripping down and peeling the leeches off that had been suckling at their raw, shivering bodies all night long. So far, Hyuk held the mission's record leech count of seventeen, barely one night's worth. Leeches weren't the only discomfort that presented itself to a hardened recon man. Sleeping on the bare ground also meant dealing with a variety of poisonous snakes, deadly centipedes, hornet and wasp nests, termites and ant mounds, and a plethora of other varmints that all called the jungle home. Then, there were the mosquitoes – huge, blood sucking airborne paratroopers of death that carried several different strains of malaria. There was very little that could be done to combat Southeast Asia's mosquito population. The standard-issue insect repellent had too much of a distinct odor for a recon team to use in the field. All they could do was pop the US government-issued malaria pills, roll their sleeves down and cover their faces, and succumb to the misery of jungle warfare. After all that, making contact with the NVA didn't seem so bad; at least they could shoot back.

Luc hissed quietly for the team's attention; instantly, everyone brought their weapons up and held their breath, watching and waiting while their bodies tensed up behind whatever cover was close by. Looking at Ethan, the little Yard tapped his crusty ear.

"Plane, *Trung-si,*" he whispered with a stale, hot breath.

A minute or so bled away before the droning of a SPAF Bird Dog could be heard to the southeast. Still somewhat amazed at the little pointman's heightened senses, Ethan grabbed the radio handset and motioned for Bruce to attach the long antenna. With that done, he then swapped in a fresh battery, just to be sure, then brought the handset up and keyed the mic.

"SPAF, this is Hollywood. Over." He hung by the radio and counted the long seconds of hushed static while waiting for a reply. "SPAF, this is Hollywood. Talk to me. Over."

"Hollywood, this is Karate. How copy?"

The sweet sound of Howard Davis's voice nearly brought tears to his eyes as it crackled through the handset.

"Karate, I read you Lima-Charlie. How me? Over."

"Same same, Hollywood. How's about that mornin' sitrep? Over."

"Karate, we're tired, wet, cold, and ready to go home. Negative contact so far, but Chuck's close; we heard 'em all night long."

"Understood, partner. Weather's break'n up; soon as this soup burns off, we'll get y'all outta there."

"Good to hear, Karate. We're less than a klick sierra of our primary LZ, hitting the road shortly. Over."

"Copy that, Hollywood. We're in the neighborhood."

"Sounds good, Karate. Out."

They broke down the long antenna and held a quick map reading session to discuss the best avenue of approach to their landing zone. The hill they found themselves on fingered nearly a kilometer to the north, petering and tapering all the way. During the visual recon flight, Ethan had spotted an old bomb crater smack-dab on the spine of the hilltop and decided it was as good a landing zone as any. Ideally, the team would arrive at the LZ right as the slicks did, so they wouldn't have to wait any longer than necessary. But with the lingering fog as it was, they'd reach the LZ long before the choppers could safely navigate through the weather. The hills in Cambodia were relatively low compared to what they experienced in Laos and were mostly covered by single and double-canopy jungle. Lots of sapling and bamboo thickets, bramble and scrub brush, coupled with light overhead foliage.

"I'm guessing it'll take an hour or two for the soup to cook off," Ethan whispered softly. "Not sure about you two, but I wouldn't mind poking around a bit before we high-tail it. Those were definitely generators we heard last night."

Eddie nodded and looked at Bruce for his input.

The Puerto Rican's eyebrows furrowed.

"I'm game," he said as he massaged his stubbly chin.

"Okay, here's the skinny," Ethan planned. "We'll cruise down the hill here, move for a few hundred meters, pull a wide clover-leaf and then beat-feet to the LZ."

"Sounds good," Bruce agreed, "just so long as the terrain stays easy-going. I don't know how far my feet are gonna carry me, and I know mine ain't the worst."

A valid concern since everyone's feet were in bad shape; their skin was beginning to peel and flake away – a sure sign of jungle rot. Blisters had worsened into open sores and were showing signs of infection, not to mention the hundreds of bites they had accumulated over the past ten days from the mosquitoes, leeches, and other bugs. Bruce had done what he could to stem the rot, but it had little effect with all the rain and no chance of drying off.

"Chuck's definitely in the neighborhood, so pay attention and worry about your pretty little feet when were back in Kontum."

Ethan looked at them as they both smiled grimy, dirt-covered, white-toothed grins that only recon men could produce. They took a few minutes to brief the Yards, then packed up and sterilized the RON site they'd been using for the past several days. It proved almost an impossible task to erase their extended presence from the spot, so they did the best they could before moving out.

With a new objective to complete and an afternoon extraction to look forward to, Ethan could feel the invigorating presence of adrenaline as it saturated his insides. It became almost too much to bear at first, affording him a swirling head and nauseous, queasy guts, partly because he hadn't had anything to eat in almost a day. His feet cried with each step carefully placed, and his jungle fatigues quickly turned his prune-like skin into raw meat where the wet fabric created the most friction. The team struggled for the first few hundred meters to regain the patrolling techniques they'd all been taught, but it wasn't due to a lack of proper training – they were simply exhausted and weather-beaten. Fortunately, the thick mulch-like compost that covered the jungle floor had soaked up so much moisture during the past week, the noise of their passage was silenced. They avoided mud at all costs since it was nearly impossible for Eddie to sterilize their tracks.

By late morning, they were well off the hill and pushing into the flatlands after having discovered several trails in the process. It was difficult to discern whether or not they were in fact trails due to the large amount of rainfall the area had received. Their surfaces were completely awash and showed evidence of extreme erosion from where torrents of rainwater had traveled downhill. What were once NVA footpaths had been reduced to deep mud crevasses knifing into the hillside. They completed the first loop of their recon just before *pok*-time without finding any fresh sign, and kept ghosting after their midday break. The temperatures had skyrocketed, transforming the underbrush into a natural sauna, but the blazing sun was quickly burning the fog off and an afternoon extraction was looking better by the minute. They continued to move with less-than-perfect technique, carving their way through the woods and around beaming shafts of sunlight. Luc's pace suddenly halted as he waited for a moment to sample the atmosphere. After a few minutes, the reserved little Yard inched forward but stopped short again and waved the team down. Ethan slowly crept up past Bo and joined Luc's side; he was absolutely soaked in sweat and appeared to have a difficult time keeping his eyes open – almost as if he were nodding off to sleep.

"Whatcha got?" Ethan whispered softly.

"Think… *beaucoup* NVA ahead," Luc replied with slow speech and a labored breath.

Ethan turned back and motioned for Bruce to come up; the rest of the team concerned themselves only with what may be lurking in and beyond the shadows.

"What do ya see?" Ethan asked, trying to keep Luc conscious and focused.

Just then, Bruce edged up beside them and immediately noticed the symptoms of dehydration and fatigue. The high humidity made it impossible for sweat to dry, which meant the body lost the ability to cool itself.

"He's worn out," Bruce whispered as he quickly examined Luc's face and peered into his eyes.

Ethan motioned Eddie to bring the team into a defensive perimeter around them while Bruce gave the tough little Yard a few salt tablets and some water.

"Will he be okay?" Ethan asked as he looked into Luc's sagging eyes.

"Yeah, I'm gonna rig up a bag of saline real quick," Bruce said. "He needs fluids."

Ethan nodded, "He thinks we're about to stumble into something."

"Dude, we're in no condition to get in a gunfight," Bruce advised. "Look at everybody; Mother Nature's kicked our asses this time. If we make for the LZ right now, we'd be lucky to get everybody there under their own power."

"I'm ready to get the fuck outta here," Eddie admitted.

"Yeah, me too," Ethan leveled. "Tell ya what, we'll take fifteen and then head for the LZ." He loosened his rucksack straps and slid out from under its weight. "I wanna move up a few more meters and take a look around real fast."

"By yourself?" Eddie hissed.

"No, you're comin' with me to make sure I don't step in any shit," Ethan smiled. He motioned for Hyuk to drop his ruck. "We ain't goin' far – I just wanna peek around one last time."

"Never satisfied, are ya?" Eddie sighed.

"Be back before dinner, sweetheart; listen for the challenge," Ethan winked, but Bruce was in no mood to joke around. "Hey asshole, would it kill ya to smile a little? It does wonders for morale."

Bruce shook his head and finally cracked a massive, toothy grin, "Hurry the fuck up, will ya?"

A quick glance at the map, a compass reading, and out the front door they went for a friendly neighborhood stroll. And after only about fifty meters, Ethan's respect for Luc had grown to exponential proportions; taking point was no simple affair. He'd never felt so vulnerable, so open to potential mistakes – the kind that would happily snatch his life away. Walking point required him to analyze everything in sight across his front, all while trying to find the safest passage through the terrain while still offering them the best cover possible in case they made contact. On top of all that, he had to be conscious of enemy booby-traps and hazardous wildlife that roamed the woods like tigers, wild buffalo and boar, elephants, a myriad of venomous snakes, scorpions, and spiders, and centipedes. He'd never run point before then and quickly concluded that Cambodia was definitely not the safest place to learn the finer aspects of the job. But there was no way he could expect any of his teammates to perform a task that he himself would not do. He'd learned from many seasoned Special Forces instructors back in Training Group the hallmarks of a successful SF soldier was to do the job at hand with professionalism, and to set the example by leading from the front.

A few hundred meters further, the woods began to thin in a peculiar way. He froze in his tracks and signaled caution to the boys behind while carefully creeping forward with his CAR-15 firmly in his clutches – eyes hunting, nose filtering, ears tuning. He caught an odd shape off to his left not more than ten meters away. He shifted his eyes and nothing more, generating as little movement as possible. It didn't look much like a trench-line at first; all the rain had flooded and caused it to cave in on itself but when he followed it with his eyes, he made out at least a half-dozen bunkers all connected by flooded slit-trenches. They were clearly at the edge of a major instillation and it was a miracle they weren't dead or running for their lives yet. His throat tightened as his heart pounding maniacally in his ears; he signaled the others and then slowly and methodically retraced his steps until the three of them were safely concealed back inside thicker brush.

Just beyond their little hide-site, the underbrush had been cleared away; they could see where tree branches had been tied together to patch holes in the upper canopy which effectively made the place invisible to aerial observation. The entire trench system that connected the bunkers had been completely flooded from all the recent weather. They identified a dozen or more structures built from a variety of materials: sandbags, bamboo and timber, even pierced steel planking, corrugated sheet-metal, and concrete. The buildings all varied in size from small hootches, to much larger dwellings that could house sizeable units moving along the Trail. Everything blended miraculously well with the environment, even the man-made PSP and sheet-metal. There was no way to tell what purpose each individual structure served but the mind had a nasty way of speculating on such things in the heat of the moment. What was even *more* ingenious was that every structure appeared to have natural vegetation actually growing from the rooftops. It appeared the NVA had used the rooftops as huge planters in which they grew small saplings, ferns, and other vegetation usually found at ground level.

It was absolutely ingenious in every way.

Looking past the immediate area, there was no telling how large the base-area was. Though they could see no enemy activity to their front, they could hear movement to the north end of the complex and assumed the enemy was working to clear the flood. From the looks of things, the encampment had been there for a long, long time and was vital for logistical support to their units, both arriving for and returning from battle inside South Vietnam.

There came a slight hint of stale sweat, and then a pungent waft of *nuoc-mam* fish sauce – a sure sign the enemy was danger-close. Chitchatting voices fluttered through the woods to the south of where the trio was hiding, maybe twenty meters off to their left, moving toward the complex. They moved loudly – both in voice and with rattling equipment and tools, obviously unaware of Ethan's team, nor worried about the possibility of being discovered. That usually meant they were comfortable there and were among large numbers.

Stoned on adrenaline, Ethan picked his little squad up and lead them quickly back the way they'd come, stopping short to buttonhook and observe their back-trail for trackers. After several uneventful minutes of observation, they moved back to where Bruce and the rest of the Yards were waiting. Ethan lightly snapped his fingers once and waited for the reply – two light snaps – and with that, they reentered the tiny perimeter.

"Dude, we just listened to a full company march past us about fifty meters out," Bruce whispered. "Sounded like they were humping tools and all kinds of shit. Must be a trail we missed somewhere over there."

"Yeah we just found a huge fucking base-area," Ethan spoke with a jumpy whisper as he was almost out of breath. His entire being was absolutely saturated with adrenaline and he could barely keep himself from screaming at the top of his lungs because of the exhilaration he felt.

"Shit, a base-area?" Bruce gasped. "That big?"

"The whole place is flooded from all the rain. Didn't see anybody but we think we heard 'em working on the other side right before that unit came strolling by."

"Probably engineers working to clear the water," Eddie guessed.

"That explains the generators."

Luc was looking much better and refused to allow anyone else to run point, so without wasting any more time, the team formed up and quietly put a few hundred meters between themselves and their new discovery. They pulled into a bamboo thicket and called in a sitrep to Karate. Ethan didn't get too chatty on the radio and spent only enough time to request the orchestration of the team's extraction.

A few hours before sunset, they hit the LZ just as the ships arrived on station. As the last man on the ground, Ethan sprinted those last twenty meters from the tree-line in record time and heaved himself aboard just as the chopper began to pull up. It was a text-book extraction and the only thing about the mission that went according to plan, but they were all alive with the knowledge and whereabouts of a high-value target. None of them could have known it then, but in barely four weeks' time, they'd be back in that same area running a bomb-damage assessment just minutes after an Arc Light strike, and they'd be fighting for their lives.

16

Had it not been for the roar of the cold evening air blowing through the chopper's open cabin, Ethan would have been sleeping like a baby. Only after the extraction did he feel the true extent of his exhaustion; his adrenaline had kept him going for the past day and in its passing wake, he was left feeling achingly drained and helplessly famished. Their teeth chattered and they shivered uncontrollably in the freezing cold, all the while struggling to keep from peeing all over themselves. CCC appeared in the distance, basking in a moody orange glow as the evening sun angled lower and prepared to dip below the mountains of Laos. A massive crowd had gathered around the helipads, waiting impatiently to greet them with open arms, warm faces, and ice-cold beer. Before he knew it, they were on the ground and all of CCC was swarming around them as they landed.

"It's good to have you boys back," Bob Howard said as they pumped fists and cut through the crowd.

"Thanks for coming out to properly welcome us back," Ethan smiled.

"Y'all look a little skinny. Gotcha some steaks and cold beer over at the mess hall, although I doubt the cooks will let y'all in smelling like that," Bob laughed.

"Don't worry," Ethan assured. "We been think'n about hot showers all week long."

"You motherfuckers look like you been on R-and-R for the past ten days!" Bill Allen shouted while filling their hands with beer.

"Shit, I wish," Ethan said as he punched a hole into the top of the can with Bill's church-key; cold suds erupted and foamed over the rim and he quickly put it to his parched lips to stem the spill.

"Y'all smell like assholes," Mark winced as he elbowed in and slapped their backs. Most of the crowd was beginning to thin but quite a few walked alongside the trio and made small-talk.

"Any other teams get stuck out there besides us?" The beer hit the bottom of Ethan's stomach and turned his insides warm and woozy, and slightly buzzed.

"Nah, Plaster's team went back and forth to Dak To for a week straight but never launched," Luke Dove said. "Zune gave them a few days' break, but John somehow got bad dysentery and had to go to the dispensary."

"How's he doing?" Bruce asked.

"He's stabilized and conscious now, but he's still over there."

They packed a small cooler of beer, grabbed their lawn chairs and dragged themselves over to the showers in full combat kit – grenades, guns, ammo and all – and began the post-mission shuffle. They set their chairs up directly beneath the showerheads, broke open cold Budweisers, plopped down and let the hot water do its therapeutic thing. It usually took about three beers for the water to flush all the dirt, grime, and mud away – plenty of time to plan and scheme for their pending stand-down. The club was already getting rowdy in anticipation of the Korean band that was scheduled to play that night.

"Hope they brought those strippers with 'em again this time," Eddie called from the adjacent shower stall.

"Let's stick around for the show tonight and jump the ash-and-trash run south tomorrow," Ethan suggested. "House 10 by *pok-time*."

"Saigon, huh? Goin' back to visit that fine little piece you smoothed a few weeks ago?"

Ethan didn't need to look up to know who it was; he could recognize that ratty North Texas drawl through an Arc Light strike. It was Randy Reynolds and he'd been drinking.

"Ain't your inbred ass supposed to be in isolation right now?"

"Tomorrow, which gives us plenty of time to play tonight," he snickered with his arms folded across the top of the stall, beers in each fist.

"Yessir, Saigon," Ethan grinned like a sinner. "Might even make a little detour through Vung Tau while we're at it, right Ed?"

"Do a bit of bronzing, some saltwater therapy, chase a few roundeye nurses," Eddie plotted from next door. "Damn shame you can't go, Reynolds."

"Yeah?" Randy scowled momentarily. "How's about I get Major Doom good'n sauced tonight, tell him ya'll practically begged me to straphang on this one," he slurred. "He won't be able to resist sending ya'll back across the fence in my gentle care."

"If that happens, we'll just cap you on the LZ," Eddie chortled. "Your Yards like us better than they like you."

Reynolds threw back the rest of his beer and let out a stale, boozy belch. That dirty Amarillo grin of his materialized on his face as he drew his revolver and made a slow, deliberate pass at their cooler for resupply.

"You gonna wear your belt buckle tonight?" Ethan teased. Texans were notoriously soft in the head when it came to belt buckles and spurred cowboy boots.

Randy church-keyed the beer open, took a big swig and flipped him the bird, "See you queers in a bit." He stumbled off towards the club, occasionally glancing over his shoulder to make sure they weren't maneuvering on his flanks.

"Well, well, well," Captain Yates chimed as he sidled up to the stalls wearing nothing but cutoffs, shower shoes and sunglasses. "I was *really* hoping the NVA had made mince-meat out of y'all three but God forbid the planets ever align in *my* fucking universe. I knew it had to be y'all coming back, too… I could smell you three from inside the club."

"Is that where you've been while we were stranded – drowning your sorrows in booze?" Ethan sneered. "And why the fuck are you all oiled up?" He leaned over the top of the shower stall and sniffed suspiciously at the good captain. "You smell like coconuts... Is that – is that suntan lotion?"

"You been working on that base tan, *Dai-uy*?!" Eddie howled.

"Your act of insubordination and backtalk is get'n old," Yates pointed at Ethan. "You fuckups better scrub extra-good cause y'all smell like shit and I ain't letting ya in my club 'till you're clean."

"You just try and keep us out, *Dai-uy*," Ethan laughed.

By that time, the mud had rinsed to clean water so they gathered up their chairs and what was left of the cooler stash and moved the show back to the team house. They began by stripping and cleaning their CAR-15s down to the smallest part with diesel and then systematically going back through them with WD-40. They repeated the process with every gun in the team's arsenal: cut-down RPDs and M-60s, the suppressed Swedish-Ks, chopped M-79s and the 60mm mortar tube, then their pistols and suppressors. While their guns soaked and glistened in oil, they moved to their combat harnesses, dumping all their magazines and grenades out on the floor. One-by-one, they emptied all the rounds from their magazines to be dried and oiled and reloaded; grenades were wiped clean, spoons re-taped, pins secured. They inspected their Claymores and det-cord, blocks of C4, blasting caps and the electrical clackers, and all their survival gear. And while everything air-dried, they traipsed back to the showers and finally cleaned their good selves. Once back at the team house, they repacked their tools and recon trinkets, all the while speculating on the evening's festivities and subsequent misadventures that surely awaited them down south. The beers had them buzzing smoothly while the AC frosted the room and "Louie Louie" saturated the airwaves.

"Hey, you two coming or what?!" Mark shouted from outside. The door swung open and all the boys piled in. "The Koreans are all set to jam."

"They brought their strippers again." Tom Waskovich and Pete Johnston were grinning like horny baboons. It was a waste of time to expect that pair to behave like respectable Army officers.

The club was packed wall-to-wall and as soon as Ethan cleared the door, the band cued up and the whole place turned at him and started singing, "For he's a jolly-good fellow," but substituted "felon" for "fellow".

"For he's a jolly-good felon, for he's a jolly-good felon," his peers all sang in unison and the band rocked. "For heeeee's a jolly-good FELLLLLOOOOONNNNN! Which nobody can deny!" They went on for a few more verses while Fuller and Reynolds and the others shoved him towards the bar. Then came the happy birthdays and the subsequent lighthearted wishes for ill-will and great misfortune, hugs and backslaps, and tongues in his ear. He was a ripe twenty-one years young and life was as good as he could imagine. Barnes poured him a deep shot of bourbon but before he could grab it, Bill snatched the glass up.

"This occasion calls for a recon cocktail," Bill grinned and spit in the glass. He passed it to Ray Fuller, and one-by-one, they all spiked his drink in the most disgusting of ways until it came around to Reynolds. And like the unsavory North Texan he was, Randy unzipped his pants and stirred the whole mess with his penis.

"Now it's a legit con-*cock*-tion," he smirked.

Ethan's stomach turned at the notion; he had his silenced .22 and considered the possibilities of shooting his way out but Reynolds must have read his mind.

He caressed the hilt of his .357 Magnum and grinned, "Drink it, pussy."

Ethan grabbed the glass and threw it back as fast as he could, and the entire place broke up into disgusted yet satisfied hoots and catcalls. He made straight for the bar and washed the whole affair down with another double-shot of bourbon, hoping and praying that none of his cohorts' germs and STDs could survive the alcohol – especially Randy's.

"So what else's been going on while we were out?" Bruce asked as he swirled his drink. "Feel like we've been in the bush for a month."

"Nothing much, really – gotta buncha FNGs in over the past few days," Mark said while swigging his beer.

"How many for Recon?" Ethan asked.

"Two or three; couple guys went to the Hatchet Force, and the rest are staff twinkies," Bill said. "I'm trying to work up a good gag to play on 'em but I got nothing."

"Defused frag across their hootch floor?" Eddie shrugged.

"You pulled that shit on me the first day I was here," Ethan laughed at Bill. "Remember that?"

Bill chuckled but shook his head, "Nah, oldest trick in the book."

"Well it scared the shit outta me."

"You were already scared shitless," he chortled.

"Fuck you," Ethan sneered.

Ken Snyder walked over and shared a hilarious little anecdote about how John Plaster had recently convinced a new guy that he had an incurable strain of syphilis after his pee had turned orange from drinking Tang.

"Biological warfare," Bruce guffawed. "I was in the dispensary when he came through. John had that poor bastard convinced he was gonna get shipped off to some island with a bunch of other infected GIs."

They laughed back and forth for a while and discussed the finer aspects of a well-orchestrated prank. The commentary was worthy of some serious laughs, and before long, they were good and drunk, and embracing stand-down. The band played on and the girls danced, and the spirits flowed.

A major from Saigon had somehow found his way into the club earlier that afternoon, and as he described it, he was "part of an initiative to evaluate and assess the effectiveness of every Special Forces installation in-country."

"Well shucks, sir," Danny Cunningham chuckled like a fool. "That was quite a string of ten-dollar words you just rattled off. Me and my companions here ain't exactly scholars."

Cunningham was a strange guy – a master of social deception, and the fuse to his temper varied in length. Sometimes the young captain would string an unsuspecting victim along with innocent banter for a while and other times he'd just knock them clean out of their knickers. Danny obviously had big plans for the poor major; they'd been pouring liquor into him all afternoon.

"Think of me as an advisor," the major slurred. "General Abrams himself appointed the directive and all he wants to know is what you guys are up to and how you can do your jobs better." That was more than enough to seal his fate but it was Cunningham's operation. The major went on to spin a great yarn about how Recon could train better and harder and run more missions. "It's all in my report," he nodded.

"Fuck you and that limp-dick tanker," Yates said of him and General Abrams, and smashed a beer bottle over his head, dropping the poor sod to the deck, out-cold. Jim had stumbled into the club mid-conversation and hadn't taken the major's assessment too keenly. The good captain did, however, have the foresight to use a bottle instead of his fist; no evidence on his knuckles meant plausible deniability.

"Now what?" Tom Waskovich laughed.

"Get him the fuck outta my club," Captain Yates ordered and the mob raged.

"Grab his legs," Cunningham giggled. "I got an idea."

Whatever it was would likely ruin the major's ticket-punching career and probably land him in a foxhole somewhere up along the DMZ, which no one seemed to have a problem with. Nobody came into the lions' den spouting such blasphemy without paying the price and learning a lesson. Ethan started to grab one of his legs but stopped himself. It had become an officers' affair and it was best to let them sort it out amongst themselves, lest Cunningham's little plot backfire and he required a victim of the junior NCO ilk to frame for the whole mess. Danny was cold and cutthroat like that. He'd shown up out of the clear-blue one day a few months ago, AWOL from Group Headquarters in Nha Trang and just never left. He didn't really seem to have a permanent slot anywhere at CCC but he was always straphanging with a team or going out with the Hatchet Force. That seemed to suit him just fine.

They gathered the cold-cocked major up off the floor, carried him down to the dispensary, gagged him, tagged his toe, and zipped him up in a body-bag. Graves Registration would pick him up in the morning and whisk him off to their collection facility in Saigon before anyone the wiser.

On they partied, into the wee hours of the morning. The band called Ethan up to the stage to have a dance with the girls but one man surrounded by a host of naked strippers was too much for anyone to handle, birthday-boy or not, and soon, the whole place was grabbing at the girls. A fight broke out, a fair amount of furniture was demolished, and Barnes had to flush the place out with a teargas grenade.

Life was good.

The next morning, Bill walked over to Utah's team house and announced that he was putting together a special recon team to run down to Pleiku for a little furniture shopping to replace the previous night's damage. No way was Ethan about to pass up on another misadventure with the RT Missouri One-Zero. He grabbed his ruck and packed a few choice items to take along – a fake NVA battle flag complete with chicken blood and bullet holes, several thousand piasters and some American greenbacks for good measure, a slew of miniature teargas, white phosphorous, and V40 mini-frag grenades, compass, camera, survival knife, his .22-cal High Standard, and his CAR-15 with plenty of extra magazines.

"What the hell do you need all that for?" Eddie asked as he wiped the hangover from his eyes while watching Ethan pack.

"Ain't no telling what Bill's gonna get us into," he shrugged.

"Fuck, I'm not sure I want anything to do with this mission," Eddie chuckled reluctantly while he packed his ruck and grabbed his CAR-15.

They made their way to the north gate where Bill, Ray, Mark, and Paul were waiting with one of the company's jeeps. Quickly, they piled in and sped off for the Kontum airfield before anyone could inquire about their "mission". Bill drove like a maniac, swerving by civilians and water buffalo-drawn carts as the jeep barreled over the Dak Bla River Bridge. Reaching the airfield, he downshifted while coming to a brake-squealing halt in front of the gates that guarded B-24, the Special Forces B-team compound located just off the airstrip. They all flashed the guards their identification and were quickly admitted entrance. Bill spun the jeep back behind a building just on the inside of the wire and parked it. Once everyone had dismounted, he chained the steering wheel to the floor and padlocked it. They passed back through the gates while a C-123 crew worked laboriously to unload its cargo under the unrelenting tropical sun. They walked across the apron to where a cluster of slicks had just started cranking their rotors. Bill casually approached the crew chief and bid him a good morning, then asked where they were heading to.

"We're head'n down to Pleiku to make our milk runs," he replied as he looked them over with a curious glance.

"Hot damn, whatta coincidence," Bill declared. "So are we; y'all got room for a few more?"

"Sure," the crew chief said, "but that's as far as we can take you. We're resupplying a few line companies out in the boonies and then playing mailman for the rest of the day."

"Perfect," Bill agreed as he waved everybody onboard.

They were airborne in a matter of minutes, heading south some four thousand feet above the war-torn countryside. Despite all the bomb craters, Vietnam actually looked somewhat peaceful from that perspective. The countryside resembled a myriad of patchwork squares divided and separated by high mountain ranges and thick, unyielding jungle, while other areas were endlessly flat with rice paddies. Lush greenery painted the terrain while the frequent spit of red clay marked the positions of US and ARVN fire support bases while rivers and roadbeds drew dirty brown lines throughout the landscape.

It would be easy to run a war from way up here, Ethan decided. *All the beauty of this country without the ugliness of modern warfare so easily visible…*

It was hard to believe that such brave young men – both Americans and Vietnamese alike – were bloodying themselves somewhere far beneath them, out of sight and largely unheard.

They sat quietly for the duration of the flight, unable to talk without shouting at the tops of their lungs due to the roar of the wind and the popping of the main rotors. The rolling countryside far below eventually gave way to the Pleiku airbase while steep purple-colored mountains loomed to the west, blanketed by dense jungle and who knew how many secrets. The chopper sunk down and buzzed over Engineer Hill before planting skids onto the PSP-covered helipads. They thanked the crew for the uneventful ride, dismounted the aircraft and followed Bill across the tarmac into a city of clapboard buildings and sandbags. The place was an absolute mud hole and the immense heat made it feel like the sun was sitting right on top of their shoulders. The noise from passing aircraft was enough to wake the dead and the place was absolutely crawling with 4th Infantry Division personnel – mostly rear-area desk jockeys and clerks, REMFs – a lot of expanded waist bands and baggy eyelids caused by smoke-filled bars and houses of ill repute. Yes indeed, the rear-area life was good for them and they were rightfully hated for it. The airfield itself was far busier and larger than Kontum's, but nowhere near the size and activity of Bien Hoa. With shouldered weapons and berets cocked and locked into position, they strutted with authority through the airbase before stopping at the PX.

"Okay, here's the deal," Bill said as he stopped them. "We need to secure ourselves two deuce-and-a-halfs for this little operation."

Everyone nodded and began to casually snoop around to see if any were sitting nearby, unattended.

"I hope you remembered to bring your paint and stencils," Ray cautioned.

"Of course," Bill said with a nod. "Wouldn't leave home without 'em."

"Good, this'll be easier if we split up, so you take Paul and Eddie, get a deuce, and meet us back at House Eight."

*   *   *

By early afternoon, they had a pair of expropriated US Army 2.5-ton trucks and were rolling out of SOG's House 8 compound with fresh white stenciling designating them to Pleiku's MACV headquarters compound. Ethan and Mark were in the lead truck with Bill behind the wheel, while Ray, Paul, and Eddie followed in close pursuit. They had all changed into new jungle shirts with MACV patches, officers' ranks, and sterile baseball caps; nothing to tie them to the 5th Group or SOG.

"So where in the hell are we gonna find furniture for the club?" Mark finally asked as Bill squeezed the rig in between a sea of Lambrettas to the right and an old International bus on the left. Diesel and two-cycle fumes choked the rutted, pot-holed road with a bluish-gray cloud that swirled around the open-air markets and vendor kiosks along the roadside.

"I ain't quite figured that out yet, but I think I know a place," he said with a devilish smirk.

A short while later, they found themselves back at the airfield as Bill rolled the truck up to the MP hut that stood guard over the main entrance. The officer on duty walked up to the side of the truck with his clipboard in-hand and peered inside the cab.

"Afternoon, lieutenant," Bill said. "Can you point me in the direction of the Air Force O-Club?"

"Yessir," the lieutenant said and mimed directions with his hands, indicating it was somewhere straight ahead, with a left turn somewhere in the mix, then on the right someplace.

Bill thanked him as the gate opened and the truck urged forward with a growl; Ray and the others passed right through without having to stop.

"Listen boys," Bill began. "Never buy anything you can either steal or barter for, but never steal from the grunt units, only from the Air Force… or the Navy." And his reasoning was simple. "These Air Force REMFs have it way too fucking good. I got respect for the zoomies who're bombing Hanoi and dropping Arc Light strikes along the Trail, and for our Covey pilots, but to hell with these jokers in the rear."

He hit the brakes and stopped short of their final destination.

"Wait here," he said as he hopped out of the cab and walked back to Ray's truck.

"This is either gonna work, or land us all in Long Binh Jail," Mark speculated.

"Whatever that nutcase is scheming, I'm fairly certain it'll work," Ethan laughed.

A few minutes later, they stood at the club's double-doors listening to Jimi Hendrix wail away at a guitar solo inside.

"Remember, just follow my lead," Bill advised.

He pushed the doors open and they crossed into the air conditioned barroom. The lights were dim and the crowd somewhat thin, but still a crowd. All eyes were on them – US Army "officers" inside an Air Force Officer's Club. They walked up to the bar while Ethan inspected the scene; nice furniture fashioned from teak wood – probably bought from a local craftsman in Pleiku.

"Afternoon, major," Bill offered with a taut salute. He even knew how to act like an REMF officer.

"Afternoon to you too, captain," he replied with a lazy salute. "What can I do for you gentlemen?"

"Sir, we'll have two of your coldest beers," Bill replied while looking at Ethan. Ethan just nodded and waited for Bill's next move.

With beers in-hand, Bill swung back at the major, "Are you the manager of this fine establishment, sir?"

"That's right, captain," he replied. His fatigues looked brand new with razor sharp creases and all his insignias neatly sewn on.

"See," Bill started, "me and my lieutenant here stumbled into our current assignment a few months ago, which is to baby-sit for in-country USO tours. We've been hauling Playboy Playmate Bunnies around in Hueys for the past two months to all sorts of outposts and firebases. They get all dolled up and put on a good show for the grunts, and it's been a pretty cushy gig for us in turn," he smiled, but waited before continuing.

"Which Playmates would they happen to be, captain?" the stiff major replied, trying not to sound too curious.

"Say Ethan, which months are those two beauties?" Ethan nearly froze as he tried to remember a measly two months out of the year.

"Uh, February and June, sir," he blurted.

"Lorrie Menconi and Helena Antonaccio?!" the major exclaimed. "You're telling me you two have been flying all over South Vietnam with Lorrie Menconi and Helena Antonaccio?"

By now, every officer in the bar was standing around Ethan and Bill with their tongues nearly hanging out.

"That's what I'm telling you, sir," Bill smiled as he threw back the rest of his beer.

"So what are they like? I mean, do they look as good as they do in the magazines?"

"Well hell, sir that's what I wanted to talk to you about. You gents can all find out for yourselves what they're like... *in* person, *in* the flesh."

"Is that a fact?"

"Well, they've been putting on shows for grunt units all throughout the country and just finished up the last leg of their tour; they fly back to the States tomorrow afternoon, but have time for one more show – but *only* for a small group of gentlemen. See major, they're tired of getting hawked at by those line doggies and Marines, and those damn Special Forces hoodlums are the worst!" At that point, everybody was nodding their heads in agreement, cursing the aforementioned professions.

"So are you asking us if we want to go to the show?" asked a plump, round-faced captain who was standing behind Bill.

"Basically, but we got a small problem."

"Name it."

"Well, we were planning on using one of the hangars over at the airfield to put the show on, but the problem is we ain't got any seating arrangements or even a stage for them to dance on. See, it's a private deal for a small group. We would need to move all your tables, chairs, and stools over to the hangar."

All eyes shifted to the major for the final word.

"We've got a jam-up speaker system and all that stuff, just no furniture for the ladies to dance on," Bill continued.

"Why can't we just do it here, in the club?" the major suggested.

"Well sir, they're tired of doing clubs," Bill shrugged. "Plus, they wanna have an Air Force themed stage with fast-movers in the background and all, see?"

The major came out from behind the counter and walked over by the doors, looking outside.

"Y'all got something to haul all this furniture with?"

"Yessir," Bill exclaimed. "I've got two deuces parked right outside the club and four more men waiting to help load everything up."

"And when will this shin-dig commence, captain?"

"Well sir, we've gotta get all this stuff over to the hangar and have time to set it up," Bill said as he looked down at his watch. "It's almost fourteen-hundred now… I'd say we could be in full-swing by nineteen-hundred, *if* we hurry."

Damn Bill's good, Ethan realized. *We've got 'em; Bill's a fucking genius!*

The major nodded and smiled, "Sounds good to me, captain. A few of my officers won't mind giving you a hand to help load up."

It took them barely twenty minutes to load everything up. Slipping past the major as he stood guard over the club's doors, Ethan moved back into the empty room to where Bill stood with the last piece of furniture. He slipped Ethan a CCC bomb-burst patch and motioned for him to pin it to the dart board that hung over by the juke box. He stabbed the colored patch with a dart and slipped through the doors behind Bill without anyone the wiser.

"Well major, I can guarantee you and your men a memorable evening," Bill smiled as he climbed in behind the wheel of the truck. "If any of y'all have copies of the February and June issues, be sure to bring 'em. They love to sign their centerfolds."

That sealed it. The major smiled broadly at that prospect and waved them on.

"See you in a few hours, captain."

17

"He didn't even ask you which hangar?!" Mark was incredulous as they blew through the airbase gates and onto Highway 14. "I can't believe he didn't even think to ask you which fucking hangar it was supposed to be in!"

"You should have been in there," Ethan laughed. "As soon as Bill said 'Playboy Bunnies' I thought they were gonna start humping each other."

"So I guess we're driving the goods back up to Kontum?" Mark inquired as Bill whipped and darted through the late-afternoon traffic along Highway 14.

"Yeah, you guys are gonna head on back to CCC with the furniture while me and Ethan head over to supply and get a few pallets of beer for the club."

They pulled over on a side street and dropped Bill and Ethan off.

"How long of a drive is it from here to Kontum?" Ethan asked he watched the trucks turn back onto Highway 14 and melt into a commotion of vehicles.

"Probably a few hours if they don't run into any trouble along the way," Bill wagered as he waved down a taxi.

"You don't think they'll get hit, do ya?"

"This time of day? Not real likely, but stranger shit has happened. But that's why they're packing iron, so don't worry about it," Bill reassured. "Hell, me and Ray have made that drive in the middle of the night, wasted. It's not that bad."

They piled into the sagging Citroen and headed for Pleiku City which sprawled just south of the airbase, and hung out downtown just long enough to grab an early dinner. They rumbled back into the airbase with another stolen deuce-and-a-half, stopped by supply and had the forklift operator load the entire back of their newly acquired deuce-and-a-half with pallets of beer and soft drinks. Bill reached into his pocket and produced a neatly preserved sheet of paper, type-printed, with a large stamp across the bottom that read "PAID" in bold black lettering.

"This is an old trick I learned while I was in the A-teams," he smirked as they pulled up to the supply terminal exit.

A skinny second lieutenant approached the driver's side and Bill handed him the piece paper. Taking the sheet, the lieutenant walked around to the back of the deuce and glanced around. Satisfied, he walked back around to Bill and handed the receipt back, then waved them through. Bill urged the truck forward until they cleared the terminal and met Highway 14 again. Once clear of the terminal, Bill handed Ethan the sheet, which was a receipt for several pallets of beer and soft drinks bought in April of 1968.

"When I was with A-333, we only paid for all that once," Bill elaborated. "We kept the invoice and just got the same thing every time we went back. The clerks never check the date – just gotta be sure to get the same thing every time."

"Pretty fucking slick," Ethan laughed. "I never woulda thought of that."

"I'm telling ya, kid. You stick with me long enough and you might just live through this fucked up war."

*   *   *

The countryside continued to roll by while they sped north on Highway 14. The sun was just beginning to slip below the horizon to the west, offering only a brief stretch of twilight before submitting to the foreboding mountains that wedged up against the tri-border region. It had been an uneventful ride up to that point but they'd made good conversation and enjoyed comparing notes on combat lore and what new tricks the NVA had recently been caught employing.

"I think I might extend my tour for another year," Ethan announced, somewhat off-topic, but none-the-less, one worth discussing.

"You do that, and *I'll* fucking shoot you," Bill warned with sarcasm. "Another year's too much; if you extend, do it in six month stints."

"Why's that?"

"Well, are you trying to stay with SOG?"

"Yeah, definitely."

"Well, I'll tell ya something, kid. There's no guarantee that SOG's gonna be in business for another year. The Saigon commandos and bigwigs in Washington may decide we've served our purpose and pull the plug. I mean, let's face it – the war's gone down the shitter."

Ethan listened as Bill expounded.

"If you extend for a year and SOG closes shop, who knows where you'll get stuck.

"Yeah, that's true," Ethan admitted.

"You're gonna wanna stay in-country," Bill figured. "The second you get back to a state-side assignment, like Bragg, you'll seriously regret your decision. You've been playing this game long enough to know the stakes. You're a good team leader and your little people trust you – there's something to be said for that. But if you extend for a year and something happens, like SOG closing the doors or the 5th Group pulling out, they'll send us all back to Bragg and we'll be stuck in permanent shit detail, and it'll be next to impossible to get out of it. There's already talk about Group pulling out soon."

He downshifted and wove around a convoy of ancient carts piled high with bamboo stalks and palm fronds drawn behind water buffalo. Ethan stared from his seat at the weathered farmers as they tended to their only means of a meager living. Seconds later, they were lost in a sea of red dust and diesel fumes.

"Besides," Bill added as he shifted gears, "if you extend for six months, that's one more month of extension leave each time; so for two six-month extensions, that's a total of two months leave… *anywhere* you wanna go!"

"Ohhh that *does* sound good," Ethan grinned.

He reflected fondly on the past eight months of his life. It hadn't been so bad in retrospect; he'd lost close friends to the grind of recon, yes, but they had all asked to be there. It didn't take much for all the emotion to flood back, bringing with it the memories of those fallen souls and their legacies along with it. He had become a part of something – something so tightly knit that it could only be described as family. He didn't have to serve in any other combat unit to know the bond that existed between those few who openly chose to run recon or fight with the Hatchet Force was unique *only* to them.

Then there was the club, a sort of tactical operations center for non-combat related affairs. It was a place where officers and enlisted men alike, from both Recon and the Hatchet Force could mix things up. It was a place where outsiders were generally not welcomed, regardless of rank and affiliation. People frequently got hurt in there, whether the source of the melee was a balled-up fist or just a few choice words from a fellow recon man. Devious mischief was carefully conjured up underneath that roof before being hatched by those who were the only people on the planet who could find the humor in such things. It was an existence that was so close to insanity, the dividing line was far too faded for most to see – a place where *everyone* shared the same dark, morbid sense of humor. Those in Recon and in the Hatchet Force were thought of as Neanderthals with an insatiable appetite for death and destruction – utter mayhem. Outsiders looking in only shook their heads in dismay, ashamed to be associated with such crude behavior and hooliganism. But the truth was, they *weren't* associated with them – it was only a *perceived* association. No one simply transferred into SOG and was immediately accepted; not Bill Delima or Joe Walker, or even Bob Howard. A seat inside that circle had to be earned, and the only way to earn it was to operate across the fence. That was the way it had to be.

"Shit," Bill mumbled. He leaned forward and squinted to get a clearer view through the bug-splattered windshield.

"What's up?"

"I think we might be running into an ambush."

"What? Where?"

"See all that shit in the middle of the road right where the bend is?"

"Yeah, looks like a trash heap," Ethan said, peering intently ahead.

"Those little fuckers block the road and make it so you can only drive through one spot. And then, *BOOM!* – you hit a mine and they assault the wreckage while your head's still spinning."

"NVA or VC?"

"Does it matter?" Bill fished a couple frag grenades from his ruck and placed them in his lap while steering with his other hand. "Here, plant your ass in that," he instructed as he pointed to a flak vest in the floorboard.

Ethan snatched the heavy vest up, opened it and put it in his seat, then folded it around his thighs.

"At least you won't get your balls blown off," Bill joked.

As they neared the roadblock, Ethan could see the way the enemy had intended for them to go – to the right, cutting the corner as the road banked. In the waning light he scanned the terrain at either side of the road where the ambush would inevitably start from. Dried rice paddies stretched out on both sides of the road with scrub and bramble and low elephant grass choking the pocket of the turn.

"Okay, get ready cause I ain't stopping for shit," Bill warned as he laid his carbine across his lap.

Ethan checked his CAR-15; double-taped magazines with eighteen rounds in each, all tracers for a psychological edge. He thumbed the selector from safe to full-auto; no need to rack the charging handle back – the chamber was always loaded. He licked his lips nervously and welcomed the fluid taste of adrenaline. His throat tightened like a snare drum as Bill downshifted and floored the truck, aiming it to the far left of the junk heap. Ethan glanced at the fearless misfit behind the wheel and noticed a hellish grin that defied the existence of any sanity. Feeling the muscles tightening in his own face, he realized he too was wearing that exact same grin.

Sparks winked at them from a dike about fifty meters out in the rice paddy as they smashed through the left side of the roadblock.

Pank! Thud! Thapp! Crack! Green tracers streaked across the hood and slammed into the windshield, and ripped through the canvas soft-top above their heads.

Ethan opened up with a volley of bright red tracers in return. Bill was lobbing frags up and over the cab with his left hand while steering with his right, pulling the straightened pins out with his teeth.

"Fucking John Wayne?!" Ethan laughed manically as he flipped the magazine over and slammed it back into the receiver. In a matter of seconds, they were past the elbow in the road with a swarm of green tracers chasing them. Bill's head was hanging out of the window and he was screaming obscenities in his best pidgin Vietnamese.

"If those motherfuckers hit my beer, so-help-me-God I'm gonna turn this fucking thing around and go back!" he stormed. He was so serious, it was funny.

"Fuck yeah, let's go back and kick their asses! Quick – tell me something to say in Vietnamese!" Ethan shouted as he ripped apart the tattered remnants of the canvas top. Bill rattled something off but Ethan was already standing up on the seat with his upper body poking through the soft-top facing backwards at the ambush.

"Uncle Ho fucks water buffalo!" he shouted as he fired a long burst at the fading dust cloud. He dropped back down into his seat, reloaded his CAR-15, and looked at Bill. The two of them broke into tears with side-splitting, gut-busting laughter.

"Uncle Ho fucks water buffalo!" Bill shouted as they laughed their way back to CCC in the growing darkness. "You're fucking crazy. I love it."

*   *   *

With great reluctance, the security detachment guarding CCC's west gate moved the old French armored car aside to allow the tattered deuce-and-a-half into the camp's perimeter. Once inside, Bill gunned the rig over to the club while blowing the horn and shouting for the rest of the recon delinquents to come help unload the booty. Soon, the entire club was standing outside – some sober, but most not.

Ethan kicked the shot-up windshield with both feet, sending the entire frame slamming down onto the hood of the truck. Everyone was laughing and cat-calling while the beer was being unloaded. Bill was personally inspecting every pallet to make sure none of his precious cargo had been shot to pieces during the ambush – all the while still vowing that if any of it was, he was getting his guns and going back. Yates was standing there with his arms folded across his chest, just scowling with suspicion.

"I don't wanna know how Recon suddenly wound up with three new deuce-and-a-halfs," he warned, "why two of them are loaded down with barroom furniture and why one is shot to shit. I don't wanna know where the new furniture came from, and I sure-as-shit don't wanna know where all that beer came from. What I *do* wanna know is where the hell the colonel's goddamn jeep is. He's been up my ass all fucking day, nagging me about which one of you shit-for-brains took it, and where the hell you took it to."

"No worries, *Dai-uy* – the colonel's wheels are padlocked up at the B-team compound," Bill smiled.

"Fuck me to tears, at least you thieves remembered to chain the goddamn thing down this time; can't have shit around here. And y'all get this heap of fucking shit outta my company area. I got half a mind to hog-tie your worthless asses, fly y'all out across the fence, and leave you there with neon-orange *chieu hoi* signs draped around your skinny necks. Let y'all be someone else's nightmare for a change."

"That's a pretty fucking specific threat," Ethan laughed. "You done that before?"

"Maybe."

The party was in full-bloom in short order and the beer was on the house. Nearly everybody from Recon Company was in attendance as were many from the Hatchet Force, along with SPAF pilots Rex Hill and Pete Johnston, and a number of the aircrews that supported them. Everyone was still laughing and carrying on about how Bill had conned the Air Force guys back in Pleiku, and it wasn't long after that when the ambush incident was recounted. The laughter rolled even harder when Bill jumped up on the bar and shouted, "Uncle Ho fucks water buffalo!" in his best impression of what Ethan had looked like. Then someone came up with the brilliant idea to mimic the gunfight scenes made popular in the movie *The Good, The Bad, and The Ugly*. There was a mad scramble for guns, and Ethan decided to use an old Smith & Wesson .38 complete with an oiled leather holster and belt he'd pilfered from supply a few months back. He grabbed a towel, cut a slit through the middle and used it for a poncho, then added his recon boonie-hat for good measure.

He strutted back to the club with his costume just as everyone was drawing straws to see who would duel who. To make things all the more fun, they took live ammo and pried the bullet from the casing, then packed the end of the case with a spitwad. With dummy rounds loaded, Ethan and Tom Waskovich put fifteen paces themselves with everybody gathered around, snickering and swilling booze. Someone began whistling the theme song to *The Good, The Bad, and The Ugly*.

"Ohhwiee-ohhwiee-ohhhh... wahhh-wahhh-waaahhhhh! "

Ethan garnished his best impression of the classic wide gunslinger stance and swept the makeshift poncho away from his right side, just like Clint Eastwood, which stirred a gaggle of cackles and hoots from the peanut gallery.

"Draw!" Bill shouted.

Pow! Pow! Fountains of sparks and flames blasted from the pistol barrels as he and Tom popped away at each other. It was too dark to be certain who had won, so they just kept shooting. And before any sober heads could prevail, everyone was shooting at each other outside the club. In typical fashion, the commotion rousted the entire camp and most of the staff personnel from the TOC, and the party was eventually broken up. Yates was fuming mad, as usual, and openly threatened to pistol-whip the next man that made his blood pressure climb. All the Yards were milling about their barracks, inspecting the ruckus and laughing at the debauchery perpetrated by their fearless counterparts. Ethan stumbled over to Nay and Hyuk, and they immediately broke into giggles at the sight of his getup.

"*Trung-si* Yok-son look like Yon Wang," Nui howled as he and Hyuk latched on to Ethan's arms and led him back to their barracks.

"You mean John Wayne." Ethan slurred and laughed.

"Yon Wang."

More giggles.

Nay stood by the door and shook his head at Ethan, "Always must make mad *Dai-uy* Yates."

"The *Dai-uy* loves me!" Ethan declared as his Yards helped him into the dingy room. Nay just shook his head and followed them inside.

Several naked light bulbs cast dirty light down upon the little peoples' room; part of the dwelling served as their common area where they cooked and ate, while the other half served as their quarters. There were several hammocks strung up on the support beams and individual cots scattered about with piles of equipment and weapons neatly organized at their ends.

Luc and Bo went back to the chicken that was cooking over a burning chunk of C4; another small fire was busy boiling a pot of rice. Luc flashed him a smile and a thumbs-up, then turned the chicken and basted it with its own blood they'd drained into a cup after killing it. Nui and Sol busied themselves with cleaning their weapons and the rest of them grab-assed while they waited for the dinner bell to ring. Ethan's stomach was rumbling like thunder at the aroma of their cooking, and soon, everyone was gorging themselves on the feast. The food was working to absorb the several gallons of beer he'd drank earlier and things were beginning to quiet down in the room. Nay took Ethan by his arm and showed him to his quarters – a hammock strung between two support pillars.

"You sleep here tonight," he smiled.

Ethan climbed clumsily into the hammock and rolled around until he grew comfortable. His little people came by one at a time just to smile and pat his arm or hold his hand for a few moments. It was customary and it symbolized a bond between them that few Americans had ever known. He watched them settle into their cots and hammocks, all except for Nay, who had taken up the nearest chair to watch over him with an almost fatherly-like presence. The lights were extinguished, all but for an old oil lamp that Nay kept by his side. He lay in the hammock, breathing in the fleeting aromas of the food they'd just shared, and he knew he would rest well among his boys. They were so simple, yet so morally and family oriented. They were his little people, his Wild Bunch, his Merry Little Band of Marauders and he loved them.

His thoughts began to drift away. He, Mark, and Paul were scheduled to leave for R&R the following morning. Bangkok and all its lustful secrets lay just a short flight away.

18

The RON was roaring and the party was in its full throes as Ethan, Mark, and Paul crept up to RT Iowa's team house-turned-bar, still wearing the custom tailored silk suits they'd bought on their first day in Bangkok. They looked like pimps with all the necessary trimmings and flair. Their week in paradise had been nothing short of spectacular: They bought the suits for dirt-cheap, selected and paid for their women, paid for a taxi driver to arrive on time at the Opera Hotel every day to serve as their personal guide, and generally ate, drank, and fornicated themselves blind for seven days.

The evening air was chilled and added a bit of twinge to the sweet revenge they'd been plotting since they'd landed at the Kontum airfield. Reynolds had forgotten to pick them up and since they'd blown every penny they'd taken, they had to bum a ride from a few guys at the B-team. No one had noticed when they finally rolled back through the gates late that afternoon, so they snuck over to the Yards' barracks and hid out until dark, deliberating on the coming retribution. They were really only out to snake Reynolds, but he was buried deep inside Iowa's little recon bar and desperate times called for desperate measures.

Oh well, Ethan snickered, *casualties of war…*

With a mini CS grenade in-hand, he nodded Mark to add the finishing touch to their ambush: a monofilament tripwire strung across the doorway at shin-level. All the boys were kicking back and cutting loose inside as Donovan's "Hurdy Gurdy Man" bumped over the sound system while the recon lies floated above the noise. Gassing a team house was a big no-no but they were out of ideas. Ethan pulled the pin on the little CS grenade and let the spoon *ping* away. He opened the door and rolled it inside, then pulled the door shut and ran around the corner where Mark and Paul were hunkered down. By the time he dipped behind the adjacent building, there was mass confusion inside the RON as chairs were being overturned and glass was breaking; suddenly, a single gunshot blasted a hole through the roof just as the door flung open and the entire commotion came spilling out onto the ground, courtesy of the tripwire. In a typical military installation, the entire base would have gone on high-alert and rushed out into fighting positions at the sound of gunshots and the whiff of teargas. Not at CCC. Even the staff commandos in the TOC were no longer alarmed at the sound of a few gunshots from inside the wire.

Teargas was billowing out from the opened door and the inside was all bleary and glowed from the strands of Christmas lights. Everyone was coughing and sneezing and rubbing their eyes, fighting for any relief they could get; some were so drunk by then, the riot gas didn't seem to have too much of an affect. Then out came Reynolds, the only one out of the whole bunch who had managed to find a gasmask. And as if that wasn't bad enough, he paused right at the tripwire, looked down, and stepped right over it.

"Dammit," Mark hissed. "He always comes out smelling like a rose."

"No shit, huh? Iowa ain't gonna be happy with us," Ethan chuckled. "Better get back to our racks and play like we don't know shit before we get caught."

With the beginning of a new month, new assignments were issued to all the active teams in rotation. Utah hadn't pulled Bright Light duty since the first of July, so they all figured they'd be heading out to Dak To in the coming days to pay their dues for a week, but Saigon had other, more pressing matters for them to tend to.

"Are you gentlemen familiar with Project Igloo White?" Major Zune asked them as he swept the veil away from the wall map inside the TOC, detailing CCC's area of operations.

"Only bits and pieces, sir; nothing solid," Ethan replied. "I know it's part of our PSYOPS program but that's about it."

Zune nodded to one of the men standing off to the side, signaling him to take the floor. Ethan could immediately tell they were all from SOG Headquarters in Saigon simply by their rigid posture and lack of personality; the tidy fatigues and mirrored boots didn't help their image either.

"Igloo White is managed by our OPS-33, Psychological Studies Branch. The project employs a range of high-tech, state-of-the-art devices that are capable of detecting both troop and vehicular movements using seismic and magnetic, and even acoustic sensors." The stubby PSYOPS major paused and turned his attention to a sheet-covered table and undressed his toys.

"These are just a few of the types of sensors we have in-place along the Ho Chi Minh Trail corridor. This particular sensor," he said as he picked one up, "is hand-dropped from passing aircraft. Upon impact the spike penetrates the ground so that only the base and antenna are left visible. As you can see, the antenna resembles a small sapling which is commonly found at ground-level in the jungle." The major returned the spear-like sensor to the table and picked up a smaller unit.

"This sensor runs off long-term batteries and measures seismic activity caused by large troop movements and vehicular traffic, and is designed to be hand-placed by recon teams." The base of the unit was about the size of a book and the antenna was flat, resembling a blade of elephant grass. "It's very easy to operate. You simply switch it on and place it by a major footpath or roadway and it does the rest of the work until the batteries die. We're also starting to use acoustic sensors which look similar to magnetic bombs, so if you see anything like that out there," he cautioned, "don't fuck with them. Leave 'em be."

"We don't make a habit of putting our guys in areas where we've dropped CBUs or magnet bombs, "Zune promised.

315

"Sir, how is this sensory data received?" Ethan asked.

"Excellent question, sergeant. We have a wall-sized map at the Royal Thai Air Force Base in Nakhon Phanom, Thailand; every time one of these sensors detects seismic activity, it transmits a signal to that map causing a light to flash, which discloses the location of the sensor and where the enemy activity is. This data is then used to determine where Arc Light strikes will go in, and where interdicting raids will be conducted by our Hatchet Forces. We sometimes like to send in recon teams to help us get a more concise picture about what's going on in a particular area where the sensors are constantly signaling activity."

"The Highway 165 corridor is teaming with seismic and magnetic sensors," Major Zune indicated with his hand on the wall map, "but it's the area just to the south of the main route that we're now concerned with. Aerial recon photos show several well-traveled footpaths and even some secondary roadway networks to the south of the highway that all cross over the border. Recon Team Illinois was targeted for Alpha-1 only a few weeks ago but the weather was shit and they never inserted.

"We know this area is hot but we need a clearer picture, and these sensors will give us that. The device your team will be deploying is the smaller version made to look like a blade of grass. You'll stage out of our secondary launch site up at Dak Pek. You guys are expert planners so I'll leave the rest up to you. Questions?"

"Will we have a Bright Light team on standby at Dak Pek?" Ethan asked. He had yet to run a mission that far north.

316

"Negative – the launch site isn't large enough to support more than one team, so plan accordingly. But if you really step into it, we'll mobilize one of the Hatchet Force companies. But don't count on that; y'all know how long it takes to make that happen."

"What about air assets?"

"SPAF-4 will be providing you with FAC support for the duration of your mission and will launch from Kontum each morning along with the other air packages."

"Who's our backseater?"

"Staff Sergeant Howard Davis," Zune said after referring to his notes.

Damn, good ol' Pete Johnston and Karate Davis, Ethan smiled. *This'll be a cinch with those two running the air show.*

"Is this one of your gentle propositions?" Ethan asked.

"Why?" Zune grinned. "You guilty of some crimes I should be made privy to?"

"Of course," Ethan laughed through his nose, "I've been in Bangkok for a week."

"I'd like to add one last thing if that's okay," the PSYOPS major broke in and moved back to the front of the room. "This technology is highly classified and top-secret, so at no point is anyone other than you three to handle this equipment, under any circumstances. Clear?" Ethan, Eddie, and Bruce all nodded silently without looking up from their notes. "Good; now, I've brought along two of my guys who will get you up to speed on the mechanics of the sensors, where to put them, and any other questions you may need answered. The three of us will also be accompanying your team out to Dak Pek to oversee the mission, and to assist in handling and maintaining the equipment." Ethan looked up from his notes to the PSYOPS major, and then shot a brief glance to Zune.

"Care to clarify *exactly* what it is that you intend to oversee?"

"Well, we –"

"Ethan," Major Zune interjected, "they understand you're in command of the ground operation; they just want to be there when you boys place the sensors." Zune's final say couldn't have come at a better time; his two cents reinforced the amount of confidence he had in Ethan as a One-Zero.

The PSYOPS major nodded in agreement, and with that, the briefing was adjourned.

The three of them strolled back to their team house to begin hammering out the details; they had four days to train, familiarize themselves with the sensor equipment, and plan the overall execution of the mission.

"We're gonna take the whole family up there," Ethan said while they scoured through several different target folders that detailed Highway 165 and the surrounding area. "Not much choice since we don't have any other means of Bright Light support. Plus, it'll be a good chance to get all the Yards into the field." His tactical brain began spinning and they spent the rest of the day discussing the formations and structure of the team. This wasn't going to be a typical "sneak-and-peak" recon mission; they would stage from Dak

Pek every day, so their time on the ground would be dictated by how fast they could place the sensors and extract.

"Me, Luc, Hyuk, and Nui will be the insertion team. Bruce – you're flying chase in case we take on wounded. That will leave you," Ethan turned to Eddie, "to lead the rest of the Yards on our Bright Light team, so y'all gotta be ready to sling some lead in case we get our tits in the wringer. Bo should do fine on point for you since he walks Luc's slack in normal formation."

With that done, they held a briefing with the Yards detailing the team's new structure and what their primary objectives entailed, but mentioned nothing of the sensors; those details were for American ears only. After that, they began laying out their equipment and weapons list.

The insertion team needed to move quickly and carry a light load, yet still have the firepower to slug it out with the NVA if need be until Eddie's Bright Light element could get to them. In typical fashion, they would all carry their CAR-15s and chopped-down M-79 grenade launchers, and Ethan would haul the radio in addition to the sensors in his rucksack.

Bo would run point for Eddie's Bright Light element and Noon would cover their back-trail; both elected to carry their chopped RPD light machineguns. As a seven-man rescue element, they would be packing tons of ammo and water, as well as a small assortment medical supplies such as blood expander, morphine Syrettes, and compression bandages. Just the bare essentials.

319

"Bruce, you're flying chase with the insertion package," Ethan said as a matter-of-fact. "You gotta be Johnny-on-the-spot if we get our asses kicked."

"I'm there," he nodded.

They loaded up in full kit, split up into their respective elements, and spent the rest of the day on the range, going through the motions. The next morning, they met with the PSYOPS experts over in the TOC for a crash-course lesson in operating and planting the sensors. The NCOs were impressively knowledgeable in regards to the sensors and it only took them an hour to cover the dos and don'ts. Ethan and the others were expecting a more in-depth briefing, but there wasn't much to the equipment. The sensors operated on long-term batteries and all that was required was to switch the unit on and stash it in the bushes.

"I don't know why those PSYOPS gurus think they have to tag along – there ain't much to those things," Bruce mumbled in his Puerto Rican tongue after the briefing.

"They probably just wanna feel like they're getting closer to the war effort or some shit," Eddie guessed. "Those dudes have spent their entire tours inside a concrete bunker down at SOG Headquarters. Hell, none of 'em have a CIB and I'd bet money they haven't even fired a rifle since Basic."

"The two techs seem like good lads to me," Ethan admitted, "but I can see that major pissing me off at some point."

The next three days were spent at the range practicing live-fire IA drills, formation movements, sensor placement, and rope and ladder extractions. Utah's morale was sky-high and the Yards were all business. The night before they flew out to Dak Pek, Karate Davis swung by their team house to discuss the mission and help plan exactly how the insertions would unfold.

"Usually, the PSYOPS guys give one of our teams a few sensors and they'll plant them during the course of a mission, so this method is pretty unusual," Karate leveled. He eyeballed a map sheet and a collection of aerial photos detailing Highway 165. "I'm guessing the brass will be watching this one closely."

Since they were getting dedicated FAC support, Karate seemed confident they could plant two or three sensors a day, depending on how long their luck held out.

"We'll fly out, pick a good spot near a trail and send y'all in to plant the sensors, then pluck you back out before the NVA can respond," Karate smiled, "and then do it all over again." He had a knack for making it sound so simple, and by the way he described things, it almost seemed *too* easy.

A little while later, John Plaster dropped by to wish the team luck; he'd lost quite a bit of weight while fighting bacillary dysentery but he had his legs under him again and was looking much better. He was also the newly appointed One-Zero for RT Illinois. John took a look at some of the aerial photographs and warned them of the abundance of antiaircraft positions that covered the highway's corridor. His concern was genuine and they thanked him for the heads-up.

Early the next morning, all twelve members of RT Utah trucked up to the Kontum airfield, accompanied by the three PSYOPS staffers, and an additional truckload of equipment and provisions they'd need to sustain a week-long mission up at Dak Pek. Since the camp was CCC's northern-most launch site, the team needed a more efficient means of transportation – a single aircraft that could get everything and everyone in a single trip.

"Howdy, Yanks!" the Australian loadmaster chortled as he lowered the cargo ramp on the back of the DCH-4 Caribou. "I reckon you're the blokes we'll be ferrying up to Dak Pek today, aye?"

"That's right, boss," Ethan smiled. He loved the way Aussies talked.

"Soon as we get everything loaded up, we'll be on our way."

It took everyone about 45 minutes to get everything packed up and strapped down. With everyone inside, the ramp was raised and the cargo bay sealed off. The aircraft assumed position and began taxiing in line to take off.

"G'day gents," a voice piped up over a jerry-rigged intercom system. "I'd like to welcome you to Flight Two-Niner-Charlie, non-stop service to Dak Pek Special Forces Camp, Republic of South Vietnam. Flight time will be short and the weather remains partly cloudy. My name is Terry Windsor and I'll be your captain today. I'd like to request that any alcohol brought onboard please be diverted to the cockpit at this time, as myself and me crew are fresh out.

"The Royal 'Stralian Air Force has designated this a non-smoking flight. Please remain seated during the flight, and try to refrain from discharging any firearms or explosives until we are safely on the ground at Dak Pek.

"Welcome aboard, gents."

The flight out to Dak Pek was short as promised and uneventful, and the landing rough. As quickly as they could, they dismounted the Caribou and formed up into an assembly line to expedite the unloading process. Everything was stacked neatly in one of the bunkers next to the airstrip, which also housed a huge stockpile of 2.75-inch rockets, 7.62mm mini-gun rounds, and 40mm grenade rounds – all of which were used to rearm the Cobra gunships.

"I reckon that's about it, aye?" the loadmaster barked as the last of the equipment moved down the line and into the bunker. "See you blokes on the return flight."

They thanked the Aussies for the lift and bid them safe passage back to Kontum.

As the Caribou careened down the runway, Ethan finally took a minute to survey the launch site and the surrounding area. Steep mountains loomed over the bare rolling hills that made up the Dak Poko Valley, while the peaks and ridgelines remained lost in passing clouds. The airstrip ran northeast-to-southwest and was constructed of a combination of PSP, gravel, and dirt. A precarious ridge jutted several hundred feet skyward just south of the runway which forced all fixed-wing aircraft to land on the north end of the strip. A failed landing approach to the south meant almost certain death since fixed-wing aircraft couldn't climb fast enough to clear the ridge. And as if that wasn't bad enough, the strip had been cut straight through by a low hill that ran perpendicularly *through* the runway, allowing only inches of clearance under the wings of taxiing aircraft. SOG's launch site was located at the northeast corner of the strip near the foot of the A-team's perimeter. The launch site itself was meager and quite crude in comparison to their primary site down at Dak To. There wasn't much to the place besides the airstrip and a few bunkers to house the team and equipment. Several large fuel bladders sat at the edge of the strip protected by sandbag revetments.

After stowing the equipment and getting the team's living accommodations in order, Ethan put a few of the boys into a relaxed security perimeter around the launch site while the others cooked food and grab-assed. The A-team's executive officer and team sergeant came down the hill to gather the three PSYOPS analysts and show them to their temporary quarters. They had made previous arrangements with the camp's commanding officer since the launch site wasn't large enough to accommodate that many people. It was the first time Ethan had been up to Dak Pek, so he joined the camp's welcoming committee and took the grand tour.

Special Forces A-team 242 had setup shop on a collection of seven hills situated on the eastern side of the airstrip. The camp had been constructed back in 1962, making it one of the first A-camps built during the war. There were three main hills, the lowest of them occupied by the twelve-man A-team and a security platoon of Montagnards. The other two hills were manned by a Vietnamese Special Forces team, and a few companies of Montagnard strikers. The only above-ground structure on the American hill was a square rock building that served as the A-team's mess hall and club; everything else was built underground and made of concrete, accessible through the mess hall/club. Dak Pek was truly one of a few Special Forces show camps in Southeast Asia. After touring the camp, they spent the remainder of the day preparing their equipment for the next day's insertions. If it had been Dak To, they could've trained a little more but the mountains were too close, and that meant the NVA were too.

*   *   *

The first two days of insertions went as smooth as Karate had planned. Every morning at sunrise the air package would thunder into Dak Pek and set down on the north end of the airstrip, top off fuel, and await the launch order. Karate would then select a good sit-down LZ and scramble the air assets. En route to the primary LZ, the insertion chopper would make a false landing about a kilometer away where they would drop off one or two "Nightingale" devices to create a diversion. The Nightingale device was another ingenious CIA-born creation consisting of a piece of wire mesh bordered by a wooden frame, and was about the size of a coffee table. Covering the wire mesh were a series of firecrackers all wired together by a time-delayed fuse. When the fuse was initiated and the time-delay expired, the firecrackers would cook off, creating an impressive illusion of a large firefight. It worked so well that it actually sounded like small-arms fire and exploding grenades from a distance.

Once the Nightingales were dropped off, Karate would then direct the Cobras in to troll for ground fire, and then send the insertion ship in. Once on the ground, Karate would stack the air package in orbit while Utah found suitable locations to plant the sensors. Because they were inserting so close to heavily-travelled sections of the Trail, Ethan elected not to lay-dog; time was simply too precious, so they moved decisively to place the sensors, but stealth was still of utmost importance. Once done, they'd quickly extract and head back to the launch site to regroup and refuel for a second pass. To keep the NVA guessing, Karate staggered their insertions at all times of the day and never in a set pattern, but that tactic only worked for the first few days. During the third day, they began receiving light ground fire from the north and west near the main highway, and by the end of the fourth day, they were taking large-caliber antiaircraft fire from the same areas. On the fifth day, they were only able to make one insertion during *pok*-time; the team got in relatively easy, but had to ride strings coming out as a tremendous volume of antiaircraft fire filled the skies.

Up until that point, the PSYOPS gurus had spent most of their time on the American hill inside the camp's wire, venturing out only long enough to monitor the insertions in the bunker down by the launch site. After discussing things over with Karate, Ethan decided to abort insertions for a few days, hoping the area might cool down in their absence. His four-man insertion team hadn't yet engaged the NVA on the ground, but they all knew it was only a matter of time.

Days six and seven were spent on a much-needed stand-down at the launch site, but they could all tell the PSYOPS major was becoming impatient with the inactivity. By midmorning on the eighth day the major was back down on the airstrip harassing the team, wanting to know why they weren't planning any insertions for the third straight day. They clearly explained the situation to him, and even had Karate and Pete Johnston, and the aircrews corroborating their assessment, but the major simply wouldn't listen.

Early the next morning, the air package arrived right on schedule and Karate reported the target-area felt much cooler than the previous days. The team was already busy painting their faces and reviewing their predetermined escape and evasion routes when the major stormed back down the hill.

"Sergeant," he barked, "quit sandbagging and get this fucking show on the road."

That was the last straw.

Ethan wrapped up the pre-mission briefing while Eddie and Bruce got the little people loaded up on the choppers. Rotors spooling and aircrews waiting, he waved the major over for a quick word. When they were close enough to speak into each others' ear, Ethan casually turned the major's back towards the bird and shoved him onboard.

"Let's go, let's go!" Ethan yelled.

The Huey was up and soaring out over the valley before the major could even react. Ethan pulled a spare headset on and shared a few laughs with the pilots before the major elbowed in on the net and proceeded to express his discontent with such a stunt.

"You're as good as court-martialed!" he vowed.

"No sir," one of the pilots laughed. "You jumped in!"

Karate called a few minutes later with an LZ near a secondary roadway just south of Highway 165.

"Are you ready to earn your CIB today, sir?" Ethan mused into the headset mic.

Ten minutes later and they were spiraling wildly down through the treetops before leveling off, flying nap-of-the-earth while the gunships trolled over the LZ. In seconds, the insertion ship flared over the hole just long enough for Ethan and Bruce to kick out two Nightingale devices. Then they were clawing for altitude while heading north for the highway. The adrenaline was there again, like it always was, but not without the fear and the uncertainty.

No time for that shit now, Ethan decided. *Let it turn to something else. Make it turn to something else.*

The gunships were drawing figure-eights over the primary LZ, but nothing took the bait.

"Karate, this is Panther Two-Five. This one looks cold," one of the Cobra pilots transmitted.

"Okay, looks like we may have us an LZ to work with here," Karate drawled. "Gladiator One-Six, you're on deck to deliver the package."

Ethan pounded fists with Luc and readied himself in the open doorway. He looked back at the major who was plastered against the bulkhead, confused about whether he should be infuriated or terrified. Ethan grinned and pulled the headset off as the ship careened down to a collection of bomb craters not more than two-hundred meters south of a secondary roadway. Before common sense could tell him that it was all a very bad idea, he was on the ground, sprinting for all his worth behind Luc while Nui and Hyuk were on his heels. They hit the tree-line and went to the ground as the choppers pulled out and took up formation to the south. He fought to catch his breath while he scoured the surrounding hills for any movement. The jungle was thick and choked with heavy bramble thickets and wait-a-minute vines, but nothing was moving out there.

"Karate, this is Hollywood. We're on the ground, moving at three-five degrees."

Without waiting for a reply, he stashed the radio handset on his shoulder strap and gave Luc the signal to move up the hillside that separated them from the secondary roadway. At the top, they discovered a well-concealed footpath that appeared to parallel the roadway, moving in an east-to-west direction. Its surface was hard-packed and showed constant use. They quickly crossed and scurried downhill and into a brush thicket that lined the roadway. Hyuk pointed out a perfect stand of grass nestled just off the road at the edge of the tree-line. The Yards broke into defensive perimeter mode while Ethan removed one of the seismic sensors from his ruck. He planted the base inside the middle of the grass patch then erected the antenna and switched the unit on.

A roar of small-arms fire erupted far to the south and for an instant, he'd nearly forgotten about the two Nightingales they'd dropped off. With that little bit of reassurance, Ethan looked nervously up and down the dirt road just beyond the edge of the jungle; the roadway was barely twenty meters to his front and fully operational despite thousands of bombs that had been dropped along its route. The immediate jungle that had once concealed it had long since been vaporized.

"Karate, this is Hollywood. We're ready for a spare-three-niner."

"Okay bro, how do you feel about coming on the same LZ?"

"Not too wild about it," Ethan leveled, "but I feel like we might be running outta luck."

"Okay I'm sending the gunships in to make a pass," Karate called. "Sit tight."

A short minute later the Cobras spun over the hilltop they'd just crossed, skimming the treetops. Gunfire crackled and tracers creased sky as they rolled over the ridge. Ethan tucked under cover and pulled the handset to his ear while the Yards surrounded him in a tight defensive perimeter.

"Karate, Cobras are taking fire from the top of the ridge we just crossed."

"We see it, Hollywood. Get small – the gunships are inbound and hot."

They got low as the Cobras zipped back in unloading their rockets and cannons; molten frag whizzed over their heads and ripped through the woods. AKs and light machineguns opened back up and chased the menacing warbirds away from the hilltop. Suddenly, the low thumping of a distant .51-caliber opened up on one of the gunships as it was turning inbound to line up for a second pass on the hilltop, and the NVA had them pegged. A large fireball engulfed the gunship momentarily and a delayed explosion reverberated through the hills only seconds later. The bird wobbled and dipped, then climbed for altitude while thick black smoke boiled out from behind it.

"Panther Two-Three, can you make it back to the lima-sierra?" Karate called.

"Karate, you gotta fix on that gun?" Ethan asked.

"Yeah, I got it spotted. About to work the area over now."

Seconds later, they could hear Cobras swarming over the gun position several hundred meters to the west, firing rockets and cannons. Things went silent in their immediate area for a few moments and then they could hear the enemy reorganizing above them where they'd found the trail.

"Karate, this is Hollywood," he whispered. "Lotta NVA still moving around on that hilltop. They're blocking our way out."

"Okay, I think we knocked that fifty-one out. I'm sending the gunships back in to clear y'all a path."

Minutes later, the Cobras swooped back over and raked the hill with everything they had before turning inbound and making a final pass.

"Hollywood, bro," Karate called again, "gunships and slicks are returning to the lima-sierra to rearm and refuel. I've got two sets of Spads and more Cobras coming up on station, zero-five mikes out.

"Beaucoup NVA that way, *Trung-si*," Luc pointed towards the hill.

"Karate, we can't see much from here, but I can still hear them moving around up there. Gimme a new LZ so we can get outta here."

"Okay... okay, there's one about four-hundred mikes at one-ten degrees from where you are."

"Roger, we're on the move. Out."

After shooting an azimuth, Ethan pointed Luc in their new direction of travel and gave him the signal to double-time it. Just then, the hillside came alive with khaki and olive-drab uniforms as the NVA broke cover and started maneuvering down towards them. They tried to slip away but the NVA had closed in too quickly.

Gunfire cracked and tracers burned past their heads. Without a shred of hesitation, they dropped to their knees and opened up with everything they had. They dumped a magazine apiece, fired their M-79s, and peeled away while Nui covered them from behind his RPD.

Ethan dumped another magazine into the NVA giving Nui just enough cover to peel off. He pitched a white phosphorous grenade rigged with teargas powder, clambered to his feet, and ran for all his worth. Muffled sounds and a dull ringing in the pit of his brain that constantly grew louder and sharper, but he couldn't worry about that. Wait-a-minute vines clawed at his face and snatched at his equipment as he smashed through the tangle and kept running. The ringing in his ears soon stopped and he was able to hear himself crashing through the woods and breathing heavily, and then there was Karate's voice crackling over the radio.

"Hollywood, do you read me? Break squelch twice if you can't talk. Spads are rolling inbound. Get your people away from that hill."

Hyuk suddenly materialized through the lush foliage in front of him, waving him past while pointing the muzzle of his CAR-15 over their all-too-obvious back-trail.

"Go, *Trung-si*," Hyuk urged with eyes wild.

Ethan bolted past the little Montagnard and quickly caught up with Luc and Nui, while pressing the radio handset to his soiled and sweaty face.

"Karate, we fired some dudes up and we're on the run," he gasped between each lungful of stale air. "*Beaucoup* bad guys behind us."

"Okay partner, hang tight while I vaporize 'em."

As quickly as Ethan heard the Spads' droning props, they were lost in a fury of deafening explosions that shook and rocked the earth all around them. A swell of concussion waves rolled out and away from the direction of the hilltop and flattened them all to the ground while molten frag and debris shredded the lush canopy to fluttering bits. A rushing breeze sifted through the leaves and over their crumpled mass, carrying with it the acrid smell of expended explosives and molten metal, and cooked flesh. Ethan's ears were ringing again while his temples throbbed and pounded to the rhythm of his heartbeat. He searched his little peoples' stunned faces for any signs of injury. Then they were up and running again, and Luc was constantly zigzagging their route of travel to stump trackers and to avoid any possible ambushes that awaited their arrival.

When his ears finally quit ringing again, Ethan was back on the radio, supplying Karate with another sitrep and the progress of their movement. The Spads were busy working the hilltop and their back-trail thoroughly over while the Cobras were making gun-runs fifty meters to their front. If they moved too fast or too slow, the risk of being hit by friendly fire was almost certain. It was an intricate display of spectacular firepower coordinated in brilliant concert to their forward progress on the ground. There was no margin for error.

More antiaircraft fire opened up on the slow-rolling Skyraiders from the north and west while sporadic small-arms pecked away at the Cobras. Karate was stacking air support by the dozens and began sending fast-movers in first since their loitering time on station was limited. Ethan monitored the radio traffic as they made passes on several spotted antiaircraft positions a few thousand meters away. They heard the fast-movers kick their afterburners first, and then came the booming concussions of 250 and 500-pounders and the *kawoosh!* of napalm as it sloshed and engulfed the jungle. The team had slowed down to a labored walk, doing their best to exercise stealth while maintaining a quickened pace. Karate reported them being just shy of the alternate LZ and that everything appeared cold from the air. Meanwhile, the Cobras had expended their ordnance and were en route to topping off back at Dak Pek just as the first pair rolled back on station and picked up where they'd left off. Accompanying the Cobras were the extraction ships, two of which carried Eddie and his Bright Light element. Karate advised them to stay high and to the east unless things got bad. The last few meters to the secondary LZ remained an uneventful jaunt while the zoomies stayed busy pounding the antiaircraft emplacements on the surrounding ridgelines. The small-arms fire had finally been stemmed by the air strikes Karate had put in on the hill and the immediate area.

They were coming down a gentle, rolling slope when the LZ began to take shape through the trees about thirty meters ahead. Two pairs of Cobras were waiting impatiently off in the distance, holding their ordnance in reserve in case the team made contact again and needed instant air support while Karate orchestrated the Spads into pattern. They silently penetrated a dense stand of bamboo just inside the northwestern tree-line at the edge of the small clearing. Beyond the bamboo and the tangle, the LZ appeared to be little more than a grass-covered clearing large enough to sit two Hueys in.

"Karate, this is Hollywood; we're at the secondary LZ, ready to go," he breathed into the mic.

"Okay sit tight. Gunships will make a pass first. Wait for me to give you the go-ahead to move into the open – I don't want the Cobras to fire y'all up by accident."

The jungle remained eerily silent around them while the zoomies kept pounding the NVA antiaircraft positions farther to the northwest. A minute later, two Cobras came trolling over the clearing not more than a hundred feet above the ground, but nothing took the bait. The gunships swung wide and pulled up, but stayed close in case the situation deteriorated.

"Hollywood, Gladiator One-Six is dropping in; get ready for a quick sit-down."

"Thanks bro, we're on the move," he whispered as he patted Luc's shoulder.

The little pointman moved forward while keeping low, allowing his eyes to track with the muzzle of his CAR-15. They could hear the rotors change in pitch as the extraction ship whisked toward the ground in a near-vertical, gut-wrenching spiral. They smashed through the tangle brush and wait-a-minute vines before spilling into the grassy LZ but met an instant problem. The elephant grass was easily about twelve feet tall and practically impossible to push through. The chopper flared out several feet over the clearing, just beyond them. The intense rotor wash worked to flatten the grass directly beneath the ship causing it to whip violently about. The thin, serrated edges sliced through their exposed skin while they fought as hard as they could to get beneath the Huey. Bruce and the crew chief were on their stomachs, waiting to pull the team onboard. The Yards had their machetes out and were hacking a swath through the tangle. Both door gunners leaned into their M-60s and began hosing the tree-line with red tracers once they knew where the team was. The pilots expertly nosed the bird closer and closer until Ethan and his little people were directly beneath them. The rotors were chewing into the overhanging tree limbs, making mulch of the sappy foliage, but the skids were still too high. Ethan motioned the bird lower while the crew chief mouthed into his headset. The chopper finally sunk lower and closed the gap. Ethan slung his CAR-15, turned and grabbed Nui and tossed him up.

Small-arms fire cracked behind them and licked the side of the chopper but the door gunners weren't letting up. Ethan and Luc helped Hyuk up next just as the Cobras rolled in and began firing up the adjacent hillsides. The major suddenly appeared in the doorway and latched on to Ethan's arm, yelling for him to get onboard. Ethan ripped his arm away and used what was left of his sapped strength to throw Luc into their waiting hands before he himself was pulled up into the cabin. The ship banked violently to the starboard side a few feet above the grass as the pilot collected airspeed before leveling off and zooming out over the treetops. The door gunners were standing on the skids and firing backwards. Ethan tried desperately to squirm into a sitting position so that he too could return fire but he couldn't get enough room to free his weapon. Once they were out of the hole, he checked his men then grabbed the last spare headset and broke communications to let Karate know they'd all gotten out clean.

*   *   *

The launch site fluttered with deliberate activity as the air package cleared the valley and sunk in towards the northern end of the airstrip. Pete Johnston and Karate Davis had already set down on the runway and were waiting nearby with the PSYOPS NCOs and both pilots from Panther Two-Three whose gunship had been crippled by antiaircraft fire earlier that day. There was also a large reaction force preparing to mount up in the Kingbees that sat at the very end of the airstrip. At a glance, the reaction force appeared to be roughly two platoons from one of CCC's Hatchet Force companies, but as the two gunship pilots explained, they had asked the A-team for volunteers since a CCC Hatchet Force would have taken several hours to mobilize that far north. Although they weren't a part of SOG, they were still Special Forces soldiers with a rabble of loyal Montagnards, and desperate times called for desperate measures. Ethan, Eddie, and Bruce spoke briefly with the four A-team NCOs who had volunteered and immediately noticed the relief in their faces when they found out they weren't going to be inserting into Laos. Regardless, Ethan knew they would have gone if the situation had been dire, and that meant as much to him and his people as the action itself.

The remaining hours of the day were well spent decompressing around the launch site; the A-team organized a small hunting party and managed to bag a few deer from the mouth of the valley. By dusk, the Yards were feverishly preparing the feast while everyone congregated around the raging bonfire they'd started on the east side of the airstrip, well away from the ammo bunker and fuel bladders. As the fire crackled and the venison simmered, the gravity of the day's events began to sink in for them all. Nearly every chopper involved in the operation had taken hits from small-arms fire, and two were inoperable – both of which had managed to limp back to the launch site.

Pete Johnston joked about Jane Fonda and put everyone in stitches while the Yards constantly streamed away from the glowing coals with sizzling delicacies and fresh fruit for their American counterparts to feast upon.

With his belly stuffed, Ethan dropped back against the small mound of sandbags he was using for a seat and stared into the flames that licked towards the star-studded ceiling. Gritty combat was still fresh on his clammy skin but all he could think about was the sheer luck the whole operation had been graced with. He pondered how long it would hold out – for himself and his teammates, but also for the others in Recon Company and the Hatchet Force, as well as the aircrews that supported them. It wasn't something he often dwelled on but combat had a nasty way of reminding a man of his own mortality.

19

"What the hell's going on?!" Ethan shouted as he followed the others toward the club.

"New York's in the shit," Mark shouted. "They uncovered a shitload of bunkers a few hours ago and tried to nab a prisoner. That's all I know."

They spilled through the doors just as Tom Lois hushed the crowd to deliver the latest news; his reluctance was evident.

"I was just in the TOC; St. Martin's hit bad and they're surrounded."

"Where's their fucking air support?!" John Plaster demanded.

"S-3 made them call Spads in on the camp before they assaulted, but they were off target. Karate's got zoomies and Cobras en route, but they're still a few minutes out. Covey's keeping Chuck's head down with marking rockets and Karate's shooting from the backseat with his CAR-15."

"Jesus Christ," Ethan mumbled; he looked back outside at the waning afternoon daylight.

"Why the fuck did they kick a hornets' nest this late in the day?" Pete Mullis raged. "And why the fuck did S-3 make 'em blow the element of surprise?"

No one could answer.

"Goddammit, I wish those fuckheads in the TOC would butt-out before they get someone killed!" Ray Fuller slung a half-empty beer can into the nearest wall.

Emotions were starting to boil as multiple debates broke out amongst the mob. Just as some were beginning to promise bloodshed over at the TOC, Norm Doney and Bob Howard entered the club with reassuring news.

"They're out and everyone's alive," First Sergeant Doney announced.

Cheers instantly erupted from corner-to-corner. Both senior NCOs quickly calmed the mob down and elaborated on exactly what had happened to New York. John St. Martin had been hit in the opening volley by three AK rounds – once in the stomach, another in his thigh, and the last in his ankle. His assistant team leader, Ed Wolcoff, charged forward and was able to drag St. Martin back to safety. The gunshot to John's abdomen had nearly left him eviscerated, so all Wolcoff could do was tuck his team leader's shirt into his pants and urge him to hold on while he and John Blaauw organized the Yards to keep fighting the NVA off until the choppers arrived.

It was touch-and-go for the young One-Zero during the next few days after having lost so much blood and going through emergency surgery in Pleiku, but he held on tight and was medevac'd back to the States where he faced a long road to recovery. Ed Wolcoff had performed heroically during the ensuing firefight, and was duly appointed as the team's new One-Zero; Blaauw had distinguished himself during the battle as well and was moved into the assistant team leader slot.

The news of RT New York's ordeal had Ethan's emotions in a headlock and from where he was sitting everyone else in the company had experienced the same thing. That was just the way it was. First came the initial shock and then came the outrage and anger; afterwards, there was nothing but a lonely feeling of total helplessness and desperation. And right when they began to accept the inevitable, suddenly, people were alive and were going to make it back, almost as if someone had been playing a cruel joke on them the entire time.

"You!" Captain Yates bellowed and pointed with a long, hotdog-like finger aimed right at Ethan's chest. Ethan looked at John Plaster to his right and then at Mark and Tom Waskovich across the table, hoping their fearless commanding officer had fingered one of them instead. "Yeah, that's right buddy, you, Ethan Jackson," Yates nodded as he and Bob Howard moved through the elated crowd and surrounded their table. "What's this shit I hear about you kidnapping that PSYOPS major the other day and forcing him to go across the fence with you yahoos?"

"Who the hell told you that lie, *Dai-uy*?" Ethan chuckled. "He volunteered, honest."

Bob just stood there with his arms folded across his rigid chest, raked smile, shaking his head while everyone at the table snickered.

"I ain't buying that shit for one minute," Yates promised. "But however it went down, he must already be over it 'cause I just got paperwork recommending you for a Bronze Star."

Ethan sighed while the others erupted into catcalls.

"Ohhh, look at this fuck'n hero right here," Mark guffawed while the others laughed.

"That's a buncha bullshit," Ethan argued.

"You sure about that?"

"Yeah *Dai-uy*," Ethan nodded, "creative writing, nothing more."

"Very well," Yates gave in. "I'll see to it the paperwork gets lost. By the way, good work up there, even if ninety percent of those sensors y'all placed got wasted by Karate's air strikes!"

He melted back into the hubbub, cackling like a wild animal at Ethan's expense.

The rest of the week was slow and uneventful for a change; the team was tired and had been run hard during the past month, but it earned them a much-needed break from the war. They mingled in the club and with the Yards, skipped company formations and slept in late, and spent their afternoons catching up on mail and watching movies over at the club. Unfortunately, other teams weren't so lucky.

Ken Worthley's RT Florida was busy poking around in northeast Cambodia's Base-Area 609 , not more than two kilometers south of where Ethan's team had gotten trapped by the weather before finding the flooded NVA encampment. Feeling the odds swing in Florida's favor, the team ambushed a small party of NVA officers and captured a leather case, then shot their way clear. They were coming out on strings when an AK burst caught them in midair. Tragically, Ken was killed instantly and two other teammates were slightly wounded.

Just as all those whose time had come before his, Ken Worthley's sacrifice was recognized and his loss mourned in the club that evening, but more importantly, his life celebrated. For the rest of the night, all anyone could talk about was how much respect and admiration they reserved for the fallen recon One-Zero. Bob Howard left to return to the States a few days later to accept his long-overdue Medal of Honor, but not before he personally escorted Ken's body back to his hometown in Minnesota.

As it turned out, the leather case Worthley's team snatched off the dead NVA colonel was stuffed full of highly-classified material which named enemy agents who had penetrated the South Vietnamese government and military infrastructure. One of the names in the documents matched that of a suspected mole who was working under the 5th Group's Project Gamma. The rumors about the NVA having eyes and ears inside Special Forces had proven true and the mole was executed, but where there was one, there were many. A few days later, Armed Forces Radio announced the death of Ho Chi

Minh, the North Vietnamese communist leader. Not a week later, Utah was back in the sling, sitting in the TOC while Major Zune gave them the rundown.

"Shit's happening fast and Saigon's not waiting," he told them. "In three days, an Arc Light is going in on this exact spot." The major's index finger pegged a valley on the wall map that looked all too familiar. "That's right, the flooded base-area y'all uncovered last month. And as y'all know, RT Florida seized top-secret documents from an NVA colonel they killed just south of this valley. We're not sure which unit the colonel belonged to just yet, but we have reason to believe he was part of the 66th NVA Regiment. In two days, Illinois will be inserted about six klicks south of this valley and they'll be digging for the 66th as well."

Zune left the map and stepped a little closer.

"Boys, the 66th is the same bunch who slugged it out with the 1st Cav in the Ia Drang Valley back in '65, and they almost overran Ben Het in March using PT-76s." The major paused for a moment to let the intelligence sink in. "These guys got their shit together. So we're gonna vaporize that base-area and you guys are gonna pull a bomb-damage assessment just as soon as the dust settles. Company A of the Hatchet Force will mobilize out to Dak To to back you up. Any questions?"

"Major fucking Doom," Bruce swore as they made for the team house. "I feel like we've been on his shitlist for months. We're fucked, Ethan. This is a page right outta Billy fucking Waugh's handbook."

"Billy Waugh... Billy Waugh...," Eddie mumbled to himself. "Why does that name sound familiar?"

"Special Forces living legend," Ethan said. "Has an insatiable appetite for suicide missions and loves to drag unsuspecting victims like us in with him.

"Where's that crazy bastard at now?" Bruce asked

"Somewhere with SOG, no doubt."

"Probably the only outfit who'd hire him on," Bruce wagered. "See, him and Major Doom go way back. Billy's got his *good deals* and our lovely Carl Zune has what he calls *gentle propositions*. Same damn arrangement, different fucking name. Either way, we're fucked."

"I knew coming here was a bad idea," Eddie sighed.

*   *   *

Ethan shoved a new magazine into his CAR-15 and dropped the bolt closed with the palm of his left hand. Green tracers split the air above his head and spun past his face as he pushed Luc and Bo into the nearest bomb crater. Luc was already returning fire as the rest of the team piled into the crater and staked out their defensive sectors. Bo was steadily chipping away behind his RPD but the NVA were maneuvering up on their flanks. Keeping low, Ethan rolled over one of his Yards and scrambled to where Nui was firing out to their far left.

"Many, many!" he shouted with a terrified look in between bursts, but Ethan could only smile at the little tribesman. The Yards had such a knack for pointing out the all-too obvious in the worst of times.

Ghost-like figures washed in and out of sight amidst the twisted trees and scorched earth – a once lush and densely-wooded valley barely an hour before. The pulverized gray earth was as fine as ash and it clung to everything as it drifted above the ground. A group quickly found cover as Ethan's burst ripped across their shuffling feet and chewed into what was left of an ancient hardwood tree. He swapped his carbine for the chopped M-79 and lobbed a grenade at them, driving them from their position right out into the open where Nui chopped them into tattered bits. The little Montagnard was perfectly happy about that and dug in even deeper behind his RPD with a gritty smile.

Ethan slapped his little Yard on the back and then scurried through the crater to where Eddie was busy reloading.

"We gotta spread out into these other holes to keep them from pinning us down!" Ethan shouted while Eddie fired at more advancing NVA. "You and Nui hold this one down and keep your radio safe. We rally on this hole!"

He rolled over and crawled to where Nay and Bruce were.

"Where's Karate with those guns?!" Bruce shouted between short bursts. Explosions were cooking off everywhere, in every direct.

"Guns are refueling and there's more on the way," Ethan promised. "Karate's staying high to the east to avoid antiaircraft fire, so we're alone until those guns show up. Take Nay and Hyuk, and get your asses into that crater over there," he ordered and pointed at a depression about twenty meters out on the far right flank. "We can't let them pin us all down in one position."

"Where are you going?"

"I'm taking Luc and Bo down to that ditch over there," he pointed thirty meters beyond them and off to the far left flank. "We'll tie off with your hole and this one here. Nobody gets through!"

"I hope those guns show up soon, or we're gonna be in some deep shit."

"They're coming, just get ready to move," Ethan assured him as he raised his carbine and readied himself.

"Hey, you know I was only being sarcastic and playfully morbid when I said we were fucked the other day," Bruce grinned wryly.

"Good to know you still got your sense of humor."

They opened up with covering fire allowing Bruce, Nay, and Hyuk to reach the depression. The boys dropped out of sight momentarily before Bruce stuck his arm up and waved back. He watched them as they worked to button up the right flank, which slowly but surely took the pressure off.

"Stay on me," he said turning to Luc and Bo.

He pitched two frags and then they were up and running while Eddie and Nui opened up with suppressive fire. They were in the cut in seconds, and as the dust cleared momentarily, the bodies briefly came into view. There was half-a-dozen scattered in and around their new position and at least twice that scattered just beyond them. Ethan dropped his rucksack beside one of the bodies and rolled him over it in hopes of keeping his radio protected. AKs barked and RPGs went zipping and whistling by but the shift was working, and all three positions had tied off with interlocking fields of fire. Ethan reached down for the radio and stretched the handset up to where he could talk and direct his men at the same time.

"Karate, what's the status on those guns?"

"Hollywood, guns are one-five mikes out. Any chance you can break contact and move somewhere?"

"No way in hell, they're too fucking close!"

The gunfire suddenly slackened as the enemy tried to reorganize, and Bo was using the lull wisely to fortify their position by stacking bodies in front of themselves. Empty magazines and spent brass were beginning to pile up all around them. Ethan reached forward and grabbed the arm of another dead NVA soldier and dragged him back. The top of the kid's head had been blown away, exposing a mushy pile of dirt-covered brains and shattered skull. The bile stench was unbearable as it wafted with the pungent odor of gun-smoke and feces. Several AKs winked from a charred log not more than twenty meters to his front but the kid's body absorbed the fire.

Ducking quickly behind the corpse, Ethan removed a white phosphorous grenade rigged with packets of teargas powder. He pulled the pin and let the spoon fly and counted to two, then lobbed it high and watched it burst directly over their heads. They broke from cover and scrambled through the billowing white cloud while frantically swatting and waving at the molten fragments that melted their flesh away. He stroked them with a quick burst from his CAR-15 and then reloaded just as a bunch of shrilling whistles pierced the air. Bo's finger was clamped over his trigger and the barrel was beginning to glow white-hot. It was a human wave assault and the NVA were absolutely everywhere. Ethan pitched grenades and fired his carbine and in seconds, another magazine was empty and he was reloading again, then again, and again. Two more empty magazines and dozens more dead NVA, but they just kept coming.

He felt no fear, no despair, no rage or guilt, or remorse; he was beyond all those emotions. All he felt was the sheer will to survive another second, another minute, another hour. He killed a man at point-blank range with a burst to the face; hair and flesh, shattered teeth and bone and brains went everywhere as he tumbled into the dirt an arm's length away. He shifted fire onto a group as they scurried through a layered-up pile of twisted trees. Three went down as red tracers cut through their maneuver. He dropped the empty magazine and grabbed another from the stack he'd laid out in front of his position; he'd never had to do that before. Didn't want to. Stacking magazines meant they were locked in and unable to break contact.

There was an NVA trying desperately to pull one of the wounded to safety, but there was nowhere safe in that valley for anyone.

Ethan lobbed a frag into their laps and moved on.

"Check your ammo, check your ammo," he ordered.

Making use of the lull, he reached forward and pulled two dead NVA back in front of his position while Luc and Bo readied themselves for the next push. He then emptied another canteen cover of magazines and stacked them in the dirt just behind his barricade of bodies. A burst of AK fire raked across the edge of the hole but found neither him, nor his Yards. Luc returned fire on semi-auto and Bo tossed a grenade, but it didn't go very far; Montagnards notoriously lacked the arm and shoulder strength. Ethan reached down and retrieved the radio handset again, praying Karate had good news.

"Triple-A is opening up and I'm trying to put air on it so I can get to you," Karate called. "Stay in the fight, bro. We're coming, I swear."

"We've got a lull here, but –"

Something blunt and hard bounced off his chest and into the dirt by his feet.

"Grenade!" he yelled while scooping it up and throwing it away. He kept his mouth open to equalize the blast pressure. It rocked the edge of the hole and showered them with dirt and debris and left him in a dazed and slightly concussed.

Another came tumbling over the edge of the hole and down beside his foot, and he looked at it with insane fascination for a split second. There was no time to throw this one away so he did the only thing he could do. He rolled the dead body off his rucksack and on top of the grenade and threw himself on top of the pile…

A bright flash and then it all went black and silent, and he was weightless. Momentum filled his being while centrifugal force transferred from his upper to lower body with each flipping spin. Something slammed hard into his back with traumatic force, but he had not the strength required to fight back. He felt suffocation creep into his body as his lungs and brain fought for air, and then he wheezed hard and long while sucking in the dirty, smoky air. He felt nothing, saw nothing, heard nothing, smelled and tasted nothing for what seemed like a long, long time. He lay there, conscious, but unable to make his limbs or senses respond to his pleading will. As the blood flow returned, his brain began to throb and pound harder and harder with each passing heartbeat. He desperately tried again to will his motor functions into action – he knew he wasn't dead, but he simply could not open his eyes or make his limbs respond.

Oh God, oh God.

He could hear himself moaning weakly but he knew at any second the enemy would be upon him. They'd press their glowing-hot AK muzzles up against his pounding temples just long enough to sear his skin before squeezing the triggers. Or maybe he'd feel the dull point of one of their rusty bayonets as it plunged slowly into his guts, but once would not be enough. They'd stick him again and again and again, and leave him there to moan and die a gritty, cold and lonely death. All he had left was the sudden intoxicating surge of more adrenaline and the taste of blood in his mouth. He rolled over and crawled a painfully short way to fetch an AK from a pile of bodies. NVA were swarming all around him but none seemed to care that much. He laboriously checked the magazine and cleared the action, then laid the muzzle across one of the bodies. The stench was ripe and thick in his world. He was behind the sights with plenty of people to shoot at but he couldn't focus, couldn't shake the spinning horizon and blurred vision. He wondered who was still alive. Luc and Bo had been beside him when the grenade had gone off and he prayed to God the blast had spared them.

A strong hand latched onto his harness and began dragging him backwards. He rolled over and looked up but all he could see was a bright blue sky and brilliantly blurred muzzle flashes all spinning and melting together in a trippy kaleidoscope.

They're... dragging me. Why am I being dragged? Goddammit, I can still walk... right?

He panicked and looked down at his legs expecting to see nothing but bloody stumps and shattered bone, but to his everlasting relief, they were still there – exactly as he remembered them. The blast had blown his boots and pants completely away.

Goddammit, he cursed, *those were my good boots – my lucky boots.*

He glanced at his bloodied, frag-peppered arms as they dragged through the gray ash-like soil. He had dropped the AK along the way, but was still clenching something in his other hand. He brought it up to his face and realized he was holding another hand – a left hand ripped from the arm at the wrist.

That – that's not my hand, he calmly convinced himself. *Can't be... See, your other hand's right here.*

He brought his left hand up and examined it, then looked up and was finally able to focus. Bruce had dragged him back and they were suddenly in a bomb crater with several other people around them.

"Hey," Ethan stammered, "whose hand is this?"

"Ethan look at me," Bruce said as he took the severed hand. Everyone's voice was heavily muffled – almost as if his head were underwater. Explosions and gunfire were still erupting all around them. "Ethan! Look at me – look right here," he indicated with his fingers to his eyes. "Stay awake! Do you hear me? Stay awake! Help's on the way, man, stay with me!"

"Bruce! Hurry man, help me! He's hit bad," someone shouted. He watched as the commotion unfolded by his side, but he still couldn't see who they were working on.

Ethan's body was numb but his head was splitting and bulging. In a moment of desperation, he wiggled his feet back and forth, reassuring himself that he wasn't paralyzed. He looked back to the man who was lying by his side and tried hard to focus on his face. He blinked several times, clearing the blur from his watering eyes.

It was Nay. The only thing moving were his eyes and nothing else. The tough tribesman watched helplessly as Bruce applied a pressure bandage to a wound underneath his right armpit. They rolled him over and lifted his shirt up, probing for an exit wound.

"That's it – I can't do any more," Bruce said as he stuck Nay with a Syrette of morphine.

Ethan's eyes locked back on to Nay's. There were tears slowly rolling down his round, smudged cheeks. He couldn't believe it, but he knew Nay was dying. He didn't want to believe that Bruce couldn't do anything more for him. He reached over with a shaking hand and collected Nay's into his own and squeezed hard, but there was nothing there. He watched him, unable to move or respond.

"Nay, can you hear me?" he stammered.

The Yard blinked twice, forcing more tears down his soiled face.

"Don't leave... Please? Nay, please?" he slurred. "You gotta... you gotta hold on..."

He wanted to cry, but he simply didn't have the energy, so he just gripped Nay's hand and held his eyes with his own for what seemed like days, fighting off the urge to black out again.

People were suddenly all around them – scary, painted faces who seemed to know him but he couldn't recall their names. Someone was standing above him, waving an orange signal panel at a sky full of birds. Men were suddenly by their sides, tying Swiss seats around their waists.

"I'm not first," he slurred while trying to fight them off. "Get everybody else out first," he demanded but nobody listened.

"You hang on to him, Ethan! You hear me? You hang on to Nay and don't you let go for shit!" Eddie shouted as he slung his CAR-15 over his back.

"I swear to God I won't let him go," Ethan promised.

He latched on to Nay's limp form with both his arms and squeezed him tight into a bear hug, locking his hands. Seconds later, they were up and soaring out above the valley while green streaks blurred past.

"I got you, Nay. I ain't letting go," he groggily vowed.

The cold air engulfed them both and he was soon freezing and shaking uncontrollably. He closed his eyes to ward off the intense windburn, but never once released his grasp on Nay.

20

Finally conscious and clutching at the bedrails while his body quaked and trembled in a cold sweat. His breathing was labored and cumbersome and he could feel his heart palpitating deep inside his chest. There was no pain at first, but soon the throbbing began to stab at his temples and abdomen again. It was dark and cool and unfamiliar, and though he recognized a clean smell to his new surroundings, his instant urge was to find his weapon. He sat up in bed and squeezed his eyes against the artificial light pouring dully into the room, but he was quickly overcome by total disorientation. He pawed momentarily at the bandage wrapped around his left arm, reading it like brail from mid-bicep to his wrist. He swung one leg out of bed and probed the darkness below. His foot touched the cold floor and he feebly attempted to stand and support his aching body, but his knees gave out and he spilled to the floor with a squeaking thud. He moaned quietly and stretched out, feeling every muscle in his body tighten with soreness. Light footsteps approached the bed from the opposite side.

"Sergeant?" a soft young voice whispered in the pale light.

"What?" His voice was hoarse and raspy and dry; he wasn't expecting a woman.

"Are you okay?" she asked as she skirted the foot of the bed and knelt down to help him up. "What on earth are you doing on the floor?"

"I fell," he sighed. "Where the hell am I?"

"Here, let me help you back into bed." Her small yet firm hands clutched at his bare shoulders. He winced as he pulled himself up with her help and fell back into the sheets. "Are you sure you're okay?"

"Where the hell am I?"

"This is the 71st Evacuation Hospital in Pleiku; you're in the recovery ward."

"Recovering from what? How long have I been here?" he asked, pressing his palms into his eye sockets, trying to smother his pounding headache.

"About twelve hours; you came in late yesterday afternoon," she softly replied.

"My head's fucking pounding like hell," he complained. "Where the hell's the rest of my team?"

"Team?"

"Yeah, seven others; two Americans and my little people. You seen 'em?"

"Little people?" she asked with curiosity. "There was one other man – Vietnamese, I think? – who came in with you on the same helicopter; you were both hanging by ropes beneath it."

"Yard."

"I'm sorry?"

"He's a Montagnard, not Vietnamese."

"Sorry, I didn't know." Her voice was brimming with innocent sincerity.

"It's okay. So where is he – the man I came in with? His name's Nay."

"I'm not sure. The only time I saw him was when you first arrived."

"I gotta find him; he was bad fucked up," Ethan said as he tried to sit back up. "He's… he's important to me… like family to me." Tears began to well up in his eyes and he could feel his face trembling. He tried to wipe his emotions away and she pleaded for him to relax and lay back down.

"You've sustained a moderate concussion and trauma to your abdomen."

"How bad?"

"Two fractured ribs," she said. "The doctors also removed several pieces of shrapnel from your left arm. Please, try not to move around so much."

He groaned as he fell back into the sheets.

"You're lucky to be conscious at all," she added in surprise as she pulled the sheets back over him.

"Why's that?"

"You passed out sometime before you arrived and that often leads to a coma if your concussion is severe enough."

Silence settled between them as he relaxed again. She stayed by his side for what seemed like a long time and he felt a great deal of comfort in her presence.

"I was dreaming."

"What about?"

"I dunno… I don't remember."

"I bet it was a good dream," she whispered, and he could tell she was smiling. Her voice was something he hadn't heard in a very long time. She was young and beautiful, educated; he was sure of all of these things simply by how she sounded when she spoke – even in a whisper.

"Sorry I swear so fucking much."

"It's okay," she laughed softly. He could feel her eyes looking him over with curiosity. "Try to get some sleep now; I'll be close by if you need anything, okay?"

"Miss… You never did tell me your name."

"June," she smiled. "June Matthews."

*   *   *

A tongue in each ear and he was wide awake, swatting and cursing at Reynolds on one side and Mark on the other.

"Dammit, c'mon," he complained as they both laughed through their noses like a pair of giddy hyenas. He could smell the liquor on them from a mile away.

"Quit sandbagging and get your lazy ass up," Reynolds ordered as Mark tore the sheets away and pulled at Ethan's leg.

"Alright alright, I'm up," he groaned. Luke Dove and Pete Johnston went racing by in wheelchairs and crashed into the door at the far end of the ward where Eddie was talking to one of the nurses.

"How ya feeling, E?" Mark slurred.

"Here," Reynolds offered with a broad grin, "brought ya something to wet your whistle."

He waved the flask away but Randy just shrugged and took a long swig.

"We came by yesterday but they wouldn't release you into our loving care until we sobered up some," Mark said. "So we went back into town and kept drink'n."

"Seems about right."

Eddie gathered the welcoming committee up and pushed them all back outside so as not to disturb the other GIs in the ward who were still recovering; he was clearly the only sober head among them.

Ethan hobbled out of his hospital greens and into a fresh new set of fatigues the boys had brought with them while Eddie helped lace his boots up. The headaches were finally gone and the swelling in his chest had nearly subsided, but the bruising was still there and his entire body was still painfully sore. And then he remembered lying helplessly in the dirt beside Nay in a distant Laotian valley four days earlier.

"He's dead, isn't he?"

Eddie just nodded.

"What happened?" He forced the lump back down his throat.

"Got hit below his left armpit. They said the bullet deflected off one of his ribs and hit his spine." Eddie shifted his weight and ran his hand through his wild hair. "We tried, man – Bruce tried, but there wasn't anything he could do for him, Ethan. I'm sorry."

"…What about the others?" he asked, sleeving his eyes dry and clearing his throat.

"They're okay – upset, but Bruce is with 'em right now."

"You okay?"

Eddie nodded again but he was still holding something back.

"I ran into my old CO while we were waiting in town for them to release you… I quit Recon, Ethan. I'm transferring back to the 75th. L Company needs a first sergeant."

"You check with Yates or Doney for a slot at the TOC?"

"They offered me one," he said and shook his head, "but it wouldn't be fair to the others who've earned those slots, y'know."

Eddie grabbed Ethan's harness and carbine off the bedpost and slung them over his shoulder. Ethan glancing around the recovery ward as the mid-morning sunlight poured through the windows making the room glow bright.

"You ready?"

"Yeah."

Eddie slung an arm over his shoulder and they made for the door.

"Ethan – ah, Sergeant Jackson," a voice called softly from behind. He turned around and there she was, June Matthews. Her hair was the color of walnut, accented by soft sandy highlights and it was pulled neatly back into a tight bun. She had deep green almond-shaped eyes and a light dusting of freckles on either side of her nose – a beautifully simple face.

"Look – uh, just, I mean… Take care of yourself out there, okay?" she said as she forced her hands deep into her pockets. It wasn't so much a question as it was a request or even a plea. Then she leaned in, palming a folded piece of paper, and tucked it into the left breast pocket of his jungle shirt. As she pulled away, she held his eyes just long enough and then applied a thin smile to melt the tension.

"I will," he nodded with a thin smile.

Out of the hospital recovery ward and into the saturated heat of Pleiku. The boys had all piled into the back of a jeep – likely stolen, considering his companions – and had finally passed out on top of one another. Ethan struggled and winced at the pain while slowly climbing into the passenger seat.

"Guess there ain't nothing I could say to change your mind, huh," Ethan figured.

"You hungry?" Eddie asked.

Ethan glanced across at him, relented a grin and nodded, "I'm starving."

*   *   *

They parted ways with Eddie at the airfield and hitched a ride back up to Kontum on an old Vietnamese-flown H-34 Kingbee. The massive nine-cylinder engine dashed all hopes of conversation and the little Vietnamese door gunner had a knack for firing up abandoned hootches with the old Browning .30-caliber machinegun mounted in the doorway. But that was all just fine and good with him for he was lost in thought about the people who had come and gone in his life so abruptly over the past few days. Nay was dead, Eddie had quit, and then there was June Matthews.

He dug the neat fold of paper from his breast pocket, opened it and carefully read her in-country mailing address, then followed on with her stateside address.

Shit, he cursed silently. *I thought I'd be able to forget about her; reckon that's not gonna happen...*

It was the ultimate cliché: a wounded soldier and a beautiful young nurse crossing paths in a hospital amid a chaotic war in a foreign land. It was the type of stuff B-grade war movies were made of and he was on the verge of starring in the lead role. He nodded his head and pocketed her correspondence while leaning back against the vibrating bulkhead. His eyes drew narrow as he relaxed, cradling his CAR-15 in his lap while letting the cool bristling wind obliterate his worries, and they were soon back on the ground at CCC by mid-afternoon.

He dumped his equipment off at his team house and swapped his CAR-15 for a suppressed .22-caliber High Standard. He hung the little pistol around his neck by way of a para-cord lanyard and tucked it into the waistband of his pants. No one ever went anywhere around camp without some sort of a weapon; that's just the way it was in an existence where one's survival was ultimately associated with guns.

He made his way over to the Yards' barracks and entered to find his little people whipping up a late-afternoon lunch. The aroma was nothing short of incredible and as he crossed the threshold of the doorway, the Yards mobbed him with gleeful delight and all manner of horseplay. They touched him with gentle hands, inspecting his bandages and the few minor abrasions that were on his face. They played with his unruly hair and lifted his jungle shirt to investigate his abdomen. He grimaced when their hands probed too firmly against his sternum and ribcage, but he was happy to be back amongst them. The reunion felt unlike anything he'd ever experienced before. It wasn't the same feeling as seeing childhood friends after years gone, or even the same as being reunited with distant relatives at a family gathering. It was something different altogether – something he couldn't quite put his finger on at the time, but he knew it was unique and special in every way, even in the most simple of ways.

Nui prepared the feast – seasoned chicken, cooked fish, and rice piled over large fresh leaves they'd plucked from the jungle, served in split sections of bamboo. But before anyone began eating, they all glanced around the dimly-lit room at one another, accepting that Nay was no longer among them in physical form.

They ate in silence and he stayed with them again that night, taking up the very same hammock that Nay had strung up for him almost nine months ago. One-by-one, his little people eased by his side to pat his arms or shoulders and smile before turning in. The naked light bulbs that hung from the ceiling were switched off and the only light that remained was that of a collection of flickering candles.

"We will take Nay back home tomorrow," Hyuk said in a soft whisper as he knelt beside Ethan. "We will celebrate his death with big feast and want you there."

He watched the flickering light from the candles as it danced behind Hyuk against the dingy wall.

"Yes my friend," he said while forcing the tears back. "I would be honored." The little tribesman smiled thinly and patted Ethan's head before moving to his cot. Luc quietly sat in his chair by the table exactly as Nay had so many times before, meticulously braiding a bracelet made from thin strands of elephant hide. He never took his dark eyes off the bracelet and there were never any words spoken between them, but Ethan could feel the weathered man watching closely over him, along with Nay's spirit. There would be no cold sweats or nightmares to stir him awake.

*   *   *

He made his way over to the TOC the next morning for a formal and somewhat belated debriefing of the BDA mission. S-2 and S-3 had plenty of speculation to offer on what had unfolded on the ground, but Ethan made it clear the mission had been doomed from the outset. Instead of being immediately inserted right after the last bomb fell, the air strike had touched off a huge munitions cache which resulted in an uncountable number of secondary explosions. Karate had sent the air package back to Dak To for fuel and hoped by the time they returned, they'd be able to insert, but the ordnance continued to cook off for nearly two hours. Soon, Pete Johnston's O-1 drew low on fuel as well and had to return to Kontum, which left no airborne eyes over the target.

"So we finally showed back up and inserted after Karate made sure there were no more secondaries."

"And you took no ground fire and saw no enemy troops before or during the insertion, correct?" Major Zune asked.

"That's right."

"What happened then?"

"We moved through the valley for maybe ten minutes and then all hell broke loose. We tried to press 'em but they were everywhere so we got small and let Karate work the Cobras around us. They drew low on fuel and ordnance and went back to the launch site while Karate moved high to the east to avoid the antiaircraft threat and waited for the other gun package to show up."

"Were the air assets taking antiaircraft fire at this point?"

"I can't say. I was too busy trying to stay alive."

"Can you recall how extensive the bombing was to the target?"

"On the way in, we saw an unearthed tunnel system and a lot of demolished bunkers, but everything else was pretty much annihilated. The Air Force was on-the-money," Ethan assured.

"What about bodies or body parts?"

"Before we made contact, no."

The staffers made more notes before continuing the debriefing. They spent a while longer discussing everything from weather conditions and soil-type, to mission-specific equipment they used, to radios and communications.

"We had an unconfirmed report that your Covey Rider, Staff Sergeant Howard Davis, directed air support for your team via a pair Spads. Know anything about that?" one of them asked with a quizzical glance.

"Sorry, I can't recall much after I was blown up," Ethan replied with a fair dose of sarcasm.

"RT Illinois was in contact about five klicks south of your team at the same time, but your team had priority due to the circumstances. Once your team and the Hatchet Force was pulled, apparently, Staff Sergeant Davis redirected those Spads to support Illinois. You are aware that fixed-wing air support is strictly prohibited from the Salem House AO, correct?"

"I am *very* aware of that ludicrous restriction," Ethan quipped, but could tell they wanted more. "Look, I don't know if Karate got us Spads or not and I really don't give a good shit. Whatever measures he took to get my team, the Hatchet Force, and John's team out of there saved our lives. Period. And we all know how notoriously inaccurate our maps are of the tri-border area. We could have just as easily been in southeastern Laos as opposed to northeastern Cambodia."

The officers and senior NCOs conducting the debriefing made their final notes before Zune asked him if there was anything else he'd like to add.

"Yessir," Ethan replied quickly. "Me and my little people saw this bunker complex up close before the Arc Light. This should have been a Hatchet Force operation, not something for a little eight-man recon team to have to deal with."

"Ahh don't feel so bad, sergeant," one of the staffers offered in a nonchalant tone. "SPAF-4 counted seventy-seven dead NVA scattered around your team's position while the Hatchet Force was being inserted. Seems like a pretty good ratio for one dead Montagnard."

Ethan started to say something but Zune cut him off just in time.

"Lieutenant, you're new here. These men are very close with their indigenous teammates and they take losses hard," Zune said. "Don't ever make the mistake of disrespecting them like that again."

The debriefing had lasted hours and the recollection of events had pushed Ethan to a jittery edge. Afterwards, he secured three-day passes for everyone on the team and spoke briefly with the colonel to assure him that he was okay.

"They've still got you on medical profile over at the dispensary," the colonel said, "so take it easy for a little while, okay?"

"I will," he promised with a thin smile.

"I'm sorry to hear about Nay. Everyone respected him deeply. You can collect the remainder of his pay from the clerk's office. There should be a small bonus included as well."

"Thank you, sir," Ethan said as he began to turn away.

"Hold up, son," he chuckled. "It's not completely official yet, but Captain Yates submitted the paperwork for your Silver Star and Purple Heart and I've already pushed it through; it won't be downgraded this time, so don't think you're going to get out of it by telling me you don't deserve it. Now, get your little people squared away and take it easy for a bit." The colonel patted his shoulder and smiled.

"I will," Ethan offered with a nod. "Thank you."

He stopped by the clerk's office and collected the remainder of Nay's pay – the equivalent of $250 US in Vietnamese piasters. He pocketed the envelope and made his way back to Utah's team house. He passed Pete Wilson, Frank Greco, and Tim Lynch on the way, and they were beaming to see him back in the company area in one piece.

He found Bruce sound-asleep in his rack, fully clothed – boots and all – which meant he'd had a long night and an early morning at the dispensary. He decided to let him sleep for a little while longer and elected to take the time to catch up on mail. He collapsed in his rack and rummaged through the stack of letters that had accumulated in his brief absence. Among all the mail was a plain white envelope with his name written sloppily across the front. Inside was $200 in greenbacks and a note.

"Give this to Nay's family. – Eddie."

Ethan opened his footlocker and retrieved a fat roll of greenbacks and promptly counted out $500. He dug into his pocket and pulled out the measly $250 in piasters that was owed Nay and put it with what was left of his stash, and closed the lid. Because of its strength in Southeast Asia – especially on the black market – the American dollar was strictly prohibited by the military; it was worth a great deal more than Vietnamese piasters and even more than MPC. Instead of paying GIs with US currency each month, the military issued new notes of Military Payment Certificates, rendering the previous month's MPC worthless. As soon as the new notes were issued, every GI in-country had to trade their old notes for new, otherwise they'd be worthless. The real problem came when civilians were paid in MPC only to have the following month's notes issued. Since they weren't allowed to swap notes, whatever money they had in MPC became worthless. Many GIs often helped their Vietnamese friends by trading the notes for them, but the US military quickly caught on. In order to curtail the unauthorized trading, they issued the new notes randomly. Regardless, American currency never lost its value and was always in high demand, especially on the black market, and Special Forces soldiers always seemed to have plenty to go around.

"That should make it an even grand," Bruce said as he handed him $300 in greenbacks. He'd been watching silently from his rack for the past few minutes as Ethan counted the bills to himself.

"Still doesn't seem like it's enough, huh? I mean, how do you put a dollar sign on someone's life?" Ethan rolled the bills up tight and wrapped a rubber-band around them, and dropped it into his pocket. He glanced over his shoulder at the empty rack and the vacant wall locker that had been Eddie's. It suddenly felt like months since he'd last seen him. Eddie was a solid recon man and a loyal friend, and as he stared at the empty rack, Ethan suddenly realized just how much he was going to miss him.

"I've gotta catch up on some of this shit," he said, turning his attention back to his mail. He hadn't written his family in almost a month and once he read through all their letters, he finally sat down to write back:

Mom, Dad, David,

Sorry I haven't written in the past few weeks; it's been pretty hectic around here. My friend Ken Worthley was killed in Cambodia a few weeks ago and another friend of mine, John St. Martin, got all fucked up in Laos, but he managed to hang on somehow. He almost had his foot shot off at the ankle and his guts literally spilled out of his goddamn shirt. They were both good team leaders. Anyways, me and my team just ran a BDA mission in Cambodia; BDA stands for bomb-damage assessment. It's when we secretly bomb target-areas in Laos and Cambodia with B-52s, then send in little eight-man recon teams like mine to scour through the wreckage and assess whether or not we killed anything. The whole mission was fucked from the get-go and we nearly got wiped out by a bunch of pissed off NVA. My senior Montagnard mercenary was killed and I got blown up by an enemy grenade; other than a few shrapnel wounds, some bruises, and a moderate concussion, I'm okay. We gave better than we got, though; I think we killed about eighty of those pricks. I know I killed at least fifteen or so myself. Well anyways, I just wanted to let you all know that I'm doing fine and everything's fuck'n a-okay.

Love you all,
Ethan

He considered the consequences of writing such a letter as he reread it silently; if he could have sent it, he probably would have. Instead, he ripped the sheet from the pad and balled it up as tightly as he could. He started over, and within five minutes, had finished his letter – a carbon-copy of all the ones he'd sent home before. They all said the same things – that he was doing well and keeping busy, but nothing more, especially not about his wounds. He knew his family hadn't been notified by the Army of his injuries as per his instruction when he had first arrived in-country. They didn't need to be any more worried than they already were; if they were notified, it'd be because he had been killed or was missing in action. No false alarms. He sealed the letter and addressed the envelope.

He wanted to eat lunch before leaving with the Yards, so he hung his suppressed High Standard around his neck and shuffled out of the door with Bruce close behind. They stopped by South Dakota's team house long enough to collect Mark and one of his teammates, then made for the club where they enjoyed steaks and cold beer and debated recon lore. Afterwards, Ethan signed out one of the company's deuce-and-a-halfs and gathered the Yards up before heading over to the dispensary.

Without a single word spoken between any of them, they solemnly retrieved Nay's body from the morgue and carefully placed him in the bed of the deuce. One-by-one, the Yards climbed into the back, taking special care not to step on Nay. They rolled out of the gates by mid-afternoon and headed south on Highway 14, bound for the Montagnard village near Plei Te.

He thought quietly back to his first visit to the village months before, back in mid-July. He'd been a guest-of-honor then and had visited under peaceful circumstances, but he secretly feared the coming visit would be far more different. He could still smell the constant waft of burning wood fires, and he could still recall the jovial smiling faces of half-naked children; the unattended livestock, the food and rice wine, but most importantly, the hospitality that had been extended to him. They had opened their homes and their hearts to him and he had felt comfortable among them because of it. By Western standards, the village was a dirty place but there existed a real natural feeling of cleanliness that no store-bought household cleaner could achieve. He searched endlessly for the right words to offer Nay's father, but he knew there was nothing he could say that would ease the news of tragedy. They traveled the uneventful twenty klicks with limited conversation while keeping weary eyes and CAR-15 muzzles trained on the passing countryside.

*   *   *

They were mobbed by dirty little children just as soon as the deuce rumbled to a dusty halt at the edge of the village. It was difficult to smile and horseplay with them when bearing such tragic news, but Ethan quickly felt warmed by their playful touches and contagious laughter. Luc promptly shooed the kids away while the rest of the team quietly huddled around the back of the deuce, staring at the black rubber bag. Finally, Bruce reached forward and carefully tugged Nay across the bed of the truck and into their waiting arms. They made it a little past halfway before Nay's father, the village chief, cleared the ancient fencing and hobbled down the hard-packed footpath to meet them. The entire village followed close behind in silence while chickens and feral dogs scampered out of their way.

Ethan and Bruce released their grasps on Nay and stood shoulder-to-shoulder as Chief Y Lap closed the last bit of distance. His weathered, leathery face already showed grief and heartbreak before Ethan and the others could tell him; Y Lap had somehow already known about the loss of his son. Ethan and Bruce both bowed their heads slightly in the chief's presence as Hyuk and Luc moved by their sides; the rest of the team stood silently with Nay firmly secured in their grips. Hyuk spoke swift, yet softly in their native tongue.

The old chief remained silent with a blank gaze but the entire village had broken down into wailing cries of devastation. He looked at the team members one-by-one, noticing the abrasions on their skin and offered a slow nod of understanding. He then fixed his heavy eyes onto Ethan and raised his wrinkled hand up, patting his shoulder before inspecting the bandages on his left arm. Then, he stared long at the body-bag. He finally spoke quietly but it was difficult to hear him over the rest of the villagers as they sobbed quietly. With the wave of the chief's hand, his immediate family rushed past him and promptly retrieved Nay from the grips of the team. They wept and moaned as they carried him back up the footpath while the rest of the village remained broken and in tears.

"I'm very sorry about Nay," Ethan said. "He was very courageous and saved all our lives many times," he added, hoping the old man would take pride in his son and find comfort and solace in his words. The wrinkled old man sucked on his unlit hemp cigar with tears streaming down his cheeks. He placed a withered hand on Ethan's shoulder and squeezed affectionately while speaking in Bahnar, then patted Bruce on his arm.

"He is saddened by the death of his son," Hyuk translated. "Nay told him many times that you are both great warriors and good men."

Ethan looked back at the old chief who stood before him wearing only a black loincloth, a heavily-soiled denim jacket and tribal jewelry.

"He has asked that both of you stay for the ceremony to honor his son," Hyuk continued.

"We would truly be honored to stay as your guests."

Hyuk once again translated and Y Lap revealed about as much delight as one could expect under the circumstances. They turned and followed him up the path while the rest of the villagers continued their mourning.

The mood remained somber for a while but the villagers soon began to embrace their memories of Nay, and the chief seemed to feel the warmth of his people as they prepared to celebrate his son's life. The rest of his immediate family continued to mourn inside their longhouse for the duration of the team's stay, as was their custom. Everyone else gathered at the center of the village and waited while several men retrieved the earthen jars that contained the rice wine. One-by-one, Utah's Montagnards slipped away to trade their jungle fatigues and boots for loincloths, but Ethan and Bruce weren't able to escape the ancient tradition like they had back in July.

"Join us," Hyuk said with a toothy smile as he handed them their very own loincloths; the rest of the team looked on and giggled uncontrollably. Ethan and Bruce exchanged a brief look of hesitation, but the Yards weren't having it.

"Come, come – you change in my family longhouse," he said while motioning for them to follow him. A few minutes later, they reluctantly emerged from the longhouse garnishing their loincloths, and for an instant, the entire village stopped what they were doing just long enough to howl with laughter at the Americans' stark-white legs.

"Wish I woulda known I'd be wearing one of these so I could've worked on my suntan," Bruce joked.

They rejoined the chief and rest of the team while one of the village elders painted their faces. Then out came the big urns filled with rice wine. The pungent taste and heavy odor of the fermented brew was still something neither Ethan nor Bruce had yet grown accustomed to, and after a few sticks, they quickly felt the sloshing effects. Ethan pulled another throat-burning mouthful and passed the jar once more while watching everyone crowd around a lone water buffalo at the village center. A short and shriveled old man pushed his way through the crowd carrying a homemade blade in one hand and a large earthen jar in his other. He wore nothing except a tattered loincloth and many brass bracelets; both ears were pierced with large circles of ivory which stretched his earlobes to the size of a silver dollar, and the middle part of his nose was pierced with a long, straight length of bamboo. He stepped from the crowd and confidently faced the water buffalo.

"Hyuk, who is that man?" Ethan slurred with a quizzical nod.

"Ahh," Hyuk smiled, "Nui's grandfather, Hahn. He is village shaman. He will sacrifice buffalo to fend off evil spirits."

The villagers grew eerily silent as Hahn reached forward with his curved blade and swiped it swiftly under the buffalo's throat. He quickly caught the spilling blood with the jar while the large beast gurgled and released its dying breath. It swayed and staggered, and collapsed on the hard-packed dirt at the shaman's feet while the villagers cheered and clapped. The man held the jar for all to see before putting it to his lips and taking a swallow. He then passed it to the nearest Montagnard who, in turn, drank the blood and passed it along.

"What will happen to Nay?" Ethan asked as he watched the tribesmen take their turns drinking from the jar.

"Because his soul is good, it will go into the ground and he will take a new form of life. I believe your word is reincarnation."

"Reincarnation," Ethan agreed. "So where do bad souls go?"

Hyuk frowned and pointed to the sky, "All the daughters of evil spirits live in the sky and bad souls go to live with them. You see, it is our religion to seek to please the bad spirits *more* than to praise the good spirits."

"What happens if you can't or don't please the bad spirits enough?"

"They will cause trouble and make mischief... kind of like you when you drink too much," Hyuk giggled.

They shared a good chuckle while the villagers quickly piled bundles of tinder and kindling all around the dead water buffalo. Hahn approached their circle with the jar of blood and handed it to Y Lap. The chief brought it to his lips and drank heartily, then passed it to Ethan. With no hesitation, he grabbed the jar with both hands, put it to his lips and threw back a large gulp; the blood was thick and heavy and tasted like sweet copper. He forced it down as far as he could before passing the jar to Bruce while wiping his chin with the back of his hand. Y Lap, Hahn, and the rest of the Yards sitting around them all smiled and chuckled at Ethan.

"Will Nay be buried?" he asked as Hyuk took his bloody drink from the jar and passed it.

He shook his head, "His family will place him in a hollow log coffin and it will remain above-ground, as is the tradition of the Bahnar people. All of us already have our coffins made." He pointed to a small hootch across the village; stored neatly beneath its stilted floor was a tidy stock of pre-made pine coffins.

The buffalo was thoroughly cooked by way of open flame exactly where it had fallen in the dirt. Nothing was removed from the animal – it wasn't skinned or beheaded or gutted. Instead, the Yards cooked the beast as it was without wasting a single morsel, and the celebration continued well into the wee hours of the night.

With a stomach swollen full of buffalo meat and fermented rice, Ethan stumbled up into the chief's longhouse with Luc and Hyuk's help where he found his bedding next to Bruce. Luc sat quietly before them and assumed his fatherly vigil while his silhouette danced in erratic flickers against the walls as the wood fire crackled and filled the longhouse with that authentic smell.

In that inebriated state of mind, Ethan pondered Hyuk's description of their burial rituals and their beliefs on life after death and reincarnation. For a moment, he wondered how the people back home would view the Montagnards, but he doubted the Yards could escape religious persecution even in the States. Ethan knew they would quickly be dismissed as simple-minded, uncivilized beasts and their animistic religion be shunned. He figured the Montagnards would be tolerated back home, sure, but what ethnicity of people wished only to be tolerated?

Everyone was slow to wake the next day, but by midmorning, the team was ready to load up and head back to CCC. Before they left, Ethan reached into his pocket and handed Nay's father the envelope of money, but he knew of nothing more to say. The old village chief embraced him and patted his head. Everyone said their goodbyes and they were on the road in short order, complete with a fresh new recruit to help fill the open void that Nay had left. He was a skinny, handsome sixteen-year-old kid by the name of Ayatt, and was a cousin to Ti Tu. He had no prior military service, but all the Yards on the team vowed that he was a superb woodsman and hunter.

"Ayatt so silent in jungle, he once sneaked up on sleeping tiger and pulled its tail," Ti Tu recounted with vividly animated eyes.

Bruce looked at Ethan as if to say, "Yeah right!" but Nui nodded adamantly.

"I saw, I saw," he beamed.

Ethan trusted his Yards and knew that if they felt confident in Ayatt, there was no reason for him to reserve any doubt. Being among his relatives and peers, it was almost certain the little Montagnard would live up to his promised reputation. Utah's little people all came from the same village and had known each other since birth, and several of them were even kin.

They rode back to Kontum with heavy hearts for Nay but somehow rejuvenated after celebrating in his memory.

21

Enemy activity across the fence was as fierce as ever and the fall months of 1969 had proved taxing and difficult for CCC. During a Hatchet Force operation in Laos in late September, Ron Goulet was killed shortly after rescuing Mike Sheppard from a burning Kingbee that had been shot down on the LZ during insertion.

A few weeks after Bob Howard left for home, Joe Walker turned his beloved RT California over to Richard "Moose" Gross, packed his gear, and trotted off to northern Laos with the CIA for a year. Gross had already spent a year running recon up at CCN and just when he seemed to find his footing with California, they drafted a remote Prairie Fire target and were hit at point-blank range by a counter-recon element. Bill Stubbs never even had a chance, and the shooting so intense the rest of the team was unable to recover his body.

Barely five days after that, Joseph Whelan and Ron Bozikis were both killed after their Hatchet Force platoon walked headlong into an ambush in Laos; Frank Belletire suffered a traumatic head wound and barely survived.

It was getting hotter across the fence and more and more difficult for teams to get on the ground. Nine times out of ten, teams were getting shot out of their third and fourth alternate LZs by large numbers of NVA who were seemingly just lying in wait beneath the Hueys. And when teams were finally able to get on the ground, it was always a race against the odds as the NVA massed to overrun them.

Though the odds of surviving on the ground weren't improving much, at least their equipment was. In an effort to make rope extractions safer and more user-friendly, a handful of SF instructors down at the 5th Group's RECONDO School developed a new extraction harness called the STABO rig. The acronym was a marriage of the phrase "stabilized body" and that's exactly what it did. It was an ingenious design that incorporated two seat straps, two shoulder straps that crossed behind the user's back, and a waist-belt – all in one. It was intended to be used both as a combat harness and as an extraction harness. At the top of each shoulder strap was a D-ring and a carabiner where ropes were attached via an inverted Y-shaped yoke. Helicopter crews would tie the ropes off to their ships and drop the yoke assemblies down to recon men or Hatchet Force members who would snap themselves in. The brilliance of the STABO rig was that it provided the user a hands-free ride which gave him the ability to fire his weapon and fend off trees while being lifted through the canopy. In order to maintain a free range of motion, all the user had to do was unhook the seat straps from the front, fold them back behind and clip them into the waist-belt. The STABO rig also provided a far more comfortable seat to ride home in and there wasn't a soul in Recon or the Hatchet Force who complained about the new harness.

*   *   *

In mid-November, Utah drafted a trail-watch gig way up near Highway 165 – a few klicks south of where they'd pulled the sensor mission, and not far from where Bill Stubbs had been lost only weeks before. No one in Recon could comprehend the logic behind the assigned target-area because it was simply too soon to send another team back up there. And for such a remote section of the Trail, that area had received a lot of attention over the past few months.

It was appropriate to label it a suicide mission and Ethan could sense it when he moved the team into isolation. The Yards were uncharacteristically quiet and their smiles seemed half-hearted and forced. It had gotten sticky before – very sticky, but this time felt different somehow. It was eerie and unsettling to know how California had been stalked up there; how the NVA had shadowed them with nary a sound and killed Stubbs at point-blank range. John Plaster's team had been slated to go in the previous week but the mission was scrubbed and Illinois never left Dak To.

*   *   *

The visual recon didn't offer up much in the way of fresh intel; Highway 165 looked as menacing and foreboding as ever from the backseat of the old Bird Dog. Thick early-morning ground fog coiled itself around the surrounding hillsides and piled up on the roadbed, smothering corners and sections of it from observation. It would be impossible to find useable landing zones down in the valleys until the sun burned the fog away, but orbiting over the target for that long would quickly draw unwanted attention.

Pete Johnston coaxed the nimble O-1 back around again while Ethan eyeballed the higher ridgelines and connecting saddles, and looked for a way in.

We really only have two options, he figured. *Early-morning insert above the fog-line, or at last-light down in a valley.*

But the more he weighed those options, the less he liked the latter. Last-light was too final – too many factors hinged on luck alone and that was never good. On the other hand, an early-morning insertion would give them all day to shake trackers and elude counter-recon forces, and if things got bad they'd have ample time to get out before dark. But going in at first-light meant going in high on a saddle or a low ridge, just above the fog. It'd be unavoidably loud and they'd need several false insertions to throw the NVA off long enough to get away clean.

"Hey dude," Pete called over the two-way cockpit intercom. "We keep drawing circles like this and Uncle Ho's bound to turn this rig into Swiss cheese. How many more passes do you wanna make?"

"...I've seen enough," Ethan said as he fingered a ridge on his map-sheet and scribbled the six-digit coordinate fix onto the Plexiglas windscreen. Without much reluctance, Pete rolled the Bird Dog sharply to starboard and the mist-shrouded mountains flipped vertical and slipped away before the border leveled out on the horizon.

*   *   *

"What'd you guys see out there?" Bruce asked as he wheeled the jeep out of the airfield and sped into a strange, bustling mix of ancient and modern traffic.

"Not much," Ethan mumbled with a light sigh. "Lots of ground fog, a few abandoned AA positions but that's about it." The sounds of midday hustle-bustle muted their brief chat but that wasn't the only reason for the lack of conversation. Seeing those bomb-scarred, fog-ridden valleys and mountains from the backseat of Pete's O-1 had stoned him with a cold eeriness. It was just too remote way up there; too deep and too shadowy, as if the warm, life-loving rays of sunlight never reached out that far.

"If we take eight, we're gonna need two birds and that's gonna be loud as shit," Ethan speculated while reviewing his map-sheets and coordinate fixes. "I'm thinking a six-pack this time: you, me, Luc, Bo, Hyuk, and Nui." He glanced up as they bounced over the Dak Bla River where Tom Waskovich and a few other lads who were busy minding a platoon of Montagnards while they practiced rappelling from the bridge. Tom's recon team had been in the midst of assaulting an NVA antiaircraft position back in April when he suddenly went delirious and collapsed with malaria. Luckily enough, his assistant team leader was able to get everyone out on strings without further casualties. Fearing that Tom might have another bout with malaria while across the fence, Lieutenant Colonel Abt transferred him to A Company of the Hatchet Force as a platoon leader.

"Operations scrubbed the mission," Bruce grinned as he swerved the jeep at Tom and gave him the finger.

"You're shitting me."

Bruce flashed his pearly teeth and shook his head, "Zune and Yates told me about an hour ago; said we're back on stand-down."

"He say why?"

"Nope, just that it was a no-go and that the colonel wants to see you when we get back."

"You think they passed it to another team?"

"Beats me," Bruce shrugged as they wheeled through the east gate. They stashed the jeep over at the motor pool and grabbed a bite to eat at the club before parting ways again. Between mission prep and dispensary duties, it seemed Bruce barely had time to sleep.

Ethan caught the colonel by himself a short while later unwinding at the horseshoe pits. Aside from going out of his way to take care of those under his command, Fred Abt enjoyed few things more than a good game of horseshoes.

"You play much?" the colonel asked while retrieving the ringers he'd just tossed.

"Every once in awhile," Ethan sheepishly admitted.

"So how was the VR?"

"Well sir, we didn't see much, really," he shrugged. "Too much ground fog."

"Well I'm sure you know by now the mission's been cancelled," the colonel said as he shoved a pair of weathered horseshoes into Ethan's hands.

"Yessir, that's my understanding."

"We mulled it over with Saigon and agreed that it's simply too risky to send another team back in there for the time being." He pitched both shoes and stepped aside to let Ethan take his turn.

"Well sir, do we have a new target yet?"

"No and you're not getting one."

"Bright Light duty then?" he guessed.

"Afraid not… your team's been pulled from active rotation."

"Sir, I know we're short a man," Ethan pleaded, "but I've –"

"You're too goddamn short, Ethan," the colonel cut him off. "Both of y'all. Your tour is up at the first of the year and Sergeant McNeil rotates out in February. Hell, I've been waiting for y'all to come to me for reassignment for the past month but you boys just keep going out."

"So does this mean we're both being reassigned?"

"Well the dispensary is simply overworked and undermanned right now, so Sergeant McNeil will be spending the rest of his time there…"

"And me, sir?"

The colonel pitched his last shoe, turned to Ethan and put a hand on his shoulder.

"Ethan, I think it's fair to say that you're a solid recon man and a great team leader. And believe me, others agree with that assessment."

"I dunno sir, that's a pretty bold statement," he replied with his best attempt at being humble. "We are among heroes here."

"We are, yes… My tour as CCC's commanding officer will end in February and I wanna be certain that whoever assumes command here next has the best men for the job at hand. I need you, Ethan. *We* need you… It's never easy to ask men to do this," he confessed with a sigh, "but your role in our war is one that is very difficult to fill."

Ethan nodded quietly and thought about the right answer to give his commanding officer but the words just didn't come.

"Listen, don't worry about it; I don't need your answer right now," he smiled and patted Ethan's shoulder.

"What about my new assignment?"

"Well Ethan, it's up to you, really. What do you wanna do for the next six weeks?"

"Sir, I'm happy to go wherever you need me," Ethan assured him, "but I'd like to stay with my team if that's all right. We could easily use this time to stay trained and fit… Maybe fly VRs with the SPAF guys a few times a week, too. Shoot some photos for the lab…"

The colonel puckered his lips slightly and nodded, "Fine by me, just so long as you keep busy."

"No problem, sir," Ethan said as they shook hands.

He left the colonel alone to finish his game in peace. And as he wandered away, listening to the clanking report of the ringers, he already knew the answer he'd give him. Too much about himself had been forged in the fires of SOG's secret war. With every mission he ran, every night he spent with the Yards, every tear he shed, and every laugh he shared, it became more and more impossible to turn it off and walk away. Few could. That was why men like Joe Walker and Bob Howard kept coming back.

He was playing with the handmade brass bracelets he wore on his right wrist as he passed through security and entered the TOC. His little people and the elders of their village had given the bracelets to him as a symbol of their undying friendship and Ethan often fiddled with them out of habit. He breezed into the administrations office, approached the baggy-eyed personnel clerk, and requested the necessary forms and paperwork required for a tour extension.

It had to be that way.

*   *   *

"They moved me outta Recon," Bruce muttered while leafing slowly through the March, 1969 issue of *Playboy Magazine*. His scheming eyes glanced up from the sex-splattered pages, searching for Ethan's reaction as the words rolled off his tongue. "I'm gonna finish my tour out at the dispensary." The Puerto Rican's round, stubble-covered face had shown a strange mix of guilt and great concentration for the past hour.

Ethan finished the sentence he was writing before pushing the letter aside and turning to face his teammate; the pause bled for several quiet moments.

"…Yeah, I know."

"How'd you hear?" he asked as the two push-broom-like mustaches he had for eyebrows fluttered inward.

"The colonel told me earlier this afternoon."

"So who's getting the team?"

Ethan shook his head, "I'm staying on. We're just gonna train for the time being until I get back from extension leave."

"You extended?! How long?"

Ethan chewed his lip for a second and grinned deviously, "Another year."

"Damn…"

"What about you? You thought about extending?"

"I've been toying with the notion of another six months," Bruce confessed, "but I haven't decided yet."

"Uncle Sam gave me a two-thousand-dollar extension bonus," he grinned.

"Damn, wonder if it's the same for six months?"

"Beats me," he shrugged as he punched a hole in the top of his beer with his church-key.

"So you ain't mad?"

"Why? You mean because you abandoned me and the Yards to relax in the dispensary for the next two-and-a-half months?" Ethan kidded.

"Fuck you," Bruce laughed and Frisbee'd the Playboy at him. "But yeah, seriously... I mean I practically begged you to gimme a slot on the team, and now I'm back at the dispensary..."

"Hey fuck that shit, okay?" Ethan demanded. "We've been through some heavy shit and not once did you ever lose your cool when it got sticky. We all counted on you for so much... probably more than was fair, but you never let us down." There was no jest in his words as raw emotions began to surge and flood inside him. Bruce hadn't said a thing but sometimes words left unsaid carried more meaning.

Ethan cleared his throat and stood up to leave.

"Hey, the SPAFs are playing poker in about ten minutes," he said as he checked his watch. "You in?"

"No-can-do, amigo; I'm back on duty at sunup tomorrow morning. Think I'm gonna slam another beer and crash."

Ethan looped his pistol around his neck and tucked it comfortably into his waistband.

"Okay buddy, see ya when I see ya," he promised as he pulled the team house door shut behind him. The night was young and the air, refreshingly cool. A tremendous barrage of artillery fire suddenly thundered overhead like an airborne freight train.

"Goddamn those fuck'n legs," he grumbled while ducking his head out of natural reflex. Firebase Mary Lou's outgoing artillery fire passed directly over the compound so low the shockwaves were frequently felt on bare skin. It had been a difficult thing to get used to and even after almost a year of it, he was still caught off-guard every now and then.

He rounded the corner of the building and gathered stride as he made way for Pete Johnston and Rex Hill's team house. It was a rather quiet evening on the compound despite the artillery fire. The telltale sounds of *The Wild Bunch* playing at the outdoor theater over by the club fluttered on a drifting breeze. He pulled open the SPAF's door and stepped in as Jefferson Airplane greeted him gently with psychedelic guitar riffs.

"There he is!" Tom Waskovich bellowed with a raised beer in one fist and a fan of playing cards in the other. "Just in time too, E, check that shit out – full house!" Tom sprawled his cards out to reveal three fives and two nines. "I *finally* win!"

"God you're swine, Woji," Rex grumbled as Tom raked his winnings in with a giggle.

"Since when did you hang out the night before a mission?" Karate asked.

"It's been scrubbed. They decided me and Bruce are too short so they nixed it and moved him back to the dispensary."

"Well, I'm glad to hear that," Pete beamed as Tom fastidiously dealt out the next round of five-card draw. "Beers are in the fridge; help yourself."

Ethan crossed the room to the little refrigerator and pondered for a moment.

"Any particular reason why y'all got this thing zipped up in a fucking flack-jacket?" he asked as he opened the body armor and retrieved a beer from inside. Tom was snickering uncontrollably behind his cards while Pete and Rex looked on with lighthearted disgust.

"When do you DEROS?" Tom asked as he stifled his giggles and tried to change the subject.

"I'm not – I extended. So what's the skinny on this armored fridge?"

"You wanna tell it this time, or should I?" Pete asked Rex.

"Go ahead," Rex laughed with a nod. "You tell it way better than me."

"Well, it started with our dearly beloved Ken Snyder," Pete began. "See, me and Rex had been flying all day, rolling over the treetops and getting shot at like the heroes we are, calling in air support for you recon dregs – no offense – and generally working miracles like we always do..."

"Boy, he's laying it on thick, ain't he?" Karate ribbed Tom with his elbow.

"So we get back from flying all day long," Pete continued, "and find a bunch of arrows stuck through our wall because Ken decided to use their side as a target for his Montagnard crossbow."

"It was legitimate research," Tom assured with a laugh. "We needed to know if a Yard crossbow was effective enough to be used in our IA drills!"

"No surprise there," Rex chuckled.

"Yeah, and then about a month later, Tommy shoots a hole through the same wall with his forty-five and the round sails through my pillow, and tags our fridge. I woulda gotten my head shot off had I been asleep."

"Hey, what'd you call it, Woji – an accidental discharge?" Rex egged on. "Ain't that how the ladies in town describe you?"

"I can just see you in there facing the wall, looking like a badass gunslinger – like Clint Eastwood!" Pete howled.

"Yeah, well the real tragedy was the fridge, even if you *had* gotten capped," Tom hissed at Pete.

They spent the rest of the evening listening to music, playing cards, discussing combat lore, and talking about the States. Tom was short and would be rotating home in the coming weeks, and Ken Snyder had taken a slot with SOG Headquarters in Saigon and was set to rotate out just before Christmas. Ethan talked to Rex and Pete about flying backseater with them for the duration of his tour. They both agreed but quickly decided he was going to need a change of codename.

"Ethan, 'Hollywood' is pretty weak for a SPAF backseater, and just plain pussy for a recon knuckle-dragger," Pete advised him.

"Sounds too much like a zoomy call-sign or a stage-name for a porn star," Rex chuckled.

"Yeah, if you're gonna fly with us, you're gonna need something... something heavier, ya dig?"

"Alright, alright, I'm onboard," he caved. "Whatcha got?" They all scratched their heads for a minute before blurting out suggestions.

"How about Chaos?" Tom offered.

"Mayhem," Rex countered.

"Hitman," Karate Davis said with a nod. "Hitman."

There was a collective silence while everyone considered it.

"It's good, *real* good," Pete admitted.

"It's dark – I dig it."

"Ethan, you're the Hitman from now on, ya hear?" Pete declared as he raised his beer in a high toast.

Ethan made his new codename official with the head-shed first thing the next morning and then wandered over to the mess hall. He drew a cup of coffee and sat down alone with a week-old copy of the *New York Times*. He read quietly for several minutes, sipping the hot brew and observing the morning rituals of his fellow comrades before they all shuffled off to their respected places of business. But something was suddenly amiss with his world; he could feel Captain Yates' presence close by. He listened for his hacking troll-like laugh and looked for his snarling visage in and amongst his fellow troopers. Yates was an elusive creature when he had to be. A choking waft of Aqua Velva drifted past in someone's wake. For some reason, the good captain was convinced he was going to meet the future Mrs. Jim Yates right there on the compound because he never went anywhere without a liberal spreckling of Aqua Velva, but the scent often betrayed him. Ethan knew he only had a split second or two to make a run for it. He half-stood and spun around in his seat but it was too late – Yates had him flanked. Ethan kept his eyes on him while he inched his gun-hand slowly across his waistline and fingered the plastic grips of his pistol.

I might be able to wing him if I can draw fast enough, he figured. *That should buy me enough time to get some more firepower and hardware to finish the job.*

He could feel a devious grin spreading across his face at the thought but Yates made it known he had the drop on him.

"Ahh, ahh," he cautioned with a gremlin-like smile while motioning Ethan back into his seat with the barrel of his Smith & Wesson.

"Look, *Dai-uy,* I was playing cards and drinking beer with the SPAFs all fucking night," Ethan sighed as the captain planted himself in the opposite chair, "so don't even think about trying to hang a bag of shit around my neck."

"Surely you don't think I'd attempt to frame or railroad you," the captain said with a sarcastic smirk. "You're one of my most loyal conscripts."

"Whaddaya want, *Dai-uy*? You're scheming and I can smell it. I'm too fuck'n short for any of your Audie Murphy fantasy missions. Same goes for Major Doom's gentle propositions, so pass the word, ya hear? Go pester Reynolds; he wants to be a hero."

"Well I figured you'd be too much of a pussy to keep run'n recon for a full twelve months so I reckon I'll let you play with the SPAFs so long as you keep those little indigenous criminals of yours entertained until your extension leave."

"How'd you know about that?"

"I'm all-knowing," he scowled.

"Doesn't that just make your black little heart leap for joy?" Ethan beamed cheekily. "Knowing that yours truly will be here to continue the chaos and utter mayhem that give you purpose in life for another year."

"Shit, the only things you ingrates give me are high blood pressure and alcoholism," he groaned with an annoyed smirk. "Now get the fuck outta my mess hall and don't let me see your worthless hide until Thanksgiving dinner. Savvy?"

*   *   *

He finally came to, slumped over the steering wheel of the old steam tractor that sat along the Highway 14, just up the road from the compound. His neck was stiff from the position he'd been left in and his sternum and chest ached from the press of the tractor's steering wheel. The inside of his throat felt like sandpaper as he groaned and leaned back, trying to shake it off. He pulled at his arms and wrists but couldn't seem to free them. He groggily rolled his eyelids back from the alcohol-induced coma and was immediately blinded by the early-morning sunlight. If he had been anywhere else, he would have fought for more sleep but the bonds that held his wrists fast were beginning to cause alarm.

"What the... fuck."

He was tied to the steering wheel.

He smacked and licked his lips and sampled the fire on his breath: a peach-flavored aftertaste on top of what he imagined the bottom of his boots might taste like after strolling through the gutter of a Saigon alley. He opened his eyes once again and glanced down at his clothing and finally realized he was dressed as an NVA soldier: pith helmet, Bata boots and all. He focused on the cardboard sign that was strung around his neck.

"*Chieu hoi,*" he slowly read to himself in confusion. He began to remember bits and pieces of the night before. The club had gone full-tilt after Thanksgiving dinner and at some point, he had passed out after indulging in too much of Bill's peach-flavored, homebrewed hooch.

"Jesus Christ, I can't believe I passed out in the club," he sighed. "God knows what else those idiots did to me." The next thing he recalled was hysterical laughter, an NVA uniform, a careening jeep ride against his inebriated will, and the steam tractor. Fuller, Bill, Reynolds, Pete Johnston, Karate, Tom Waskovich – they were all in on it.

He began working his hands loose while assembling a litany of criminal charges against his suspects…

Attempted poisoning via Bill's peachy concoction, premeditated kidnapping, larceny, grand theft auto, probably some form of molestation since Reynolds was involved, he shuddered. No jury in the world would fail to convict those cutthroats. But he wasn't interested in judicial proceedings. No, he had greater aspirations than that; legal action was too soft a punishment for the nefarious rabble he was dealing with.

With his hands free he woozily climbed down from the ancient steam tractor and straightened his act as best he could. The morning traffic offered him sideways glances and double-takes, and he received the common accusation of, "You numba one, *beaucoup dinky dau,* GI," followed by heaps of snickering from the locals.

"Oh I'm crazy alright," he laughed maniacally at them as he bristled back towards camp. "Just wait 'till I get my guns and the rest of my hardware," he vowed while clapping his hands for effect.

Lord knows Woji and the damn SPAF Sisters were in on it. Thick as thieves, those three… I could probably get Tom's 201-file and doctor his mental health evaluation to include a diagnosis of delusions of grandeur or some sort of abnormal, psychotic nervous tick. And I may as well throw in a few STDs for good measure while I'm at it.

He giggled at his own devilry. Nothing would railroad an aspiring young officer's Special Forces career better than a psychological disorder and a host of venereal diseases.

And maybe I'll pay that stumpy personnel clerk at the head-shed to forge some reenlistment papers for Reynolds; get him sent to some leg outfit for a year, or maybe to an MP detachment somewhere real nasty, like Hue or Quang Tri.

Yes, retribution was going to be fun indeed.

He was lost in the fantasy of revenge as he closed the remaining distance to the camp's northern wire. The Yards pulling security offered him mushy giggles and arm pats as he trudged back into the perimeter.

Ah the Yards, he remembered with an adoring smile. *My little pirates; they're the only true friends I have among all these criminals.*

His little people had seemed strangely crestfallen the day before when he'd told them the mission was cancelled and the team had been taken out of active rotation. Usually, they would have been animated and relieved because they always knew when they were going into a hot target. But the Montagnards were simple, not stupid; Ethan had been with them since he'd arrived at CCC and they knew his time in Vietnam was coming to a close.

"You leave soon, *Trung-si?*" Nui had asked with a little brother-like expression on his warm face. He patted and stroked Ethan's forearm gently the way he always did but there was something pleading about his eyes. All their eyes looked that way. There was no coming and going for them; they were fighting and dying on the very soil they had known their whole lives while foreign armies had shuffled in and out for centuries.

"I'm not leaving just yet," he tried to reassure them. "I still have almost two months left." Bo and Luc and the others went quietly back to their game of cards. He begged them to hear him out, but they were too busy giving him the indigenous version of the silent treatment. When he finally got their attention he explained that he was going home to see his family for a short while and then coming back.

"You come back to run team again," Bo pleaded.

Ethan could see the gravity of the question as it hung from all their faces.

"Yes," he nodded. "And then we'll go back into the woods and hunt Uncle Ho's cousins again," he promised. And with that, their umbrage melted into a fluttering, child-like exuberance with wide smiles, more arm pats and cheek sniffs. All was well in their world again.

22

For the next six weeks, Ethan roamed the volatile skies above the Ho Chi Minh Trail in the cramped backseat of a SPAF Bird Dog. They rolled low and slow, skimming the treetops while working feverishly to sniff out enemy truck parks, way-stations, base-areas, antiaircraft positions, and ammo and fuel depots. And when they stumbled onto targets of high-value, they mustered up whatever immediate air assets they could and pounded the NVA until there was nothing left but pulverized earth.

Just a few days before Christmas, he pulled Ray Fuller's team out on strings after they'd been discovered counting trucks fording a riverbed just north of Juliet-9. Since Rex Hill's O-1 was the only airborne FAC within earshot of RT Oregon's desperate calls for help, Ethan went from being a visual reconnaissance photographer to an on-the-fly Covey Rider. Rex ordered up Spads and fast-movers by the pairs and stacked them accordingly while Ethan directed Fuller and his people to the nearest useable clearing. And when Rex banked the little plane over the LZ, Ethan was able to see his friends sprawling out in a pair of bomb craters a few hundred feet below, reloading their weapons and stacking magazines, readying grenades and preparing to fight for their lives. And in that instant, he wanted to be down there among them where he belonged, where he felt he could best influence the fight and control the outcome.

While Oregon dug in, Ethan began directing gun-runs all around them, slowly and methodically working the fire out and away from them with each new concentric pass. Hidden antiaircraft batteries chugged away from the surrounding hillsides and valleys in mixes of .51-caliber and 23mm. While Rex juked and dodged swarms of green tracer-fire, Ethan put the fast-movers to work on the heavy guns where they could drop 250 and 500-pound bombs and napalm-death without the possibility of hitting Oregon by mistake. Every time a hard-bomb hit the deck, a quick ring of concussion swells rippled away from the bubbly-orange flash and rolled through the tangle like a stone had been dropped into water. And when the zoomies hit the enemy gun emplacements spot-on, all that was left was vaporized jungle, coils of black smoke, and secondary explosions as the ammunition caches cooked off. The cadence of destruction was horrifically beautiful and as spectacular as anything Ethan had ever witnessed, and he was strung out by the power he commanded with just a bank of radios.

Christmas and New Year's 1970 came and went, and as his one year tour pared down to only a few weeks, parties were thrown and farewells were bid to friends who were going home or on to new assignments. Tom Waskovich had already left for the States at the beginning of December and Ken Snyder dropped his gig at SOG Headquarters in Saigon for the Army's stateside flight school. It didn't take long for Ethan and the others to miss that duo and their antics, but it was good to see them make it out in one piece and with *most* of their sanity intact.

He was back in the skies above Laos a few days after the new year in the backseat of Pete Johnston's O-1 Bird Dog, photographing a stretch of Highway 165 that had been heavily bombed the night before. The emergency radio frequency suddenly crackled with a faint cry for help.

"You get that?" Pete called.

"It's somebody's indig," Ethan said. "Definitely not American."

It wasn't good; indigenous teammates weren't allowed to make radio transmissions unless something had gone horribly wrong and their American counterparts weren't able to do it themselves. Thankfully Covey was already on the scene trying to sort through the details, and the extraction package was en route, but the radio traffic was difficult to understand.

"Whose team is it? Do they know yet?"

Pete broke in on the net and asked Covey for an ID on the team, and that's when bad news turned worse.

"SPAF-4," Covey transmitted, "I'm being told by Guerilla it's RT Georgia. Still waiting for White Horse to confirm. Over."

It was Paul's team, and as if that wasn't bad enough, Mark had thrown in as a straphanger at the last second on what was supposed to be their last time out before extension leave. Pete had turned south and was pushing the Bird Dog for all it was worth, but things were unfolding quickly and it sounded like Covey was going to get them extracted before they could get there. The indigenous teammate finally identified himself as Bao, the interpreter, but there was a lot of traffic on the net making it difficult to keep track of the situation. Meanwhile, Reynolds and his people were gearing up for the Bright Light just as soon as more slicks arrived at Dak To. Then Covey called back with a fix on their position and said the target looked cold and that he was going to pull them.

"Cobras are zipping around down there but I don't see any ground fire," he reported. "Okay, one slick in… looks like… looks like five or six onboard." He then ordered the second slick to go in for the rest but the first bird called back with a troubling development.

"Covey, the six we just scooped up are saying they don't know where the others are. Over."

"What the hell, we're missing people?!"

"Roger Covey, we got six indig onboard, no Straw Hats."

"Bro, what the fuck?"

"They're saying they got hit this morning and got separated and don't know where the Straw Hats are."

So Covey did the only thing he could: He ordered the whole show back to Dak To for fuel while he remained over the target-area incase Paul or Mark came up on the emergency frequency or signaled him.

"Pete, I need to get to Dak To," Ethan pleaded. "I'll take the heat, just get me on the deck."

Thirty minutes later, they bounced onto the far end of the airstrip just minutes behind the extraction package. Ethan grabbed what little he carried with him – his CAR-15, two bandoleers of loaded magazines, assorted grenades he carried inside a Claymore mine bag, his treasured Gerber Mk II fighting knife, camera, and a STABO extraction harness he was already wearing. He stripped his helmet off, kicked the door open and jumped out, stumbling as the Bird Dog continued to taxi across the runway. Pete yelled after him but he had not the time. He bolted past the choppers, across the drainage ditch and into the perimeter of the launch site where Randy Reynolds, Pete Mullis and their little people were all geared-up, waiting to go in.

"What the fuck's going on?!" he demanded.

"Fucking Kontum is sending up a Hatchet Force company," Reynolds complained.

"Fuck that, let's help them finish refueling those birds and get on the ground before they get here."

"Ethan, we don't even know where to look yet," Captain Shepherd interjected. "The interpreter says they got hit early this morning in their RON, and they're not even sure what direction they moved in before we got to 'em."

"Captain, let us go in before the Hatchet Force gets here."

"C'mon sir," Reynolds urged. "They ain't got much time out there."

"I can't order the launch and just send you guys in without knowing where to look," he reasoned. And he may have been right, but Ethan wasn't interested in waiting.

"How the fuck did Covey not know Paul and Mark were missing *before* he pulled them out? This whole thing smells like shit!"

He hustled over to where Paul's Vietnamese teammates were being questioned by one of the launch site staffers and his interpreter.

"Ask him how far they moved after they got hit. I need to know where to look."

"He ain't sure," the staffer sighed. "I already asked him."

"Well when was the last time you saw 'em?"

"We hit early," Bao's eyes searched, "…did not see where they went. Not sure what way we move… Got on radio, call helicop. *Beaucoup* NVA."

Ethan turned and trotted back towards the gate; he didn't like it. Captain Shepherd and the others called after him but he didn't have the time and neither did his friends. He sprinted across the drainage ditch and onto the tarmac where the aircrews were topping their birds off and found the ship that pulled Paul's little people out.

"I need you to take me back to where you extracted them."

The whole crew looked at him like he was crazy.

"C'mon, we're wasting time!"

Minutes later, they were off the ground and soaring out over the valley, heading west for Laos. He pulled the headset on and heard a flood of radio traffic ordering them back to the launch site.

"Just tell 'em I got a gun to your head," Ethan advised.

"Would that happen if I turned this ship around?"

"Please, sir," he begged, "don't make me do that…"

The tension settled and Ethan cleared the net so he could talk to Covey.

"Hitman, go ahead."

"Please tell me you got something – a mirror, a flare, traffic on the emergency freq – *anything*."

"Hitman, bro… I got nothing. But I'm still looking and I got plenty of fuel."

"Okay… okay, what assets you got for me?"

"Whaddaya need?"

"Well I'm one slick, no guns. I'll take whatever I can get," Ethan leveled.

"Jesus, dude… Wait one."

He quickly looked his equipment over and tried to imagine exactly what he intended to do once they reached the LZ, but there really wasn't much to consider.

"Hitman, Covey."

"Yeah go."

"I got a pair of Spads three-zero mikes out."

"Roger that, can you describe the area to me?"

"Okay, there's a wide draw facing west and at the bottom of that draw was where they were monitoring trail traffic. The LZ we pulled 'em out on is about three-quarters up the draw on a shelf."

"That woulda put their last RON somewhere downhill near the trail, right?"

"Yeah roger that, Hitman. And there's a north-to-south blue line paralleling the trail."

"Shit ain't adding up, Covey. The interpreter said he wasn't sure which way they moved after getting hit."

"They moved east. Only way they coulda gone. You'll see what I mean."

The crew chief came over the net and told Ethan they were a few minutes out and Covey gave them the all-clear.

"Roger," Ethan said. "I'm switching my emergency radio on now. Out."

He pulled the headset off, powered his URC-10 on, and gave his weapon one final check. The crew chief reached over and handed him a stick of camouflage which he used to paint his face and the backs of his hands. He made quick work of what was usually a meticulous pre-insertion ritual, then waved them a thumbs-up and made ready in the portside doorway. The valley had opened up beneath the slick and he could instantly see what Covey had described. The bird hit short-final, flared, and he was out and on the ground, running for the tree-line while the Huey thundered up and away without taking a single lick of ground fire.

Alone. Utterly alone, right as the gravity of the situation and what he was attempting finally hit him. He was plenty scared – not for himself but for his friends.

"Covey, I'm on the ground, moving downhill to the west. No contact. Over."

"Roger Hitman. Spads are on station and the Bright Light is en route."

He stashed his URC-10 in his thigh-pocket and slowly began canvassing the hillside until he was able to pick up Georgia's back-trail. It wasn't hard to find.

They musta been on the run because they sure as shit didn't cover their tracks, he reasoned.

He retraced their passage, stopping every few steps to listen to the jungle and to smell the air while letting his eyes search and his muzzle track. The fauna was beautifully vibrant and green, and the place alive with all manner of creatures. Farther downhill he moved, skirting past shafts of dusty sunlight and always moving with solid cover in reach. He scanned the ground where he intended to place his next step, making sure there were no surprises; deliberate and calculated movement while searching for spent shell casings or empty magazines that may have been dropped in the heat of battle, but there were none. No chopped-up fauna, no fired brass or empty magazines, no bodies or blood trails, or even the faint smell of expended gun powder and ordnance. It was as if nothing had happened at all. The NVA should've been all over him by then but he didn't even feel their presence, not even so much as a hint or a whiff of them lurking about. He was a little more than halfway down the draw when this all occurred to him. He threw caution to the wind and started moving faster as the panic mounted. He wanted so badly to scream their names so they could call him to their predicament, but deep down, Ethan knew they weren't there.

Panic turned to frustration, and then to anger and rage.

He wanted contact. He wanted the NVA to be there so he could kill them but they weren't. And worse yet, neither were Paul and Mark. They were gone and he knew it, and none of it made any sense.

He reached the bottom of the hillside and found the trail to be a hard-packed affair with only a few minor scuff marks showing recent use. Luc might've been able to read tracks from it but Ethan wasn't that good. He paralleled the trail until he found their RON site. It was a good spot from what he could tell – one that he would've hoped to find had his team been there for the same purpose. There were signs of recent activity in and around the site as well, but nothing that suggested any real struggle and certainly no evidence of a firefight having taken place.

His emergency radio suddenly crackled.

"Hitman, this is Covey. You alright down there?"

"I got nothing, Covey," he calmly replied. "It's a fucking mystery. They just vanished… I dunno."

"I'm inserting the Bright Light in zero-five mikes."

"Roger, I'm moving back up to the LZ."

When Randy's team got on the ground, Ethan pointed them in the direction of Georgia's back-trail and told them where to find the RON site.

"You're not gonna help us search for 'em?" Randy asked with a bewildered gaze.

Ethan couldn't find the words to tell him they were gone, and that his Bright Light was too little, too late.

"Be careful," he said as the second Huey slid in overhead. "No hero shit."

"Hero shit? You fucking kidding me?"

The slick dropped into a perfect hover and out came Pete Mullis with the rest of RT North Dakota. Ethan shielded his eyes and climbed onboard, and they were out in a rush. He watched from the open doorway as Reynolds consolidated his people and slipped into the woods.

One-man Bright Light, Jesus Christ... What was your plan, dude? Fight off a thousand Nguyens with a few hundred rounds and some frags? What the fuck would you have done had you actually found them? What if the slick had gotten shot down? No medical supplies, no water... Fuck, did Georgia even get hit like Bao said?

And right then, he had an epiphany. He realized Bao's story had been a complete fabrication. They never got hit. Ethan remembered how his eyes had cut back and forth when he had pressed him for details back at Dak To. Bao had acted cagey and shocked but Ethan had been so consumed by getting on the ground and going to the aid of his friends, he'd missed it.

Bao and the others were the only ones who could solve the mystery.

Ethan pulled the spare radio headset on and cleared the net.

"Guerilla, this is Hitman. How copy?"

"Loud'n clear, go."

"Guerilla, are Georgia's indig still there?"

"Negative Hitman, White Horse ordered 'em back home for an immediate debrief. They left about ten minutes ago."

The aircrew bypassed Dak To and took him straight to CCC, and he was mobbed by a happy yet reserved welcoming party. The mystery surrounding RT Georgia and Ethan's subsequent one-man Bright Light had circulated through camp. He ignored all their questions, backslaps, and offerings of cold beer – not because he was ungrateful, but because he only had one priority and that was to get face-to-face with Bao and the rest of Paul's Vietnamese teammates.

"Get your ass in the TOC right fucking now," Captain Yates ordered.

"Are they in there?"

"They're being debriefed."

"They're lying, Jim; their story is fucking bullshit. I found their RON site… Jim, they were *never* in contact."

"They've been separated, isolated, and are being individually debriefed, and they haven't been found guilty of anything yet. Don't forget that. Now get in there and talk to the S-2 and S-3 people."

Those were orders he didn't intend to ignore, and he told them exactly what had transpired from the second he and Pete heard the call while shooting photos up north, until the moment he landed back at CCC.

"So what's going on – what have they told y'all?" Ethan probed.

"We don't know; we haven't been made privy to those interrogations," one of the S-2 staffers shrugged.

"Wait – so they're being *interrogating* now?"

"Interrogate was the wrong word," he backpedaled. "It's a debriefing as far as we know. They're debriefing them all separately. If their statements aren't congruent, they'll be in a world of shit."

By the time he was dismissed from the debriefing, it was well after dark and the past fourteen hours had whittled him away to almost nothing. The loss of Mark and Paul had yet to really set in, but Pete's team and the Hatchet Force were still on the ground searching and as it stood, his friends were listed as missing in action.

He was hungry and tired; a steak and a stiff drink at the club was all he required but he just couldn't deal with any more questions. He crossed the company area under a moonless sky and headed for the Yards' barracks. They were sure to be cooking up a feast as usual and the comfort of his hammock, and their genuine company was beginning to best even what the club could offer. He was just about to knock on their door when he glanced down the line and saw a few shadows lurking in front of RT Georgia's indigenous barracks. He could feel his hands tightening around his CAR-15 as he started making his way down the row, and then he could see a few cigarette cherries glowing in the dark by the doorway.

"That's far enough," an American ordered. "Who is that?"

"Sergeant Jackson, Utah, One-Zero."

"Whatcha look'n for, sarge?"

"Look bro, I just need to talk to 'em."

"Forget it," he said as he stepped into the flickering ghost-like light of a parachute flare. "Strict orders. Nobody goes in, and they don't come out until the CO says so."

"What the fuck's up?"

"Look pal, that's all I know," he admitted. "They were individually escorted from the TOC back here and I was told to maintain security all night until their escort shows up tomorrow morning to take 'em down to Saigon."

"Shit," Ethan sighed. "Look, I lost some friends today and those guys in there are the only ones who know what happened to 'em."

"I'm sorry man, but I can't let you in there."

"Here," Ethan said, handing him his carbine, "take it. That ain't why I'm here. Just walk in there with me and lemme ask 'em straight up so I can tell their families the truth. They deserve that much."

"Goddammit," he sighed through his nose while giving Ethan an uneasy glance. "I'll do it because I respect what y'all do out there, but please don't make me regret this."

"After you," Ethan offered.

The guard handed one of his Yards Ethan's CAR-15 and motioned for them to keep a keen eye out. He knocked on the door, turned the knob and pushed but was only able to crack it slightly.

"Hey… hey, open up."

"Is it locked? What's the matter?"

"Feels like dead weight – like something's blocking the door down low."

"Shit."

Ethan grabbed his carbine and signaled the Yards to circle around to the back of the building. Then he and the guard threw their shoulders into the door once and then twice before it splintered at the bottom and caved in with them falling in on top. He scrambled up, groping for the light switch for a few long seconds before finally turning it on.

"Oh fuck!"

They were all dead, all but two: Bao and Chien, the indigenous team leader.

"How long were they all in here?"

"An hour? Maybe more," he figured. "Fuck!"

"Go get the CO," Ethan ordered. "Now, go!"

He moved across the room, stepping carefully while searching his foot placement for tripwires and toe-popper mines. They were all dead in their racks, throats cut or strangled, two even had small-caliber gunshot wounds to their temples and light burns from the suppressor. Then he found their escape route – a narrow trapdoor cut into the bottom of the sidewall right behind one of their bed racks. He bolted out of the barracks and around the side to where the Yards were examining the escape hole. He saw flashlights and heard shouting voices and a lot of commotion heading his way but he had no intentions of getting swept up in the evidence collection process. Bao and Chien had a good long lead on him and he couldn't waste any more time. To the motor pool he ran, hoping to find an unattended jeep to steal but they were all locked down, and it was too late. The entire camp was lit up, perimeter security at full strength and both east and west gates locked down; no one was coming in or going out, and Bao and Chien were as good as gone.

*   *   *

Five days later, he was sitting in a jeep on the tarmac at the Kontum airfield waiting for his flight to taxi back across the apron, while the sun boiled and the heat radiated off the blacktop. Bill stubbed his cigarette out and threw Ethan's duffle bag onto the hood of the jeep.

"I oughtta stomp your ass for extending another year," he scolded with a smirk.

"Whenever you think you're ready," Ethan encouraged him, "you just say so."

Karate snatched his arms from behind while Bill drummed on his abdomen. They hammed it up for a few more minutes like a couple of kids on a playground but the mood went sour again. The Bright Light had stayed on the ground for four days and turned up nary a clue or a sign of any kind, and Saigon had no choice but to pull the plug. Mark and Paul were officially listed as missing in action.

"Hey, any of you guys know a Sergeant Jackson?" the loadmaster called as he trotted over.

"Yeah yeah, that's me," Ethan said as he fended Bill and Karate off one last time.

"Well look, pal," he said as he jerked a thumb towards the waiting Blackbird, "this rig's all fueled up and ready to go and we gotta schedule to keep, ya hear?"

"Yeah, be right with ya," Ethan promised as he situated his jungle shirt and adjusted his beret.

"Watch your ass in Nha Trang," Karate warned as he slung an arm around Ethan's neck. "Lotta couch commandos and armchair generals hang around that joint. They'll probably give you some shit for that long-ass hair of yours," he snickered as he pawed at the locks bristling slightly below the edge of Ethan's beret.

"You guys keep an eye on my little people while I'm gone?"

"Quit worrying about the boys and go catch your flight, will ya?" Bill ushered.

"Yeah, yeah; I'll see y'all in a month."

He shouldered his duffle bag and walked with Pete and Randy down the tarmac to the blacked-out SOG C-130. The crew chief took his bag first and then Ethan carefully handed him the other two bags he was travelling home with – one packed with Mark's personal affects and the other with Paul's. He'd had a local tailor sew their name-tapes to the outside, and special arrangements had even been made with the airlines to reserve a pair of seats for them on the flight home.

"Safe travels," Pete offered as he and Ethan hugged.

"Take care of them," Randy said.

"Thanks, I will," Ethan nodded. "I'll see y'all in a month. Stay safe."

*   *   *

Surprise and recognition lit her face as she waved to catch his attention from the opposite end of the ward. Nervousness suddenly struck him like a bolt of lightning and anchored him fast in his steps.

She's gonna ask me what I'm doing here… Shit.

He took a few steps forward but stopped short, afraid he'd somehow disrupt the recovering wounded in what little bit of peace they'd managed to find there. He waited as she worked her way towards him, moving among her patients with genuine care and comfort, and he could see they greatly appreciated her devotion and attentiveness. And before he knew it, June Matthews was hugging him with both her arms and all the might her five-foot-four-inch frame could muster. He hugged her back, tuning his senses to the sexy press of her slender body and the intoxicating smell of her hair – a brilliant marriage between peaches and aloe with an Asian signature.

"Ethan! Are you okay, are you hurt?" she asked, pulling away and giving him a quick, but concerned look over.

"No, no I'm fine," he promised.

"Well, it's good to see you again," she confessed. "What are you doing here?"

"Well, I'm supposed to be down in Bien Hoa," he smiled, "waiting for my flight back to the World."

"Your tour's up? That's great," she beamed.

"Well yeah, but it's just extension leave; I'm coming back."

"So why aren't you in Bien Hoa?"

He shrugged, "Got sick of all the REMFs so I thought I'd take a little road trip to kill some time."

She smiled and shook her head, "Yeah that seems about right. I hear most of you SF-types like to make your own rules... Are you looking for somebody in the ward?"

"More or less," he shrugged with a smile. It felt like years since a girl had made him nervous like that.

"My shift ends in a few hours..."

"Pleiku has good food, ya know..."

"Meet me out front in an hour," she smiled.

*   *   *

He lay beside her that night, listening to the thunder roll across the countryside while a steady rain pitter-pattered on the tiled roof of her downtown apartment. Lightning occasionally flickered through the windows and danced on the walls, and in those quiet hours, he realized how much he desired a woman's companionship; all the subtleties and intimacy. He needed to know that he was capable of feeling those emotions again – emotions that weren't inspired by the brutality of combat; emotions other than elation or distress or raw lust.

"You awake?" she whispered.

"Yeah."

She rolled over on her side and faced him in the dark and he ran his hand gently down the contour of her naked body.

"Is it a hard thing to do?" her voice softer and more apprehensive than the question.

"The first one or two," he admitted, "…but not now – not anymore."

She trembled slightly from a sudden chill in the air and nestled in against his bare chest.

*   *   *

His homecoming was a bitter-sweet and a somewhat emotional affair. His family had left the Christmas tree and all the decorations up for his return and although it was a heartwarming surprise, it was a great deal to take in. The women all had joyful tears, and repeatedly accused him of being too thin while the men in his family hugged him and proudly shook his hand. Whenever both sides of his family gathered under one roof, they spent most of their time passionately arguing and debating over everything from politics to sports. They did their best to make him feel at home again but his preoccupation was impossible to hide, and he spent a great deal of time thinking about the Yards and the others back in Kontum. Even still, he enjoyed the quiet solitude of his basement bedroom and spent a lot of time shooting pool with his father and his older brother, David, while catching up on some of the happenings he'd missed during the past year. The basement of his parents' home had pretty much been a sanctuary for him and David when they were growing up. Their rooms were at the far end of the hallway and the common area was big enough for a TV, living room furniture, and a pool table. They'd since added a record player and some speakers, a small refrigerator, and a hot-plate, making the place self-sustaining for late-night pool tournaments and jam-sessions. It quickly became the hangout that everyone needed during their high school years and their parents rarely objected.

David tried schooling him on the basic ins-and-outs of the stock market, but Ethan eventually just gave him a few months of combat pay and told him to invest it as if it were his own money. It wasn't that he lacked interest; he simply found it pointless to prepare for the long-term when the only foreseeable future he had was running recon.

A few nights later, the two of them wandered off to a house party on the far side of the neighborhood where Ethan ran into old friends and schoolmates he hadn't seen in over three years. Most of them were unaware that he'd joined the Army and the few he'd told seemed to have forgotten. Most were consumed by their college careers and a few had married and started families of their own, yet it felt good to catch up with them again.

When they asked him where he'd been and what he'd been doing with himself, he simply smiled and dismissed the opportunity to talk about it.

"Ah not much," he lied, "just working a lot. What about you?" And with that, the conversation would flip and probably for the better.

They partied the night away to The Doors, Janis Joplin, and a fresh new English rock band by the name of Led Zeppelin. Most of the music reminded him of CCC and the many unruly nights he'd spent in the club and he soon found himself suppressing his inner rowdiness for the sake of the greater good.

When the scene finally grew stale, the brothers casually slipped away – each with a freshly liberated ice-cold six-pack underarm. They struck out against the wet chill of a late-January night through the backyards and streets they'd grown up in, but no matter how familiar the neighborhood was, Ethan never took his eyes off the shadows. It was just one of the subtle changes he'd come to notice about himself. No matter how relaxed he'd grown during the previous weeks, he was always on edge, always expecting *something* to happen at any second. He slept unsoundly, usually in hour-long fits, sometimes waking in momentary confusion about where he was. He carried scars caused by everything from sucking leeches and wait-a-minute vines, to tiny bits of molten-hot frag. There were other scars, too – deeper than what his skin could bare.

When things grew completely silent, he could hear a constant ringing in his ears – exactly as it sounded after a firefight, only fainter. He carried his father's .45 and two spare magazines everywhere he went; when he ate, he always kept his eyes up and forward and his back as close to the nearest wall as possible. The reasons for that sort of behavior were impossible to explain in Charleston but back in Recon Company, it was normal. He looked forward to getting back – back to where things like that all made sense.

And he still had Mark and Paul's duffle bags. He made a conscious decision to keep them until he knew the whole truth behind the mystery, but he certainly had his speculations. In his mind, they'd gotten themselves surrounded and the NVA had cut Paul's indigenous teammates a deal: their lives for the two Americans. Neither Paul nor Mark spoke a lick of Vietnamese, and before they knew what was happening, the team had mutinied for self-preservation. No shots fired, the NVA took them and cut the others loose and moved quickly out of the area, knowing a Bright Light would soon be landing to search. That explained the lack of antiaircraft fire and why the NVA weren't waiting for him and the rest of the Bright Light effort. They had what they wanted and didn't feel like sticking around to get pasted by American airpower. Ethan had also learned the statements Bao and Chien gave during their debriefings hadn't matched. He remembered how John Plaster had fired all the Vietnamese on his team after they had reacted sadly to the news of Ho Chi Minh passing away back in September. Their somber reaction had led John to suspect them as communist sympathizers and he no longer trusted them, so he fired them and hired Montagnards.

The war in Vietnam was a chaotic conundrum; a war without borders or boundaries. Enemy agents and communist sympathizers had managed to penetrate the South Vietnamese government and military including even the most classified projects like SOG. Ethan knew he'd find Bao and Chien sooner or later. Strange things like that had a way of happening in the midst of a war...

GLOSSARY & ACRONYMS

A-1E Skyraider

Vintage WWII prop-driven airplane used extensively in support of SOG teams

AA, AAA

Antiaircraft artillery; most common enemy gun calibers found along the Ho Chi Minh Trail consisted of 12.7mm (.51 caliber), 23mm, and 37mm

AAR

After-action report; chronological documentation of a specific military operation drafted by a unit leader afterwards

AK-47

Soviet-designed automatic combat rifle

AO

Area of Operations; a specific area tasked to a military unit for which it is responsible for

Ao-dai

A traditional French-inspired Vietnamese dress consisting of a brightly-colored, long silk top (usually white) worn over loose-fitting black silk trousers

Arc Light

Top-secret B-52 air strikes conducted on heavily fortified and secret enemy positions

ARVN

Army of the Republic of South Vietnam

A-team

Basic twelve-man US Special Forces detachment responsible for unconventional guerilla warfare operations

AWOL

Absence without leave

Azimuth

A compass reading and/or heading

B-40

Shoulder-fired rocket-propelled grenade

B-52

Long-range winged aircraft designed for making high-altitude bombing raids.

B-team

Special Forces detachment tasked to provide support to a number of nearby A-teams

Bac-si

Vietnamese meaning doctor

Base-area

NVA enemy strongholds located along the Ho Chi Minh Trail network

BDA

Bomb-damage assessment

Beaucoup

French for very or many

Binh Tram

Vietnamese meaning base camp

Blackbird

Top-secret SOG-operated C-130 cargo transport aircraft

Blue-line

Streams and rivers marked on topography maps as blue lines

Bra

Infamous CCC target-area located inside Southeastern Laos; heavily-fortified and fiercely defended by enemy troops

Bright Light

Code-name given to rescue operations conducted by SOG commandos

C-4

Plastic explosive material shaped into one-pound blocks; burns smokeless and odorless and is generally harmless until a blasting cap is installed

C&C

Command and Control

CCC

Command and Control Central

CCN

Command and Control North

CCS

Command and Control South

CAR-15

A sub-machinegun version of the M-16 rifle favored by Special Forces and SOG commandos

Chase medic

SOG Special Forces medic who flew in on insertion and/or extraction helicopters to provide expedient medical treatment to wounded recon or Hatchet Force members before reaching rear-area medical facilities

Cherry

A soldier who is new to a unit and untested in combat

Chicom

Chinese-communist

Chieu hoi

Government program implemented to encourage enemy soldiers to defect over to the South Vietnamese side

Chinese-Nung

Ethnic Chinese mercenaries hired by US Special Forces to serve as recon team members within the Special Projects

CIA

Central Intelligence Agency

CIB

Combat infantryman badge; US Army decoration awarded to a soldier for having been engaged in a firefight with enemy forces

CID

Criminal Investigations Division; responsible for investigating criminal activity within US military

CIDG

Civilian Irregular Defense Group; indigenous civilians armed and trained by US Special Forces

CISO

Counter-Insurgency Supply Office; designed and produced a wide variety of untraceable field items for SOG commandos including knives, rucksacks, indigenous rations, and more

Clacker

A handheld detonator used to manually trigger explosives

Claymore mine

A curved antipersonnel mine filled with hundreds of ball-bearings and C4 plastic explosive

CO

Commanding officer

COSVN

Central Office for South Vietnam; a heavily-occupied Vietcong staging area located inside the "Fishhook" region of Southeastern Cambodia

Counter-recon team

An NVA unit trained specifically to hunt and kill SOG commandos

Covey

Call-sign given to US Air Force FACs that flew in support of SOG ground operations

Covey rider

A former recon team leader who flew with FAC pilots in support of SOG ground operations

CS

Teargas in the form of a hand grenade or as packets of powder

Daisy-chain

A demolitions procedure in which multiple Claymore mines are linked together by det-cord to achieve a simultaneous explosion

Daisy cutter

A huge 10,000-15,000 pound bomb dropped from the cargo bay of a C-130 aircraft; used to create useable LZs in dense jungle

Dai-uy

Vietnamese meaning captain

DEROS

Date of Expected Return from Overseas

Det-cord

Detonation cord; milky-white fuse cordage used in demolitions to link explosives together or to enhance a single explosion

Di-di

Vietnamese meaning to run or move quickly away from

DMZ

Demilitarized Zone

Dung-lai

Vietnamese meaning to freeze or to halt

Dust-off

Medical evacuation by helicopter

DZ

Drop zone

E&E

Escape and evasion; a preplanned route used to elude, escape, and evade enemy forces and immanent capture

EOD

Explosive Ordnance Disposal

FAC

Forward air controller; aircraft flow by US Army and Air Force pilots used to coordinate air strikes and air support for ground units engaged with hostile forces

Fast-mover

Jet fighter-bombers

Fire mission

A request for artillery support

Fishhook

Major NVA base-area located in Southeast Cambodia

Fix

Specific map coordinates used to pinpoint a unit's position or a hostile target

FOB

Forward operating base

FNG

Fucking new guy; a new, inexperienced soldier

Frag

Fragmentation; can also mean to wound or kill a fellow soldier

HALO

High altitude, low opening; parachute tactic for covertly inserting commandos behind enemy lines without detection; jump is made at 15,000 feet with an approximate fall-time of seventeen minutes

Hanson rig

Modified A7a military cargo strap used for helicopter extractions; developed by One-Zero Bill Hanson of CCC; bridged the gap between Swiss seat and STABO rig

Hatchet Force

SOG's platoon and company-sized raiding elements

H&I

Harassment and interdiction; artillery fire procedure used against suspected enemy locations, routes of travel, and staging points

HE

High-explosive ordnance

Head-shed

Slang term used to describe a base's command post or the tactical operations center.

Heavy team

Larger recon team carrying heavier-caliber weapons

High Standard

A silenced WWII-era .22-caliber pistol favored by SOG commandos

Hillsboro

Call-sign designation for the US Air Force C-130 airborne command post that orbited the skies over Laos during the day

Ho Chi Minh Trail

A vast, intricate network of roadways, bike paths, base-areas, way-stations, truck parks, weapons caches, and foot trails that ran from North Vietnam down through Eastern Laos, and Eastern Cambodia, branching off into South Vietnam all along the way; heavily fortified and fiercely defended by the North Vietnamese Army

Hootch

A dwelling or living space

Hophead

Junkie; a soldier who abuses hard drugs such as opium and heroin

Horn

Radio or telephone handset

Hot

Heavy enemy activity in a specific area

Hump

Patrolling or moving through hostile terrain while on a combat operation

IA drill

Immediate-action drill; recon team tactic designed to respond instantly to enemy contact

I-Corps

Northernmost military region in South Vietnam

II-Corps

Central Highlands military region of South Vietnam

III-Corps

Densely-populated and fertile military region of South Vietnam

IV-Corps

Southernmost military region within South Vietnam; characterized by the marshy terrain of the Mekong Delta

In-country

To be deployed in a warzone

Indian country

Term referring to hostile, enemy-controlled territory

Jody

A state-side person who swindles a soldier's lover away while they're at war

KIA

Killed in action

Kingbee

Sikorsky H-34 Choctaw helicopters flown by South Vietnamese pilots in supported SOG ground operations

Kit Carson scout

Former enemy soldiers who defected to join US combat units

Klick

Kilometer

LAW

Light antitank weapon; disposable, single-shot rocket launcher

Launch site

Top-secret forward staging areas that SOG teams used to launch ground operations from

Leg

A derogative term used to refer to non-airborne qualified soldiers

Leghorn

Top-secret SOG radio-relay site located in Southeastern Laos; call-sign "Heavy Drop"

LLDB

Luc Luong Dac Biet; South Vietnamese Special Forces

LRP

Long Range Patrol

LRRP

Long Range Reconnaissance Patrol

LZ

Landing zone

M-16

Lightweight automatic combat rifle used by US and ARVN forces in Vietnam

M-60

Lightweight, belt-fed machinegun used by US and ARVN forces in Vietnam

M-79

Lightweight, single-shot, breech-loaded 40mm grenade launcher

MACV

Military Assistance Command, Vietnam; command element which ran the Vietnam War from Saigon

MACV-SOG

Military Assistance Command, Vietnam – Studies and Observations Group; separate command element solely responsible for commanding SOG's secret war

Mag

Ammunition magazine

McGuire rig

Nylon sling attached to the end of a 120-foot rope used to extract recon team members by helicopter from dense jungle where landing zones were not readily available

Medevac

Battlefield medical evacuation conducted by helicopter

MIKE Force

US Special Forces Mobile Strike Force used to reinforce and support other Special Forces units or camps under attack or engaged with the enemy

Moonbeam

Call-sign designation for the US Air Force C-130 airborne command post that orbited the skies over Laos at night

Montagnard

Primitive hill tribesmen of the Central Highlands; superb hunter-gatherers and fiercely loyal to US Special Forces, but ostracized and despised by the Vietnamese

MP

Military Police

MPC

Military Payment Certificate; payment script issued to US soldiers instead of American greenbacks

NCO

Noncommissioned officer; enlisted soldier

Nightingale

CIA-developed diversionary device consisting of time-fused fireworks which closely mimicked an actual firefight

NKP

Nakhon Phanom Royal Thai Air Force Base; top-secret SOG launch site for Northern Laos and North Vietnam target-areas

Number one

Slang for very good; the best

Number ten

Slang for very bad; the worst

Nuoc-mam

Foul-smelling, fermented fish sauce

NVA
North Vietnamese Army

O-1 Bird Dog
Small recon planes flown by US Army and Air Force FAC pilots

O-2 Skymaster
Twin-boom recon plane flown by US Army and Air Force FAC pilots

OV-10 Bronco
Recon plane flown by US Army and Air Force FAC pilots; replaced both the O-1 and O-2 models and featured thicker armor and a heavier weapons system

OD
Olive-drab (green)

One-Zero (1-0)
SOG recon team leader

One-One (1-1)
SOG assistant recon team leader

One-Two (1-2)

SOG recon team member; typically carried the team radio

One-Three (1-3)

SOG recon team member

OPS-31

(SOG) Maritime Operations

OPS-32

(SOG) Air Operations

OPS-33

(SOG) Psychological Studies Group

OPS-34

(SOG) Special Operations

OPS-35

(SOG) Ground Studies Group/Ground Reconnaissance

OSS

Office of Strategic Services; American WWII-era "cloak-and-dagger" efforts against the Nazi regime; precursor to the CIA

Parrot's Beak

NVA stronghold inside Cambodia, just northwest of Saigon; Tet Offensive of 1968 was staged there

Piaster

Vietnamese currency

Pointman

Soldier who walks at the front of a combat patrol

***Pok*-time**

A two-hour lunch break the Vietnamese take every day at beginning at noon

POW

Prisoner of war

PRC-25

Standard-issue FM field radio

Prairie Fire

Code-name designation for all SOG operations conducted in Laos

Prairie Fire emergency

Radio code-name used by SOG commandos to declare an urgent and immediate tactical emergency

Project Delta

US Special Forces reconnaissance unit that operated exclusively inside South Vietnam

Project Eldest Son

SOG OPS-33 psychological warfare project that introduced booby-trapped ammunition into NVA supply lines

Project Ford Drum

SOG OPS-32 photo surveillance project that instituted aerial reconnaissance over-flights of the Ho Chi Minh Trail

Punji

Sharpened bamboo stakes typically placed inside a pit and smeared with human excrement

PX

Postal Exchange; military-run goods store

R&R

Rest and recreation

Radio relay site

A stationary team or site with the primary duty of relaying radio transmissions

Redleg

Standard call-sign issued to US artillery units.

REMF

Rear echelon motherfucker; soldiers whose duties kept them safe in rear-areas

Ricky-tick

Slang meaning "right now"

RON

Remain overnight position; a safe place for recon teams to hole-up in and spend the night while out in the field

Roundeye

Non-Asian women

RPD

Lightweight Soviet-made, drum-fed machinegun

RPG

Rocket-propelled grenade

RTO

Radio telephone operator

S-2

Intelligence shop; responsible for compiling and analyzing recently collected intelligence

S-3

Operations shop; responsible for assigning missions

S-4

Supply and equipment shop

Safe-house

SOG-owned and operated facilities located in several major cities around South Vietnam where SOG personnel could safely stay without dealing with conventional military personnel and procedures

Sapper

Highly-skilled NVA and Vietcong soldiers trained in engineering, sabotage, and demolitions

SCU

Special Commando Unit; SOG-employed indigenous soldiers

SEAL

US Naval Special Warfare commando

SF

Special Forces

Short-round

Artillery rounds that fall short of their intended target

Signal panel

A rectangular-shaped fluorescent-colored vinyl panel used to signal aircraft from the ground

Sitrep

Situational report

Six

Radio call-sign designated for a unit commander; also used to refer to the position directly behind someone

Slick

Troop-carrying helicopter

Spad

Nickname given to vintage WWII-era, prop-driven Skyraiders

SPAF

Sneaky Pete's Air Force; unofficial name given to the small detachment of US Army O-1 Bird Dog pilots of the 219th Aviation Company who flew exclusively in support of CCC's ground operations

Spectre

AC-130 gunship platform armed with mini-guns, Vulcan machineguns, and a 105mm howitzer

Spider-hole

Well-concealed, one-man fighting position

STABO rig

Innovative combat and extraction harness worn by SOG commandos; was designed to replace the Swiss rappelling seat and the McGuire extraction rig

Stay-behind

Technique where a larger force is extracted but leaves behind a small recon team to begin or continue a mission

Straphanger

One who operates outside of his assigned position in order to reinforce or fill a specific role for a mission

Swiss seat

Hand-tied rappelling harness; also used for rope extractions

TAC Air

Tactical air support

Tail-gunner

Very last man in a recon team formation whose job is to cover the team's back-trail and erase their passage from the terrain

Target-area

A very specific area selected for an operation

Target folder

Folders which contain the most up-to-date intelligence about a specific target-area

Tiger-stripes

Fatigues characterized by irregular black and green stripes designed to mimic jungle foliage and shadows

Time pencil

Delayed fuse used with explosive charges

TOC

Tactical operations center

Toe popper

Small pressure-detonated antipersonnel mine designed to maim

Tracer

Ammunition containing a small pyrotechnic charge that glows when fired, enabling the rounds to be seen by the naked eye

Trung-si

Vietnamese meaning sergeant

Un-ass

To move out of a place or area very quickly

URC-10

Small FM survival radio carried by SOG commandos and the aircrews

VR

Visual reconnaissance

Warning order

Official notification that a recon team had been assigned a new mission

White Mice

Slang for Vietnamese Military Police

WIA

Wounded in action

Willie-Pete, WP

White phosphorous; extremely hot-burning chemical that burst into molten spray when mixed with oxygen

XO

Executive officer

Yards

Short for Montagnard tribesmen

Zero-One (0-1)

Indigenous recon team leader

Zero-Two (0-2)

Indigenous assistant recon team leader

ABOUT THE AUTHOR

Born and raised in Charlotte, North Carolina; moved to Wilmington in pursuit of higher education, and graduated from the University of North Carolina at Wilmington with a Bachelor of Arts in Communication Studies in 2006. Currently working and residing in Wrightsville Beach, the author spends most of his free time surfing between home and abroad. He is also an uncompromising supporter of the Constitution and the Second Amendment, and a vocal supporter of the veterans of this great nation.

Gentle Propositions is his first novel, and will soon be followed by its sequel(s).

Jason is active on social media so feel free to follow him on Instagram @jseconomos, and drop him a line with any criticism, comments and/or questions you may have on Facebook.

46102724R00261

Made in the USA
Columbia, SC
22 December 2018